SO MUCH
LIFE LEFT
OVER

SO MUCH LIFE LEFT OVER

Louis de Bernières

Pantheon Books

New York

Copyright © 2018 by Louis de Bernières

All rights reserved. Published in the United States by Pantheon Books, a division of Penguin Random House LLC, New York, and distributed in Canada by Random House of Canada, a division of Penguin Random House Canada Limited, Toronto. Originally published in hardcover in Great Britain by Harvill Secker, an imprint of Vintage Publishing, a division of Penguin Random House Ltd., London, in 2018.

Pantheon Books and colophon are registered trademarks of Penguin Random House LLC.

Library of Congress Cataloging-in-Publication Data
Name: de Bernières, Louis, author.
Title: So much life left over / Louis de Bernières.
Description: New York : Pantheon, 2018.
Identifiers: LCCN 2018010018. ISBN 9781524747886 (hardcover).
ISBN 9781524747893 (ebook).
Subjects: BISAC: FICTION/Literary. FICTION/War & Military.
GSAFD: War stories.
Classification: LCC PR6054.E132 S67 2018 | DDC 823/.914—dc23 |
LC record available at lccn.loc.gov/2018010018

www.pantheonbooks.com

Jacket image: *View Near Point de Galle, Ceylon.* Copyright © British Library Board. All Rights Reserved/Bridgeman Images

Jacket design by Kelly Blair

Printed in the United States of America
First American Edition
2 4 6 8 9 7 5 3 1

In memory of
my grandparents, Audrey and Kenneth,
who tried to start a new life in Ceylon.

Chacun de nous a sa blessure
Son coin de paradis perdu
Son petit jardin défendu

Georges Moustaki, 'Alexandrie'

Contents

I

Gun Snap

The crackle of gunshots bounced between the mountainsides, the percussion fading with each return of echo. Daniel Pitt and Hugh Bassett sat side by side on a small level patch, playing gun snap. They had on the table before them two decks of cards, a box of ammunition and two Mark VI service revolvers. Fifteen yards away was a gibbet with two rows of six tin cans suspended from it on pieces of string.

The idea was to be the first person to put a bullet through every can. Sometimes, for a change, they went down to the valley, threw bottles out into a lake, and sank them with rifles. These were fine ways for two old fighter pilots to pass the last hour of the day as the mist rose up and supper was cooked in the bungalows.

Daniel Pitt and Hugh Bassett suffered from the accidie of not being at war. Even in a land as beautiful and surprising as Ceylon, they missed the extremes of experience that had made them feel intensely alive during the Great War, in spite of its penumbra of death. Neither of them missed the killing, and if they went out after duck or small game, they never returned with more than their families could eat. They had both, many times, seen the way in which the light suddenly goes out of a man's eyes as he passes out of the world, and it was just the same with an animal. There was no longer any triumph in the kill, the guilt was as intense as it had ever been, but still they yearned for the passionate oblivion of the hunt.

There is a kind of man who, having been at war, finds peacetime intolerable, because he cannot develop the civilian's talent for becoming obsessed with irrelevant details and procedures. He hates the delays and haverings, the tedious diplomacy, the terrible lack of energy and discipline, and, above all, he hates the feeling that what he is doing is not important.

If you have struggled for the freedom of France, or have fought to keep Zeppelins out of the skies over London, what else can seem important thereafter?

Daniel and Hugh were fortunate to be involved in the manufacture of tea, because everything in that industry depends upon good timing and good teamwork, and strictly understood hierarchies of responsibility. Daniel loved the huge and beautiful machinery in the factory, and could not resist rolling up his sleeves and helping the Singhalese engineers when it broke down. Machinery was so much easier to deal with than people. There was always a precise set of reasons why a machine may not be working, and there were always completely logical solutions. People were slippery and elusive, changeable and moody. You thought you understood them and then found out that you did not. You thought they loved you, and then they suddenly turned spiteful or indifferent.

Daniel enjoyed the sheer reasonableness of the machinery, but he also enjoyed the brotherhood of mechanics, and he reflected quite often that he had more in common, and more enjoyment, with the engineers than he did with those British people who congregated at the club. He had picked up some Singhalese, in addition to the Tamil of the tea workers, and was finding that the more languages you know, the better you understand your own. He realised that languages divide the world up differently from each other. He was half French, and had often wondered why it was that his French personality was different from his British one. In French he was more emphatic and rhetorical. Somebody had told him once that in Russian there was no word for blue. There was bound to be a word for pushrod, or tappet, though.

It was very fortunate for him that he had the company of Hugh Bassett, who had spent his war flying Sopwith triplanes and Camels over France, in the Royal Naval Air Service. The RNAS had been operating out of airfields alongside the Royal Flying Corps, and they had an inexhaustible amount to talk about, to mull over, to repeat. Both had binged beyond the borders of sanity, knew the same jokes and ribald songs, had overflown the same strip of desolation month after month; fought the same battle to keep flying sickness disorder at bay, to remain optimistic, to perform over and over again the impossible trick of trampling their own fear underfoot every time they sprinted to the cockpit. Daniel wondered if he had ever been truly courageous at all, but had rather been seduced by the wondrous beauty and excitement of flying, consoled by the airman's simple fatalism. If today's the day, then today's the day. Goodbye, world, it was good to know you. All I ask is to die a clean death, one that's not by burning.

But now he and Hugh, and the rest of those who had survived, had so much life left over that it was sometimes hard to cope with. Some became drunks; others fell quiet and imprisoned themselves inside themselves; some foresaw a brave new world and strode out towards it; others returned to what they had been before, and turned the war into the memory of an outrageous dream from which they had at last awoken. Most were as proud of what they had done as they were amazed to be yet alive.

2

Archie and Esther

In late May of 1925, Archie was delivered to Taprobane in the early evening, with the intention of spending the first two weeks of his annual three-month leave with his brother, and then going snipe shooting in the wetlands west of Trincomalee.

He had havered over the invitation for some time. The fact was that his long unrequited passion for Daniel's wife made it painful for him to be with them. He felt cut off and safe in Peshawar or Simla, or in the Hindu Kush. In those places Rosie was a remote and beautiful dream, and that she existed at all was a kind of joy to him, and a pleasure. He could bivouac in a nullah, with his sepoys slumbering about him, and gaze up at the stars, remembering Rosie sipping tea, Rosie as a little girl, Rosie playing tennis, Rosie at prayer in church or talking earnestly about poetry in the conservatory at Eltham. Archie cared not a whit for poetry, beyond 'How Horatius Kept the Bridge', but Rosie's bright-eyed passion for it almost made him believe in its importance. The way she talked about it, you'd think that it was as vital as bread. He loved her blue eyes, her chestnut hair, her freckles, her bohemian armbands, and the way that her hips moved when she walked. He loved her soft voice, and the shadows of sorrow in her eyes that had never quite gone away, even after marrying his brother.

That wedding day had provided the most painful hours of his life. It had been completely unbearable to think of her in Daniel's arms, night after night, for all the years to come, raising the children that he would never have, and would so much have wanted. On the boat back to India he had written a long confessional letter to Daniel: '... One has dreams. It is very hard to endure the sight of them fluttering away like a flock of sparrows. It leaves a taste in the mouth like licking an old penny.' He had concluded the letter by asking to be buried in Peshawar.

Archie thought a great deal about death. One saw a great deal of it on the North-West Frontier, and the tribesmen seemed to find a value in it much higher than any they attached to life. To them, the latter was just an irksome anteroom to paradise. Archie thought they yearned for death because their religious fanaticism made any enjoyment of this life completely *haram*. Life was not to be enjoyed until you were dead, and in paradise.

The fun in Archie's life was of the unenduring, self-destructive kind. He drank too much, and too much enjoyed the danger of being up in the mountains, always in imminent jeopardy of avalanche, ambush, capture and torture. But the most destructive pleasure of his life was thinking of Rosie, becoming paralysed by dreams.

It was therefore with great misgivings that he had agreed to come to Ceylon instead of taking ship straight back to Southampton, and now that he was out on the terrace with Rosie and Daniel, sipping tea as they watched the mist rise up in the valley below, those misgivings became even greater. This was too much like paradise, and something was bound to go wrong.

Rosie was talking animatedly about her work in the clinic: '... and the natives don't trust our medicine at all, because they've got their own, and so they only come to us when they're desperate, and obviously by then it's too late, and they die anyway, and of course that means they trust our medicine even less.'

'Damned awkward,' said Archie, puffing on his cigarette. He smoked Abdullas when he could get them, and was enjoying the first of a pack he had bought in Colombo before setting off.

'Worse than awkward,' said Daniel. 'You build a lovely expensive clinic for your workers, and then it's only a few Europeans who use it.'

'It's so frustrating!' said Rosie.

'There must be something you can do,' said Archie.

'What do you do in India these days? It seems like a lifetime since I was there. Has anything changed?' asked Daniel.

'No, it's just the same. On the North-West Frontier, the only medicine they believe in is the bullet, if you don't count things like swallowing a verse of the Koran. It's completely different in Calcutta or Delhi, obviously. The more sophisticated Indians use both systems at once, as far as I can see, depending on the expense. Rosie, my dear, will you be using the clinic ... on the day?'

'What day?'

'Well, I see that ... forgive me ... I know one is not supposed to draw attention to such things, but ... Well, it is quite evident, if you don't mind me saying.'

Rosie patted her stomach happily. 'Oh, you mean this!'

'Yes. And congratulations. I imagine it's due quite soon?'

'Six weeks,' said Rosie. 'We're so happy about it, aren't we?' she said, turning to Daniel.

'We are indeed. Poor little Esther isn't, though. She doesn't want the competition. She's very grumpy, and says, "Daddy, make it go away." She says she's going to give it to someone else.'

'So will you be having the baby at your clinic?'

'One normally gives birth at home,' said Rosie. 'I expect we'll get the midwife in, and hope that she's here on time.'

'I can't imagine what it's like, giving birth,' said Archie. 'Must be hell. Strange how easy it is for cats and dogs, eh? And such damned hard work for you. The curse of Eve, eh?'

'I'd rather not think about it,' said Rosie.

'Sorry. I'm just glad it's not something I'll ever be called upon to do.'

'Well, I'm glad I don't have to creep about being ambushed by Pathans,' said Rosie.

'We have a lot of fun too,' said Archie. 'We put on a new Gilbert and Sullivan every six months, and once we did a mock *Romeo and Juliet* with our largest officer as Juliet. You should have seen him mince. The sepoys think we're mad, of course. And then there's the Peshawar Vale Hunt.'

At that moment Esther came out in her nightdress, with her thumb in her mouth. 'I can't sleep,' she announced. 'You're too noisy, and I'm not tired, and it's not even dark.'

'I think the plan failed,' said Daniel to Rosie. 'I did say there wasn't any point in sending her to bed early.'

'Well, I thought that Archie might want us to himself on his first night here. Children can be such a distraction, and then they take all the attention, and you can't talk about anything else.'

'Oh, you shouldn't have done that for me,' exclaimed Archie. 'My niece is adorable, and I see her so little.' He beckoned to her, saying, '*Viens, chérie*, come and sit on my smelly old knee.'

Esther settled herself onto his knee with much aplomb, her thumb never leaving her mouth, and he put his hand to the side of her head, pushing it against his shoulder.

'Suffer the little children,' he said happily.

'You do smell cigaretty,' said Esther.

'Nothing like a child for honesty,' said Archie. 'Is "cigaretty" nice or nasty?'

'A bit of both. Daddy doesn't smoke.'

'Everyone thinks I'm very strange,' said Daniel. 'I don't smoke, and to make matters worse, I'm half French, though it doesn't much show. I prefer coffee to tea, and I'd rather be at home than at the club.'

'You are strange, little brother,' said Archie. 'I always did say so.'

'Uncle Archie?'

'Yes, *chérie*?'

'Why's your moustache orange in the middle?'

'Cigarettes. There's something orangey in the smoke.'

'If I go to bed, will you tell me an *histoire*?'

'As long as you promise to get so bored that you go to sleep.'

'I will when it's dark.'

'Dark soon,' replied Archie. 'Look at that sun, sinking like a ship.'

'It's on fire,' said Esther. 'It's a wheel on fire.'

'Come on, my darling,' said Archie. 'I'll carry you in. Why don't you pretend to be a wounded soldier, and I'm carrying you to safety?'

He stood up, and Esther flopped in his embrace. 'Oh, I am *blessée*,' she cried, 'and I think I might die. Kiss me hardly.'

'Say goodnight to Mummy and Daddy,' said Archie, presenting her in turn to Rosie and Daniel for a kiss on the forehead. 'I hope you're cured by the morning,' said Daniel.

'It's prob'ly fatal,' said Esther.

Archie carried her indoors and laid her in her small bed. 'There,' he said, pulling the covers over her.

'Now you've got to tell me a story.'

'I'll tell you one about Ali Anei, the elephant. I was told it by someone called "The Mad Major".'

'Why's he called Ali?'

'Because he is a Mohammedan elephant.'

'And why is he called Annie?'

'Because Anei means elephant.'

'But Annie's a girl's name.'

'Not Annie. Anei.'

'Uncle Archie?'

'Yes?'

'What's a Mohammeding?'

'A follower of the prophet Mohammed. Look, it would take hours to explain. Do you want a story or an explanation of an entire religion?'

'Story, please. Uncle Archie, does Mohammed like elephants?'

'I've no idea, *chérie*. He was very fond of his camel, and it's said that he liked cats, and he had one disciple who loved cats so much that his nickname was "Father of Kittens", and I believe that in his will he left only one white mule. Can I tell you the story now?'

She nodded her head solemnly.

'Once upon a time there was a big bull elephant called Ali Anei, and this elephant was the biggest and strongest in all Ceylon, and he lived with his wives and friends and relatives by a huge lake that was full of crocodiles, at the very edge of the jungle.

'Now, one day in the dry season, he went down to the water to drink, and it so happened that there was a crocodile just under the surface, and when Ali put his trunk into the water, the crocodile said to itself, "Oh goody goody, a big grey wiggly sausage!" And he grabbed hold of it with his dreadful sharp teeth.'

'Uncle Archie?'

'Yes?'

'What was it called?'

'The crocodile? It was called Lord Palmerston.'

'No it wasn't!'

'Was!'

'Wasn't wasn't wasn't!'

'Was was was!'

'Not!'

'All right, it was really called Lieutenant Colonel Aloysius Reginald Arthur Quibbling Crockersnapper. Don't you want to know what happened? Well, Aloysius the crocodile pulled hard on the trunk, and Ali Anei pulled back. Ali was much bigger, so he began to drag the crocodile out of the water.

'Now, Lieutenant Colonel Crockersnapper's best friend happened to be passing by, so he thought he'd lend a mouth, and he grabbed Crockersnapper's tail in his jaws, and heaved backwards, but Ali was still too strong, and then Crockersnapper's second-best friend came along and grabbed hold of the crocodile's tail, but Ali was still too strong, and before you knew it there were ten crocodiles trying to pull him into the water so they could gobble him up.

'Now, you might be wondering why Ali's friends didn't come to help, even though he was bellowing with pain and indignation. Were you wondering that?'

Esther shook her head.

'Oh, never mind then. So, when there were ten crocodiles pulling, Ali felt himself beginning to be overpowered, and just then he noticed that he was next to a rubber tree, and he wrapped his tail around it.'

'Trees aren't rubber,' said Esther. 'They're made of wood.'

Archie sighed resignedly, and said, 'Very well, there was a wooden tree, and Ali wrapped his tail around it to anchor himself, and they all stayed like that for five hours because it was a complete stalemate.

'Ali racked his brains for a solution to his predicament, and then he had a very good idea. He breathed in and breathed in and breathed in until he could inhale no more, and then, with all his might, he blew through his trunk, which by now was right down the crocodile's throat. He blew so hard that the crocodile swelled up as round as a football, and he blew so hard that the crocodile expanded so much that quite suddenly it exploded – bang! – and all his friends fell back into the water with a big splash.

'So that's how Ali Anei defeated the crocodile, and he went back to his wives and friends and relatives, and showed them his wounded trunk, and he said, "You wouldn't believe what just

9

happened to me," and he told them the story I have just told you, and they said, "Stop making things up," because they really didn't believe a word of it. But we know it's true, don't we?'

Esther looked at him sceptically in the gathering darkness and said, 'Will you stay with me 'til I fall asleep?'

'Of course I will.'

'Uncle Archie?'

'Yes?'

'Where's my birthday?'

'Where? Don't you mean "when"?'

'No. Where is it?'

'Um, well, I suppose it's waiting for you just round the corner, and when it comes it'll be here. Here in Ceylon. At Taprobane.'

'Which corner?'

'At Daddy's tea factory, I expect. But don't go looking for it, because it'll see you coming, and just nip round the next corner.'

'Why don't balls have edges?'

'Gracious me … I suppose that a ball is a solid body with only one edge if you think about it. Or perhaps it's the only geometrical solid with no edges at all … I'm afraid you've got me there.'

'Uncle Archie, how big is air?'

'How big is air? Good Lord … well … um … it's a big blanket a few thousand feet deep, and it wraps the earth up completely. I expect your father would know how big it is. He used to be a flyer. Ask him in the morning.'

'Uncle Archie, why is "brought" not "bought"?'

'Well, "brought" means "did bring", and "bought" means "did buy". Does that make sense? Do you think you'll remember that?'

Esther nodded, and said, 'I'm going to sleep now.'

She turned on her side and closed her eyes. Archie sat on his chair, leaning forward with his arms on his knees and his hands clasped together. He watched the child fading away into her dreams and thought he had never seen anything so beautiful in his life. He put out a hand to stroke the side of her head, but then withdrew it.

He would have loved to have had a child like this, and he wondered again why it was that he had quite deliberately cut himself off from any chance of living from a full heart. 'Had it beaten out of me at Westminster,' he said to himself. At prep school and then at public school he had learned to close himself off so completely during his ten years of thrashings, spartan training on the sports fields, and the Hobbesian war of all against all, that he knew he had become like the prisoner whose cell door has fallen open, but cannot go out into the light. 'Why didn't this happen to Daniel?' he asked himself. Daniel had been thrashed and bullied and half starved as well, but he had emerged with a heart open to the world. His own was in the darkness out of choice, it seemed. At home in England there was Rosie's sister Ottilie, a good woman who loved him, with whom he could have enjoyed domesticity and children, but at the back of his mind was the knowledge that anyone who adored him as sincerely as she did must have something wrong with them, and should therefore be avoided. It was easier to love Rosie because she would never love him in return.

Archie observed the sweet little girl breathing softly and peacefully in the half-light, and felt tears well up. He closed his eyes and muttered, 'Dear Lord, let this child live a long life full of happiness, and may she never suffer harm, and defend her from wars and disasters, and watch over her and protect her.' He paused, then added, 'And as far as I'm concerned, I don't mind if you take me as soon as you like. Amen.'

After an hour had passed, Rosie came in to look for him, fearing that something was amiss. She put her head round the door, and saw Archie in the darkness, stock-still in his chair with his hands clasped together and his head bowed. 'Is everything all right?' she whispered. 'Is she asleep? Supper's ready.'

Archie looked up at her with sorrowful eyes, and said, 'Tickety-boo. Perfectly splendid. Along in a minute.'

3

Archie and Rosie

As usual, Daniel left for the tea factory just after dawn, and when Rosie came out onto the terrace an hour later, she found Archie at the table with a pot of tea and half a dozen weapons laid out in front of him. One of them was dismantled, and he was pointing it at the sky in order to peer down the barrel.

'Gracious me, what an arsenal,' she said. 'Is there a war on?'

Archie said, 'Good morning, my dear, and what a lovely morning it is too. It's splendid to see the mist burn off in the valley. It's all so marvellously green, and the air is so breathable that I don't even want to spoil it by smoking.'

'Oh well, Ceylon is the second Garden of Eden, don't you know,' said Rosie. 'According to the natives, Adam was sent here after the expulsion from Paradise. His footprint is on Adam's Peak, but I haven't seen it yet.'

'The natives? I thought they were Hindus and Buddhists. What's Adam to them?'

'We've got plenty of Roman Catholics and Mohammedans too. It's obvious from the names. Fernandos and da Silvas and Mohammeds in batches of a dozen. I think the Hindus even have Jesus as one of their gods. That's what I've heard. What's this very slender gun for?'

'Snipe. It's a close-range business, and you don't want to make them inedible by blasting them to bits with a big dose of shot. It's wonderful snipe shooting here; you can bag a thousand in a day.'

Rosie was horrified. 'A thousand in a day? A thousand?'

'Yes, indeed.'

'Oh my goodness!'

Insensitive to Rosie's horror, Archie ploughed on. 'And this gun is a twelve-bore, but it's got one smooth barrel and one rifled barrel, so you can put shot or a ball in one barrel and a bullet in the other. You know, a crocodile with one barrel and a peacock with the other.'

'Crocodiles? Peacocks?'

'Mm. And this one is good for dogs. You can use a dead dog as crocodile bait. There's nothing a crocodile likes more than a dog. I understand that people do eat them in China. Never tried it myself, and never will, no doubt, unless I'm in China and having to be polite.'

'Dogs?'

'Yes, and this is the best of the lot. My pride and joy. It's a Jeffery Nitro Express .600. Look, I even had my name engraved on it. It's got Krupp barrels and a truly wonderful ejector mechanism.'

'It's absolutely huge. It must weigh a ton.'

'It's *magnifique*. The strike poundage is 8,700 pounds, and the velocity is 2,050 feet per second, and the safety isn't automatic, so you don't get caught out when the beast is charging straight at you and you've got no time for messing about. I'll show you a bullet, if you're interested. They're absolute whoppers, packed with cordite, nickel-covered for penetration. Eighty-eight shillings a hundred. You don't waste them.'

Rosie had a horrible suspicion, and asked, 'So, is this an elephant gun then? Is that what you mean by "the beast"?'

'Yes, bang on, my dear. It's an elephant gun. It's surprising what you can do with an elephant. You can make the feet into walking-stick stands, and I know someone who used a section of trunk to sheathe a biscuit tin. One always keeps the tail. If there is one, of course.'

Rosie sat down heavily and trembled. Archie looked at her with concern. 'What's the matter, my dear? Are you quite all right?'

She suddenly lost control of herself. 'Crocodiles? Dogs? Peacocks? A thousand snipe? Elephants? I can't believe my ears. Are you completely mad? What is the matter with you? Walking-stick stands? Trunks for biscuits?'

'My dear —'

'Don't you know that people love dogs? And peacocks are too beautiful ... and ... and ... a thousand snipe in a day?'

'But, Rosie ... my dear —'

'I am not your dear! Don't call me that! You're despicable! A bloodthirsty maniac! And elephants! Don't you know that elephants live in families like us? And they're intelligent and sensitive, and the natives use them for work? And you're going round making them orphans and widows? Archie, I'm sorry, but you utterly disgust me.'

'But, Rosie!'

'I've said what I feel. All this slaughter of innocent animals is utterly vile!'

Archie stood up slowly, devastation written all over his face. 'Rosie, listen,' he said, with desperation in his voice. 'Innocent animals? But, my dear —'

'Don't call me your dear. I'm not! And I like to be called Rosemary. How many times do I have to remind you?'

Archie went to the table and picked up his precious Jeffery.600. He went to the edge of the terrace, took the gun by the ends of the barrels, and hurled it out over the hillside. It turned lazy circles through the air as it described its arc down into the bushes below.

'I'll be off now,' he said, turning round, and taking out his silver cigarette case. He removed a cigarette and, with shaking hands, put it between his lips. He took his lighter from his pocket, and pressed the lever several times. When it failed to ignite he flung it over the hillside in the wake of his rifle. 'Please ask Daniel to forward my possessions to the Grand Hotel in Nuwara Eliya.'

Leaving Rosie open-mouthed on the terrace, he went inside and found Esther standing behind the door, where she had been listening to her mother shouting. Archie kissed her on the top of her head and said, 'Goodbye, little darling. I've no idea when I'll see you again.'

'Uncle Archie, don't go,' she said.

'Got to,' he replied. '*Pas de choix.*'

'Uncle Archie, were you alive in the olden days?'

That evening, Daniel came in and gathered Esther into his arms, carrying her out to the terrace.

'Uncle Archie did go,' said Esther.

'Go? Where?'

'Down the hill.'

'Where's Archie?' he said to Rosie, who was sitting somewhat rigidly in her wickerwork chair, hands clasped across her distended stomach.

'I believe he's walking to Nuwara Eliya,' she replied.

'What? Walking? To Nuwara Eliya? It's bloody miles!'

'Yes, he asked me to ask you to forward his things. To the hotel.'

'Why? What's happened?'

'I'm afraid we had a falling-out. I got angry about him killing all the animals, and he threw his elephant gun over the hillside, and he just went.'

'Oh God,' said Daniel, 'you know how he feels about you! And you've been shouting at him, I suppose?'

'Well, I did shout a bit. You know I can get heated. When I feel very strongly.'

'About shooting elephants?'

'And other things. Snipe, crocodiles. He even said he shoots dogs for crocodile bait.'

'You shoot rabid dogs, and you shoot pariah dogs who are taking livestock, at the request of the villagers,' he said stonily. 'No one shoots them for fun.'

'Oh, really? Oh dear. But elephants! They have families, and they're so sweet and intelligent. And such useful workers.'

'Well, the solitaries aren't.'

'The solitaries?'

'The rogues. The periya aliens. The ones who've been expelled from the clan. They've often lost their tail in a fight. They rampage in the villages and trample the huts. They're an absolute menace. In the absence of lunatic asylums for mad elephants, you have to shoot them. Archie shoots rogues, and it's always at the request of the natives or the local authorities. You need a special licence to kill any other kind of elephant. It costs a hundred rupees, and you have to get one for each province. Archie can't afford to go round spending a hundred rupees at a time, can he? He had a request when he was in Colombo. There are two rogues in the jungle behind Trincomalee. In the Eastern Province. Didn't he tell you?'

'Oh gosh,' said Rosie, putting her hand to her mouth.

'You have to shoot from virtually point-blank. The shots have to go straight into the elephant's brain or the beast just keeps on charging. You only have two bullets to fire before you're trampled to death. I wouldn't do it for love or money. Archie's braver than I am, that's for sure. It's heroism of the first water.'

Rosie's eyes began to fill with tears. 'He said … he said you can take a thousand snipe in a day. A thousand!'

'The bag,' said Daniel coldly, 'is distributed to the villagers. It's their one chance of a good feast, once in a blue moon. And there are literally millions of snipe around every tank. That's why it's so easy to get a thousand of them.'

'And the crocodiles?'

'I think you know the answer already, don't you?'

Rosie nodded, but Daniel continued anyway. 'Some of them get a taste for children and dogs. They can pull a grown man under and drown him before they eat him. And they're eminently edible, especially the tail.'

'Well, it seems a shame to kill peacocks,' she said feebly. 'They're so beautiful.'

'So are pheasants. Peacocks are just the local pheasants. I've seen you eat pheasant. Gaskell used to bring them to The Grampians when she came back from the estate.'

'Oh goodness, I've done a dreadful thing,' said Rosie, beginning to cry, and wiping her face with the back of her sleeve. 'I was so foul and horrible to him. Can't you go after him and ask him to come back, and tell him how sorry I am?'

'How little you know him. I'll go after him and take him to Nuwara Eliya. I know he won't come back. You say he threw his elephant gun over the hillside?'

Rosie nodded. 'And that silver cigarette lighter you gave him.'

'That gun was absolutely his most prized possession. It cost him something like ninety pounds, for God's sake. If we can find it in the morning I'll have to get it repaired myself.'

'It was absolutely massive,' said Rosie. 'I can't believe it would be much damaged.'

'It's very easy to dent a barrel.'

'Oh, Daniel, I'm so very sorry. Do you think he'd be able to walk to Nuwara Eliya?'

'He's a Frontier Scout,' replied Daniel. 'But all the same, I'm going to take the Henley and go after him.'

'But it's getting dark!'

'Well, then. Even so. God knows when I'll be back.'

'I'm going to write him a letter,' said Rosie, hanging her head. 'With any luck I can get it to the hotel before he leaves for Trinco.'

'You do that. But you'd better put Shompi to bed first.'

'Yes, of course.'

Daniel went to the hallway to retrieve his gauntlets and goggles, and returned to the terrace, where Rosie was sitting glumly, watching as the sun went down. 'I used to have three brothers,' he said fiercely, 'and now I only have one. Two brothers lost to the Empire. Both killed in South Africa. My father is dead. Archie is the only brother I have left.'

'What are you saying?'

'You know how Archie adores you. If anything happens to him … if he's prompted to … do anything … You know how little he values his life … Well … if anything happens, I'll never forgive you. And neither will my mother.'

'He wouldn't, would he?'

'He lives his whole life in the hope of losing it,' said Daniel. 'He's always been disgusted with himself. I thought you knew that.'

'Oh, darling, please don't be so angry with me.'

'I am damned bloody angry,' he replied, and left.

After the roar of the retreating Henley had faded into the darkness, Rosie knelt in the drawing room and tried to calm herself with prayer, but was immediately interrupted by Esther.

'Uncle Archie did go and now Daddy's gone,' she said, with her thumb in her mouth and her first and second fingers crooked over her nose.

'Yes, but Daddy's coming back.'

'Good,' said Esther. 'Can I *faire dodo* now? Can I have an *histoire?*'

'Mummy's no good at French,' said Rosie. 'In fact I seem to be rotten at lots of things. I'll tell you one in English, if you don't mind.'

'Can I have "Le Petit Chaperon Rouge"?'

4

Poor Child

Rosie's waters broke just an hour after the midwife arrived from Nuwara Eliya in her rugged, beaten-up little Riley. Daniel and Rosie were delighted by the fortuitous good timing of it all, and the three of them sat on the terrace drinking tea, whilst Rosie, bright-eyed with both fear and excitement cradled her vast belly in her hands. 'I really think I've got to walk about,' she said.

'Maybe you should jump up and down,' said Daniel.

'Oh, be quiet. It's no laughing matter.'

'Yes, I remember the last time.'

'I hardly remember it at all,' said Rosie. 'It was just one terrible nightmare that was suddenly over, and there I was, weeping, with Esther wrapped up in my arms. Wasn't she tiny? You forget so quickly.'

'You were awfully weepy and low for the first few days,' said Daniel.

'That's what usually happens,' said the midwife. 'But as this is your second, it shouldn't be nearly so prolonged and painful. One can be grateful for that. The labour might be just five hours or so.'

The midwife was a wide-hipped practical spinster in early middle age, with gunmetal hair organised into tight practical curls, who wore sensible shoes, and was armed with a black Gladstone bag. She had never given birth herself. Instead she had devoted her life to giving birth by proxy, and there was nothing she did not know about joy, suffering and tragedy. It had given her the kind of stoical outlook that accepts misfortune and smiles knowingly at good. She always liked to remind herself that man that is born of woman hath but a little time to live, and that every tiny creature she delivered was offered to life for a certain time only.

'Where are you from?' asked Daniel.

'Oh, I'm from Dorset,' she replied. 'Dorchester.' Her voice was cheerful and a little crackly, like someone who has been tippling on whisky.

'It's a lovely little place,' said Daniel. 'It reminds me of some of the towns in France.'

'Every town reminds you of somewhere in France,' said Rosie. 'I've lost count of the number of times you've said, "Oh, this is just like Abbeville."'

'Very true,' he replied. 'Apart from Colombo or Calcutta.'

'You're going to start labour in a minute,' said the midwife. 'I think I'll go to the room and make sure that everything is in place.'

'I'm certain it is,' said Rosie. 'The servants have been wonderful, and I've checked everything off on the list that you sent me.'

Rosie's labour commenced in the early evening, and she groaned suddenly. 'Oh my, here we go,' she said.

'Anything I can do?'

'Just let me hold your arm whilst I stagger about.'

'Shouldn't you be lying down?'

'Absolutely not. I can't think of anything worse.'

'You're going to miss supper.'

She gave him a baleful glance. 'I'm trying to get something out, not put more in.'

'Well, when are you supposed to go and lie down?'

'When I can't stand or walk any more. And stop fussing. We've got a midwife for that. Can you fetch her from the kitchen?'

'I do admire your courage,' said Daniel.

They walked round and round the terrace, Rosie flinching and crying out with every pang, 'Oh God, oh God.'

'It was hell last time,' said Daniel. 'You don't know how horrible it is to be locked out whilst someone you love is apparently being tortured to death for hours.'

'I am full of sympathy,' gasped Rosie.

'If it's a boy,' said Daniel, 'would you like us to call him Ashbridge? I'm just wondering. I mean he was my friend too. I wouldn't mind, I really wouldn't.'

'It's a girl,' said Rosie, 'I'm sure of it.'

'Ashbridgette doesn't sound too good, does it?'

'There's nothing wrong with Bridget.'

'Brigitte is even better.'

'Let's just wait and see what she's like.'

'Yes, of course. Do you think Esther will be all right, staying with Hugh?'

'Well, I wouldn't want her here, listening to me screaming and swearing.'

'Do you really intend to swear? You didn't last time.'

'I'm going to be cursing you at the top of my lungs.'

'I'm man enough to take it. You can apologise when you've cooled down, in a year or two.'

'I think it's coming.'

As Daniel escorted Rosie to their bedroom, they were surprised to find all four of the servants lined up in a row against the wall of the corridor. One by one they held out a hand to be shaken, smiling broadly and saying 'Good luck, missy' and giving a little bow.

'Oh gosh, they're so sweet,' said Rosie as she lay down on the bed; 'I could almost cry.'

'I fear they may have a long night.'

The child arrived at half past two in the morning. Just as the last time, Daniel paced up and down, sat with his head in his hands, raided the whisky bottle, and cringed with sympathy every time that Rosie yelled. It reminded him of pulling broken airmen out of the wreckage of their aircraft. The servants took turns to bring him sustenance, saying, 'Master need more tea, master need more tea, master need mutton chop, master need snack.'

'Thank you, but I really don't,' Daniel would say, accepting the offerings anyway, before resuming his striding about.

Preethi, Esther's ayah, came out of the kitchen and smiled at him. Her huge brown eyes seemed to sparkle with the pleasure of anticipation. 'Oh, how she lives up to her name!' thought Daniel, as he did every time he saw her.

'If master go out, baby come quicker,' she said.

'Go out?'

'Yes, master go out for walk, baby come. Always happens. Missy crying more often now.'

'A long walk?'

'Just factory and back, maybe two, maybe three times. Maybe down to village, come back up.'

'I might have to anyway. Otherwise I'll go mad.'

'Missy very strong, very brave,' said Preethi. 'Master not to worry.' She went to the hall stand, and presented him with his hat.

There was a light rain when Daniel went out, and it was extremely dark. He waited a few minutes for his eyes to adjust, and then set off for the factory. Once there he sat on a crate, and soon realised that the water was soaking through to his skin. He walked round the factory perimeter, and then further down the road to the bungalow where Hugh lived with his wife. All the lights were off, so he stood outside the window of the room where he thought Esther might be sleeping.

'Sleep well, my little darling,' he said softly, and then turned on his heel and returned to Taprobane.

Five minutes before he returned, the midwife delivered the child, took one look at it, wrapped it hastily in a towel, and ran to the bathroom, leaving Rosie both exhausted and bewildered, her hair knotted with sweat, the afterbirth slipping out unattended.

Sensing movement, Daniel put his head round the door, and beheld the midwife, stock-still, standing back from the basin. 'I'm so very sorry,' she said.

Daniel came in and looked at the child in the basin as, beneath its caul of blood and slime, its body began to turn from crimson to blue. The face was very beautiful, its tiny mouth turned up at the ends as if it were suppressing a smile. It was a boy.

'Don't look too much, sir,' said the midwife; 'you don't want to be having nightmares.'

But Daniel looked anyway. He had seen many horrors during the war, but he had never realised that such a thing as this might be possible. 'Oh God in heaven,' he said, his eyes welling up.

'I'm going to go and tend to Mrs Pitt,' said the midwife.

'You do that,' said Daniel.

He took a sponge and washed the dead child clean, and then wrapped it in a towel and took it out onto the terrace. He sat down in one of the wicker chairs and hugged it to his shoulder. 'Oh Christ, oh Christ,' he said, rocking with the grief of it. 'You poor little mite.' Although it was dead, it smelled as a baby should, warm and sweet.

The ayah came out, and stood in front of him. Daniel said, 'Preethi, the child is dead.'

She put her hands to her face and ran indoors. Soon he heard all the servants wailing together in the kitchen, so he stood up and carried the child into them.

'Please stop,' he said, speaking in Tamil. 'Think of missy. Go to bed, all of you.'

The servants scurried out, wiping their eyes and glancing at the dead baby's face as they passed, each one saying, 'So sorry, master, so sorry.' Preethi was last, and as she left she kissed the tips of her fingers and touched them to the child's forehead. 'God bless,' she said.

'Thank you,' said Daniel. 'Goodnight.'

As he stood alone in the kitchen with the baby wrapped up in his arms, the midwife entered, saying, 'Oh, there you are.' She tried to take the dead child from him, but he grasped it more tightly. 'But, sir,' she said.

'It's my child.'

'So it is, sir, but what are we going to do about Mrs Pitt?'

'What do you normally do?'

'You tell them straight away that it's dead, and then they're so exhausted that they fall asleep anyway. And then you tell them why in the morning when they wake up. It might be better, sir, if I take it away and she doesn't have to see it. It's what one normally does.'

'No.'

'Honestly, sir, it is better if they don't.'

'I know my wife very much better than you do. She was a nurse in the war, and there's almost nothing she hasn't seen. She'll need to see for herself or she'll never come to terms with it.'

'I'm sorry, sir, but you're quite wrong about this –'

'Am I employing you or are you employing me?'

'Well,' she said crossly, 'you may have it your way, and regret it at your leisure.'

'I suggest that we see if my wife is asleep, and then go to bed ourselves. I'll keep the child.'

Daniel slept that night with his dead child wrapped up in a towel beside him in the bed. His dreams were vivid and terrifying, and when he awoke in the morning to see that it was still raining outside, it was a moment before he remembered the stiff little bundle that had slept so deeply next to him. He shaved and dressed, and then went to see Rosie, who was sitting up in bed with the midwife holding her hand.

Daniel bent down and kissed his wife on the cheek, saying, 'Do you know?'

She nodded dumbly and bit her lips, looking at him piteously with her large blue eyes.

'Do you know why?'

'I told her it's better not to know,' said the midwife, looking up at him, 'but she's very obstinate.'

'I want to see him. All of him.'

'It's not pretty,' said Daniel.

'I don't care,' said Rosie. 'He's my child.'

Daniel went back to his room and returned with the baby, laying it before her on the bed.

Rosie unwrapped it hastily, paused, then said, 'I see.'

The child's dark brown liver and kidneys, its yellow intestines, all of its internal organs lay on the outer surface of the abdomen, protected by nothing but a thick white, translucent membrane.

'It's called an omphalocele,' said the midwife. 'I've only ever seen it once before in my life, and it wasn't nearly as extreme as this. They tried to operate but it died of peritonitis. I don't think this one's even got a stomach cavity. This must be the worst it can possibly be.'

5

The Reverend Williams

Daniel stalled his machine outside the church by pulling out the choke, and lifted his goggles onto his forehead. He dismounted and walked through the lychgate, trying to shake off the stiffness of having been riding for so long.

Holy Trinity Church, of Nuwara Eliya, sat on the hillside facing across the valley to the terraced slopes opposite. It had a small external belfry with a single bell. The building was rendered and painted in cream, with a corrugated-iron roof, and had chunky buttresses whose sole function was to announce to the world that this was a place of worship rather than a bungalow. By the road outside there was a stand of eucalyptus, and in the large graveyard, an enormous monkey puzzle tree. The yard itself was awash with ochre-coloured day lilies that gave it a bright and happy appearance, and two gardeners were clipping at the grass around the tombs. Daniel wished them a good morning, and they smiled and bobbed in delight, replying, 'Morning, master. Morning, master.'

He walked around the church until he found the one door that had been left unlocked, and went inside. Rows of pews were set across the rough-hewn, gappy floorboards, and a small harmonium served the place of an organ. The walls were hung with brass and marble memorials, and Daniel read them, one after the other. They only increased his melancholy.

He looked at the curved rafters of the nave, and then at the stained-glass windows above the altar. They seemed both sombre and Pre-Raphaelite, and too small, as if Rossetti had been obliged to come to a compromise with another artist of impeccable Victorian respectability.

Daniel knelt before the altar rail and began to pray, but soon gave up. He had long felt envious of Rosie's ability to find consolation in her personal conversations with God, but whenever he

25

tried it himself he had the ineluctable sensation of speaking to no one, across a void. He could sense the Deity only in His extreme absence.

He stood up, and said, 'I don't think You're really much concerned, are You?'

He returned to the door, and went back out into a light rain that reminded him of home. Nuwara Eliya was often called 'Little England'. He took another lychgate through into the garden of the vicarage, a bungalow with the inevitable metal roof, and a lovely croquet lawn whose hoops had been freshly aspinalled.

The Reverend J. L. Williams, Anglican vicar of Nuwara Eliya, was aroused from his napping on the terrace by his wife, who came in and shook his shoulder, saying, 'Darling, there's someone here who wants to see you urgently.'

'Oh drat,' said the clergyman wearily, sitting up in his reclining chair. 'Send him in then. And can you fetch Fernando? We've got a monkey in the garden again. Damned nuisance.'

'Can I get you a cup of tea?' she asked Daniel, as he took off his motorcycling gear in the hallway and handed it to a servant to be hung up.

'I practically drown in tea every day,' he said, 'but yes please, Mrs Williams. Is there any chance of having it *à la française*? Weak, with no sugar or milk?'

'How very unusual,' she said.

'I am half French,' he explained apologetically.

'How fascinating,' she said flatly, and then passed the request on to the servant, in Tamil.

Daniel was shown out to the terrace, and the Reverend Williams got awkwardly to his feet in order to shake hands. He was a slightly corpulent gentleman of about sixty years, with two clumps of grey curls sprouting out of either side of an otherwise bald head.

'Daniel Pitt,' he said, and the Reverend Williams replied, 'Yes. Yes, we have met before. Though not often. Your wife, I believe, is very much more active as a … as a … as a …'

'Christian?'

'Well, as a member of the congregation, shall we say? She comes here when she's in town.'

'I see you have a monkey in the garden,' said Daniel.

'Damned nuisance. This one throws its, er, excrement at the windows, and if you leave one open, it comes inside and steals things, and tears up my sermons and so on.'

'An infidel monkey,' said Daniel. 'I suppose you've got the monkey man coming?'

'Of course. Anyway, do sit down. What can I do for you?'

Daniel sat down on the edge of the chair and asked bluntly, 'Do unbaptised babies go to hell because of having inherited original sin?'

'What? Gracious me! Why do you ask?'

'Because yesterday, Rosemary, my wife, gave birth to a child that died immediately. She is utterly distraught because she thinks it will go straight to hell.'

'Oh my goodness. Is that what you think?'

'I have no faith at all, I'm afraid. To me hell has as much reality as Atlantis. I am just very worried for the sanity and *bien-être* of my wife.'

'I see your point, I see your point.'

'Well, what do you think?'

'Well, we Anglicans have no settled doctrine on the matter. In some churchyards they have unhallowed ground for the burial of the unbaptised, but we don't do that here. She is an Anglican?'

'Very High Church.'

'Oh dear, the awkward squad. Well, the Romans believe in limbo, don't they? You don't go to hell but you don't see God either. I don't think it's official doctrine, though.'

'Please will you do me a very big favour?'

'Well, I will if I can, of course.'

'Will you conduct a service for the burial of the child, and will you come with me to talk to my wife? Pray with her perhaps? She is still in bed. I don't mind what you tell her as long as it's comforting. As long as you tell her that the baby is not going to suffer torment. I have my combination outside.'

'A combination? How exciting. I love riding in a combination. I shall have to cancel the Ladies' Bible Study Group, but, to be honest, I will not be much aggrieved. My wife can look after them. She usually does. Aren't you nearer to Christ Church in Varleigh, though? Shouldn't the body be buried there?'

'I couldn't find the vicar. I think he must be on leave. I don't mind where it's buried as long as it's in hallowed ground, and you tell Rosie that it's not going to hell. What if we bury it in one of those roadside cemeteries on the plantation, near to our bungalow? Then we could visit it more often.'

'My dear boy, those are Roman Catholic. For Tamils. I think it would cause more trouble than it's worth. Rosemary might not consider it properly hallowed, and the natives might think they have an unwanted intruder. One has to be terribly sensitive about the natives. Things tend to backfire.'

'Oh, I hadn't realised. I never snooped in one. I just saw all the crosses.'

'Well, if you do, you'll see that all the names are Portuguese. I suggest we do the burial at Christ Church. I'll sort out the formalities afterwards. No one'll be any the wiser. But how will the grave be dug? I've no idea who the sexton is. Perhaps we could slip a few rupees to a native.'

'I'll dig it myself,' said Daniel. 'He's such a tiny little mite, it won't take long. Do you think I could borrow a spade?'

'Well, of course. And you'd better take a pick as well.'

'It's a fair distance. I suggest that you stay the night. It'll give Rosie more time with you. I promise to feed you well.'

'Mutton chops, I suppose,' said the vicar.

'I'm afraid so. It's a wonder there are any goats left on the island.'

'You should take the opportunity to try some of the native foods, you know. Porcupine is absolutely delicious. Of course, one has to wait until one's wife is away, and then ask the servants, and then you have to put up with their incredulity and disapproval. They hate it when we go native. It's like having trespassers in one's garden. Or a damned monkey.' The Reverend Williams laughed quietly, and Daniel said, 'What are you laughing about?'

'Oh, I have a sweet boy who's my *podian*, and he writes out the menus for dinner, and yesterday my wife called me and said "Look what Ahilesh has written!" and she showed me the menu, and it said "Roman Cream" which is perfectly fine, but above it, he'd written "Wilderness".'

'Wilderness?'

'Yes. He'd looked in our dictionary to find another word for "desert". Anyway, I'll just pack a few things. I expect your wife would like communion.'

'I'm certain she would.'

'And may I ask you something? You seem very concerned about your wife, but how are you bearing up yourself? I don't mean to intrude, but ...'

'Well, Father,' replied Daniel, 'it hasn't properly sunk in yet, and I haven't slept for two days. At present I feel a strange combination of anger and numbness. I think of these dreadful things as natural mishaps. My wife thinks of them as acts of divine retribution. Sometimes, however, I think of them as evidence that God doesn't give a fig about any of us. And please don't tell me that God moves in mysterious ways.'

'No, I shall desist.'

'Thank you. It would only make me more angry.'

'Of course, of course.'

Twenty minutes later Daniel and the clergyman were out on the roadside, with Daniel lashing the spade and the luggage to the rack on the back of the sidecar. He removed a small rectangular box from the seat and handed it to the vicar, saying, 'Do you mind travelling with this on your lap?'

The vicar was about to shake it to see what was inside, when he suddenly realised what it was. 'Did you make this yourself?'

'Had to,' said Daniel. 'I can't wait for a coffin. I made it this morning, in the factory workshop.'

'You've done a marvellously neat job.'

'Well,' said Daniel, 'it's for my son. One has to do one's best. Do you know where I can get a headstone?'

'They have to be ordered from home, I'm afraid. It takes months. Why don't we bury the poor little mite here, in this graveyard? In Nuwara Eliya? Wouldn't that be more convenient for everyone?'

'It's too far to visit with any frequency. It wouldn't feel right.'

As Daniel put on his flying helmet and goggles, the vicar rubbed his hands together with anticipation. 'I went up in a balloon once,' he said. 'It was marvellous.'

'I was a scout pilot,' replied Daniel. 'And that was even more marvellous.' He turned to face the clergyman. 'Please remember that I would like you to tell my wife that the child has gone straight to heaven.'

'But I actually don't know where it's gone,' he protested.

'Put it this way,' said Daniel. 'The baby's departed. There's absolutely nothing we can do for him. What we do for the dead is really for ourselves.'

'Let the dead bury their dead?'

'Exactly so. My concern is for someone I love who is very much alive, and completely desperate. If you must, then cross your fingers and tell her lies.'

'You can't lie if you don't know the truth,' said the Reverend Williams. He looked up at the hills opposite, waved his right hand, and said, 'Soteriology. It's all a complete mystery, really. I'm really terribly sorry for your loss.'

6

At Christ Church

The little church was set back from a curve in the road that ascended through the hills, beside the plantations. On the left-hand side they passed stupendous waterfalls whose cataracts ran beneath the road and on down the slopes, until they united with the lakes and rivers thousands of feet below.

It was a difficult drive for Daniel, not least because of the slow bullock carts heaped with jackfruit, or hay, or scarlet mangosteens, and usually topped off with a few small, dark, laughing children, whilst the adults plodded beside. The road was secure, but not well surfaced, and inclined to be damaged frequently by landslides and heavy rain. Everywhere there were parties of coolies making them good, and Daniel often thanked the God in whom he did not believe that he was neither an ox nor a coolie. He had to stop three times to adjust the carburettor to the changing altitudes.

When they pulled in, Daniel cut the engine by means of both the choke and the advance/retard lever, and it popped and banged as it struggled, and then gave up. The Reverend Williams and Daniel dismounted and shook the stiffness out of their limbs.

'I do love this little church,' said the clergyman. 'They keep it so beautiful, and in July that flamboyant tree is a real pleasure.'

'We'd better walk about and find an empty spot,' said Daniel.

'I have to warn you that you still might find bones. Sometimes there was never any headstone. We'd just have to put them back after we've lowered the coffin.'

'I've seen a great many bones,' said Daniel. 'They're the most beautiful sparkling white when they're freshly exposed. They have a tint of blue.'

'Ah,' said the clergyman, 'yes, I can hardly imagine what you must have been through.'

'Old bones would be positively relaxing by comparison.'

They found a small space by the wall on the right, and Daniel began to dig. The red earth came up easily enough, and when the hole was about three feet deep, he looked down into it as he leaned on the spade, puffing from the exertion, and said, 'It's not really practical to dig such a small hole any deeper.'

'Normally you'd go for six feet,' said the Reverend Williams. 'Would you let me do some digging? I feel shamefully redundant just standing here watching you slaving away. I'm still quite hale.'

'It's very good of you, but I'd like to be selfish if you don't mind.'

'Selfish?'

'Yes. I want to do this for my son. For my little boy. It's all I can do, all I'll ever be able to do.'

'I do understand. But let me know if you change your mind.'

At a depth of four feet, Daniel climbed out, saying, 'I really can't dig any deeper. There isn't the space for getting any leverage on the spade.'

The Reverend Williams peered down into the hole. 'It looks deep enough to me,' he said. 'In any case, no one will ever know how deep it is, will they?'

'What's the point of the six-foot rule anyway?'

'To deter thieves and ghouls? I don't really know. I do know that the deeper the body is, the more slowly it rots. Perhaps it's just to make the flesh last a little bit longer. I suggest we draw stumps. This is a perfectly good grave as it is. Let's do the burial service, shall we?' He took his Book of Common Prayer from his pocket, and thumbed through it until he reached the Order for the Burial of the Dead. Daniel reached for the little coffin, and placed it at his feet. It seemed unbelievable and atrocious that his beautiful little child lay still within it, having had no chance in life at all. Rage and sorrow, rage and sorrow.

Daniel scrambled out and stood beside the Reverend Williams. He looked over his shoulder. 'Have you read what it says at the top?' he said.

Here it is to be noted, that the office ensuing is not to be used for any that die unbaptised, or excommunicate, or have laid violent hands upon themselves.

'I suggest we ignore it,' said the Reverend Williams.

'Really? And you a clergyman?'

'This is between God and us. In the end, I'm a Protestant. You look a little shocked.'

'Well, one expects priests to be somewhat fanatical and exigent. To have more exacting standards than the ordinary man.'

'This may seem strange to you, but I am confident that I know what God expects from me. God isn't the God of the Old Testament any more; He's not even an Elizabethan. This is the twentieth century. I don't believe in original sin, and I'm damned if I'm going to consign a stillborn child to unhallowed ground without any kind of blessing. If the Good Lord is offended, He'll let me know at some future date, if I manage to breach the Pearly Gates, and I shall try to explain myself as best I can. I would just ask you not to proclaim in public what I've done. It might get back to the Bishop.'

'I'm not convinced he was stillborn. I think the midwife may have stifled him. He was hideously deformed. All his guts were on the outside.'

'Oh my goodness. She murdered it?'

'I don't really know. I came in and she was standing there over the dead baby. She had a pillow in one hand. I can't prove anything. The idea only occurred to me as I was driving here.'

'Aren't you going to do anything about it?'

'It would have been a mercy killing. Without witnesses.'

'Even so ...'

'Well, Father, I can't be a hypocrite. I've shot three of my friends, and two enemies, who were burning to death in the wrecks of aeroplanes. It takes a desperate fight to overcome oneself, to commit such acts of mercy. It still troubles me, almost all the time, but I know it was right. She must have known it was right. Perhaps she saved me from having to do it.'

Father Williams stared into the tiny pit, and said softly, 'I think that on this occasion I shall have to defer to you.' He lifted his head, closed his eyes, and without looking at the prayer book, began to recite: 'Man that is born of woman hath but a short time to live, and is full of misery. He cometh up and is cut down, like a flower; he fleeth as it were a shadow, and never continueth in one stay ...'

At the end, the priest bent down and threw a handful of earth onto the little box, and Daniel did the same. They made a light, hollow rattle. Then Daniel took the spade, and set about filling the grave. His anger and grief gave him an unnatural, decisive energy.

Afterwards, they sat quietly for a while, side by side in the front pew of the little church, and then Daniel asked, 'That new grave, with five children in it, near the front gate. What happened?'

'Yellow fever.'

'My God, this country really is a white man's grave,' said Daniel.

'We've still got yellow fever at home in England,' replied the Reverend Williams reasonably, 'and my grandfather lost six children in one flu epidemic, in Manchester. They had to begin again. I'm descended from number seven.'

'Even so, have you ever walked around the old cemetery in Kandy? Behind the Temple of the Tooth? There's barely a soul who reached forty. There must be a dozen who never got to twenty-five. We come here and live like kings, and then we die suddenly of something foul. What on earth do we think we're doing?'

'It's the natives who have the hard short lives. Not us. They get yaws. I dare say that we're as well off here as we would be at home. The people who reached their threescore years and ten were the ones who went home to retire, and settled into damp little cottages in the Cotswolds, with names like "Adam's Peak" and "Trinco". That's why the ones who got old aren't in the graveyards of Ceylon.'

'I have my doubts. Has anyone collected any statistics?'

'I've no idea, old boy. Anyway, what is upsetting you is the recent misfortune with your poor little boy. You can't blame that on the Empire. And I imagine you haven't slept for quite a long time.'

'Only a little. I do feel a kind of drunkenness. Like the woozy disconnection that had everybody reeling during Bloody April.'

They sat in silence for a long time, and then the priest broke it. 'If you think of how long eternity is, and put everything into perspective, then you and I haven't lived any longer than that poor little boy.'

'I know that, Father, but you're talking like a mathematician. You and I don't live in eternity. We live in what seems like a fairly long portion that we borrow from it. '

The Reverend Williams laughed softly. 'You know, for some reason, I always get on much better with agnostics than I do with the faithful.'

'My brother-in-law, Fairhead, always says that. He was a military chaplain and now he's working in a hospital. He sometimes finds believers very tiresome, just as narrow-minded and foolish as atheists. He's probably my best friend these days.'

'Yes, well, thank God for agnostics, that's what I say. Let's go out and find flowers for your little boy, and then we'll see what we can do for your poor wife.'

7

The Beatitudes of Oily Wragge

The architect of The Grampians had designed it so that it would have a dignified and impressive set of steps up to the front door. The consequence of this was that the ground floor was a good six feet above ground level, and beneath it was a system of passages that meant one did not have to lift any floorboards in order to perform maintenance on the wires and pipes. It was dark in there, but not too damp, and it had been a wonderful playground for the house's children. With their flickering matches, candles or torches, they had crept around in the cold shadows, frightening themselves with thoughts of spectres and creepy crawlies, and enjoying the absolute absence of adults, with their 'be careful' and their 'never let me catch you doing that again'. If you were very still, you could hear the adults walking and talking above, oblivious to you crouching in the darkness, all your senses alert, like a fox at night. When they were childhood sweethearts, Ashbridge and Rosie had met in there in order to be deliciously and poignantly alone.

Back then there had been a whole tribe of children, who called themselves 'The Pals'. Archie and Daniel Pitt lived next door; Rosie, Christabel, Ottilie and Sophie in this house; and Ashbridge and his brothers on the other side. But now the children had grown. Ashbridge and his brothers were dead. Archie was on the North-West Frontier. Christabel had struck up an unconventional friendship with a green-eyed artist who comported herself like a man, and moved between Lewes, Hexham, Chelsea and Bloomsbury, mounting successful and controversial exhibitions all over the country. Sophie had married her chaplain, and Rosie and Daniel were planting tea in Ceylon. Of the children, only Ottilie remained, the most sensible and quiet of all of them, with her big eyes, her wide hips, her brown bob of hair, and her unkissed lips that would have been so adept at kissing. She was still waiting for Archie, who was himself consumed with a painful and impossible passion for her sister, Rosie. Ottilie was too grown up now to venture into the dark passages beneath the house, and so she stayed upstairs with her increasingly peculiar mother and her genial father.

The entrance to the labyrinth was at the back of the house, inside a large tenebrous cave beneath the conservatory; a room full of garden implements, piles of sacking, the wheelbarrow and the mower. It was here that Oily Wragge had his lair.

He had returned at the end of the war, escaping at last the malnutrition and enslavement of his labour on the Ottoman railways, but too sick to carry on soldiering. He had been skeletal, his eyes glowing with sickness, his mind whirling with the horror of his memories, his intestines all but ruined by enteritis and typhus. Sometimes his head still spun in response to the hundreds of blows from rifle butts. He still heard the slavers' cries of 'Yallah! Yallah!', his back would forever bear the scars of the floggings with plaited hide, and he would always walk a little gingerly because of Commandant Musloom Bey's enjoyment of the basti-nado.

Oily had married before he left for the war, because the woman was pregnant, but upon his return four years later he had found her gone. The neighbours said she had absconded with a Gordon Highlander. Oily had never known his child. He was told he should write to the Colonel of the Gordons, because the officers were good at sorting out these kinds of things, but he put it off because of a strange terror, and because he could not write.

Oily was a Norwich boy. When he wanted to say 'I'm going', it came out as 'Oi'm a gooin'. Nowadays his surviving comrades of the 2nd Battalion, the Norfolk Regiment, were trawling the endless desert roads of Mesopotamia and the plateaus of Anatolia for the scattered bones of their friends, but Oily Wragge had found himself work at The Grampians as a gardener, and lived contentedly in the dank cave of tools under the conservatory until Mr McCosh discovered him there, and told him he might only stay for as long as it took to find decent accommodation.

Oily Wragge had never minded living the troglodyte's life beneath the conservatory. There were no lice or fleas, as in the hovels he had inhabited in Anatolia, and, in the absence of the other slaves, it seemed incomparably and wonderfully roomy. How pleasant it was to stretch out one's legs, roll a cigarette made with proper tobacco, and knock back huge mugs of tea with real milk and sugar. It was cool in there in the summer, and not as cold in winter as the Anatolian plateau, nothing you couldn't cope with by piling up the sacks and drawing over a greatcoat. There was no comrade doubled up with intestinal spasms, taking days to die, and no Arab or Kurdish tribesman to strip him naked, beat him and leave him for dead.

Mr Wragge was content in his modest paradise. After the death marches, and the months of tunnelling in the mountains with a pick, this English garden was indeed a dream of Eden, and therein he set about pulling himself together. He pruned fruit trees and roses, and forked out weeds. He mowed militarily immaculate rows of stripes across the lawn, and then along it at right angles. He cleaned and oiled the mower, and took it to bits twice every summer to decoke it. He had a tin with his eponymous oily rag in it, to wipe the tools clean each evening so that they would not rust. He marked out the lines of the tennis court, and left a white spot in each place where a croquet hoop should be, were the family to tire of playing tennis. He cleaned and polished the moletraps, even though there were no moles. In the autumn he laid up the apples in the apple shed, with the keepers at the back, each one meticulously wrapped in its own piece of brown paper. He made weak cider for himself by pulping a share of the apples and squeezing it through a cloth. Every day he would release the gas with a quick twist of the screwcaps, until there was no more hiss, and he knew it was ready to drink. All those years of slavery and torment without one drink of alcohol, and now he could linger over each appley mouthful until his tongue and cheeks began to tingle and his eyes rolled with delight. It was bliss.

Oily Wragge bought a Primus stove and a brown teapot with his first wage, so that he would not have to depend on Cookie's limited generosity for tea. He bought a small skillet so that he could cook himself fried bread and sausages for lunch.

Even after finding lodgings, Oily Wragge thought of the tool store as his real home. There was one small cracked window, overgrown outside by a climbing rose, so it let in very little light, but Oily made a curtain out of a sack, and each morning he drew back the curtain when he arrived for work, and closed it again each evening when he left. Sometimes, especially in summer, he reverted to staying there at night, gazing in wonder at the stars as he staggered out, woozy from cider, to urinate in the rose beds.

Oily Wragge was determined to salvage his sanity out of the purgatorial experience of captivity. He attempted slowly and deliberately to come to terms with his war in Mesopotamia and his enslavement in Anatolia, by sorting his memories into the least painful order. He tried to look at them, as it were, from the outside, as if he were a spectator, and not someone to whom they had happened. Eventually he began to consider that the ordering of his recollections was in fact not the most important thing; what was important was the final memory, the one he deliberately kept 'til last, the one that would be nearest to salvation, the one that blazed with light. This memory would have to cancel out the darkness and lift his spirit from the slough.

When he was not busy in the garden, Oily Wragge climbed into the wheelbarrow and went to sleep, his head lolling on a wad of sacking. He instinctively knew that it would require an eternity of sleep to restore his peace, for the world had to be excluded in order for him to wake up and go back out into it again.

Oily Wragge dreamed of Mespot, which is the arsehole of the universe, where Basra is the arsehole of the arsehole, and Kut is the arsehole of the arsehole of the arsehole.

The many months of siege, when we confidently knew that our provisions would not run out before the relief force arrived. Us placing bets on the day of their arrival. Then the floods that cut us off.

The dust flies, sunstroke, the stomach cramps, the dysentery and sweat, the flies in every orifice, on food and water. The shamal wind that blows for weeks and covers and fills the world with dust. Oh, Oily, I can't see a thing.

The Arabs selling us eggs. The Marsh Arabs concealed in the reeds, shooting us down for fun. Townshend's regatta. The hard bites of the sandflies. No medicine, no quinine, no vegetables, no castor oil, rumours of sharks in the river. The wounded at Vital Point, the camel thorn shrubs that ripped our clothes and flesh, the ammunition dumps aflame, our mate Bill shot nine times. Oh, Oily, they've made me a bloomin' pepper pot. The ranks of the wounded laid out in the bazaar, the incessant frenzy of digging in, the water carriers picked off one by one by snipers, the Turkish corpses bloating on Corpse Hill, the star shells and Very lights throwing the night into absolute light and total shadow. I remember how lovely the star shells were.

The daily Hymn of Hate, the fighting all day on Christmas Day, the gangrene, the ceasefire when the Turks came with iron hooks on long poles to drag the corpses to pits, the corpses that fell to bits or exploded.

The Tigris in flood that made us almost an island, the implacable wind and rain, the rain that marinaded the corpses all the better for the sun to come out after and cook them. The obsolete aircraft dropping relief parcels that fell in the river and wouldn't have been enough. Atta bread and horseflesh. The Hindu soldiers dying more quickly than us, fifteen a day from scurvy, because there were no vegetables and they wouldn't eat horses and donkeys, the Muslim soldiers dying more quickly than us whilst waiting for fatwas that let them eat horses and donkeys.

Tetanus, scurvy, beriberi, our legs swelling up and then the rest of our bodies, and when at last our heads swelled up, that's when we died. Mesopotamian mud that clings like the grip of drowning men. Starvation, scorpions, slugs. Eating the pretty starlings. The Last Post, the Reverend H. Spooner in his white surplice, tireless at burial. The desert covered in graves. The natives stealing the wooden crosses for cooking, a cloud of flies so dense that nothing at all could be seen. Fanny the giant antique cannon of Ctesiphon, her shots that always fell short.

Eating a bitch and her five pups. Oh, Oily, I never thought I'd sink to this.

The rumble of cannon, the skirl of pipes in the distance, mirages, the vivid lightning at night, the jaundice, the starvation that one day brings the eerie silence of surrender, the total destruction of all our useful kit. Bonfires of saddlery, documents, bedding, chairs, guncotton in the breeches of the guns, the handing over of officers' swords, the cholera, the black biscuits, the evacuation of General Townshend's dogs, the biblical plague of fleas, our interpreters hanged in rows in the square, an Arab about to be hanged who throws me his prayer beads, the flogging and hanging of Sheikh Abbas.

The first death march, the hundred-mile trudge to Baghdad.

Starved and ill, in heat so scorching it can't be imagined or told, without food, without water, we are driven along by Arab horsemen. The beatings with rifle butts, the trampling of the dying, the theft of our boots and clothes. Enteritis. *Yallah! Yallah! Yallah!* Move on, move on. Shit running down our legs, pains like childbirth in our guts. Oh, Oily, I'll never make it, I'm falling out, I'm going to die down there, in the stones. Goodbye, old son, if I make it back I'll try to get a message to your mum.

The stripping of the dead, the skipping of vultures, the bark of jackals, the rivers of black beetles, the rain, a plague of inedible frogs.

Septic sores, oedema.

And after Baghdad, it's six hundred miles, twenty miles a day to Ras-el-Ain. Two thousand two hundred and twenty-two dead on the march, stripped naked, starved, bayoneted, beaten, left behind in the road. The horsemen galloping past, holding their guns by the sling, swinging the stocks at our heads. This is a game, their own special kind of polo, they whoop with delight, to hell with the filthy infidels *Yallah! Yallah! Yallah!* The villagers throwing stones as we beg for food, the women and children hissing, the drawing of forefingers across the throat, the real thing from the guards, just for the practice, just for the entertainment.

The vast dogs set upon us by their shepherds, attacking in pairs. The floggings and shootings at Ctesiphon. Wrapping puttees round our feet to replace our stolen boots, wading waist-deep in mud to reach the high road, Crosse & Blackwell jam tins for cooking all the food we didn't have with water we didn't have, the jibes of the Arabs, 'English finished, English finished', the sick camp by the river, no floor, no walls, straw mats up on poles. No water, no medicine, no food, no latrines. The unwashed bandages, the unsterilised blades. Oh, Oily, I'm shitting myself to death.

Blessed are the dying for they shall soon be dead.

Paraded for Enver Pasha's satisfaction, our bodies wrapped in blankets and left.

Nineteen deaths per day.

The march, the never-ending march, a road just travelled by Armenians. The wells filled with mutilated women and children, the hovels packed with Armenian bones, the houses destroyed, the naked skeletons by the roadside cleaned up by jackals and vultures, the Armenian women with horseshoes nailed to their feet, the escorts who can't count higher than a hundred, and count us over and over.

The flour and wholemeal at the end of the day, without any means to cook it, we're too ill to cook, there's no water, our tongues swell up in our mouths. A bivouac of all we possess, and we sleep around in a ring, to stop the Arabs from stealing. Sandfish a penny each. Oily, can you spare me a penny? Has anyone got a penny? Ain't nobody got one penny?

Naked except for our feet. The vast burns festering on our shoulders. The dying stripped and thrashed, and left to the tribes. The Turks hiding the dying from General Mellis. At Jolahi, the massacre by neglect. At Nisibin, a doctor giving us poison.

At Bagtche a loaf and a week's rest, and water that ran to reach us through six Armenian cemeteries. At Taurus, the burial of the dying along with the dead.

Being forced to buy water from a dogskin, only five hundred yards from the river where the water ran for nothing.

Two thousand miles on foot.

Processions of the insane, the maddened Armenians, gibbering, eating dirt and falling, emaciated babies that clung to the necks of dead mothers, naked lacerated trembling women striped all over with weals, seeping with pus from the piercing of bayonets.

At Afion on Thursdays, the weekly floggings to death.

Malaria, rheumatic fever, typhus.

The Commandant Musloom Bey, who flogged us and starved us and opened a shop to sell our clothes, and dragged the youngsters away to fuck them from behind.

Lying in his wheelbarrow in the twilight of his cave under the conservatory, this is what Oily Wragge remembers of his war in Mesopotamia, the arsehole of the world, and of his slavery in Anatolia. He remembers either in order or in no order at all, but before he shuts them out he remembers the following things:

General Mellis who tirelessly bullied the Turks and gave us money and found us food and refused to leave us, until the Turks lost patience and sent him away by another route.

The women of Kersheba who let us wash our feet and gave us yogurt.

An American priest who came with carts and took away the dead.

In Mosul the gift of half a pound of raisins each, from an unknown hand.

Mr Brissell, the American Consul, who sent us disinfectant and sheep, and died of the cholera he caught from us.

The Benedictine nuns of Baghdad.

Armenians in towns who gave us dates and cigarettes, knowing they'd be flogged to death if caught.

Dr Illia, the Turkish doctor, who tried to help.

The Anatolian Greeks in the mountains and deserts who knelt in the stones and prayed for us as we passed.

Blessed are the dying, for they shall soon be dead;
Blessed is General Mellis;
Blessed are the women of Kersheba;
Blessed is the unknown American priest;
Blessed are the Benedictine nuns of Baghdad;
Blessed is the giver of Mosul;
Blessed are the secret donors of dates and cigarettes;
Blessed is Mr Brissell, the American Consul,

For the gift of disinfectant and sheep;
Blessed is Dr Illia, and
Blessed the Anatolian Greeks
Who knelt in the stones
And prayed for us as we passed.

8

Samadara (1)

This is what happens: sometimes the *dorai* falls in love with a native girl, and sometimes he just wants to put himself inside her until he gets bored. If he has children he usually falls in love with their ayah, and if not, it is a girl from amongst the tea pickers. The ayah in *dorai* Pitt's house was called Preethi, and she was my second cousin, and there was no one more pretty and nice than she was, and she used to talk to me about *dorai* Pitt, and there was nothing I didn't know about what went on in his house. Nothing ever happened between her and *dorai* Pitt, but I don't know the reason for that. She loved him, but she also loved *dorasani* Rosie, and perhaps she thought of him as a daughter would. Mainly she loved Esther, the little girl, and she had a great deal of freedom with her, so often Esther played with the native children, and learned some Tamil from them. I knew that Preethi would be a very good mother one day, from watching her with Esther, and in that I turned out to be right.

You know, we Tamil girls are brought up to be very nice and obedient and when we are young many of us are beautiful. We are small and slender, and we are dark, but it makes our teeth look more white and our tongues more pink, and when we like a man we look at him with our brown eyes and he catches us looking, and we look away, and then we cast our eyes to the ground, and then we look up again, and if he is still looking we smile and look away once more. We know how to glance out of the side of the eyes and we know how to wear sparkling jewellery because this place is very rich in precious stones and there are places where you find amethysts in the gravel of the road. Also, we are shy, and this makes us tempting.

Many of us have bad fathers, because it is our mothers who do all the picking, and work from muster at dawn, and if our fathers have nothing to do, they take the money from our mothers and go and drink it all away, and they come home drunk on arrack every night until they die from it. Almost no fathers do any picking. Sometimes our fathers and mothers take their daughters to a *dorai* and say, 'Do you like any of these? You can have one if you like.' And then the family gets money from her, and she lives in a nice house a long way from the house where his wife is, and he comes to stay very often and their children go to a school at Hill House in Nuwara Eliya that is specially for them, and the man has two separate families, and sometimes more than that because the two wives are not enough for them, and their native wife is happy because she has children to love and sufficient money for herself and her relatives, and she has times when he is not there to trouble her, and when he does arrive, then they are glad to see each other, because they do not wear each other's patience out by living together continually.

My father was not a bad father who drank my mother's money, no, he was a good man, he was a devout Catholic like most of us Tamils up here in this plantation, and he devoted himself to St Joseph because St Joseph was the father of Jesus. We had a picture of St Joseph on the wall, with the baby Jesus in his arms, unlike the others, who always had a Mother of God, or a Jesus with the Bleeding Heart. My father worked in the tea factory on the drying machine, and because of him the tea was never attacked by mildew, and because of him we had more money than most people, and he and my mother put their money together so we could afford to cook indoors on a petrol stove instead of on twigs and prunings, which was a blessing in June and July and October, and my father and mother had nice shoes for Sunday instead of chappals.

My grandparents came from India. They were Adi Dravida, the lowest caste, and life at home was a misery greater than anyone can imagine, and they heard there was work in the mountains of Ceylon and they came in little dhonis, which are the ones that have a little extra hull out on one side, and they came here to pick coffee, because before there was tea all the plantations were coffee, until the coffee all died of disease and something else had to be grown instead. And the coffee-picking season was at the same time as the north-east monsoon, and my family were in four boats, and only one of them arrived at Mannar, and all the rest were drowned at sea. And these survivors walked along the sand to Puttalam, and then they entered the jungle along the Deduru Oya River, and they walked through this jungle towards Dambulla, and there was a *dorai* called Cornelius Bassett, and he was the grandfather of the master we have now. When this *dorai* Bassett wanted workers, he would take his horse and ride to Dambulla and Matale, and he would find a high place and look out for the smoke of campfires, and when he found the camps he would come and recruit the coolies.

In those days the forests of the hills were still being cleared by fire and axe and elephant, and there was the shouting of mahouts and a great smoke over the mountains. And they were given rice, but it was paid for from wages so they had almost nothing at the end of the season.

And there were those who went home to India after the season, and then they came back the next year, and my grandfather said, 'This is not for us. Why should we walk 150 miles every year? And why should half of us be lost in the sea every year? And why should we go home to a place that is worse every year, and where we are treated with contempt?'

And the Singhalese who were here already blamed us for bringing smallpox and cholera, and they hated us. There were coolies dying on the roadsides in those days, and on the long walk through the jungle two of my grandfather's brothers died of malaria. And because of all this the *dorais* collected money and built a hospital for us in Kandy, but we don't go there very much. We have our own doctor who is skilled in Ayurveda.

My grandparents saw how good it was to be a coolie here, and they decided never to go back to India, because here the treatment was better and there aren't any Hindus on this estate who treat us like filth, and the Buddhists stay down below and laze about. They say that we Tamils are like the Jews, but we don't know Jews, apart from the ones who are mentioned in the Bible. They must be picking tea somewhere else, like this China that I have heard of, where the tea came from in the first place.

My grandparents became Christian because a preacher arrived, and he said, 'In God's Kingdom there is no Adi Dravida, there is no caste, there are no Dalits and untouchables, because in God's eyes all are equal, and God loves you all the same, and if you believe in Him He will admit you to paradise where there is no more pain and all the dead will rise again on the last day, and you will see again all those you lost on your long journey.' And he washed their heads in water, and said that the bread he was giving was God's body, but in the form of bread, and that the wine was God's blood, but in the form of wine. We are very dark, but this preacher was of a light brown colour because he was descended from the Portuguese, and he had learned Tamil especially so that he could speak to us, and we took Portuguese surnames, though many of us kept our Tamil first names, or we used both, and because we were all Adi Dravida we were already nearly equals, and so we liked this new religion, and we did not go home to India ever again, and my father says, 'Why would we go home to hell?' and this preacher was named Fernando da Silva, which is why many of us are called da Silva, because he was like a new father to my grandparents, and they were like his children.

It wasn't the custom for the *dorai* to come down to the lines. When they wanted to see us, they called us to muster with a horn, or whistles, and drums. We liked it when the muster was called, because it meant that something was going to happen. The *dorais* made our little ones go to their school and we got one free meal and we had a native schoolmaster. Ours was not very nice, he would strike our knuckles with the thin edge of the ruler, and throw the blackboard rubber at us if we smiled, but he is the reason that I am able to write lists and add things together accurately, and also he is the reason that I know about Queen Victoria and King George, and a poem in English about an eagle. We did all our writing in little trays of sand with our fingers, and I still think about how nice that was, the fingers moving in the little crystals that sparkled if you held one grain on the end of your finger and put it up to the sunlight.

The *dorais* gave us the little rainproof houses with one room, and they left us alone, apart from when the government inspectors came to make sure that we were well, and then there was much scurrying about, making everything clean and tidy. We lived together as people who live in a village. When I was a child we had no sanitation at all, and we had to go out into the woods or the plantation, and this was not a good thing for the women because there were bad men and drunken men who might wait for them. I didn't like it because I am frightened of *poochies*, especially spiders, and there were very many *poochies* everywhere. If there was a *poochie* in the house I used to call my brothers to get rid of it, because boys like *poochies*, and they put them down your neck when you are not looking, and run away laughing. We did have water from a tap, but we also had a stream running down the mountain, and that water was much nicer.

It was *dorasani* Rosie who broke the custom and began to come down to the lines. She was concerned about our health, and already worked in the new clinic that *dorai* Bassett had set up, but we never trusted their medicine and we used our own and only went to theirs when our cures failed, and *dorasani* Rosie said we should go to theirs first because theirs was better, and it only did not work because we always went too late. Sometimes she was very angry with us and had no patience, we frustrated her, but she was a good woman who was doing her best for us when she did not have to, and she tried to persuade us to have inoculations so that illness could not strike us down, but what really killed us was the hard work and childbirth for the women, and the alcohol amongst the men. We women had terrible pain in the neck and shoulders in old age because of the tea sacks we carried on our heads all our lives, but we didn't like the new ones that *dorai* Bassett tried to make us use, and we just left them hanging on the pegs and used our old ones because it was so easy to toss the leaves into them.

Dorasani Rosie had brown hair and very blue eyes, and the kind of skin that reddens in the sun and has freckles, which look like a kind of disease, but not a serious one, and you do get used to seeing them and you stop noticing. She was taller than us, but not fat, and she liked to put on shoes and go walking on the estate with her little girl and she was a very sweet little girl who liked to hold our hands, and she had a toy bear that was called French Bear, and usually she had her thumb in her mouth. For quite a long time she only miaowed like a cat, instead of speaking. *Dorasani* Rosie let her play with our children, which was not

49

normal for the masters although it did happen, and little children don't notice what colour anyone is, or not for very long.

It was *dorasani* Rosie who decided that we must have sanitation, and because it was too lengthy to put one device in every house on account of all the pipes and the digging up, she had a block of latrines put at one end of the lines and another at the other end, and near each of them was dug a very deep pit and we were paid for digging the pits which we enjoyed doing until we hit the rock, and then a pipe was sent from the latrines to the pit, and another pipe was put at the top which ran some way down the mountain in case the pit was to overflow. The idea was that the excrement would soak into the earth. We did not believe that it would work, but it did. Every year the pits were emptied out and the dung was spread on the vegetable patches. This was all *dorasani* Rosie's innovation, and we were very grateful to her and very fond of her, because she was a good woman who seemed to love us. And it was true that afterwards we had less illness in our stomachs, and the women were safer.

And so I swear by the Virgin and all the saints that I meant her no injury.

Dorasani Rosie and *dorai* Pitt were very happy together when they arrived. In their garden they would hold hands when they looked at the roses. *Dorai* Pitt often had the little girl on his shoulders. They played tennis together on Sundays after church, and he went to Nuwara Eliya to play golf, but he never stayed long at the Hill Club or the other one, and he was always back soon on his motorcycle, and when he came home he would toot the horn so that *dorasani* Rosie and Esther could come out and kiss him. At that time they were an example of how to be married without unhappiness.

Then *dorasani* Rosie gave birth to a monster which had all its guts on the outside, and after that nothing was the same. She became very quiet and although she carried on her working at the clinic, her servants said she spent a lot of time praying and was becoming a holy woman who was disconnected from the world. It was Preethi who mostly looked after Esther, and she stopped being interested in telling the servants what they had to do, so the head servant had to make up the orders, and write in the beef book, and organise the beef box that was delivered every week, and make sure that *dorai* Pitt's letters were given to the *tappul* who is the letter coolie, and buy things from the *tambies* who come from India to peddle their spoons and whistles and allsorts. He said that the masters got through very many goat chops, and called it mutton, and he did not understand why they did not want to have more variety.

It was at this time that much of the happiness slipped out of their door and left the house, and it even affected the little girl, because this was when she began to talk by miaowing instead of speaking. I know this because at Christmas we take our presents to the masters, and they give us presents in return. On that Christmas we gave them half a goat, and fourteen coconuts and some bread, and they gave us steel pans and some fireworks and a small cake each. I saw the little girl, and she miaowed at me, so I pretended to comb my whiskers, and she laughed. *Dorasani* Rosie was often very angry with her because of the miaowing, but *dorai* Pitt seemed not to mind very much at all, and sometimes he would miaow back, and they would have a strange conversation in this manner. We often thought that the white masters were a little mad. For example, no one could see the point of all the sports they liked to play, such as tennis, which is the hitting of a hollow ball back and forth over a net which would be better used for fishing, and croquet, which is the hitting of a wooden ball with a large wooden hammer through hoops set in the ground, and golf, which takes a great deal of land out of cultivation, just as the tea took away the forests, but the course does look nice, and every night they remove the flags from the holes because otherwise people come in and steal them, and quite often the little boys go and look for lost balls and sell them back to the players, and every year the rich Singhalese who are white apart from their colour come from Colombo and play all at the same time, and then they leave Nuwara Eliya again. That week is called Blackberry Week by the white masters.

It was explained to me that the point of the sports was to have fun and to keep the body well, if you are an idle person who has no real work to do. I have never played sport, so I don't know if it would be good for someone like me, and in any case, I am a woman, and I was always tired from the picking and the walking about on hillsides, and the carrying of the sacks of leaves.

There was a day when the flamboyant trees were all in blossom, just after the new moon celebration, and *dorai* Pitt came down with *dorasani* Rosie, and I could see that a wall had come up between them because they were walking apart though side by side, she did not have her arm through his, and they were talking only in little morsels, and looking away from each other. I thought he seemed angry and that she was sad.

Now, I was squatting by the doorway, shaving a block of jaggery with a knife, because I wanted the sweetness in a drink, and I looked up and realised that *dorai* Pitt was observing me. He was curious about everything, and always wanted to know how everything was done, and so I knew he was watching me not as a woman but as someone shaving a block of jaggery.

Then our eyes met, and I felt fate like my father's hand on my shoulder. I looked down, because I am modest, but then I looked back up, and our eyes met again, and he smiled at me. Then he made me laugh by twitching the end of his nose, and I put my hand to my mouth.

Dorasani Rosie said something sharp to him, and he turned away and they continued down the lines, and she was pointing to the roofs, where they were torn, and he was making notes in a small book, and she was pointing to the ground and making gestures, and so I am sure she was talking about improvements, because not long afterwards some materials arrived in hackeries, and we were put to work to improve our houses and dig a channel for the rain down the middle of the path, lined with concrete and covered over with slabs for walking upon. After that the road was much less messy for us when it was wet.

Now, ever afterwards, when *dorai* Pitt and I crossed in our paths he would raise a hand and greet me with a smile, and I used to arrange it so that there was more chance of our paths crossing, which was easy because there was a routine the *dorais* liked to enforce, and usually one knew where they were.

I didn't do this because I am shameless, but because I was enchanted. Everybody was surprised that he had not taken up with the little girl's ayah, because Preethi was very beautiful and very sweet, and so, when I looked at him, it was with a heart that was open, because his had not been closed. He was quite thin, so he seemed tall when he was not, and his legs did seem very long. His eyes were blue, like *dorasani* Rosie's, and he had a neat black moustache, and he had his hair held down with some kind of grease that smelled quite nice, and I don't know what it was, it wasn't coconut oil, and his hair was shiny black, with a little grey at the temples. His hands had long fingers with the tips a little bit like spades, and when he talked he waved them about much more than the other masters did. When he was annoyed he swore in a language that was not English or Tamil. They were not words that any of us understood. Sometimes when he went for long journeys on his motorcycle he would come back sunburned apart from the place where his goggles had been, and this gave his face a funny appearance that made me smile when I saw it.

I am a small woman, and my mother said I had the bones of a bird, but I am strong, and I can carry my load all day as well as any other woman. A man could get his thumb and forefinger around my wrist without touching me. My hair was long and very black, and when I brushed it, it was beautiful. I had coconut oil for it.

Now, I knew that *dorai* Pitt had been a hero of the war that had taken so many white men away from the Ceylon Planters Rifles, and so I was not only in love with his appearance and his manner, but I also admired him, because bravery and honour are very great things.

One day I encountered him alone on the mountainside. It was the day after a thunderstorm when none of us could go out, and the lightning had been flashing across the sky, and the thunder had been making big echoes that went from mountain to mountain, it always filled us with awe, even though we had known these storms all our lives, and the sun had disappeared behind the blackest clouds, and the rain had come down so hard that it made little mists that rose out of every corner, like ghosts. On the day after this, he was sitting on a rock, enjoying the sunshine above the tea bushes, looking out over the valley, with his hands on his knees, and he was throwing seeds to a little squirrel. I believe that a man who is kind to small animals must have a good heart. When I saw him I stopped, like a wild animal that has suddenly seen the hunter. A woman fears to be alone with a man to begin with, even if she likes him. But then he saw me before I could leave.

'Samadara,' he said, '*vanakkam.*'

I knew he had been learning Tamil because he understood us without speaking to us very much, but somehow I had not expected him to speak to me in my own language. I said, '*Naan nandraak irrukkiren, neengal?*' and these are all pleasantries about 'how are you' and so on, such as one always says.

I said, 'Look at all these butterflies!' because the butterflies were so many that it was a green snow, like the white snow when the pods of the cotton trees break open and the wind is blowing.

He said, 'Yes, these butterflies are very beautiful.'

Then I did something I would never have expected of myself, because I am modest and quite frightened, but when he stood up out of good manners, which I had not expected, I said, even without thinking about it, '*Neengal azhakaaka irrukireerkal.*' Sometimes my heart makes my mouth speak, and my mouth speaks before my brain tells me to be more careful.

He looked astonished and asked me to repeat what I had said. I cast my eyes to the ground and repeated it very quietly. He stood up and he did something I have never seen before, and it was so touching. He took my right hand with his right hand, and kissed the back of it very softly, and then he stroked my cheek just as softly, and he looked at me tenderly and said, 'It isn't me who is beautiful.'

We stood facing each other, and I said, '*Naalai ennai sandhikka virumpukireerkalaa?*' which is 'Would you like to meet me tomorrow?' and he said, '*Ennaku thirumanam aakvittadhu,*' which is 'I am married', and I just shrugged and said, 'Nonetheless', but I don't think he knew the word in English. I believe he understood me, because he kissed my hand again, and turned suddenly and walked away back towards his bungalow.

And the next day I thought to bring him the gift of a mango, and he was there at the same time.

9

A Letter from Fairhead

Paleo Periboli
Manor Way
Blackheath
Kent

27 October 1927

My dear Rosie and Daniel,

I am writing to congratulate you on the wonderful news that you are expecting again. Sophie and I do most heartily wish and pray that this time you will find yourselves with a healthy child, and that this will help to recompense you for the terrible bad luck last time. If not, of course, then you still have the immense good fortune of having such a sweet little daughter, though she must be getting less little by the day, and I wonder if I will even recognise her when I next see her.

Sophie and I have been hoping for a long time now that we might have similar good fortune, but nothing seems to happen. It is impossible for me to think that a woman as lively and healthy as Sophie could be barren, and one of these days I suppose I must summon up the courage to find out if I am 'firing blanks' so to speak. I am not certain how one would go about it, and I hesitate to ask my doctor, out of sheer embarrassment. I don't suppose you know, do you? It is causing us no little distress.

Apart from that sorrow, our lives continue much as before, and we find great happiness in each other, and in living in this pleasant place. Every weekend in the summer we hear the clonk of bat and ball and the cries of 'Howzat?' and the polite clapping when someone comes in after making a duck, because of living opposite the cricket ground. We often pop over and watch it ourselves, and when there is no cricket, we walk the dog there.

The dog is a dreadful little stray that Sophie found when it was trying to get into our dustbin. It has the most pernicious mange, which we are treating of course, and it has an ear that sticks up and another that flops. We are splattering it with a sulphur preparation, and the veterinary surgeon has recommended raw red meat, and something called 'violet rays'.

It is a medium-sized animal that seems to be a mixture of every kind of breed there's ever been, and it has beady black eyes. We believe that if it were not for the mange it would probably have curly black and tan fur. At present we don't allow it in the house because of its stench, its disease and its bad habits, but we keep it in the conservatory, where we have a stone floor, as you will probably remember, and where it has a rug and a heap of old jumpers to sleep upon. We are bribing it to behave with biscuits, and this is working quite well so far. Sophie has named it 'Crusty' for obvious reasons, and we hope that eventually it might become a handsome and domesticated creature that we can call 'Rusty'.

I have pleasure in enclosing the latest volume by Mme Valentine and myself, entitled The Silver Tunnel. This time we have worked very hard, to collect interesting and suggestive stories of those who have come back from death, or near-death, because, as you know, we are convinced that the prospect of surviving death is a great comfort to those who fear it and to those who have lost their loved ones, as so many of us did not so long ago. This is now the fifth volume by 'Valentine Fairhead' and it may possibly be the last, for two reasons. One is that dear Mme Valentine is steadily finding more work as a cellist. The prejudice that many orchestras have traditionally held against female players seems to be slowly but steadily fading away. This seems to have happened out of necessity, as so many fine musicians perished in the Great War. All the extra work means that Mme Valentine no longer feels the need to exploit her talents as a medium. As you know, she always was troubled by it, and frequently had worries about being a fraud. I have never thought that she was, but it seemed I could do little to reassure her. She puts her musical success down to finding a source of higher-quality cello strings, but of course this is nonsense. She is a fine musician, and sometimes when she plays I can feel my eyes welling up, and have to suppress it. She says that she knows an oboe player whose tone is so sweet and plaintive when he gives the A at the beginning of a concert that several members of his orchestra habitually weep – but that is by the by.

The other reason is that only last week I was summoned to Lambeth Palace to be carpeted by no less a personage than the Archbishop himself. I was told merely that His Grace wished to see me, and I was invited to tea, so I put on my smartest and most starched dog collar, polished my shoes, and presented myself at the palace last Thursday at 4.30 pip emma, in the confident expectation of scones.

There were indeed scones, and we sat and ate them with butter and strawberry jam, and sipped tea, whilst the Archbishop and his wife talked about the weather, and synods, and such things. Then the Archbishop said, 'Edith, my dear, would you be so good as to leave us for a while? There is a private matter that I must broach with the Reverend Fairhead.'

'I'll go and see if the servants are behaving themselves,' she said, and exit stage left Mrs Lady Archbishop.

Now the Archbishop is about seventy-seven years old, and he has formidable eyebrows. These he waggled at me, and then he said, 'I'll come straight to the point. You must abandon all this necromancy.'

'Necromancy?' I repeated.

'Necromancy. All this summoning of the dead and writing about it. If I had known that you were one half of Valentine Fairhead, I would have intervened long ago. The books are fascinating by the way. I must congratulate you. Four is it now? You are positively exceeding Sir Oliver Lodge, a very fine fellow. Do you know him? But it has to stop, Fairhead! Necromancy is explicitly forbidden in the Bible.'

'In the Old Testament,' I replied.

'Yes, indeed.'

'Well,' I replied, 'I am a New Testament Christian, and Our Lord says nothing whatsoever about necromancy.'

'So you admit that it's necromancy, Fairhead?'

'Yes, Your Grace. It can't really be honestly construed as anything else, can it? But the Lord didn't forbid it.'

'And what do you mean, Fairhead, by a New Testament Christian?'

'I mean that the God of the Old Testament is a vile old tyrant who sanctions massacres, takes bets with the Devil, invents inexplicably arbitrary rules under sanction of death, and tells people to sacrifice their own sons.'

'Takes bets with the Devil?'

'The story of Job. It's a story about a bet with the Devil, whereby they torment Job and kill off everyone he loves, just to see if he'll lose faith. It's despicable.'

'God is despicable?'

'That God is. I would go so far as to say that He actually is the Devil, pretending to be God.'

'My God, Fairhead! You are an Albigensian!'

'I follow the Gospel of Jesus Christ,' I replied, 'and I even have doubts about some of that.'

'I see you are an intransigent heretic,' he said, but in a very kindly and thoughtful manner. He finished off his cup of tea, and said, 'If you publish any more of these necromantic tracts, I will be obliged to summon you before an ecclesiastical court. You will probably be defrocked. It will be my duty. Is that clearly understood?'

I nodded vigorously, and wondered whether I should defy him any further, but then I thought, 'Well, he is an old man now,' and it occurred to me that by the time the next book comes out, he might even be dead.

Suddenly he said, 'Do you have any children, Fairhead?'

I said, 'No, Your Grace. It is something of a sorrow to my wife and me.'

He said, 'Yes, my wife and I have suffered similarly. When I die my baronetcy will lapse. It seems such a shame. I have never been very fit, Fairhead.'

'I am sorry to hear that, Your Grace.'

'Yes,' he continued. 'I was in a shooting accident when I was young. Very nearly lost a leg. As a result I have had a hernia for most of my life. It has been a torment. It always drops when I am in the middle of preaching. The worst possible time.'

As you can imagine, I was somewhat taken aback by this information, and then he said, 'I am thinking of retiring.'

I was appalled, and said, 'But, Your Grace, archbishops don't retire!' and he replied, 'One has. The question is, to whom do I send my letter of resignation?'

'The King, presumably.'

'His Majesty is the Supreme Governor, but he doesn't do any governing, or take any decisions. Certainly I would have to write to him, but I am not clear that that would actually do the job.'

I said, 'Your Grace, I think you might have to set up a special body, so that it can be the recipient of your letter.'

'Damned good idea, Fairhead. I'll do some thinking about that. A body of about three ought to do the job, eh?'

I said, 'I would be very sorry to see you leave office,' and he replied, 'And I would be very sorry to see you giving up writing about necromancy. I wish you all the best with it. But it has to stop. Do you understand?'

'No,' I replied.

He waggled those agreeable eyebrows and said, 'Write under another pseudonym, damn it, so that I don't know it's you.'

With that, I was shown out of the palace, and I walked over to Westminster to visit the dead poets in the Abbey.

Now let me see what further news I can come up with from dear old Blighty – Ah yes! Mr Wragge, known to all as Oily, very nearly resigned as gardener and handyman for the third time last week, because your mother/mother-in-law is becoming increasingly capricious about what she wants, and very critical of him. The altercation this time concerned the correct size of a spade. She insisted that he use a larger one, because then the work is done more quickly, and he countered with the adage that one 'should never use a big one when a little one will do', because a smaller one is less tiring, and therefore more work gets done. It was a most recondite subject, and it was temporarily resolved when our heroine seized his small spade and hurled it over the wall into the garden of the Pendennises, whereupon he resigned and went home, whither Mr McCosh proceeded some two hours later in order to placate him and re-employ him.

Our dear Mr McCosh is very much his usual self, except that he is somewhat breathless these days, and only manages nine holes at a time. He continues to invent intriguing gadgets for golfers. He has an idea for a mechanical hat which has a brim that automatically revolves to shield the eyes from the sun when taking difficult shots into direct sunlight. The problem is that no such mechanical light detector has been invented by man, although sunflowers know how to do it without any forethought at all. He has therefore written to Professor Smithells at Victoria University to offer to fund research into the mechanism whereby flowers achieve heliotropism, and to investigate its industrial applications.

He is also contemplating the installation of miniature radio transmitters in golf balls, so that one cannot lose them. He says, however, that no one knows how to build valves small enough, so they would not smash when the ball is struck. He is contemplating the manufacture of luminous ones, so that one might go and find one's missing ball after dark.

Christabel and Gaskell spend much of their time in Hexham, where they have made a studio out of the ballroom. When they are not there, they are travelling, or associating with the bohemians of Bloomsbury, who are a funny lot. It seems they are somewhat overemotional and sexually omnivorous. Sophie informed me of the latter point, and I have gone into it no further, as I enjoy my prelapsarian naïveté and would not like to have to give it up on account of achieving knowledge of any forbidden or inadvisable fruit.

Sophie is very well, and has become involved in a project which involves giving riding lessons to orphans. She is regarding it as an oblique way to learn to ride herself. I expect she'll tell you all about it when she writes.

Now, let me see ... ah, yes. Young Edward is thriving at the golf club, and shows every sign of soon becoming a professional, despite his damaged legs, and we hear from Canada that Millicent and Dusty Miller have had their second child. Sophie sent them a woollen shawl for it, and a christening mug.

I have saved the greatest news for last. Sophie and I are increasingly convinced that Ottilie has fallen in love! Yes, indeed!

Ottilie puts on her best clothes and does her face carefully and beautifully. A hansom arrives at The Grampians almost every evening to take her away, and she comes home a little tipsy and radiant, rather improvidently late, full of happy chatter about plays she has seen and new dances she has learned. She can swing dance quite gloriously these days, and the gramophone scratches away almost continually in the drawing room, where she likes to practise in the afternoons.

We all have our fingers crossed. Apparently he is a civil servant from Madras, over here for several months' furlough.

Enough drivel! We send you all our love, and Sophie appends a postscript.

Yours ever,
Fairhead

PS Dear darlings, or drooling dearlings here is the newds how we good-night ladies are all still prostrated with anguish and grief over the demise of poor Rudolph Valentino two months and the black armbands may have been removed from our arms but how they still encircle the afflict-erated soul and Harry Houdini has shuffled off this mortal someone burst his appendix apparently and how sad to die on account of something for which one has no need there's a war in China and religious riots in India and we are all still enchantillated by Winnie-the-Pooh I expect you can get a copy in Colombo but if not I will post you a copy and someone's just flown to Australia and back in only fifty-eight days and Mother has learned a new tune on the violin and is as batty as ever and Daddy missed a hole in one by half an inch and Wragge has fetched the spade back from next door and Ottilie is in love and Crusty is a very pitiful dog and Germany's joined the League of Nations chiz chiz Caractacus was sick on the carpet because of licking the butter and it's time to go must rush I have punctuation classes to attend toodleoo your very own bear of little brain Sophie.

IO

Samadara (2)

It is always obvious to everyone when something begins to happen between a coolie girl and a *dorai*. Every tree and clod of this red earth has eyes, and our tongues are never still for a second. There is no point in attempting secrecy.

So I went to my father, and I said, 'Father, I must tell you something, and you must tell me what I must do.' This was before there had been any touching between me and *dorai* Pitt.

My father talked to my mother and to my cousins and uncles, and most of them saw an opportunity, but the better Christians amongst them said, 'No, it would be a sin, and it would be adultery and fornication,' and others said, 'But it is clear from the Bible that the patriarchs had many wives,' and others said, 'The Bible does not have answers for everything. Whoever wrote it did not know of our customs.' Others said, 'If she goes to confession she can commit the sin without endangering her soul, because all she has to do is confess it before she dies,' and others said, 'The sin would be worth it. Think of all the benefits to the family.'

There was no one who said, 'But she might end up with a broken heart.'

My mother said, 'I am very confused,' and my father said, 'What shall we do?' and my mother said, 'You should go to Nuwara Eliya and consult an astrologer,' and my father said, 'Astrologers have to be paid,' so he asked the family to contribute some coins, and in the end we had enough for the astrologer.

There were times when the drying machine lay idle, and so my father waited for these days, and he asked *dorai* Pitt if he could go to Nuwara Eliya. *Dorai* Pitt said, 'I will need you back by the end of the week, and please will you take this letter to the Reverend Williams?'

So my father went to Nuwara Eliya on a hackery loaded with mangosteens and jackfruit and he carried the letter to the Reverend Williams, and then he went to see the astrologer.

He said that the astrologer looked at charts and scratched his head, and asked questions about dates which my father was not always able to remember, and he spelled out our names to work out the numerology, and finally he announced that both good things and bad things would happen, but there would be more good things. He said that to make sure of this I should wait for a month before allowing *dorai* Pitt to embrace me, and he named a particular time and day when I should permit it in order to maximise the good, and he gave warnings of omens that I should watch out for, because if I saw any of these, I should not go ahead.

It was on the day Father came home that I realised *dorasani* Rosie was pregnant again. Everybody was happy for her, because she had lost the last child and perhaps this would be a healthy one, but neither she nor the master seemed happy. At least, they were both very happy when they were with their daughter, but not when they were alone together. *Dorai* Pitt said to me after we became lovers that he did not want to talk to me about his wife, because it was a painful subject and he did not want to dishonour her in my eyes, that she was a good woman, and he knew how bad the gossip was amongst the tea pickers, so it was better for him to be silent. But I knew perfectly well what the problem was, which was why it was so easy for me to seduce him.

I did not do it for the advantages. I did it because that is what my heart moved me to do. I took the advantages and I passed them on to my family, like a good daughter, but I never pretended to feelings I did not have or did anything that I was not moved to do. I loved him and prized him, and I gave him back some happiness that he had lost, and he brought me comfort and a great deal of pleasure such as I had not imagined, and he treated me with kindness and often asked me if I was contented and if there was anything I might need.

He moved me to a little house on the road to Nuwara Eliya, near a waterfall, quite close to the plantation. This small house had everything I needed, and for one week I was happy there, but then I said to him, 'Beloved, I miss the women and my family and the tea-picking,' and he said, 'What? You want to go back to work?' and I said, 'Beloved, I can't have nothing to do. It makes every day into a year, and it will force me to live longer than I intended. Until I have children, I will go back and pick tea, as before. When I have children, I will be busier, and I will pick tea less often.'

He was amused. He said, 'What? You will hang our children up in a tree in little hammocks, to rock in the wind, as the other women do?' and when I said 'Yes' he laughed and said, 'Well, why not? I have spent much of my life in the air.'

I knew that my beloved was trying to avoid our having children. We had a great many other ways of taking pleasure that would make it less likely. But sometimes one gets so oblivious that it is impossible to be sensible at that moment, and one is carried away. It was these moments that I loved the best and most looked forward to, and, as for me, I was not trying to avoid having children.

Those were the best years of my life, even though my beloved had a little son who was born to *dorasani* Rosie, and who turned out not to be a monster like the last one. This child was called Bertie, and my beloved would sometimes say, 'She tries to keep him from me. Why is she trying to keep him from me? When he cries and I pick him up, she takes him away. When I try to play with him she finds reasons to take him away.' And I said, 'It is not always easy even for a woman to understand another woman, so how is a man to understand her?' He said, 'I don't find you difficult to understand,' and I said, 'I am not *dorasani* Rosie,' and he said, 'She even tries to keep me away from Esther, but Esther's old enough not to let her get away with it.' I said, 'Beloved, does she still take you in her arms?' and he shook his head and said, 'I have only you for that,' and I said, 'Is it enough?' and he said, 'If not for you and the children I would be very lonely and miserable.' I said, 'I am glad I bring you happiness,' and he replied, 'I just hope I am not setting you up for disaster.'

But he did not understand that we are not like his people. Our disasters are bigger than theirs, and the ones that are so big for them are very much smaller for us.

I tried to learn to cook to the master's taste, but it was useless. I made mashed potato and it didn't seem right so I put curry leaf and mustard seeds in it, and my beloved said, 'I want to eat the same things as you. I like the coconut and the fruit and spices. You know, I am half French, so I have higher expectations than most, and I'm sick of mutton chops,' and I said, 'I will make you a mutton curry,' and he liked that very much and he told me that *dorasani* Rosie did not like the smell of the spices on him and said he was 'going native', and he said, 'If you don't want to go a little bit native, there wouldn't be any point in being here.' I made him congee many times, and he brought me trout from the special white man's lake in Nuwara Eliya.

My beloved came to me once or twice a week and he would have come more often, but he had to have good excuses to give to *dorasani* Rosie. Sometimes he arrived on horseback, and sometimes on his motorcycle, and one day I said, 'I would like to go in the motorcycle,' and he said, 'We can't be seen together,' and I said, 'Let's go at night,' so one night when there was a moon we went out, and I got into the sidecar, and he gave me goggles and told me to wear all my clothes, and we went out in the dark with the lights on, and it was like magic to me. The throb of the engine was nice, it was strange to see the black silhouettes of all the houses and think that everybody inside them was asleep, and the smell of the petrol was pleasant, and the smell of the flowers that blossom at night, and we saw many animals in the headlight, I didn't know we had so many, and I had never seen a waterfall by moonlight before, and then we stopped at the waterfall and watched it in the silver light, all glittering. He took my hand and then we embraced and I said, 'I will remember this all of my life,' and it wasn't cold, so he fetched a rug from the box on the back of the sidecar and we lay on it behind some trees, and we were there for some time.

Further down the road we stopped at Christ Church, and he took a torch and showed me where he had buried his first boy, and we looked down at the little circle of light and the headstone, and he was so quiet that I wanted to say something, but when I looked I knew he wanted no speaking, so I took his arm and stood with him, and that is all we did. Then we collected jackfruit from the enormous tree nearby, and we put them on the floor of the sidecar and I had to bury my feet under them so as to fit in when we set off again.

Of all the times we spent together, this was my favourite, when we rode in the darkness, and lay on the rug, and came home at dawn, with the jackfruit rolling about at my feet.

II

Fairhead's Good Idea

O ne Saturday morning Sophie went downstairs to feed Crusty and put him out in the garden. The dog had largely recovered from his terrible mange, but would assuredly never be handsome. He had turned out to be an expensive addition to the household, what with all the sulphur ointments and the olive oil, and even a course of violet-ray treatment, but Sophie and Fairhead loved him nonetheless, and to a small extent, as so often happens with the childless, he had taken the place of a child. Fortunately he had turned out to be a dog with reasonably good manners and clean habits. Whilst Fairhead was at the hospital Sophie amused herself by training it in French.

This she did partly to provoke her mother, who was often heard to comment that the most extraordinary thing about France was that the dogs understood French, and must therefore be uncommonly intelligent. When challenged, she liked to say that English was the natural language of dogs, and when asked why she thought this, she would say, 'Because, clearly, my dear, all other languages are foreign.'

So Crusty already knew 'assieds-toi', 'couche-toi', and 'viens' and 'dis bonjour', and now Sophie was working on 'vas chercher' with the aid of a tennis ball thrown into the rhododendrons.

Sophie pulled the newspaper through the letter flap, and glimpsed at it as she made tea, then she tucked it under her arm and carried the cups upstairs, with a langue de chat biscuit in each saucer.

Fairhead sat up in bed and drank his tea. He read an item about how, if you were earning more than £400 per annum, you could definitely afford a car, and then he began one about the first ever talking picture, but halfway through he gave up, because Sophie was lying alongside him, running her hand up and down his chest, inside his pyjamas. He tossed the paper onto the floor, and slid down to face her.

'My darling,' she said, 'as you're a priest and fully qualified holy sage, will you answer me a question theological?'

'You elevate me somewhat, my dear. Fire away.'

'What if God is really the Devil? What if the Devil rules this world, and, after we die, we go to hell for being good? I mean, what if Good is Evil, and vice versa, and we've got God and the Devil the wrong way round?'

'Oh my goodness. You're too far ahead of me. Going to hell for being good? What do you think? You asked the question.'

'I think we should do good, even if it's wrong and we go to hell for it.'

Fairhead thought about this, and said, 'I think you might just have proved that God and the Good are logically distinct. You should send your idea to Bertrand Russell and see if he can make use of it. I expect he's in Cambridge, or something.'

'You want me to give succour to sceptics?'

'I like sceptics. They keep me on my toes. I think I might even be one. Just as there's a conservative inside every socialist, and vice versa.' He kissed the tip of her nose and said, 'Today you only have one eye, from so close up.'

'And you have only one wife, from so close up.'

'That's what you think. I may have a wife in every suburb of the mighty metropolis of Blackheath.'

'I think I'd better take this opportunity to tire you out.'

'Better not miss the chance,' he said.

Afterwards, Sophie said, 'I think we've just got to face up to it.'

'I'm afraid we might have to,' agreed Fairhead. 'It's been ten years now, hasn't it?'

'It's not as if we haven't tried,' said Sophie. 'We've scaled many an alp, broken many records, established unprecedented precedents, both in frequency and in ecstasy.'

'We have never tired of making attempts. Our feats have been heroic.'

Sophie propped herself up on her elbow and kissed him softly on the mouth. She said, 'My darling, I'm frightened that if we get too desperate, it'll just spoil everything. It's already spoiling things. Let's give up trying.'

'Give up trying?'

She saw the look of horror on his face, and laughed. 'I don't mean give up the frolics. I mean give up doing it because we're getting desperate. Please can we just frolic for fun? For its own sake? It's spoiling things, isn't it? Then if something happens, it's just an unexpected stroke of luck, like finding a half-crown on the pavement.'

'Well,' said Fairhead, 'what about adopting? The world is full of orphans. We could start going to orphanages to see what they've got.'

'I don't know,' said Sophie. 'It wouldn't feel right, somehow. What would we do if we adopted, and it turned out to be a fiend? Are you allowed to give them back?'

'We've got Crusty.'

'Crusty is a regal treasure, a jewel in the crown of our contentment, but he's hardly as good as a child. And dogs only last about ten years.'

'I think you should go straight for being a grandmother.'

'How so, beloved?'

'Well, grandparents universally agree that the nicest thing about having grandchildren is that one can hand them back at the end of the day. All the pleasure, none of the toil.'

'I perceive the luminous intelligence of your idea, but it has one tiny teeny-weeny bijou flawlet.'

'It has no flaws,' said Fairhead.

'How will I skip motherhood, O sage of Blackheath?'

'You can open a dame school.'

'A dame school?'

'Yes.'

'Where?'

'In the drawing room. A dame school can be as small as you like.'

'I'll need some tiny chairs.'

'You'll need a blackboard, a yardstick for pointing to the blackboard, chalk, slates, crayons, pads of paper, exercise books …'

'And lots of lavatory paper and cotton handkerchiefs.'

'And a slipper for biffing the naughty ones.'

'There'll be no biffing in my dame school. Children will be hugged into submission in my vice-like embrace.'

'Your cruelty knows no bounds. You could call the school "Mrs Sophie Fairhead's Biffless Academy for the Children of Busy Mothers".'

'I prefer "apathetic mothers",' said Sophie. 'Do you think we could get an old wreck of a car, and teach them to be mechanics?'

'I thought you'd had enough of that in the war. Too many broken fingernails.'

''Tis true, but every five-year-old should know how to mend a magneto and crank an obstinate engine into life. How else will they cope in adulthood when their horseless carriages break down halfway across Dartmoor?'

'I think you should acquire a patron. King Zog of Albania springs to mind.'

'He'll be busy. He's only been king for a month. 'Tis sad but true. Where shall I find my pupils?'

'Advertise in the *Lady*. And the *Blackheath Gazette*. Put notices up in shops and the porches of churches. Pin papers to trees.'

'And the *British Journal of Engineering*, and the *Tablet*, and *Lepidopterists' Monthly*, and the *Taxidermists' Hebdomadal*.' She sat up in bed and clasped her hands around her knees. 'I've been getting dreadfully fed up with being a lady of leisure. It's all very well taking orphans out on ponies, and going out and about doing charitable things, and calling in on the sick, and it's fun for a while, but then you start to get bored with yourself, and simply desperate for something to get your teeth into. As we all did in the war. How much should I charge?'

'I've no idea. Let's find out what everybody else charges, and charge exactly the same. Or a farthing less.'

'I'm going to get started on Monday,' said Sophie. 'The weekend is for gardening and eating roast beef, and frolicking of course.'

'My darling, you've got to give me time to recoup my resources.'

'I'll give you until tomorrow. Let's get up and eat eggs with soldiers. Your turn! I did it yesterday.'

'Other men lounge motionless whilst their wives bustle about them.'

'Silly man, you chose the wrong woman.'

'I like boiling eggs and making toast, fortunately.'

'I hope you're grateful that I allow it.'

'Forever grateful. Do you remember our first night, in that hotel in Dover?'

'How could I forget? The Dover sole was delicious.'

'Well, our tenth anniversary is coming up.'

'You remembered! So?'

'Let's book into that hotel, and demand the same room. If it's sunny in the morning, we might see more dust that falls from dreams.'

12

Hugh

One morning at dawn I arrived at Taprobane Bungalow on horseback, leading another pony on a rein. Daniel was waiting for me, as arranged, and we set off to hack around the estate as we usually did at least once a month, to check that all was in order.

We enjoyed these rides. We had a pair of bay horses who knew the estate like the back of their, well, not hands exactly. Hooves? Like the front of their forelegs, shall we say? They became quite disconcerted if one didn't follow the usual route, and you could just feel them thinking, 'What, doesn't he know what he's doing? Silly man.'

I've always loved horses, especially a good gallop, and I've won a few cups at Nuwara Eliya in my time. I feel about a horse the same way as Daniel felt about his motorcycle. That is how you fly without an aircraft. Horses have a toasty smell, and a kind of warmth of spirit as well as of body. Some are intelligent, and some are dense, some are frolicsome and some are staid.

Daniel and I usually talked about the war, and developments in modern aircraft. We were both interested in the idea of setting up some kind of air service in Ceylon. We thought that there was immense potential in seaplanes, and so, of course, we were in exactly the wrong place, up in the highlands. There should have been a service between Colombo and Trincomalee, for example, and Jaffna always seems cut off from the rest, arbitrarily stuck onto the tip, so to speak. The big frustration was that there were the tanks, huge reservoirs, the most marvellous and obvious places to land floatplanes, but they were constructed in the first place by a civilisation that had been entirely destroyed by malaria. Until we got on top of the malaria there would be no future in setting anything up on the tanks.

We talked quite a lot about the Empire. Daniel was preoccupied with the notion that it was bound to fall away, and I had thought a great deal about that myself. I told him that Ceylon had not been anything like a democracy when we arrived, so the natives didn't see any difference over who dominated them, and there was still some residual gratitude for the abolition of compulsory unpaid labour, but even so, it's obvious from history that all empires are exhausted after a couple of hundred years. I remember saying this to him when he and Rosie first arrived, and I'd gone to meet them in Colombo. Daniel and I both had pangs of conscience about whether we were really entitled to be there. In my opinion we were a hell of a lot better than what we replaced, but that's just about all the justification I could come up with, and my pious hope is that perhaps we'll leave something worthwhile behind us when we go. It was only last year that Canada and Australia and New Zealand and South Africa and Newfoundland got independence, and the Empire began to turn into a Commonwealth. Sooner or later the brown peoples are going to notice. In fact they already have. If you raise a native elite to play cricket and golf and recite 'Daffodils' and drink sundowners and be just like yourselves, and then don't let them into your club, you can expect trouble. It turns them into Bolshies. Who's next? India, no doubt. We've created the same stroppy elite there.

More often than not, Daniel and I just rode in silence together, because, to put it bluntly, men don't seem to need to fill a pleasant silence with chatter, as so many women do. Men only become garrulous when drunk, apart from the ones who fall into the complete opposite and won't say a word.

There came a day, however, when I was obliged to speak to him as tactfully as I could manage, because there is a certain modus operandi when it comes to native women and having affairs with them, and I was not certain that Daniel knew what was what. We did the usual rounds of the estate and then decided to go to our little range where we played gun snap. I'd tied a sack of cans to my saddle to use as targets, and we rode along to the accompaniment of a gentle hollow rattle. Once there, and before we settled down to the game, I said, 'Daniel, old boy, I'm afraid I have to speak to you,' and he said, 'Yes, I know you do. I thought you would.'

73

I said, 'I did warn you about native women on your first day here.'

'You did. It seemed a very unlikely prospect at the time.'

'You know there is a protocol about these things? So that a certain decency is maintained?'

'You mean so that we don't unduly annoy the natives and turn them against us? Samadara tells me that she has the full consent of her family. Apparently it all got discussed in a kind of grand council. One can only imagine what it must have been like. I've put her up in a little house well out of Rosie's way.'

'You do realise that you are supporting her whole family?'

'Yes. But I don't have any doubts about her. She's not an actress. All her feelings are on the surface in plain sight.'

'And you do realise that if you have children she can take you to court for maintenance, and she'd win? Our magistrates are dreadfully puritanical. And it would all become terribly public?'

'You told me that in Colombo.'

'And if you leave Ceylon, you'll have to do the decent thing, and arrange for a lawyer to pay her a stipend? And the children will have to go to Hill House, and that's quite an expense?'

'Yes, I know all that. Everything seems to have been laid down by custom.'

'I blame Maitland.'

'Maitland? The Governor back in the old days?'

'Yes. Turn of the last century. He took a mistress called Lavinia. She was a dancing girl from a caste whose women were forced to go bare-breasted. He abolished that rule, and set her up in a house near his, and had a tunnel dug so they could go back and forth without too much public scandal. That's why Mount Lavinia is called Mount Lavinia. It seems he set a pattern for the rest of us to follow.'

'Us? You mean, you too?'

'Why do you think I warned you?'

'But your wife? What does she think? Does she know?'

'Daniel, don't be shocked. And don't be a hypocrite. And I don't know if Gloria knows. She acts as if she doesn't, but on the other hand she may not care very much. Rosemary strikes me as the kind of girl who would mind very much, and demand to go home.'

'She doesn't seem to give a damn about me any more,' said Daniel. 'Now that she's got the children, I'm just the one who brings home the bacon. I'm a useful ghost. Anyway, she's had too many things to get over.'

'And what about you?'

'You mean, what are my feelings for her?'

'I know it's not my business. Of course you don't have to say anything. But we have become good friends, and it's a great salve, having someone to talk to. I would like to think I could talk to you.'

'Women think that men don't talk to each other,' said Daniel. 'They live in ignorance of how much they get discussed. But I'm no better at all this confidential stuff than the next man. One tends to keep private things private. However, as we're pals ... and I'm fairly sure you won't bandy this about, the answer to your question is that I am exasperated with her, she ignores me apart from when I am trying to play with Bertie, in which case she tries to prevent me, but I love her as much as ever, and I am having to come to terms with the certitude that for the rest of our lives I will be living with her as a brother and not as a husband.'

'That's a good way of putting it,' I said. 'British women are best at being sisters. Always have been as far as I can see.'

He came back with 'So I assume that you are in the same situation?'

I said, 'In this case a pragmatic compromise is better than a principle stuck to. Principles are made for angels, not for us. If you want any kind of life worth living, there doesn't seem to be any choice, does there? Let's play gun snap, shall we?'

13

Ottilie

One day Ottilie realised that she was going to have to renounce her devotion to Archie. She had this revelation when sitting by the Tarn, throwing stale bread to the coots. All sorts of metaphors occurred to her. Loving Archie wasn't exactly throwing pearls to swine, because no one could ever think of him as a pig, but it was offering something to someone who could not possibly appreciate it. He had been besotted with Rosie ever since they were children, and was clearly not going to give up, even though Rosie had never given him the slightest encouragement. There had never been even the most fleeting moment of flirtation.

In the early days Rosie had promised herself to Ashbridge, and after he was killed she had married Daniel. Ottilie could only imagine how much Archie must have been hurting, to think of his brother with her in perpetuity. It was not really surprising that Archie had redoubled his addiction to the bottle and scuttled back off to the North-West Frontier. In fact, Ottilie thought, he had always shortened his leaves so he could get back sooner to his Pashtuns and his Masouds. He really did seem so much more at home with the tribesmen, with their religious fanaticism and their blood feuds, their absolute misogyny, and their insatiable appetite for sadism and robbery. Archie simply could not cope with the subtleties of civilian life, or with anything that brings out the natural unruliness of the heart.

Ottilie looked up at the March sky, and a small flock of dry leaves whipped past like a sprinkling of sparrows. She hugged her coat to herself, and said, 'Ottilie, you're getting older and time's passing you by. You can't keep waiting for someone to notice you who's never noticed you in twenty-five years. And if you married him, what next? Wouldn't he just carry on drinking, and carry on wishing he was with Rosie, and volunteering to go to Waziristan for months at a time? And wouldn't he just leave me to stew with the children in some bungalow in Peshawar or Simla?'

'First sign of madness,' said a cheerful, tattered old man, passing by with his dog, whose collar was attached to his hand by a long piece of thick brown string.

Ottilie looked up with a puzzled expression, and he explained, 'Talking to yourself. First sign of madness. That's what they say.'

'Oh, I am really quite mad,' she said. 'You shouldn't worry about me.'

'Best way to be,' he said. 'I'm mad myself. Only got this dog, and I'm happy as Larry.'

'It's a nice dog,' said Ottilie, even though it was scruffy and ugly, of no nameable colour, with a clumsily docked tail and dull, watery eyes.

'No, it's not a nice dog. It's called Nipper, and it nips. But not me. I don't get nipped.' He paused, and then, anxious not to end the conversation, said, 'I see that Major Segrave has broken the land speed record.'

'I read it in the paper,' said Ottilie. 'Nearly 204 miles an hour!'

'Wouldn't fancy it myself. I'm for Shanks's pony, I am, and that's about it. Well, goodbye then.'

Ottilie watched the old man go, and rubbed her hands together inside her muffler. 'I don't have to stop loving Archie,' she thought, 'I've just got to love him in a different way. I've got to love him in a letting-go-forever kind of way.'

Quite suddenly she thought of the metaphor she needed. 'I've been barking up the wrong tree,' she said to the two mallard ducks at her feet.

Not long afterwards, Ottilie went to a lecture about theosophy, to be held in Lambeth. She had missed the one the week before, because she had been embarrassed by the topic, which was Free Love, and she had been a little frightened of what the rest of the people in the audience might be like. She had envisaged bug-eyed men in brown raincoats, with dribbles of saliva coming from the corners of their mouths.

She had washed her thick dark hair the night before, and spent a good many minutes brushing it until it shone. She looked at herself carefully in the mirror, and put a little eyeliner on to emphasise the luminosity of her eyes. She put on a long dove-grey skirt, and the matching jacket that slimmed her waist and accentuated her breasts. She had chosen a cambric shirt with a lacy collar, and pinned a large bloodstone brooch at the throat. She put on her sensible shoes with just enough heel to make her look a little taller. She put on her favourite hat, which she liked to think of as her '*amuse tête*', because it was really more of a decoration than a hat, with its jaunty pair of pheasant feathers and its silver buckle. Because it was cold and windy she put a fine Kashmir shawl over her shoulders.

On the train into London she thought about how rotten it was to be the only one of the sisters left behind at The Grampians. Christabel had turned into a terrible bohemian and was off with Gaskell doing disreputable things in places like Hexham and Bloomsbury and Lewes. Rosie was in Ceylon, and Sophie was in Blackheath with Fairhead. Ottilie felt that she had drawn the short straw, even though it was often quite a lot of fun being at home with a dotty mother and an indulgent father. There was never quite enough to do, however, what with the Honourable Mary FitzGerald St George attending to Mrs McCosh, and Cookie doing all the cooking, and most of the housework too these days. Ottilie knew it was time to go forth and re-establish herself in the world outside, and in the meantime she was going to go to lectures and learn about all sorts of things that were of no intrinsic benefit to her. Her mind was still reeling from a talk about relativity two weeks before; she had thought she had understood it at the time, but now had no recollection of it at all, beyond the bafflement. She had not told anyone about the lecture on Fabian Socialism, because she knew that her mother would think it even worse than Free Love.

As she was leaving the lecture in the early evening, a young man next to her slipped on the wet steps of the hall, and fell backwards. She had noticed him earlier, because of his rather striking profile. 'Thirty years old,' she had thought, 'officer class, probably served in the navy. Receding hair, a bit too thin for his own good. Tennis player, I should think. I wonder what he does now.'

There was a general rush to raise the fallen man to his feet, during which he insisted volubly that he was perfectly all right, and please don't anyone make any fuss, after which he was left standing face-to-face with Ottilie. She looked up at him with her big dark eyes. 'You're not all right, are you?'

He winced and said, 'No, no, perfectly all right. Really and truly.'

'Then why are you grimacing and holding your left wrist in your right hand like that?'

'Just a bit painful, that's all. I used that hand to break my fall.'

'On wet days you should wear rubber-soled shoes,' said Ottilie.

'I didn't know it was going to be wet.'

'Move your fingers,' said Ottilie. 'Waggle them.'

'I don't think I can. Nothing seems to be happening.'

'You've broken your wrist,' she said, removing the Kashmir from her neck, and throwing it around his shoulders. She caught the scent of his cologne, and he noticed the sweet aroma of freshly washed young woman's hair.

'What are you doing?'

'I'm making a sling.'

'Gracious me. I'm sure I'm all right. Really, I don't need any help.'

'I was a VAD in the war. You've broken your wrist, and now you're going to hospital to get it put in plaster.'

'Are you certain about this? I mean, it's a lovely shawl. How will I get it back to you?'

'I'm coming with you to the hospital to hand you over, and when I leave I shall make sure that I take it with me.'

'You might leave me your address, so that I can forward it to you. And I do think I'd like to come and thank you in person. How are we going to get to the hospital?'

'We'll hail a hansom cab. Obviously.'

'Oh yes. Stupid question.'

'You're paying for it, though,' she said. 'It's your fault. You're the one with the slippery leather soles.'

'Of course.'

A week later Frederick Ribaud, a civil servant from Madras, arrived at The Grampians with one arm in a sling, and a bunch of twenty-four red roses tucked under the other. It was Ottilie who answered the door.

'I've come to sweep you off your feet,' he said. 'Excuse me for not removing my hat. I don't have enough available arms.'

'What would you have done if it had been my mother?'

'I would have given her one of these, and taken advantage of her moment of confusion to ransack the house for you and a vase.'

'Come in,' she said. 'No need to ransack. I'll raise your hat for you.' She lifted his hat a couple of inches, and plopped it back down again, so that the brim fell over his eyes. 'Mind the step. Don't trip up,' she said.

14

Samadara (3)

One day my beloved came into the house. I had been waiting for him on the terrace because there was a big hairy *poochie* in the kitchen, and I needed him to get it out. I was listening very hard for either the hammering of his motorcycle or the clopping of hooves.

But when he arrived he was very distressed, and he said, 'I have terrible news,' and he sat down next to me on the step of the terrace and he put his head down into his hands, and I said, 'My beloved, what is it?' and he said, 'My wife wants us to go back to England,' and I said, 'What? Has she found out about me?' and he said, 'That's what I thought at first, but she hasn't, she doesn't suspect anything,' and I said, 'Why would she want to leave when all the white men say this is paradise, and all the women have nice houses with servants and gardens, and the gardens are full of flowers and the flamboyant trees blossom on the hillsides, and there's so much fruit?'

He said, 'Sometimes it's boring to be in paradise. My wife wants more to do. She says the coolies don't use the clinic and there's no point in her trying to work there any more. She says that she can't write poetry here because the life is too easy and you can't just keep writing about how beautiful it is.'

I said, 'She should write poems with stories in. And with memories.'

He said, 'And she thinks that Esther and Bertie should be at school in England, even though the schools here are just as good. What's wrong with the one in Kandy?'

And I said, 'There is nothing wrong with the school in Kandy that I know of.'

My beloved said, 'But these are all excuses and false reasons. The real reason is that she fears that her father is going to die soon, and she wants to be with him when he dies. Then her mother will be alone, and she thinks she should look after her mother.'

I said, 'For everyone in this world it is the family that matters most. I would want to be there when my father dies.'

'My mother is quite old,' he said, 'but she wouldn't want me to come back if I was happy and successful here. And I am.'

'Does her mother want her to come back?'

'Her mother is more than a little bit mad. She's mainly preoccupied by the royal family. What she wants the most is for Their Majesties to come to tea.'

'And her father?'

'Her father would definitely not want her to come back for his sake.'

'Then you must write to her father and let her father write to her.'

My beloved was pleased and said, 'My darling, you are sometimes very wise.' Then he said, 'I think my wife loves her father more than anyone else. He's much more important to her than I am. I don't blame her. He's a great man. He's a wonderful father.'

After we had drunk coconut milk we went to the bedroom, and I lay down with him with a heavy heart, because the white women are very powerful over their men. The white men go out and stand up to rogue elephants with only two bullets in the barrels of their gun, but they tremble before the fury of their wives, who are armed only with words and self-righteousness. After we had had our pleasure he lay back with his arms behind his head and said, 'I'm damned if I'm leaving Ceylon. I'm damned if I'm leaving you.'

I said, 'Brave talking is more easy than brave doing.'

When he went back to his motorcycle he embraced me so strongly that I thought my ribs would crack, and he said, 'You know I love you, don't you? You have the sweetest heart of any woman alive. I've never loved any woman as I love you,' and it was those words, and the way in which he said them, so much like a farewell, that made me know I was going to lose him.

15

Ottilie and Frederick at the Tarn

The trees about the Tarn were in blossom, and Ottilie and Frederick sat side by side on a bench, watching the old ladies throwing bread to the ducks.

'How's your arm?' asked Ottilie. 'Still a bit achey?'

'Very achey, but I shall be brave.' His wrist was still in plaster, but he had abandoned the sling unless the pain became too much to bear, which usually happened in the evenings. 'This is a lovely spot, isn't it?'

'Yes,' said Ottilie. 'There's a local legend that it has no bottom.'

'Ah, like Cunegonde.'

'Cunegonde?'

'You know, the woman in *Candide* who has her buttocks eaten when her companions get hungry. Or was it just one of them?'

Ottilie laughed. 'I've never read Voltaire. I know I should. You're a very silly man. Your humour is most indelicate, quite unsuitable for a simpering little thing like me. Did you know that it was here at the Tarn that Rosie decided to marry Daniel? He went into the water to rescue a drowning dog, and that was what made her mind up.'

'I'm looking forward to meeting them. Are they really coming back?'

'That's what Rosie says in her letter. Daddy's furious. It's obvious that Daniel doesn't want to, and she's bullied him into it.'

'What fearsome sisters you are.'

Ottilie smacked him gently on the back of his hand. 'Watch out, you! But isn't it funny how things turn out? I mean, Christabel used to be a typical English rose, but since she's been Gaskell's companion she's turned into a sort of tropical orchid. A bromeliad or something.'

'A frangipani blossom? Bougainvillea perhaps?'

'Oh, do be quiet, silly man. And Sophie, well, Sophie's just Sophie, isn't she? Her tremendous depth lies in her apparent silliness.'

'I adore Sophie,' said Frederick. 'When you're with Sophie you can't help having a smile on your face.'

'Everyone loves her. She doesn't have a single enemy. She was a driver on the Western Front, you know. Changing tyres under fire and that sort of thing? I think she knows as much about engines as Daniel does. Who would have believed it? She seems so terribly feminine, doesn't she?'

'And Rosie?'

'Poor Rosie's too complicated for her own good. She doesn't even understand herself. She's got a heart of gold, and she'd do anything for anyone, but you know, I think she's still got shell shock.'

'Shell shock? Was she at the front?'

'Well, as I told you, her childhood sweetheart was killed in 1915. They were engaged to be married. And then she worked herself to the bone at Netley just to try and forget, but every wounded soldier must have reminded her of Ash, and every death must have reminded her that Ash was dead. And then she married Daniel on a sort of gamble that it might be the right thing to do and she might really learn to love him.'

'Oh dear. It doesn't sound very encouraging.'

'I'm expecting fireworks when they come back. I'm really rather dreading it.'

Frederick put his hand on top of hers. She was not quite sure how to react, so she left her hand where it was, and just looked down at it.

He said, 'I've never been in love. Until now.'

He turned and looked at her, and their eyes met. Suddenly her face crumpled, and she burst into tears. Frederick was confounded, and could think of nothing to do but put his arm around her shoulder, and say, 'Ottilie, my dear, my dear ...'

She fumbled in her handbag and brought out a small handkerchief, dabbing her eyes.

'Is there any hope?' asked Frederick. 'Is there any hope?'

Ottilie said nothing, but nodded vigorously. Suddenly she looked up and said, 'I thought I'd be an old maid. I am an old maid.'

'What terrible nonsense, and even if you were, I'd feel the same.'

'Would you?'

'I would. Cross my heart and hope to die. What about you?'

'Me? What about me?'

'I wouldn't want to be a gamble.'

'You wouldn't be.'

'You know I'm asking you to marry me, don't you?'

'Are you?'

'Well, don't be so surprised. There's no woman sweeter in the whole world.'

'There are millions sweeter than me.'

'I don't know any of them.'

'You haven't done enough research.'

'I've done exactly the right amount. Will you marry me and come to India?'

'There've been riots in Lahore. Sikhs and Muslims at each other's throats. Fourteen dead. It doesn't sound very peaceful.'

'Lahore is nowhere near Madras. The tea pickers are Tamils and they're Hindu if they're not Roman Catholic, and the educated Indians in town are a delight. I've got photographs. You'll see how beautiful it all is. I know you'll just love it. I've got a nice little residence in the suburbs, and a beautiful big bungalow on a hillside.'

'You don't have to bribe me.'

'I fear I may not be enough on my own. I'm nothing special after all.'

'You fought at the Battle of Jutland.'

'So did thousands of others. I'm not special, there are lots of old seadogs like me, and lots of people with nice bungalows. All I've got is my certainty. About you.'

Ottilie began to cry again. She had recently had her hair trimmed in fashionable shingles, and the spring sun was sparkling in the tips.

'Have you loved before?' asked Frederick. 'I probably shouldn't ask, but I need to know who to be jealous of.'

'Of whom I should be jealous,' said Ottilie.

'Of whom I should be jealous,' repeated Frederick.

'I loved someone for years and years and years,' said Ottilie, 'ever since I was tiny. But it was completely hopeless. He only ever had eyes for Rosie, and now he's on the North-West Frontier, still trying to get over her. I decided to give up quite recently, and just settle for being an old maid. So I did give up. And after a while I began to feel like a liberated city. Like Ypres, perhaps. Somewhat ruined, but calm, and hopeful. In case you're wondering, it was Archie, Daniel's brother. There, now you know. And you don't have to be jealous. The poor man is a tormented soul, and he's foolishly brave, and he's pretty much a dipsomaniac, and you'll probably never meet him, and he's in the Frontier Scouts. I'll always be fond of him, but I really have given up. And you're here now. Is there a clinic on your estate? I'd quite like to get back to nursing. There must be an awful lot one can do for the natives.'

Frederick laughed resignedly. 'Well, yes, there is a clinic, but you'd mostly be tending to whites, except that we're all terribly brown from playing tennis in the sun, and you'd hardly tell us apart from the natives were it not for the clothes and the tennis rackets.'

'I'm absolutely not going if there's nothing to do. I really can't abide idleness. Perhaps I could teach the natives reading and writing. Sophie's little dame school is doing terribly well.'

'Do I take it that you've agreed to marry me?'

'I'm not racy enough to live in sin.'

'So, is it yes?'

'You haven't asked me properly.'

'You want me to kneel in a park? In front of all these ducks?'

'Yes.'

16

Farewell to Samadara

Daniel and Samadara were on the terrace behind the little bungalow that he had bought for her. She had been putting out curry leaves to dry, and they lay in a patch of sunlight on a small sheet.

They sat opposite each other, leaning forward with their hands joined. 'What are the choices, then?' she asked.

'There seem to be a great many,' said Daniel. 'I could bring you over to England.'

'To be a wife or a concubine?'

'I don't know. The question is, would you want to come to England?'

Samadara bit her lip and said, 'I have no family there. I would be a dark woman amongst the white ones. Who would I go to? Who would befriend me? Who would be with me on the ship? Am I to be a servant?'

'You wouldn't be a servant. I'd look after you.'

'Who would talk to you if you had a dark woman?'

'I really don't care.'

'I think you will care in the end. One day you would send me back.'

'I fear that one day you would demand to come back.'

'Only the future knows the future. What else can we do?'

'I can stay here, and *dorasani* Rosie would go home with the children.'

'Why must they go with her? You are their father. You are the commander of your family. You tell her to go home and leave the children. Tell her she can come back, perhaps for three months a year. Tell her she must do as you say.'

'That's not how it works with us,' said Daniel. 'I can't order her to abandon the children.'

'Of course you can. You are the man.'

Daniel sighed. 'I can't think of any white man who would order his wife to abandon her children. It's not our custom any more. You would only take them from her if she was vicious in some way. And there's something else.'

'And what is that?' asked Samadara impatiently.

'I have to think of the children. My duty is not to you or Rosie but to the children.'

'And who gave you this duty? Why is it your duty? Did God give you this duty?'

'Please don't be angry with me. It's a duty I choose for myself. What matters is that the children must be as happy as I can make them.'

'Children are like dogs. They accept whatever happens to them,' said Samadara. 'Children live in a little world where they don't understand anything until they are grown up and look back on it.'

'You're right, I'm sure. But when my children look back, I don't want them to think that I destroyed their family so that I could be with a woman who was not their mother. I don't want to be remembered like that.'

'You are thinking of honour and dishonour, then?'

'Yes.'

'You will treat me with dishonour because it's more important to be honourable to others?'

Daniel said, 'There's something else you must understand.'

'And this is?'

'Both the children love their mother. Esther might be able to live with me without her, but I know that Bertie couldn't. *Dorasani* Rosie is his whole world, and I hardly feature at all. I can't take him from his mother.'

'Then do what King Solomon would do.'

'King Solomon?'

'Yes. Obviously. You keep Esther, and you send her home and let her take Bertie.'

'I said that Bertie doesn't care for me. I didn't say that I didn't care for him. And she loves Esther even if Esther prefers me. Sometimes you love someone and they don't love you in return. It's probably very common with parents and children.'

'You are saying that you prefer your son to me.'

Daniel sighed. 'My darling, if you have a child, you always love it more than anyone else.'

'Perhaps now I won't have children. Perhaps now I won't be married. Perhaps now nobody will want the discarded concubine of a white man.'

Daniel wanted to say that the fact that he would leave her an allowance would be sufficient attraction, but realised that it would enrage her, even if it were true. 'I want you to come to England. Please.'

'You're talking like a dreamer. Like a drunkard. How am I to come? On the same ship as you and your frozen wife? Where are my papers that say that I can come? Am I to become British, just like this?' she said, clicking her thumb and forefinger.

'I'm sure it can be arranged. There must be a way of doing it. I can find out in Colombo.'

'What about my family?'

'You want me to bring your family? How big is it?'

'It's as big as our families always are.'

'How many would I have to bring?'

'I would have to discuss it with my family. How can I be in England with no family?'

'We would have children.'

'You have always tried to avoid having children with me.'

'I would stop avoiding it.'

'They would be neither white nor dark. What world would they belong in?'

'To the future. All this rubbish about races is going to come to an end one day.'

'I see no sign of it. The half-castes here are like birds in a cage with invisible bars.'

'Please come with me. We'll sort it all out somehow.'

Samadara waved her arm round at the trees and mountains. 'This is my home. Here is my family. Here is the red earth I will lie in when I am dead.'

'Your grandfathers moved. They came from India.'

'For us, India was hell. This place is not hell. Here we are on our knees thanking God for the fruit and the rain and the work and the safety. If you loved me you would stay here.'

'I do love you, and I do want to stay, but most of all I want to do what is most right for the children.'

'The children would be happiest here.'

'I know that. But Bertie doesn't. Please come to England.'

'No.'

'Then we'll lose each other, probably forever.'

'Yes.'

'Please.'

'No.'

Daniel clasped his hands together and hung his head. 'Then we have to say goodbye.'

'We don't have to. You chose it.'

'I never chose it. It's been imposed on us.'

'You cannot be imposed upon unless you choose it,' said Samadara gently, her anger having suddenly died away. 'You've chosen your wife and children over me. It's simple. And I will tell you something.'

'Yes?'

She stood up, walked away, and turned round to face him, her hands on her hips. Then she raised a finger, narrowed her eyes, and pointed at him.

'You will always love me. You will always wish you had stayed with me. You will always regret giving me up. If you lie with other women, a time will always come when you begin to wish she was me, and it will be me moving beneath you. You will wonder if you did what was right, and then one day you will realise that you didn't. You will begin to miss the handsome children we would have had, and their children's children. When you are at the moment of death, you will remember me, and you will see that you laid my heart to waste and poisoned your own life.'

Daniel stood up, trembling. 'Is this a prophecy, or a curse, or a blessing?'

She held up three fingers, tightly together, and clasped them with her other hand, saying, 'All these things.'

17

Rosie (1)

Before Daniel and I left Ceylon, we went to visit the grave of our stillborn son.

Things had become very bad between us, because I had grown desperate to go home, and he was equally keen on staying. He loved the very active life, with all that time on horseback, the getting up at dawn, the expeditions down to the tanks to shoot duck, and the tennis parties on Sundays. He played golf at Nuwara Eliya just for fun, without bothering to compete for any of the cups and medals. In the evenings he liked to sit out on the terrace and read to Esther, who was always on his lap with her thumb in her mouth, and French Bear clamped to her side under one arm. I confess I often felt jealous of their affection for each other, and it was as if she had come between us. Of course, I adored Bertie, and he would be on my lap because Esther kept him off her father's.

Daniel also loved the machinery in the factory, which was beautifully maintained and had a kind of grandeur on account of its sheer size and pristine cleanliness. He would drink gallons of his own tea with the Singhalese engineers as they arranged schedules for servicing, and so on, and would come home and talk away merrily about cranks and grease nipples. I don't know why he thought I might be interested.

I did have some friends, such as Hugh's wife, Gloria, but in general we all just drank sherry, talked about each other, and about home, and about what we had done in the war. It was as though we were already eighty years old in our thirties. There was no one there who was very interested in literature or art, and somehow it wasn't enough to get batches of books from Cave's, read them, and then have no one to talk to about them. Gloria only read romances and old editions of the *Lady*. Daniel actually did understand poetry, because it had been beaten into him at Westminster, but for that very reason he was not an enthusiast, and his comments about a picture might be just 'Oh that's nice, I like that one'. He read books about machinery, and old editions of *Punch*.

I was fond of the servants and they were fond of me, but their whole lives were rooted in practicalities, and I found their kind of Catholicism annoyingly superstitious. I suspected that they thought of it as a kind of powerful magic. No doubt they would have found mine very dry. It wasn't their fault, because they'd had only a minimal education, and so the fault was ours, of course. There was a fear that if you gave them too much education, they wouldn't stay on the plantations. Hugh used to say that the educated ones would be the ones to force us out in the end.

I had a lot of reasons for wanting to go home, but I was mainly concerned about what would happen to my parents after Ottilie left to get married, and my principal worry was what it had always been, which was my father's health. It seemed to me that I was the only one who would be able to care for him properly.

The fact is, I couldn't bear the anxiety, and I had become terribly bored and listless in paradise. Looking back, I think that perhaps I should have taken more interest in the wildlife, and gone on more expeditions.

Daniel actually wept the night before we left. He sat on the steps of the terrace, his head in his hands and his shoulders shaking, with Esther standing next to him saying, 'Daddy, don't cry. Daddy, don't cry.'

On the morning of our departure all the servants lined up to shake our hands, and they were all weeping, particularly Preethi, who didn't want to have to say goodbye to the children. Her wailing followed us down the road. I was the only one not in tears when our little convoy set off on the long journey to Colombo. I was the guilty one, and I felt ashamed and excluded, but obstinate.

On the way to Nuwara Eliya I saw a small and very pretty young Tamil woman standing by the side of the road, stock-still, decked out beautifully in scarlet wedding finery, with gold bangles. She cut a very striking figure, as she was on the left side, silhouetted against the sky. She had a rosary in her left hand. As we passed she stared at me so intently that I felt as if her eyes were boring into my soul. I looked back, and she had gone down on her knees, sitting back on her heels with her arms crossed against her breast, as if she were dead, and her head bowed.

We had to pass Christ Church on the long winding descent, and I tapped Daniel on the shoulder and indicated that I'd like to stop. Hugh had the children and all our luggage in his car, and he stopped behind us and waited whilst we visited the grave.

Daniel was trembling. He and I stood side by side and looked down at that tiny little plot on the mountainside, with its equally tiny headstone, and 'The Stillborn Son of Daniel and Rosemary Pitt' inscribed on it. Gloria had suggested that we put 'God Wanted Him for an Angel' but Daniel and I both hated the idea. He thought it was sentimental rubbish, and I thought it was presumptuous.

I don't know what God could have been thinking. After that, I still depended on Him completely, but I loved Him a lot less.

I said, 'Who will look after the grave?' and Daniel said, 'I've left some money with the gardener. He said the job's pretty much hereditary, so the grave should be tidy forever.'

'Poor little thing,' I said, but Daniel said nothing. When you look down at a grave it is impossible not to think about what state the body might be in. You wonder if it's mummified, or if it's a skeleton, or whether the bones have turned brown and yellow and crumbled to nothing. I had only a vague memory by then of what the baby had looked like. I just remembered his rainbow-coloured entrails packed under that membrane.

I felt completely empty, and reached out sideways and took Daniel's hand. It was strong and warm, and he squeezed mine gently. We stood in silence for about twenty minutes in that perfectly beautiful place, utterly stricken with regret, hand in hand for the first time in months, for the last time.

18

Returning

D aniel and Rosie returned in the spring of 1928 and in some ways it was the mirror image of their outward journey. They were back on the SS *Derbyshire*, which had recently been refitted and smelled of fresh paint. As before, Rosie was seasick until she had been at sea for several days and, as before, the smell of turmeric and perspiration drifted across the sea as they passed Bombay. They suffered the appalling heat of the Red Sea and the Suez Canal. Bertie was miserable and grizzled continuously. At Port Said Rosie and Esther once again fell ill with gippy tummy, leaving Daniel to walk the sordid streets alone, fending off the little boys with 'feelthy pictures' of their 'sisters', and others with their blobs of shoe polish, who at all times seemed ready to pounce on his feet, so that his progress resembled a dance.

They had travelled out to Ceylon with optimism in their breasts. Rosie and Daniel had come to know each other very much better and to find that they had a great deal in common. Daniel had finally had the opportunity to bond closely with his little daughter, and they had made friends with a distinguished Egyptian gentleman, Ali Bey, from whom they had occasionally received an elaborately eloquent letter in a beautiful hand that had clearly benefitted from having learned to write Arabic first.

This time, however, Rosie was feeling guilty, but obstinate and helpless, and Esther was in a constant rage about having had to leave behind her beloved Singhalese ayah, Preethi, and the sweet-natured Tamil servants, the beautiful garden, and the pet mongoose that belonged to the Bassetts. She was still not at all delighted by her new baby brother, now a year old, oblivious to anything except his own sensations and appetites. She was still inclined to ask: 'Why can't we just put it back?' On this melancholy and ill-tempered voyage, Daniel was having to look after the infant as well as Esther, as long as his wife remained too seasick to move.

Daniel was angry and resentful, but not because of having to take care of the children. He had loved Ceylon, and had prevised a wonderful future for himself and his family, thinking that one day he would be master of an entire estate, and dreaming of setting up an aerial postal and passenger service with a small flotilla of floatplanes and a fleet of motorcycle combinations. Just as a golfer cannot help looking at the landscape and thinking of how it might become a golf course, Daniel was incapable of noticing any morsel of flat land without thinking of how it might make an airstrip.

He was also galled to the bone about having to leave Samadara. He had grown tired of being virtuous when there was no reward for it, and tired of having virtue thrust upon him by force of circumstance. He had, in a fit of pique coloured by a kind of loneliness, finally dropped his principles, and understood that sometimes a married person needs to take a lover if they are going to have any kind of romance or intimacy. He had vivid memories of his old friend Fluke advising him to find a 'dusky maiden', or at least to find a wife in France, and Samadara had lived up to all the sumptuous reveries that white men have about native girls. She had indeed been sweet-natured and sensual, and, above all, lovable. Daniel had given in to an impulsive desire, had quickly grown to love her, and it was all too bitter to have to leave her behind. He would remember his own guilt and her grief all his life, as she sat on the floor of the little house that he had arranged for her, hugging her knees, tears streaming silently down her face, biting her lip, looking up at him pleadingly with her huge brown eyes. He had turned out to be just another damned Pinkerton, and he hated himself for it.

He frequently wished that he had been able to send Rosie home without it being automatically assumed that Esther and Bertie would be sent with her. Other men sent their wives and children home. He could not have borne to be apart from Esther and Bertie, however, and being with Rosie was the price he had to pay. They had enjoyed a few months of blissful marriage in Ceylon, but now it all seemed like the kind of rose-tinted dream that comes upon you just before you wake up. He often found himself leaning on the ship's rail, looking out to sea, muttering 'damn, damn, damn' to himself. He felt that he wanted to get in a fight so that he could burn off some of this anger and disappointment, and he could hardly help but treat Rosie coldly.

In place of Ali Bey, Daniel made friends with a young Greek gentleman in a tight black suit with shiny patches at the elbow and knee, who had been employed to serve as ship's doctor. Just like Ali Bey, this man had become enchanted by Esther, and always took the opportunity to chuck her under the chin and pat her on the head whenever they met on deck. 'Pretty *koritsi*!' he would exclaim, and '*Filakimou!*'

The doctor was then twenty-four years old and had had no medical training whatsoever, but had taught himself English in order to read and memorise in its entirety *The Concise Home Doctor*, a massive two-volume encyclopedia of diseases and treatments of humans and animals that he had picked up in Monastiraki market on his first trip to Athens as an eighteen-year-old. He had gazed at the strange Roman letters, the pictures and diagrams, and known in that instant what his vocation must be. This was confirmed when, in the same market, on the same day, he found a large and equally dilapidated Greek/English dictionary. From his point of view, it was triply confirmed when, having painfully mastered the foreign alphabet, he was blessed with a revelation that struck him almost like a bolt of lightning. He would never forget the moment when, in the *kafeneion* back in his village, he had suddenly realised that the entire technical vocabulary of medicine was Greek. It was as if he had been born with all the knowledge, and would hardly have to learn anything. He had gone out into the blinding sunshine, overwhelmed with happiness, and kissed the young Father Arsenios on both cheeks, saying, 'Patir, for just this once, I am a believer.'

Fortunately he had a good doctor's natural healing touch, and learned very quickly from experience what he had not learned from his books. Such was his obvious skill and knowledge that, to the very day when he perished in an earthquake, not a single person ever challenged him to produce evidence of qualification.

Having encountered Esther for the first time, and made a fuss of her, the doctor straightened up and held out his hand to Daniel, saying, 'Dr John.'

Daniel took his hand, saying, 'Daniel Pitt.'

'Greek,' said the doctor, tapping his chest. 'You?'

'Half English, half French. *Moitié français, moitié anglais.*'

'*Vous parlez français?*'

'*Mais oui, bien sûr.*'

'*Moi aussi, je l'ai appris tout seul, sans école.*'

'*Alors, nous pouvons parler français. Ou anglais. Ou un mélange.*'

'*Ou un mélange!* Ha! *Oui,* but it is English I am wanting to practise. I learn from English book. I am ship doctor.'

'Are you really called John? It doesn't seem very Greek.'

'Only for English. Real name Iannis.'

'May I call you Iannis? John doesn't seem right. You don't look like a John.'

'OK, but when you call me you say "Ianni", no Iannis.'

Daniel puzzled for a moment, and said, 'Ah, that's the vocative?'

'Vocative, yes. *Klitiki.* Or you call me Iatre. *Iatre* is "Oh doctor".'

'Oh doctor. I like that. I shall call you, what was it? Iatre? Come and sit with us, Iatre. We're ready for the deckchairs, I feel.'

They sat side by side looking out over the seemingly infinite ocean, and Iannis said, 'You know Greek?'

'They made me do ancient Greek at Westminster. It's one of our venerable public schools, for duffers. I really was a duffer, I'm afraid. I didn't pay much attention. My brother Archie was terribly good at it.'

'Is very funny, English ancient Greek. I laugh very much. Sometimes English come to Greece and go to ruins. Is talk in strange funny voice and many dead words. Is all wrong.' He paused, and then said wistfully, 'This my last voyage. I enjoy. Then finish.'

'Oh? Why is that?'

'Wife tuberculosis. She very ill. I doctor can do nothing, nothing. She not live too long. She cough blood, she turn white and she get too thin. Very sad. I very sad. Have to go home. I work in village now. I get donkey perhaps. One day car perhaps. I love your daughter. She very sweet. *Poli glyka.* She called Esther. Esther from Bible. No? She about seven? I have little daughter. She three only, and soon, no more mama. Is terrible. So I go home. I look after daughter. I not give her to aunties or nothing. I make her doctor like me. Only lady doctor in Greece one day! I love your daughter because she sweet and pretty like mine. Soon I go home and I take her on knee and I never go out in ship again.'

'I'm so sorry about your wife.'

'Yes, she very good wife. I am loving her too much, too much.'

'And what is your daughter called?'

'She called Pelagia. Is nice name. It mean ocean. Is possible Esther sit on my knee? I miss my Pelagia. You know she smell so nice. She only three. Very pretty, very sweet, very intelligent. Also very strong. She get angry, she stamp foot, like this, she shout, and she throw *kouklaki*. She very Greek. I more like Italian.'

'Would you like to sit on the doctor's knee?' asked Daniel.

Esther looked up at the pleasant, handsome face with its eloquent brown eyes and beautifully groomed black moustache, and, with her thumb still firmly in her mouth, she nodded solemnly. She slid off her father's lap and into the arms of Dr Iannis, who cradled her in his left arm and kissed her on the forehead, bouncing her a little, and saying, 'Ah, Estherakimou.'

Afterwards the doctor had a go at holding Bertie, saying, 'I try little baby boy. I not have boy. Boy different?'

'Not really,' replied Daniel. 'Boys smell just as nice.'

'Is not different,' said Dr Iannis after a few minutes.

Dr Iannis dealt efficiently with Rosie's seasickness. He talked a great deal about the vagus and vestibular nerves, the semicircular canals and acidosis. He was quite keen on the idea of bromide or chloral suppositories, but Rosie firmly vetoed the idea. He mused aloud about atropine, belladonna and strychnine, but there was none on the ship anyway. Instead he carefully packed her ears with sterile gauze, right against the eardrums, and made her drink glucose every two hours. He bound her stomach in a kind of tight cummerbund, and told her to lie on her right side with her knees drawn up.

It worked, but it made Rosie feel very strange to be almost completely deaf, and confined to her cabin. She wondered if this was what it was like in the womb. She found herself revolving the same memories, having the same obsessive thoughts, and fighting against the strange, simmering, implacable anger that she felt towards her husband, and which she knew was steadily destroying her marriage. She asked herself over and over again whether she really loved him, and answered herself as many times that she truly did.

It was all very well telling herself that her heart had become overcomplicated because of Ash, and her natural impulses thwarted by her faith, but now she began to wonder if the truth was that she did not want to have to live with a man at all. What she dreamed of was a peaceful life alone with the children. She had the terrible thought that she might even have reached this stage with Ash, if he had lived and they had married. The idea seemed utterly preposterous and horrifying, but it nagged at her nonetheless, and she lay for hours on her side, her eyes wide open, and her heart pounding.

Daniel found that he required very little conversational skill in Dr Iannis's company. The doctor was a tireless talker, obsessed with the history of everything and anything. 'I from Cephallonia. Is Ionian Island, not in Ionian Sea, is between Greece and Italy. Was Venetian. You know Veneto?'

'No, but I do very much hope to go there one day.'

'Is very good, very nice. They give music, understand. They bring *kantades*. Is man with accordion, man with guitar, man with mandolin. They sing in *plaka* and *kafeneion*. Is polyphon, yes? Most Greek music monophon, but Cephallonia music from Veneto. Is very pretty songs. I sing you song about ant. I sing it to Estheraki.'

Esther sat solemnly on his knee whilst he sang to her, a simple tune in march time, ideal for bouncing her on his knee. When he had finished she said, 'Can you sing "This is the Way the Gentleman Rides"?'

'I not know that one. Is English?'

'I'll show you,' said Daniel.

He handed Bertie to the doctor, sat Esther on his knee and bounced her up and down to the different rhythms of the gentleman, the lady, the soldier and a great many other improvised characters, until at last he came to the farmer, and exclaimed, 'Down in the ditch!' as she fell to the deck, laughing and kicking.

'Is good!' said Dr Iannis. 'I try to remember, for Pelagia. She like very much.'

During the stop in Malta, strolling about in Valletta with nothing to do and nothing to say to each other, Daniel and Rosie felt as gloomy as they had been cheerful on the way out. The spring weather somehow made it all much worse, as if the rest of the world were going ahead without them. Daniel was holding Esther's hand, and Rosie was pushing Bertie in a large cream-coloured perambulator that they had acquired in Colombo on the eve of their departure. It was only the presence of the children that prevented them from lapsing into a continuous acrimonious argument.

'Just think, we'll be home for April,' said Rosie, trying to make conversation, and Daniel said morosely, 'O to be in England now that April's there. Have you any idea what I'm supposed to do when we get back? I have precisely one hundred guineas left. Have I got to go to Henley and beg for my job back?'

'Well, I'm certain they would give it to you, if you asked.'

'I'd have to go back to Birmingham. Are you coming with me this time?'

'Oh well, I'd have to think about that. You could open a branch in London, perhaps.'

'I've a good mind to rejoin the RAF.'

'Would you?' she asked, a little too enthusiastically.

He detected this, and said, 'Looking forward to some long absences, then? Hoping I'll be posted abroad?'

'I just want you to be happy,' improvised Rosie, and Daniel gave her a sour sideways glance, and said, 'I believe you.' A few moments later he added, 'I want to live with the children. I don't see any point in having children if you're not there whilst they're growing up. It'd be different if there was a war on. Anyway, peacetime in the services is a damned dry run. It's just polishing and saluting and stamping and following procedures.'

'You probably won't rejoin, then?'

'Probably not. Even though it's obviously where I belong. Though I did love it in Ceylon.'

The conversation was interrupted by Dr Iannis, who had spotted them from a distance, and came hurrying towards them waving his panama hat, crying out, 'Ah, my friends, my friends! I show you round. I know history. I tell you history of everything. We go eat rabbit. Rabbit very good Malta …'

It was the persistent but congenial company of this Greek doctor that prevented Rosie and Daniel from quarrelling violently and falling out with each other, and they were grateful to him. Neither of them was ready to face the inevitable storm that would be the aftermath of their return, and they thought of this period as the ominous prelude to a crisis, like the condemned man who spends the night of his execution playing cards with his jailers.

As they approached the docks in Gibraltar, Dr Iannis leaned on the rail with his pipe in his mouth, and told his friends, 'Is last time here. After, I go home Cephallonia. Here one big bordel for English sailor, like Malta, but I like anyway. I like big warships. I go see monkeys for last time. You seen monkeys?'

'One of them stole my handkerchief last time,' said Rosie.

'I go see them again,' said the doctor sadly. 'I say goodbye monkey.'

'If you're going back to Greece, why not have dinner with us tonight?' proposed Daniel. 'We can have a farewell meal. We're staying at the Bristol.'

'Ah! Nice hotel! Best hotel! Beautiful garden! But Grand Hotel also good. Moorish patio! I stay in Cecil. I like reading room, many newspaper, many language. I enjoy. We eat *huevos a la flamenca*. Is topical. You like paella? Is rice with everything kind of thing.'

'Like a risotto?'

'Is better. Is more flavour. Is *krokos*. You know *krokos*? Is yellow. Is nice, is delicate.'

There was little to do in Gibraltar but walk about enjoying the life in the streets. There seemed to be meditative, sun-browned pairs of men playing accordion and cornet mournfully on every street corner, and there were acrobats in the square outside the cathedral of St Mary the Crowned, including a little girl no more than five years old, who was doing backflips and walkovers, and then handstands on her father's shoulders. Esther was mesmerised, and wanted to watch for hours. Here began her passion for cart-wheels, which was to end only with adulthood.

She also loved the slightly mad donkeys that brought their own kind of chaos to the streets, with their constantly slipping burdens and small acts of rebellion, and she had to pat the noses of every one they passed. Dr Iannis expatiated on the Genoese nature of the architecture, and the perfection of the rhythms of arches, the symmetry of the elaborate patterns on the Moorish tiles. He wanted to show them the Flemish synagogue, and Bedlam Court, because of its sash windows. He also felt he had to show them all the chandlers' in Irish Street, and the cemetery where there was a victim of the Battle of Trafalgar, and he made them walk up to the Moorish castle above Casemates Square. In those days the square itself was not the grand piazza it became forty years later, but a parade ground. As they stood outside, Daniel looking at the soldiers wistfully, and thinking how ridiculously young so many of them were, Dr Iannis said, 'Is place where bad soldiers hanged. Rope on neck. Bye-bye.'

'You should have been a historian,' said Daniel, 'rather than a doctor,' and the doctor looked at him as if he was mad and replied, 'I both. A man is many thing. Like soldier poet. Like Byron! We like Byron in Cephallonia. He stay with us a long time. He two thing.' He tapped his own chest. 'I many thing. I doctor, I father, I historian, I traveller, I Greek, I cosmopolitano, many languages and other thing. In my country, all doctor is historian.'

'It's true,' said Rosie. 'No one is ever only one thing. Inside one person there are so many different people, and quite often they're at war with each other, and sometimes one of them is winning, and sometimes another. We're all so hard to understand, aren't we? I don't even understand myself. It'd be so much easier to be a dog, don't you think? Or one of these donkeys? I just wish so much ...' She looked away, leaving the words unsaid, and the doctor said quietly, 'Is true, is very true. I remember this to tell my daughter one day. But I know one thing, if no one love you and you not love no one, then ...?' He spread his hands apart and thrust his head forward with his lips downturned. 'Is all life no good. Dead is better.'

'I'm quite looking forward to being dead, as long as it's oblivion,' said Daniel. 'I'm completely fed up with the insane chatter I have to live with ... I don't mean the chatter of other people ... I mean, you know, my own thoughts thinking themselves, round and round. Hopes and complaints, and things you plan to say to somebody one day ... I just wish it would all stop and let me have some peace.'

'It shuts up when you're asleep,' said Rosie sensibly. 'At least, when you're not dreaming. And then you might as well be dead. You are sort of dead, when you're asleep, aren't you? And then you wake up and it's like coming back to life, being reborn.'

'That's what worries me about death,' said Daniel. 'I really do not want to go through that ordeal, and then wake up and find I've got to carry on living with myself, even in heaven.'

'Well, I believe in the life hereafter.'

'Of course you do. You still have your faith. I'm often very envious.'

'If you don't mind,' said Rosie, 'that reminds me. I'd so much like to go and see inside some of the churches. Why don't you and the doctor go and see the monkeys, and we can all meet back at the hotel for drinks at seven? You take Esther and I'll hang on to Bertie. I'm sure you can find a hansom cab these days.'

As the three of them set off towards Irish Street, the doctor said, 'Is the same rule for wifes and monkeys. You touch them first, they get angry. You wait for them to touch you, is OK.'

At the top of the rock, they endured the astonishing insolence of the monkeys, who rifled through their pockets, throwing away anything inedible, having tested it first. Esther was completely delighted, and did her first cartwheel. The macaques were visibly alarmed and impressed, backing away and chattering, so Esther did it again.

'Estherakimou is little monkey now,' said the doctor.

Whilst Esther entertained the monkeys, Daniel and the doctor took in the astonishing view of Morocco across the strait, almost an arm's length away, it seemed. 'I been there once. I not like it. Woman, she try to sell me her daughter. Daughter only five, maybe six. I get very angry, and woman think I mad. Over there, is too poor, too much poor people.'

'Did you like Ceylon?' asked Daniel.

'Oh yes, Ceylon. I like. Is *paradeisos*. How you say? Old Eden Garden? Too many beautiful women. Men very nice, very polite. I like fruit. I like rice. Colombo too busy, but still nice.'

'I am going to miss it forever,' said Daniel.

Down at the baroque Roman Catholic church, Rosie parked
Bertie in his pram at the bottom of the steps and paid one of
the street children sixpence to keep an eye on him. Inside, she
listened to the officiating priest conducting communion and sat
unhappily in a pew at the back, trying to understand herself, and
wondering how she could keep asking God to forgive her if it
never made any difference and she never managed to change, and
never realised until it was too late the difference between real
virtue and the selfishness that disguises itself as such.

The following day, down at the docks, Dr Iannis kissed Rosie's
hand with elaborate elegance and then did the same to Esther,
who held out her hand like a real lady, loving the theatre of it.
He bent down and kissed the sleeping Bertie on the forehead,
and then kissed Daniel on both cheeks and hugged him to his
chest. Daniel noticed that he smelled pleasantly of cologne and
pipe tobacco, and he felt a pang in his heart that he would probably never see this kind and interesting young man ever again.

Dr Iannis reached into his breast pocket and brought out his
portefeuille. He presented Daniel with his card, which was somewhat grubby, but beautifully designed. The doctor noticed Daniel
attempting to decipher the Greek script and took it from him,
turned it over and returned it. It read '*Poste restante, Argostoli,
Céphalonie, Isles Ioniennes, Royaume Hellénique*'.

'I'll write,' said Daniel, 'and I do hope that everything works
out for your wife.'

'I say goodbye to wife soon,' replied the doctor mournfully.
'Maybe one year, maybe two. Maybe six month. Is me and my
koritsi now.'

As the SS *Derbyshire* left the harbour, Daniel and Rosie stood
at the rail, waving to the doctor, until finally there was no point
in it any more. Daniel turned to Rosie and said, 'Too many
damned goodbyes. Halfway through my bloody life, and all I ever
do is say one damned goodbye after another.'

'We'll be back home soon,' said Rosie, looking up at him
apologetically.

'Home? Where is home? Have I got to live with your damned
mother again?'

'Don't call her my "damned" mother,' said Rosie. 'I don't talk about your mother like that. You're altogether too free with your damns and bloodies.'

Daniel picked up Esther and hoisted her onto his shoulders. He looked hard at his wife. 'Well, my mother is going to give you hell,' he said, 'and so will your father.'

19

An Interview with Mrs McCosh

M rs McCosh poured tea from her second-best teapot, and said, 'One sugar or two?'

Lieutenant Commander Frederick Ribaud replied, 'Just the one, please.'

'You should not say "just the one", you need only say "just one". It is very important for one's speech to be *comme il faut*. It says so much about one's state of refinement.'

'Quite so, Mrs McCosh.'

'I understand,' said Mrs McCosh, 'that your name may be of French origin. I do already have one son-in-law who is half French. Another would be quite *de trop*.'

'I believe we were French some centuries ago, but now we are as British as the royal family.'

Ottilie very nearly spat out her tea, and dug him in the ribs with her elbow.

Frederick said, 'The name is apparently of Germanic origin, from a word meaning "to live licentiously", and then it came to mean "the lowest class of servant", one that carries out the most menial and demeaning duties.'

Ottilie said, 'Oh, come on, Frederick, do be serious.'

'I am serious. I was told by an etymologist.'

'And what would an expert in insects know about such things?' demanded Mrs McCosh. 'Really, one has a duty to be a little sceptical of irrelevant expertise.'

She adjusted her lorgnettes, and gazed at him imperiously.

'I understand that my dear husband has consented to your marriage to Ottilie. Without consulting me.'

'He has indeed done me that honour, Mrs McCosh, but naturally I am hoping that you will also find it in your heart to give me your blessing.'

'Well, I agree that that would be preferable. What are your prospects?'

'He's going to become a provincial governor, one day,' said Ottilie.

'I may have to leave India eventually,' said Frederick. 'All the talk these days is "India for the Indians". I'd say the writing's on the wall.'

'Impossible!' cried Mrs McCosh. 'How would they ever manage without us? Now, young man, tell me about your family.'

'My mother is from Derbyshire, and her father was a clergyman. My father comes from a long line of naval officers, of whom not one ever became an admiral.'

'Not one? Not one? Such a pity.'

'I have a brother who's gone to South Africa to look for diamonds, and a sister who's married to a barrister.'

'Barristers are intolerable people,' she said. 'Unbearable blatherers. One cannot trust people who earn a living by merely talking cleverly and throwing Latin tags about like confetti.'

'I'm inclined to agree with you,' said Frederick.

'You have no aristocratic connections?'

'No, I'm afraid not.'

'He knows Prince Albert,' said Ottilie.

'Prince Albert? Do you? Good gracious!' Mrs McCosh's nostrils flared like a cavalry charger at the sound of a bugle. She put down her teacup and looked up at his face adoringly.

'Frederick was on HMS *Collingwood* at Jutland,' said Ottilie proudly.

'Prince Albert was a midshipman. In command of the forward turret.'

'No doubt he sank a great many enemy ships.'

'I believe we lightly damaged a battlecruiser. That's all, I'm afraid.'

'No doubt the range was too great.'

'Undoubtedly.'

'Frederick used to call him Bertie,' said Ottilie mischievously.

'We all did,' said Frederick. 'All the officers, I mean. He had a terrible stutter. I'm afraid we called him BeBeBeBertie behind his back.'

'How shockingly disrespectful! And are you inviting him to the wedding?' asked Mrs McCosh.

'We can send him an invitation,' said Frederick. 'I very much doubt if he'd come.'

'He must be invited! He must be invited!'

'Mother, calm down, do.'

Frederick was amused. 'Do I take it, Mrs McCosh, that you find me a suitable husband for your daughter?'

'Oh! Most suitable! Most suitable!'

That evening Mrs McCosh collared Ottilie on the upstairs landing. 'My dear, my dear, I have committed the most dreadful faux pas.'

'A faux pas? Mother, what could it be?'

'My dear, I served him tea from the second-best teapot! It's plated! And some of the plating has gone so that one can see the brass underneath. And the butter knife was also the plated one, and his scone fell to pieces, and one of the saucers was chipped!'

'I honestly don't think he would have noticed.'

'My dear, I should have used the best. You're very remiss. I do wish you'd told me he knows Prince Albert!'

20

A Letter from Archie

Care of the Political Agent
Waziristan
Third tent on the left up a nullah,
out of the firing line of snipers

13 June 1928

My dear Ottilie,

I have just received the news of your engagement. Your dear sister Christabel was so kind as to write and let me know. He sounds like a very fine fellow, and of course one cannot but be in awe of naval types. I am certain it was the blockade that brought the Kaiser to his knees.

I don't have long to write this, as we are up at dawn to do a patrol in search of the tribesmen who stole rifles and grenades from the armoury by blowing a hole in the back of it. We'll have to get them back before they are used against us, and luckily we have excellent trackers. These are exciting times for us on the North-West Frontier, but then they always are. One expects to be killed at a moment's notice, and is glee-fully surprised when one isn't.

My dear, there is no subtle way to put this, and so I shall eschew subtlety.

I am so heartily glad and joyful that you have found a worthier object of your affections than I was. I have always known about the inclination of your heart, and I have always been bewildered as to how to deal with it. You know the reasons, and there is no need to go over them. What I do know is that if I had ever had any sense, my affections would have settled on you. Of the four sisters, you are the closest to being an angel, and I am certain that your fortunate husband will find the touch of your hand a balm to the spirit.

But, Ottilie, my dear, I have never been, and never could be, good enough for you, and I would have remained painfully myself. You could not have been my salvation, because no one ever will be. I am one of the damned. I am reconciled to experiencing love only in my imagination, and reconciled to my fate here in this most godforsaken and lunatic corner of the Empire. This is where my destiny lies, and I have made a point of letting everyone know that one day I would like my bones to rest in Peshawar, in a grave where in spring it will be covered in peach blossom.

Ottilie, my dear, I wish you the most profound happiness with your husband. May he treat you with care and reverence. You have taken steps to free yourself of me, and I only beg you to ensure that you do it resolutely and absolutely, so that you may live to attain the happiness with him that you so richly deserve.

Yours ever, your old Pal from next door,
Major Archie P

21

In Which Frederick and Ottilie Abscond

F rederick and Ottilie sat side by side on a bench at the Tarn, as they so often did when they wished to escape from The Grampians and have a little time to themselves.

'All this bread really can't be good for them,' said Frederick. 'It's not as if ducks feed on bread in the wild. Shouldn't we bring seeds or something?'

'Haven't you heard of evolution? These are ducks that have evolved over the centuries to live on the Tarn and eat a dreadful diet. They're called Duckus Elthamiensis Breadophagus.'

'Sounds plausible. What are we going to do about the wedding?'

'Oh gosh, I don't know. I mean, the last one, when Sophie and Rosie had a double wedding, it was such a wonderful affair. Daniel was still in the RAF, and his whole squadron came and stunted for us, and it was a beautiful day, and my father was perfectly well, and my mother wasn't nearly as mad. And of course my father paid for it all.'

'What are you saying?'

'I'm saying we should do something that's altogether different. I mean, poor Mother is off the rails, and Daddy can hardly breathe, and it's bound to rain, isn't it? And Daniel and Rosie don't get on any more, so it would be difficult for them, and Sophie and Fairhead will be thinking back on it and being sad that they can't have the children they'd hoped for. So we've got to do something different. But terribly romantic.'

'We could do an Oriental.'

'An Oriental?'

'Yes. I'll send in my brothers to kidnap you, and a few days later I'll send the bride price to your father. It's a wonderfully efficient system, and it would save your father from having to give you a dowry.'

'He wouldn't anyway. And you've only got one brother, and he's in Burma. What about coming in the middle of the night with a ladder?'

'I don't have a car at present, and I don't think I'd get a ladder onto the train.'

'You could borrow our AC Six. Or get a hansom.'

'How does one get a ladder into a hansom?'

'You strap it to the roof, silly. Actually I think we might have a ladder in the storeroom under the conservatory. Where Wragge sleeps in the wheelbarrow.'

'And what about the honeymoon? Where shall we go? Normandy?'

'I want to go to Scotland. I am Scottish after all, but I might just as well be English. I haven't got one trace of a burr, and I hardly know the place. I have *nostalgie de la patrie.*'

'Inverness is lovely. And what about St Andrews? It's got a road on the waterfront and two streets, and you can walk down one of them in the rain, and then back up the other in the rain, and then down the other in the rain, and then you can sit in the rain and watch the sea, or go and laugh at the golfers on the Old Course, playing in a gale.'

'I'd love that. I've never been to St Andrews. We could dine on porridge and kippers, and tatties and haggis and neeps, and cock-a-leekie soup.'

'It's quite hard to catch a haggis. Are you sure they're in season?'

Frederick threw the last morsel of bread to the ducks, crumpled the brown paper bag in his hand, and put it in his pocket.

'If we're going to honeymoon in Scotland, what about doing the most romantic thing of all?'

'The most romantic of all? Do tell.'

There was something out of kilter about The Grampians in the days thereafter, but no one could quite put their finger on it, until one morning Rosie said, 'Ottilie, what's happened to Frederick? He hasn't been here for days. You haven't fallen out, have you?'

'Haven't you noticed that I've been weeping buckets?'

'You seem positively blissful and serene.'

'Isn't one always, when one's beloved disappears?'

'Oh, Ottilie, I know you're up to something.'

'*Moi?* Little me? Have I ever looked more innocent?'

'You certainly have. You've put on a very obnoxious air of smug self-satisfaction.'

'Smugness is always self-satisfied. It's part of the definition.'

'Clever clogs. You're just trying to avoid the question.'

'All will be revealed,' said Ottilie. 'Just for now, I am being mysterious.'

Three weeks elapsed, and then Ottilie disappeared overnight. Cookie, who was always up first, found that the ladder from Wragge's storeroom under the conservatory was leaning against the morning-room windowsill, and the sash was wide open.

There was a note from Ottilie on the dining-room table that said:

Darlings,

Don't worry about me at all. I have eloped with Frederick and will return in a fortnight, a respectable married woman, having honeymooned in Caledonia.

Sorry about the ladder. It just seemed so awfully banal to leave by the front door. You wouldn't believe what fun this all is.

I am so excited!

My bestest love to you all, the soon-to-be Ottilie Ribaud

When, a fortnight later, she and Frederick did finally reappear, glowing with happiness, none of the family had the heart to remonstrate, despite their confused outrage in the interim.

'Did Prince Albert come?' Mrs McCosh wanted to know.

'No, Mother. We were married by a blacksmith. Over an anvil.'

'A blacksmith! An anvil!'

'Yes, Mother. It was rather moving, in its way.'

'Is it really a proper marriage?' asked Rosie.

'It's perfectly legal,' said Frederick. 'Otherwise we wouldn't have dreamt of doing it. I even stayed up there for three weeks to fulfil the residency requirement.'

'So that's where you were.'

Rosie was dissatisfied. As far as she was concerned, a marriage that was not a religious ceremony in a proper church was not a marriage at all. 'I thought that all this Gretna Green stuff was just for romantic novellas,' she said. 'I had no idea that it really goes on.'

'Well, it is in romantic novellas,' said Ottilie. 'That's how everyone knows about it, isn't it? Anyway, our blacksmith was very charming, and he had the most enormous muscles in his arms, and he was just as good as a vicar, and the anvil was beautifully clean and polished up, and really not too dented. It was rather huge, too, but not as big as an altar.'

That evening Mr McCosh took Frederick aside and said, 'It was very good of you to spare me all that expense, my boy, but I would have been perfectly happy to give you a proper wedding. I feel as confident in you and Ottilie as I did in Sophie and Fairhead. Very confident indeed.'

'It wasn't done to save money, sir,' said Frederick. 'It was to give Ottilie as much fun as possible. And, besides, all my family are in India and Burma. The groom's side of the church would have been almost empty.'

'If you keep that up,' said Mr McCosh, 'you'll have a good marriage. Life is short, eh? Just as well to remember that, and, as you say, have as much fun as possible. That's what I've always tried to do. It's a pity you don't play golf. Couples who play golf together stay together, in my experience, unless she's much better than he is. I can give you plenty of tips, if you'd like to learn.'

That evening Fairhead and Sophie came from Blackheath in her noisy little car to congratulate the couple and stay for the night. At supper, Mrs McCosh said, 'I am just terribly sorry, Ottilie, that I did not have the opportunity to talk to you about the nature and duties of marriage. I did so with Sophie and Rosie, and I trust it has stood them in good stead.'

'Fabulously good stead,' said Sophie mischievously, 'the steadiness has been invaluable. And consternate not, Mother, I passed on your sagacious counsel to her myself.'

'It was priceless,' said Ottilie, and she and Sophie began to giggle, whereupon Rosie cast them a disapproving look.

'I am so glad to hear it. And what did you do in St Andrews?' asked Mrs McCosh.

Sophie and Ottilie caught each other's eye again, and the latter spluttered and nearly choked on her soup. When she had recovered, she said, 'We walked up and down in the rain, Mother. And we went and laughed at the golfers trying to play in the gales. It was bliss.'

22

The Proposition (1)

In August of 1928, three months after returning to England, Daniel received a letter at his lodgings in Birmingham, marked 'Strictly Private and Confidential' in a beautiful italic hand he recognised as being that of Christabel's companion, Gaskell.

Hexham

3 August 1928

My dear Daniel,

I am writing to you on Christabel's behalf, because she doesn't have the courage to write to you herself. I don't want to write to you at any length at this point, because what we have to say to you is deeply personal and really can't and shouldn't be disclosed in writing.

Please will you come and stay with us for a weekend? I have in mind the third week of this month. We need to speak to you alone, so please, on this occasion, do not bring Rosie and the children with you, much as we love them. You can all come up together another time.

Do say yes. We are somewhat desperate and feel that you are our only hope. And you really must be desperate to be reunited with your aeroplanes. Let's take them up, one after the other! There isn't any shooting at this time of year, apart from pigeons, but it would be so nice to go out with you and the two retrievers and come back with a bunny or two. I've got a new long-barrelled Jeffery that I can't wait for you to try. I swear you can get a bird at eighty yards with it.

You could come by train, or it would be a pleasant drive at this time of year, or I could simply come and fetch you in the Avro. You'll see what a splendid flyer I've become, and how well I've absorbed your advice never never never to try to turn back when your engine conks out on take-off. Is there a cricket pitch in your village? We can use that if I promise not to land on the actual sacred bit. Or are there too many trees?

I remain your devoted Green-Eyed Monster, much love,
Gaskell

PS Wonderful news about Lindbergh, eh? But how did he see where he was going, with no windscreen in front? Was he navigating by looking out to the side? How do you land a plane like that? Apparently the crowd that was waiting for him simply threw aside two companies of soldiers who were supposed to be keeping them out! And he got $25,000 for it! Didn't you wish it was you? O brave new world!

PPS Apparently, eighty thousand people turned up to see the inauguration of the Menin Gate. How I wish I could have been there, but how I would have wept!

PPPS If you haven't seen it yet, you really must go and see Garbo and Gilbert in Flesh and the Devil. My goodness, how they smoulder! Christabel and I were in raptures! They're going to do Anna Karenina next. Can't wait!

More love, G

Daniel looked at his maps and worked out that it would probably take all day to get to Hexham on his combination, and when he went to the railway station to find out how to get there by train, he could not find the stationmaster, who was enjoying a mug of thick milky tea in the signal box, since no trains were expected in the village for another hour. Accordingly he wrote back to Gaskell:

3 August 1928

Beloved Green-Eyed One,
How wonderful it would be to see you and Christabel again after five years! Can you believe it? Tempus fugit, whereas I haven't flown at all. I am so glad to learn that my little fleet is well, and I had been at the

very point of writing to ask if I could come up and be reunited with you and my buses.

I am very much agog to find out what you two want to divulge. I have cleared you for landing on the cricket pitch with the club and the parish council, and will put out a large white sheet so that you don't accidentally land at Wootton Wawen. I think they consented mainly because they all wanted to see a lady aviator, and you can expect the whole village to turn out to welcome you. I'm afraid I may have made things worse by telling them that you are also an eminent artist. A good landing will be de rigueur!

The easiest way to find the village would be to pick up the Stratford-upon-Avon Canal, and follow it down to where it crosses the Alne. You'll see the white sheet a quarter of a mile due east. The prevailing wind here is west. Can you give me an ETA?

I still have all my flying gear, because I use it for the motorcycle, so you don't need to bring me any kit. I'll have a drum of juice lined up for the bus. Don't come if the weather turns foul, we'll just pick another date.

I recently had the honour of unveiling the village war memorial, along with the vicar and the Lord of the Manor. An old soldier sounded the Last Post and Reveille, and it brought a terrible lump to my throat. The stone makes the most horrible reading. Five Sylvester brothers gone, four Treachers, three Wagstaffes and two Mardels, along with about twenty others from this tiny village. It turned out that the Lord of the Manor is the father of the dead Wagstaffe boys. Apparently their mother was too upset to come at all. I had to make a speech about sacrifice and was miserably afflicted by the absolute inadequacy of words. I felt abject afterwards. It's almost certain that just about all of them died ingloriously under shellfire.

I can't wait to see you.
Your devoted admirer,
DP the GB (Grounded Bird)

The day turned out to be a very fine one, and Gaskell found herself circling a field which was much too crowded, leaving too small a space for making allowances. Below her a thoroughly alarmed carthorse was leaping and bucking in a neighbouring field, and next to that a small flock of sheep was hurtling from one end of their paddock to another as the shadow of her wings passed over them. 'Oh, silly innocents!' she exclaimed, waggled her wings, and then banked to make the final run, calculating that the villagers would probably have the sense to make space for her.

They duly did, and she landed neatly just to one side of the pitch. She cut the engine, removed her goggles and gauntlets, and stuffed them into the map case. When she climbed out of the cockpit and stood on terra firma, shaking her long limbs to rid herself of the stiffness, it was to be presented with a bouquet by a tiny girl in a bulky blue frock, with a huge blue ribbon tied into her hair. The child suddenly took fright, threw the flowers at her, and ran away. Gaskell was delighted, to the relief of the embarrassed villagers.

She waved when she saw Daniel, and he came up and embraced her, kissing her on both cheeks, and laughing.

'It's been ages,' he said, 'much too long. How I missed you! And you've hardly changed at all. They've laid on a lunch for you in the pavilion. *Noblesse oblige*, I'm afraid.'

'Oh my goodness, will I have to make a speech?'

'Usual stuff,' said Daniel. 'It's an honour, et cetera.'

The villagers were captivated and mystified by this tall, trousered woman with her hair cut in a shell, who spoke in a languid drawl and smoked Turkish cigarettes from an immensely long cigarette holder. Most of all they were bowled over, as everyone was, by her large, luminous and spectacularly beautiful green eyes. She found herself very much monopolised by the 'gentry', and tried to make a point of shaking hands with the more humble folk as well. 'Daniel darling,' she said *en passant*, 'this is what it must be like to be royalty.'

'And do you like it?'

'No doubt it's fun for an hour or two.'

'You pull it off magnificently.'

'You know what I'd really like? I'd like to have a go in the nets. Do you think they've got any bats and balls in the pavilion?'

'One can always ask.'

Gaskell would be remembered for years afterwards as that extraordinary woman who faced up to the village's fast bowler,

Mr 'Puffer' Harrison, and landed a six into the village pond, twenty yards beyond the boundary. The children were sent into the water to feel for it with their bare feet.

There is a sepia photograph in the pavilion of Gaskell standing with a cricket bat over her shoulder in front of the Avro 504, which is adorned with the seven or eight little children who were clambering on it. Only a few can put a name to any of them any more. Next to her is a good-looking man, a little shorter than she is, who is remembered simply as the Ace. At the bottom it says 'Visit of Miss Gaskell, 20th August 1928,', and in a small glass case on a shelf next to it is 'The Ball'.

23

The Proposition (2)

Gaskell urged Daniel to fly the Avro home and overcame his attempts to demur, pooh-poohing his diffident 'But I haven't flown for years' with 'Come on, darling, it's like riding a bicycle. You never forget.'

With the help of a few men from the village they wheeled the aircraft to the end of the field where it could be turned to face the wind. Daniel and the blacksmith held up the tailplane so that there would be no drag from the skid, and then Daniel tossed his gloves into the cockpit, climbed in after them, and tightened the chin strap of his helmet.

He was surprised by the knot of fear in the pit of his stomach, but as soon as Gaskell swung the prop and the engine fired up he was suddenly filled with the same joy that had never left him during the war, even on freezing dawns at the times of the greatest strain, when he was half dead from a hangover. Castor oil! Exhaust fumes! The roar of the unsilenced engine! He waited for Gaskell to climb in, lowered his goggles, and turned to give her the thumbs up. What a pity it was only an old Avro that could scarcely do eighty miles an hour, with an old-fashioned skid on the undercarriage, but even so, in a crate like this you didn't really want to throw it about. It was like going for a hack on a cob; you just relaxed and watched the land go by. All being well, the journey would take about three hours, and then, when he was safely at his destination, he could go up in his Snipe and his Pup. As he pulled the stick back and the machine lifted into the air, he realised that he had not been so happy since Bertie was born.

They stopped in a field near Holmfirth, and then again at Brough, because the villagers had filled them up with prodigious quantities of tea, and in any case it was good to stop and stretch one's legs. As they overflew the sublime landscape of the Peaks and then over the North York Moors enjoying the sudden bumps from the updraught, Daniel experienced a renewed sense of what he had been fighting for. It was the same feeling he had known over the Western Front, that lethal brown strip that had divided and defended France from the aggression of a tyrant. A country was its people and its culture, but it was also a beloved earth.

When, in the late evening, they finally touched down at the airfield where Daniel's planes were kept, he leapt down from the cockpit and lay down on his back, spread out his arms, and laughed.

'Darling, what ails you?' asked Gaskell, removing her helmet and allowing her hair to shake free.

'Happiness,' said Daniel. 'It's only happiness. Can I go and see my buses now?'

'They're in the East Hangar,' said Gaskell. 'It'll be locked up. There doesn't seem to be anybody about at all; we'll have to leave the Avro out overnight.'

'What's the weather forecast like?'

'No idea, and anyway it's always wrong.'

'Oh well, if the wind comes up, we'll have to nip back and tie her down.'

'We'll come here in the morning and give the other two a little spin. Come on, the car's over there.'

'Oh my goodness,' said Daniel, 'you've got a Bentley Speed Six!'

'Don't be too impressed. I swapped it for four pictures. It was a mad American. I couldn't possibly have afforded it otherwise.'

'You must be doing spectacularly well if four pictures buys you a Speed Six.'

'My preoccupation with death and decomposition and general sordidness is very much in the spirit of the times. I expect I'll go out of fashion ere long. The field will be left to Helen Allingham.'

'Well, I like her paintings,' said Daniel. 'They remind me of where my mother lives.'

'Red brick, milkmaids with churns, and roses round the door. Bucolic prettiness.'

'Exactly. No chilblains on the milkmaids, no children dead of diphtheria.'

'Let's go,' said Gaskell. 'Christabel's been dying to see you. She's very excited. I'm afraid it's not like the old days; we don't have a panoply of servants to line up and greet us at the door any more. There are only three left, and that's because they refuse to go. Oh, and we have someone to look after my poor old parents. They're both gaga, I'm afraid.'

'Comes to us all.'

The Great Hall was an elaborate expression of Victorian Gothic, in red brick that reminded visitors of the architecture of Gilbert Scott. It did have a somewhat dilapidated appearance compared to when Daniel had last seen it, but it was still very grand and dignified, and it gave out the air of a building that ideally should be populated by headless wraiths drifting about in their shrouds. He noticed that there was a small buddleia growing from the mouth of a gargoyle, and that the paving stones had weeds growing in the interstices. The lawns still looked wonderful, though, and the enormous redwood tree in the middle might well have been the tallest outside of California.

'How nice to be back,' he exclaimed as Gaskell pulled out the choke to kill the engine. 'I see you still have a fabulous rookery in the elms.'

'The biggest rookery for miles,' said Gaskell. 'Noisy buggers. The villagers used to come and shoot the young ones for rook pie. No one eats rook pie any more. And the poor old elms end up as seats for Windsor chairs.'

Christabel came to the door, and Daniel saw that she was still the lovely English rose that she had always been, despite her height and angularity. She held out her arms and Daniel ran to embrace her, kissing her on each cheek, and saying, 'You look as marvellous as ever!'

'Silver hairs amongst the gold,' she replied, laughing. 'And you have a little less thatch than you used to. It suits you. Men are so lucky. They age so much better than we do. My skin is turning to leather. I have to oil it as if I were an old boot in need of dubbin.'

Tea was brought in to the drawing room by the butler, a frail man of seventy with broken veins on his face, and very large and florid ears, whose father had been butler before him. His hands shook so much that he spilled tea from the pot into the saucers as he poured, repeating, 'I am so sorry, madam. I am so sorry, madam.'

'Never mind, Dunston, it can't be helped,' said Gaskell, taking her cup and pouring the tea into it from the saucer. Daniel and Christabel did the same.

'Will there be anything else, madam?'

'You've forgotten the crumpets and the walnut cake.'

'I'm so sorry, madam. I'll go and fetch them immediately.'

'You really don't need to keep saying sorry, Dunston.'

'I'm so sorry, madam.'

After he had gone, Christabel said, 'Poor old Dunston. He spends all his time apologising.'

'Where are your parents?' asked Daniel.

'I've given them an apartment in the east wing, on the ground floor, so they don't have to cope with stairs. My mother tries to do embroidery even though she can't see, and my father is writing his memoirs. He's written the first page several hundred times, I should think.'

'Oh, why?'

'Because he's forgotten that he's already done it. They're both quite happy, and that's the important thing.'

'Will I see them at dinner? I was very fond of them.'

'Oh yes, but they'll be fast asleep by the main course. With their faces in their plates, like the dormouse.'

'And when are you going to ask me this question that was too important to be put in writing?'

'Not now,' said Christabel. 'Now is for small talk. We were hoping to broach the subject with you after a bottle or two of burgundy and a glass of Armagnac. After dinner.'

'When we're all a little bit mellow,' said Gaskell. 'How are Esther and Bertie?'

'Here beginneth the small talk,' said Christabel.

'Can we go and see what's happening in your studio instead?' asked Daniel. 'I want to see what you two have been up to.'

'Christabel's done some wonderful contemporary portraits. H. G. Wells, Conan Doyle, Dora Carrington, Augustus John, Bertrand Russell, and so on.'

'I had a conversation with Bertrand Russell on a train once,' said Daniel. 'We talked about relativity, I seem to remember.'

'Funny little man,' said Christabel. 'He was perfectly miserable. He said he was thinking of writing a book about happiness.'

'And I'm doing a huge oil painting of that dreadful nightmare you told me about, that you kept having every night.'

'The procession of the dead?'

'Yes, that's exactly what I'm calling it. Do you still have it?'

'Much less often. Perhaps once every three months.'

The old ballroom had been converted into a large and exceedingly chaotic studio, with Christabel's section at one end, and Gaskell's at the other. A French window and a clerestory bestowed a generous bounty of natural light.

'It's an absolute bloody mess,' said Gaskell, rolling her eyes theatrically.

It was true. At Christabel's end was a home-made darkroom, taking up an entire corner, cobbled together out of sheets of plywood, painted black on the insides. Outside it, clipped onto sagging parallel lengths of string, were drying the dozens of photographs that she had developed that day. Daniel had to be careful not to collide with them as he ducked underneath.

At the other end of the ballroom, Gaskell had been clearing her brushes of paint by daubing it on the walls, so that there were now thick, brown-green ridges running diagonally side by side, like maps of ranges of hills in relief. The lower walls had half-finished paintings propped up against them, and half a dozen easels stood with canvases upon them in various states of completion. Gaskell had always done several projects at once, so that sometimes she had no paintings to sell at all, and then suddenly she would have enough for an exhibition.

'I love the smell in here,' said Daniel. 'Oil paints and photographic chemicals.'

'The smell of busy and contented women of independent means,' said Gaskell.

'We don't have independent means!' protested Christabel. 'We work damn hard and earn every penny!'

'Well, we've got the house for nothing,' replied Gaskell.

'Where did the family originally get its wealth?' asked Daniel.

'Slaves,' said Gaskell bluntly. 'It was the good old golden triangle. Trinkets for Africa, exchanged for slaves, exchanged for cotton and tobacco in America, and then back to Liverpool to pick up more trinkets for Africa. My wonderful house and my fabulous estate are all the fruit of untold human misery. One day I'm going to ask the RAF to bomb the house and spray weedkiller on the grounds. Just to wipe out the shame.'

'Where's the picture of my nightmare?'

'Right in front of you.'

'But it's just an enormous white canvas!'

'Well, I always paint the canvas white before I start. I'll get going after you've gone.'

'I'll have an excuse to come back.'

'Darling, you don't need an excuse.'

'Let's call it a reason, then.'

Daniel pointed to a picture which portrayed three people, a woman and two men, hand in hand, and dancing in a circle in the middle of a drawing room. 'This is very jolly,' he said; 'who are they?'

'Oh,' said Gaskell, 'just three friends of ours. It's Vanessa and Clive Bell and Duncan Grant.'

'It has a hidden meaning,' said Christabel.

'Oh, and what is that?'

'I couldn't possibly tell you. The point is to work it out for yourself.'

'Is it that inside every adult there's a child that wants to have fun?'

'No.'

Supper was both convivial and strange, as it is so often in England's provincial countryside. Gaskell's aged parents were wheeled in in their wicker bath chairs, and helped to their seats by the two women. Both were bent double with age, and supported by thick walking sticks. The old woman was nearly as bald as her husband, but both of them exuded the kind of radiance that is only possible for a very old person who has survived a hard winter and has understood that the present is all there is left to enjoy.

Sir Herbert stood clutching the back of his chair, and announced that he was going to say grace, drawing a breath, and beginning 'For what ... for what ... for what ...'

'For what we are about to receive, may the Lord make us truly thankful,' Gaskell supplied.

'Oh, yes, that's it, well done, yes, that's it.'

As they were drinking their soup, the old man asked Daniel, 'Now tell me, my boy, was it you or your brother who was killed in the war?'

'Neither of us, I am glad to say,' replied Daniel. 'But I had two brothers who died in South Africa.'

'So sorry to hear it. I imagine they've been buried already?'

'Very much so. I've never even seen their graves. I have a picture of them, that's all.'

Lady Charlotte said, 'Gaskell is going to make the house into an artistic colony. It'll be such fun. Just imagine, sculptures everywhere! And young people! Gaskell was my only child, you know.'

'Really?' said Daniel, raising an eyebrow and looking at Gaskell.

'Oh yes, we're thinking of it. It's such a shame to have an enormous establishment like this with nothing very much happening in it. Of course, such communities always turn into a nightmare, I hear, but it seems worth a try, just for a while perhaps.'

'All those bohemian types with turbans on their heads, talking about free love, and accidentally committing suicide.'

'Just the ticket,' said Gaskell.

'It gets very much worse,' said Christabel; 'Gaskell's thinking of ordering a lion from Harrods.'

'What? A lion?'

'Only a little one. The cubs are so delightful, like a kitten multiplied by twenty.'

'But it'll grow up!'

'Well, the estate is terribly big, and we have a simply enormous number of deer. They got out of hand during the war, and nobody seems interested in poaching any more. It's apparently become passé amongst the rural larcenous classes. Nowadays they steal motor vehicles and dismantle them to sell the parts.'

'Gaskell, you can't be serious, you'd have to fence in the whole estate! And have warning signs everywhere.'

Gaskell shrugged. 'Fun though.'

'You know they behave exactly the same as domestic cats? But when a cat goes barmy and climbs up the curtains, it doesn't matter very much. When a lion does it, it's goodbye curtains. And imagine what they do to the furniture … they don't just pull out annoying little loops in the upholstery.'

'We've thought of that. We're going to give him a scratching tree.'

'Him? Have you seen how enormous they are? What if it wants to curl up in your lap?'

'Oh, Daniel,' said Christabel, 'how unlike you to be so negative!'

'If it all goes wrong, you'd probably have to shoot it,' said Daniel.

'Apparently lions can't purr,' said Lady Charlotte distractedly. 'You know it was most awfully galling to be called Charlotte when I was young. Because of what it rhymes with. None of my friends tease me about it at all any more. I wonder why.'

'All your friends are dead, dear Mother,' said Gaskell drily.

'Are they? How very disappointing. Of course, I am grateful for getting old, but it does leave one terribly left behind.'

Sir Herbert put down his spoon, wiped his mouth with his napkin, and said, 'Awfully sorry, can't stay awake a moment longer. Very tired. This damned palsy makes eating such a trial. Throwing soup all over myself, as usual. Had to give up shooting.'

'Don't worry, Daddy, we'll get you to bed,' said Gaskell. Turning to Daniel, she said, 'Perhaps you could give him your arm. Christabel and I will get them all tucked up, and then come back for the main course. It should be about half an hour.'

During supper they drank three bottles of burgundy between them, followed by port, and a tot of Armagnac each. Outside, the hot August night settled down into its own embrace, and a nightingale struck up in the redwood tree. As they relaxed into their armchairs, Daniel swilled his his drink in the brandy glass, sniffed at it deeply, and said, 'This is absolute bloody bliss.'

'It's just so lovely to have you here again,' said Christabel. 'I wish you could be here all the time.'

'Christabel's always had a passion for you,' said Gaskell.

'I believe you.'

'Can we have our say, now?' asked Christabel.

'Fire away.'

'Well, this isn't going to be at all easy, or … or … conventional.'

'I am all ears, and ready to be agog. I have faced Spandaus in my time. And flaming onions.'

'Well,' said Christabel, 'Gaskell has had deep friendships before, and they've always come to an end because the women concerned wanted babies.'

'And for that they had to get married,' said Gaskell.

'And so they had to go.' Christabel paused. '… Gaskell has been through the most terrible pain … more times than anyone ought to. You can only have a broken heart so many times before it stops healing itself.'

'Yes?' said Daniel.

'The point is that we want to have babies. You know, it seems to be built into us, and we're simply yearning, and we can't help it. It doesn't seem to have any effect if you try to fight it off. But we don't want to get married. We don't want to be parted. Ever. You know we are very happy together, but this business … this business …'

'It would seem impossible,' said Daniel.

'But it isn't,' said Gaskell boldly. 'It's perfectly obvious that you and Rosie have a *mariage blanc*. One only has to be faithful to someone who is faithful in return. And not even always then.'

'Fidelity isn't just not going to bed with other people,' said Christabel. 'It's also about going to bed with the one you're with.'

Daniel hardly knew what to say. It sounded terribly French, exactly like something his own mother would have said.

'Christabel and I want you to be the father of our children,' said Gaskell.

'We both love you so much,' said Christabel.

'And I couldn't bear to think of her in bed with anyone but you. It's you or it's nobody.'

'And we couldn't bear not to have any children,' said Christabel.

Daniel looked at Gaskell and asked, 'It would be Christabel, and not you?'

'Could any man imagine doing it with a woman like me? Just look at me! I'm *un homme manqué*. If only I wasn't. But that's what I am.'

'You're not unlovable. I've always loved you, you know, like a sister. And you're very attractive. Your green eyes have brought entire nations to their knees. And my father-in-law too. And with Christabel, wouldn't it be incest?'

'With me?' said Christabel. 'It wouldn't really. We're not blood relatives, are we?'

'Isn't it forbidden in the Bible? Or the Prayer Book, or something?'

'Look, this is the twentieth century. Who really cares what it says in the Bible? The Bible tells us to kill witches, and thinks it's meritorious to bang tent pegs through people's heads, and wipe out entire nations, including their animals.'

'It would still feel like incest,' said Daniel. 'Even if it wasn't. And it's still infidelity.'

'Don't be silly, darling,' said Gaskell. 'And doing it the other way round wouldn't seem right. I really don't think I could countenance doing … that … with a man … but Christabel is not like me. She really could … And take pleasure in it too. She's very lucky. Much luckier than me.'

He looked at Gaskell. On the surface of things, she was a preposterous creature, so tall and long-faced, with her Norfolk jacket and men's plus fours, her tartan tie, her monocle, her drawling, artificially lowered voice, her immensely long cigarette holder with the gold band at the tip. Today she was, in addition, wearing a large dark green tarboosh with a maroon tassel. Androgynous she may have been, but Daniel was very much attracted to her. However much she aspired to manhood, Daniel could not be convinced that she amounted to anything like a man. It would have been easier to lie with her, because she was not his wife's sister. He suddenly felt impelled to say: 'I do envy you two.'

'Oh, why?' asked Christabel.

'You're not accountable to anyone. You don't have to explain yourselves. You do as you like, you earn enough money from work that you love to do. You have each other. You travel as much as you like, you have a beautiful place to come home to.'

'We are ladies of independent means,' said Gaskell.

'And independent mores,' added Christabel, raising an eyebrow waggishly.

'We are looking for a new way to live,' said Gaskell. 'There must be a better way of doing things.'

'You're a real pair of bohemians, aren't you?'

'It isn't always marvellous, being us,' said Gaskell, and he saw the melancholy well up in her face. 'There's always something missing, isn't there?'

Daniel had begun to feel a kind of panic rising up in the pit of his diaphragm. He said, 'I don't think I want to go along with your idea. I don't know why, but I'm frightened of it. To be frank, it would be easier with you, Gaskell, just because you're not my wife's sister, and I don't seem to see you as you see yourself. It's such a huge step. For all of us. And how will you avoid the social embarrassment?'

'Oh, it's terribly easy,' said Christabel. 'When it all begins to look obvious, we go to northern France to make pictures of the battlefields as they are now, and when we come back, lo and behold, we have ample material for a new exhibition, and have adopted an abandoned child that was found at dawn on the steps of a church in Bernières-sur-Mer by a priest. And we shall be roundly praised.'

Daniel's feeling of panic did not subside. 'I'm not convinced I could manage anything. And how do you expect me to father children and just walk away from them? Leave them to somebody else? You know how much I adore Esther and Bertie. What you're asking is impossible. You haven't thought of me at all.'

'We have thought of you, darling,' said Gaskell. 'We know what an awful sacrifice it would be for you, and we're only asking you because we love you and have no alternative, and we hope that you love us enough to make the sacrifice. Christabel only wants to give herself to someone she loves, and the only man she loves quite enough is you. And we would ask you to be their godfather, and come here as much as you possibly can, and we'd send them to stay with you and Rosie whenever practical.'

'Them?' said Daniel. 'There'll be more than one?'

'We'd like at least three,' said Gaskell.

Christabel added, 'And you'd have to swear an inviolable oath of eternal secrecy. For the children's sake.'

'And what about your parents? What happens to them whilst you're away?'

'We've got Dunston, and the other two, and we'll hire in a nurse,' said Gaskell.

Daniel sat silent for a while, and then said, 'Do you have any idea what you're asking of me? I really don't think I can father a child and just abandon it. I'm afraid the answer must be no.'

'Please think about it. For as long as you like,' said Christabel, leaning forward in her seat.

'I've thought about it, and the answer is no.'

Christabel and Gaskell fell very quiet, and Daniel began to find guilt replacing the anxiety that had been making him sensible. He had to sit there dumbly whilst both women hung their heads and wept silently into their hands. He felt he could do nothing but leave the room and prepare for bed, muttering 'I am very sorry' as he turned at the door. He walked up the wide staircase with a heavy heart.

He spent some time in the bath, mulling the whole strange scene over, listening to the nightingale in the redwood, and imagining what it would be like to make love with Christabel, or even Gaskell. He had been led astray by his loins quite often enough, in his own estimation, and he began to think sadly of Samadara, and what it would have been like to have abandoned Rosie and begun again with her. They would have had Eurasian children who were neither one thing nor another, and that would have been difficult for them. And what would have become of Bertie and Esther? But there is certainly nothing in life more wonderful than to have children, of that he was certain. The prospect of more of them filled him slowly with excitement.

When the water had cooled and he saw that his hands and feet were becoming white and puckered, he got out of the bath, dried himself, and put on his pyjamas and dressing gown.

He walked thoughtfully down the corridor, and turned the handle of his door. He had not gone two steps into the room before he realised that the room was filled with yellow candlelight, and that Christabel was in his bed, in a lacy nightdress, with a small blue bow at each shoulder. Her heavy golden hair, released, was spread across the pillow, and she was biting her lip, looking up at him with her blue, supplicating eyes. She sat up suddenly and held her arms out to him.

He realised that he was about to have no choice but to surrender his common sense. He remembered something that Dr Iannis had said to him on the boat. 'In Greece we think it very bad manner to refuse woman. This is *philotimo*, this is the Greek Way.'

Daniel stood for a moment, and said, 'I'm not promising anything.'

'But I am,' she said. 'You've no idea how much I've been hoping. How much I've been looking forward. How much I'm going to do my best.'

He raised the cover and slid into the bed beside her. She leaned over him, and he felt her hot breath on his face. She put her hand through the gap between his buttons, and lightly stroked his chest. He felt the tingle running down to his feet and back up his spine to his neck. She snuggled up to him, laid her head on his shoulder and laughed softly, saying, 'You're such a darling.' She laid the side of her knee across his thigh, and propped herself up on one elbow. She looked into his eyes, and kissed him lightly on the lips. She pulled back for a second and said, 'You know this isn't just about children, don't you?'

24

Young Edward

I am leaving 'cause I have nothing very much to hold me here any more.

I owed everything to the McCosh family.

I was one of the first two to be knocked down by a car in Court Road. That's quite a distinction, isn't it? Or 'innit' as I used to say before I got taken on by Mr McCosh. We kids were playing British Bulldog when this drunk in an AC Six mowed us down and I got pinned to the wall. We were only little kids, and my mate Freddie got killed because he smacked his head on the wall and it caved his skull right in. Crushed it like an egg. You could see the bones and the brains.

I got me legs smashed and it was Miss Rosie and Miss Ottilie who came out of the house and did the first aid, and thank God they'd been VADs in the war, because whatever they did, they must have done it right. And then Captain Pitt came out and thumped that bastard drunk in the nose, and kicked him over, and he would have killed him if that copper hadn't turned up.

As it turned out, Mr Hamilton McCosh paid for my hospital treatment and then he paid for my education, which is why I am somewhat good with my letters these days, because before I could only just about write my name. And he tried to keep that all secret from my mum. And then when I could walk a bit, he said, 'You're going to be a caddie, and that'll get your legs working, laddie' and I thought, 'Blimey, he talks in rhymes,' and he got me work at the Royal Blackheath, which is, so they say, the oldest golf club in the world, been going since King James the First, and what is still more stuffed with Scotch than English, like the one at Wimbledon, and to be honest it's more like a drinking club than a golf one. Straight up. They have these massive binges they call 'Wee dinners' after the trophies.

That's how I got so good at golf, starting off as a caddie, and mainly living off the tips from those Scotch blokes. Mind you, I always handed most of it to me mum. I wasn't full-grown, and Mr Hamilton McCosh gave me a set of cut-downs. I loved them clubs. I had a driver and a spoon, and a mashie, and a mashie niblick, and a niblick and a putter, all different makes, and that's all. I still use that putter. I grafted an extension on it when it got too short. It's got a slope on the back so you can get out of awkward lies under a bush by playing left-handed, and that way you don't lose a stroke. That was a tip from Mr McCosh. He said, 'Always have a left-hander in your bag, laddie.'

In the end I was winning all the artisans' and caddies' matches, despite my poor old legs, and I started winning a few bob here and there, and to tell the truth, I was thinking of leaving anyway. I mean, it's a lovely course, but it's not much of a challenge, is it? It's parkland. It's not hilly and it's not exactly a links, and I know that Mr Braid designed it, but there's not much you can do when you haven't got the space and the roly-poly, is there?

Mr Braid came to see how his course was getting on, and he brought Mr Vardon with him, and it was like as if two heroes had turned up, the way they got greeted and treated. Well, I had the honour to play a round with them, and they were very complimentary, and it was after Mr Vardon had got TB, and it messed up his putting because of the nerve damage, so he got the yips on the short putts, and he and Mr Braid put a guinea on the match, and believe it or not they finished on exactly the same score, so they took a guinea each and gave it to me, and I was only three strokes behind them. I don't know how Mr Vardon managed to play, with a smoking pipe stuck in his gob like that all the time, coughing and wheezing like a steam train. Mr Braid gave me his address and said he thought he knew a club up north that needed a professional, and that in his opinion I was the man, and he was prepared to give me a recommendation.

I said I'd have to talk it over with Mr McCosh.

I was going to do it after the Bombay Medal. That's the one before the last Wee Dinner, and that's really a bloody great binge, excuse my French. I didn't get the chance, though.

Mr Hamilton McCosh wasn't very well. It was his heart. He didn't often do more than nine holes, and he reckoned he was going to invent an electric cart for fatties and old buggers like him, but there weren't batteries light enough for that kind of thing unless you wanted to go round in a milk float. That's what he said.

But he was determined to win that Bombay Medal. It was the medal sent by the Bombay lot when their club was founded. That was 1843, and they were all Scotch 'n' all, with ginger bollocks. Mr McCosh said this was his last tournament, and then he was going to hang up his clubs, meaning he was going to pass them on to me, and then he was going to go home and take to his bed and die of sadness. I said 'You'll live forever, sir' and I was honestly hoping he would, because I loved that man, and no one in my whole life did me more favours than he did. I reckon maybe it was because he didn't have any sons. He would've liked a son or two to play golf with.

Well, Mr Hamilton McCosh never got to go to bed and die of sadness. He died of blooming happiness. On the sixteenth hole. It's a par three with a great big green, and even if you get on in one, you might well do three putts.

Anyway, he was very tired and breathless by then, and I handed him that mashie of his that he loved so much, and his idea was to lay the ball up at the front of the green. He took a nice slow backswing, and brought that club down hard and smooth, and he followed through just like J. H. Taylor. That ball made a beautiful arc and it rolled straight and true, and it ran for the flag, and it hit the pole and skipped up in the air, and then it popped back down into that little hole.

Mr McCosh did a dance on the tee, whooping and raising his arms, and stamping and cavorting, and then he handed me the mashie and he actually ran to the green, and we saw him fall on his knees and bend down to look at that little ball in the hole, and he looked like he was praying, and then suddenly he jerked a bit and fell sideways.

By the time I got there he was all but gone. I was kneeling over him and his lips were blue, and his face had a terrible paleness, and he had his right hand over his chest, and I rolled him onto his back, and he was gasping for breath, and he opened his eyes and raised his right hand, like it was a blessing, and said 'Dinna fash, Edward laddie' and then his eyes rolled back, and that was him dead as a doornail on the green of the sixteenth on a beautiful day. I do hope I go like that.

We got Dr Scott, who was on the eighteenth, and Captain Pitt, who was on the twelfth, but Mr McCosh was well and truly gone. Captain Pitt gave me his clubs and set off at a run for the house in Court Road. He was that kind of a bloke, a bit of an athlete.

Mr McCosh is buried up against the wall at St John's. Everybody came, even Mr Ives the grocer, and Oily Wragge the gardener, and all the old Scotch drunks at the golf club, and quite a few women in black who nobody knew who they were, and I'm going to put a big bunch of flowers on his grave before I go up north, because I took that job that Mr Braid came up with, and I'm taking my mum because Dad was a wheelwright what got killed in the Horse Artillery, and my little sister died in the influenza, and I can't leave my mum on her own, can I? And when I get there, up north, I've got high hopes of finding a lass who wants to settle down.

My mum reckons she can take in washing wherever she is, but I say, 'Mum, I'm a professional now, you don't have to take in another set of long johns as long as you live,' and she says, 'But I can't do nothing, can I?'

So there you are. Mr Hamilton McCosh has died of happiness, and I'm off now, and I'm a professional.

The funny thing is, that AC Six what ran me down ended up belonging to Mr McCosh, because the owner never did come back to get it, so I saw it quite often, and every time I did, I felt that ruddy great pain in my leg bones all over again. Still, it was a lucky accident for me, wasn't it?

I owe everything to Mr Hamilton McCosh. And that bleedin' AC Six, I suppose.

I really loved that man.

25

Rosie (2)

I brought us home because in the end I couldn't bear to be apart from my father when I knew he had hardly any time left to live. I did love it in Ceylon, but somehow it wasn't really me. Nuwara Eliya was like England, in fact they called it 'Little England', but it was terribly exaggerated beyond Englishness, like when an artist uses too strong a shade of blue for the sea, when the sea is actually green. And I hated having to go to the Hill Club. They didn't allow lady members, and to get to the ladies' entrance we had to step over an open gulley, go through a nasty little alley, and then we were confined to one end of the clubhouse. And despite being treated like that we were expected to go there! It was almost compulsory. Compulsory humiliation!

The races were fun, but you didn't go to watch the racing, you went to see who was wearing what kind of hat. I went to support Hugh, really. The best thing was going to that beautiful post office that was rather like a cake, to see if anyone had written or sent a parcel. And try as I might, I never learned to love playing golf, as Daddy did. Daniel thought it was a lovely course.

I adored the servants, but it was like having three grown-up children, always squabbling and coming to me for adjudication, and doing strange things like buying a pot of orange paint with their own money, and painting the stuffed monkey in the hallway because they thought it would make it prettier, and leaving orange splashes on the parquet.

And it was entirely annoying trying to be helpful to the natives, and them just putting up with it, as if I were some tedious old lady who had to be mollified. I think they were pleased about the improvements to their accommodation, but they didn't come near the clinic unless they were at the point of death. It was so frustrating waiting for someone to appear, with all your medicines lined up and instruments carefully sterilised, knowing that they were out there somewhere suffering away for nothing, and depending on numerology and astrology and strange concoctions.

Every day was the same. Daniel was out at dawn, and often not home until long after dark. He'd taken to the native food and his breath was not at all pleasant. He was always bad-tempered with me because I didn't want to have any more children and he wouldn't accept what the obvious way not to have them was. He said there were alternative ways of 'having fun' as he put it, but it's a sin if it's only done for fun, everyone knows that, and it's not as if I am a lady of the night who exists for just one purpose. In any case, we had had several years of 'fun', and it had begun to pall on me, as most pleasures eventually do. I couldn't see why he didn't want to settle for being good companions. I spent all my time supervising the servants and making lists, and I didn't even have very much time with Esther and Bertie, because the ayah was always there, and I couldn't leave her with nothing to do.

Every Sunday we played tennis after church. Every Sunday exactly the same, and jolly good fun, but always the same, with Daniel always winning the men's and me always coming second to Gloria Bassett in the women's, and then Daniel and I always beating Hugh and Gloria in the mixed doubles.

Sometimes the men would disappear for a week, to go duck or snipe shooting, and I'd be sitting in front of a blank sheet of paper wondering why I couldn't write poetry any more. Once I went to Colombo with Gloria on that magnificent train journey, and we spent the whole week going to tea with people and then out for drinks, and getting much too hot and uncomfortable, and going for walks on the promenade, and taking a hansom to Mount Lavinia, and talking sociable nonsense. I went to Cave's and came back with a big parcel of books that just made me feel even more cut off, because I was wondering what was really happening in London with all the new poets and the new kind of poetry that was being written. I bought Mary Webb's poetry, and there was one lovely poem in it called 'The Lad Out There' which came to mean a great deal to me. 'Ah, powers of love ...'

Daniel was furious when I started demanding to go home.
One night he went out into the garden and was so angry and
frustrated that he stood roaring across the valley like a mad
wild beast. Sometimes I almost feared he was going to hit me.
I knew he wanted to, but he was too much of a gentleman.
He kicked the table over and took a chair and hurled it down
the hillside instead. It reminded me of when Archie threw away
his elephant gun. Daniel really did love it in Ceylon. He loved
his workers and his mountains and his huge machinery, and his
expeditions up Adam's Peak the hard way with Hugh Bassett.
I also think he was a little dissatisfied, because producing tea
can never be as important as helping to win a war. He should
have stayed in the RAF, really. He loved his motorcycle, but it
wasn't an aeroplane.

I spoiled everything for him when I forced him to come home.
I know it.

I told him that Esther and Bertie should be properly educated
at home, but, if I am honest, I knew they would do just as well
in Ceylon. They have schools that are more British than the
British ones. I said it just to add weight to my case. I sometimes
criticise myself for this kind of thing, because it is a form of lying,
and I wonder if there will ever be a time when I live up to my
own ideals and truly become the sort of person that I think I
really am. I fear that one can only know oneself properly in the
painful light of retrospection. That's when I begin to despise
myself.

I had a feeling that if I was where I belonged, at Court Road,
then the poetry would come back. Poetry is like a stream that
has to have a source.

It didn't come back though. Sometimes I sat in front of a
blank sheet of foolscap, but the spark had gone. I'd do a few
doodles, and that was it. I wasn't even reading much poetry
any more. A lot of the new stuff just resembled cryptic cross-
word puzzle clues, the music was absent and there was no one
writing with any passion any more. There were no equivalents
to Rupert Brooke. I didn't read anyone except for T. S. Eliot,
and I couldn't write like him. I often tried, and it came out
stilted and pretentious.

Esther was just as furious as Daniel about having to leave Ceylon. She adored Preethi, her ayah, and Hugh Bassett had promised her a pet mongoose like the one that he had. It was extremely charming and naughty, and she often went to his house to visit it. Sometimes it came round to visit us, and I would find Esther playing with it on the terrace, as if it were a funny kind of cat. Hugh had commissioned a coolie to go out and find a baby one, but without success.

I suppose I was being very selfish, but what was eating me was the thought that when my father was dying, I would not be there to hold his hand and receive his blessing, and be the one to bend over and kiss his forehead, and close his eyes.

I did love my mother, tiresome though she became, and of course I loved my wonderful sisters, but I loved my father more than anyone. I don't say 'more than any man' because the love I had for Ash and for Daniel was of a different order, and besides, I didn't love them in the same way. Romantic love is not like daughterly love.

How can I put it? It was the thought of my father that put the warmest glow in my heart, and still does.

Daniel was right about one thing. Father was absolutely furious with me for demanding to come home. When we did, he summoned me to the dining room and gave me a tremendous dressing-down. He was actually shouting at me for ruining every-thing. He said I had been preposterously selfish and unreasonable, and I had wrecked things for Daniel and the children. Then when I began to cry, he let me explain that I was frightened he was going to die, and that was why I had to be here. He didn't know what to say. He knew that his heart was very weak, but it doesn't seem to have occurred to him that he might die young. He just said, 'Oh, Rosie bairn, you shouldna have come hame just for me.'

Gran'mère Pitt came to visit because she wanted to see Daniel and the children, and especially Bertie, whom she'd never met before, and she simply cut me dead for a whole week. She spoke not one word to me, but just appraised me with a kind of contempt in her face, and passed the butter to me at table without even looking at me. It was very hard to take, being made to feel so guilty.

And when Father did suddenly drop dead on the golf course, I wasn't with him at all. I was sitting at home at The Grampians, not writing poetry, but taking the place of my distracted mother as mistress of the house, cleaning the silver and making lists.

26

The Will

The five women went together to see the solicitor in Eltham.
Christabel had come down from Gaskell's estate in the north,
Sophie had come from Blackheath in her own motor car, and
Rosie and Ottilie came with their mother from The Grampians.
Mrs McCosh was dressed entirely in black, and her steps were
unsteady, so she leaned on Rosie's arm.

The day was overcast, as suited their feelings, and they felt
curiously numb as they stood outside the offices of Gilbert, Cadge
and Catchpole in the high street. Rosie rang the bell, and looked
dumbly at the shining brass plate.

Ottilie said, 'I think it's about to rain.'

Mrs McCosh said, 'A lady must always wear a hat.'

'I am wearing a hat, Mama.'

'It's a cloche hat.'

Unsure what to make of this, Ottilie said nothing.

'I'm sure it's very becoming,' continued Mrs McCosh, leaving
the 'but' unsaid. 'At least you're wearing a cloche hat.'

'I am quite happy with an umbrella,' said Christabel, who knew
that this remark was directed towards her bareheadedness. She
had bundled her hair up in a careless heap, and bound it together
with a red strip of chiffon.

'Well, you may be happy with just an umbrella ... And I do
believe you are beginning to become a little tubby. It's most unlike
you. You should perform callisthenics for half an hour each day
at your age. Before an open window. Even in winter.'

They were greeted by Mr Horatio Cadge himself, a small,
round-shouldered man with a worried expression, and wisps of
greying hair on his otherwise bald head. He breathed with difficulty, having endured a gas attack in 1917, and his voice was thin
and weak.

'You are wearing a spotted bow tie,' said Mrs McCosh.

'I am indeed, Mrs McCosh.'

'It's a lovely tie,' said Christabel, shooting a meaningful look at her mother.

'Beauty is in the eye of the beholder,' said Sophie brightly. 'Sometimes it's so hard to get it out. One needs to invest in so much eyewash. It's most peeving and vexatious.'

The women sat before Mr Cadge who fumbled with the will as he drew it out of its envelope. He peered at them over his half-moon spectacles.

'As you know, I, er, have tried to warn you that you may find the contents of this will, shall I say, dare I say, somewhat untoward, somewhat alarming. Indeed, I have tried to dissuade you from reading it at all. I do appeal to you to read it privately, and alone rather than together, so that you may ... you may ... compose yourselves before discussing it. Mr McCosh has not come up with, shall we say, a conventional approach to his bequests. It's all most unusual.'

'*Mysterium tremendum*,' said Sophie.

'We're here now,' said Rosie.

'Shall we get on with it?' said Christabel. 'All I need to know is that Mama will be well taken care of.'

'My dear,' protested Mrs McCosh, 'you really should not conclude a sentence with a preposition.'

'It's something one has to put up with. And be ready for,' said Sophie.

'And you shouldn't start a sentence with a conjunction,' declared Mrs McCosh.

'Mrs McCosh is well looked after by the will, I am glad to say,' said Mr Cadge. 'It's in one way fortunate that he died when he did, because his finances were, shall we say, somewhat cyclical, and he departed at a very high point. If you don't mind, shall we start on this most ... difficult ... not to say embarrassing task?'

The women nodded, and the solicitor coughed into his hand to clear his throat, and read:

'This is the last will and testament of me Hamilton McCosh in the county of Kent.

1) I revoke all former Wills made by me

2) I appoint Messrs Gilbert, Cadge and Catchpole solicitors of Eltham in Kent to be the executors and trustees of my Will

3) To my mistress Eliza Sarah Girdlestone of 17 Eaglesfield Road in Shooters Hill I devise and bequeath the sum of two thousand pounds whereof one thousand is to be divided equally amongst my four children by her and I devise and bequeath to her the house in which she lives

4) To my mistress Molly Heycock of 81 Rowley Avenue in Sidcup I devise and bequeath the sum of one thousand and seven hundred and fifty pounds whereof seven hundred and fifty is to be divided equally between my three children by her and I devise and bequeath to her the house in which she lives

5) To my mistress Agnes Whiteley Rump of 5 Robin Hood Lane in Bexleyheath I devise and bequeath the sum of one thousand pounds and the house in which she lives

6) To Agatha my daughter by my deceased mistress Patricia Feakes of 26 Parkside Avenue in Barnehurst I devise and bequeath the sum of five hundred pounds and my house in Notwithstanding in the county of Surrey

7) To my former mistress Marianne Theresa Goodin of 42 Links View in Dartford I devise and bequeath the sum of one thousand and five hundred pounds of which five hundred pounds is to be divided equally between my two children by her

8) To my mistress Rebecca Esther Weinstein of 9 Park Road in Chislehurst I leave the sum of one thousand pounds and the house in which she lives

9) I give to my wife Caroline Wentworth McCosh my furniture wearing apparel and all other effects in and about my residence at my death absolutely subject to the payment of my funeral and testamentary expenses and debts (other than mortgage debts)

10) I devise and bequeath all my real and personal estate not hereinbefore otherwise disposed of unto my trustee UPON TRUST that my trustee shall sell call in and convert into

money the same or such part thereof as shall not consist of money and shall with and out of the moneys produced by such sale calling in and conversion pay my mortgage debts and shall stand possessed of the residue of the said moneys IN TRUST to invest the same in any investments authorised by law for the investment of trust moneys with power for my trustees at discretion to change such investments for others of a like nature and shall stand possessed of the investments for the time being representing the same and of annual income thereof UPON TRUST to pay the said income to my said wife during her life and after her death I direct that the capital and income of the fund shall be held IN TRUST for such of my legitimate daughters by my said wife as shall be living at my death in equal shares

11) I declare that my trustee may postpone the sale and conversion of my residuary estate or any part thereof for so long as he shall think fit and that rents profits and income to accrue from and after my decease of and from such part of my residuary estate as shall for the time being remain unsold and unconverted shall after payment thereout of all incidental expenses and outgoings fall into and form part of my residuary trust moneys

IN WITNESS thereof I have hereunto set my hand this twelfth day of December One thousand nine hundred and twenty-two. Signed by the above named Hamilton McEwan McCosh as his last Will in the presence of us both being present at the same time who in his presence and in the presence of each other have hereunto subscribed our names as witnesses.'

After Mr Cadge had finished, he pushed the will across the desk and Rosie took it up.

'I can't believe that Daniel witnessed it,' she said. 'And Fairhead too. Sophie, did you know about Daniel and Fairhead witnessing this?'

'Oh yes, he told me.'

'He actually read this and witnessed it?'

'Oh no, neither of them actually read it. They just signed the end when Daddy asked them to.'

'I don't think it's the done thing to read it when you're witnessing it,' said Ottilie.

'I was going to kill both of them,' said Rosie.

'The 12th of December in 1922 was very sharp. A very cold wind,' said Mrs McCosh abstractedly.

'Fancy remembering that,' said Christabel.

'It seems that we have ten or eleven half-brothers and -sisters,' said Christabel softly, looking around at the others.

'It's all completely nonplussing,' said Sophie. 'What a pother. Do we have to get to know them, do you think?'

'Let's just be us,' said Rosie. 'I'd be much happier if it was just us.'

'Me too,' said Ottilie. 'I just want to remember Daddy as ours.'

'I don't think I'll be able to avoid being curious,' said Christabel.

Sophie suggested, 'Perhaps you should do a scouting expedition, and report back to us.'

Mr Cadge coughed politely, and the women stood up, taking the hint. 'Thank you for coming,' he said. 'I am sorry, very sorry indeed, if this has all been something of a shock. Normally a man, you know, a man finds another way to cater for these, um, irregularities, and then of course there's no, there's no …'

'You mean it all stays under wraps, even after death?' asked Ottilie.

'Oh yes, oh yes. Really, it's greatly preferable if it is, as you say, under wraps. If it's any comfort to you, if I may make the suggestion, your father had to choose between being a dishonourable rascal or an honourable one, and he, of course, as you might expect if you knew him as well as I did, took the latter course, although much against my best advice. Please do allow me to show you out, and I shall keep you informed of the progress in executing the will. Good day, good day, good day.'

To the astonishment of the sisters, Mrs McCosh set off immediately towards the florist, saying, 'We must have fresh flowers for his grave. Yesterday they were looking quite past their best.'

'Are you going to carry on visiting it every day?' asked Ottilie.

'Of course. Why on earth wouldn't I?'

'Just to be respectable?'

'Of course not. I have never cared for respectability, as you know. I shall go out of loyalty. And gratitude. He bought me the most beautiful violin. And a complete leather-bound set of Thackeray for our thirtieth anniversary. And we had a great many very enjoyable games of golf.'

'When I was in the Snapshot League,' said Christabel, 'I did get to know an awful lot of out-of-the-way places.'

'And?' said Rosie.

'Well, I can't help noticing that all these women live next to golf courses.'

'How very like Daddy,' said Sophie, 'always a man for two birds with one stone. Duopoulic but monopetric. But polypoulic really, if you think about it.'

'Sophie, you're talking to yourself,' said Ottilie.

'He was never a man with only one thing on his mind,' said Mrs McCosh proudly.

At St John's, Mrs McCosh laid a new spray of flowers on the grave. 'One day I'll be in there with him,' she said, 'and it'll be me and not anyone else.'

That evening they sat together by the fire in silence, still trying to come to terms with the bewildering revelations of that morning. Rosie was reading her prayer book, and Mrs McCosh was studying a little book entitled *How to Manage Without Servants* whilst Sophie and Christabel played mah-jong. Ottilie sat quietly with her hands in her lap, apparently doing nothing.

'Why are you reading that book?' she asked her mother.

'Because we don't have any servants.'

'But we still have Cookie. And the Honourable Mary.'

'Mary is a companion. And Cookie is hardly one of the servants.'

'She's a permanent fixture, like the plumbing,' said Sophie, 'or the banisters.'

'Mama,' said Rosie suddenly, 'why aren't you more upset? About Daddy. What he got up to. I mean, I would have expected —'

'Nonsense,' said Mrs McCosh. 'I was perfectly happy with four children. Four was quite enough. Just right. And your father and I were somewhat dissimilar in some respects. Under those circumstances, a wife has to make allowances.'

'You knew all along?' asked Ottilie incredulously.

'A lady does not know more than she chooses to know or needs to know. I dare say I would have been quite furious and humiliated to find that one of his mistresses was a Jewess, but it's too late to make a fuss now, and it does go to show how very broad-minded he was. At least he had the decency not to encumber you with any Jewish siblings. Apart from that, he was a very good husband.'

'What?' cried Rosie. 'How can you possibly say that? He broke his vows!'

'He was a wonderful father to you,' replied Mrs McCosh. 'I am certain he was a good father to all his other progeny. He was always a very kind and affectionate husband who respected my wishes even when he mocked them. And, as I said, we did have some glorious rounds of golf.'

Six weeks after Hamilton McCosh had been piped to his grave to the tune of 'The Flowers of the Forest' Rosie was in the house alone when a letter for Daniel was delivered, from Ceylon, and she recognised Hugh Bassett's handwriting. She took the letter to the conservatory and held it up to the sunlight, but could not make out the writing inside, so she went down into the kitchen and put the kettle on the hob. When it began to steam she held the fold of the envelope near the spout, and then very carefully began to prise it open. The soggy paper ripped suddenly, and she realised she had gone too far. She hesitated, wondering what to do, but as there was no turning back, she tore the envelope open and read the letter.

My dear Daniel,

I have news for you of some import, and I am sorry that I did not inform you of this before, but I had no idea until yesterday that anything was afoot.

I am certain you would want to know that Samadara has had a son that she has called Beloved Daniel. I have no doubt that you did not know of her condition when you left, and that you will be as surprised by this news as I was. I anticipate that you will be both shocked and delighted.

This throws up tremendous complications for you, but I would like you to know that, whatever happens, I shall ensure that both of them are as comfortable as possible. I actually have no idea if this is still your forwarding address, or if you will ever receive this letter. I can only hope. My intention is to look after the child and his mother as if I were you, and as I know you would want. I shall ensure that he goes to Hill House and receives an excellent education, and I shall try to find a suitable match for Samadara, after some consultation with her family. They seem to be reasonably pleased by the arrival, because they know that he will make their economic position more secure, and will eventually find a post in the Civil Service, or some such thing.

If anything should happen to Samadara, then I shall ensure that the child is looked after by someone else, whom I know extremely well, and who has light brown children of her own. I think you probably catch my drift.

Do reply by return of post if you should receive this letter. I am certain that you would wish to take appropriate actions on your own account.

Dear Daniel, how we miss you, and how we wish you had never left. What fun we had! I shall miss our games of gun snap, our tennis on Sundays, our snipe shoots, our swipings and airshots and slicings on the golf course, our dawn rides around the estate, and I shall always regret never having had the chance to set up our aviation business together. It would have been a hoot.

Yours ever,
Hugh B

PS Your replacement is nowhere near your calibre, unfortunately. If you were a rail-mounted howitzer, he is a .177 Gem air rifle.

Rosie read the letter several times, and a curious numbness overcame her. All men were the same, it seemed. Hugh and Daniel and her father, all the same. Still, she was not going to let some native girl queer her pitch.

She did exactly what her own mother would have done, and burned the letter in the grate, watching with hard satisfaction as it curled and browned and crumbled to ash. She said nothing about it to anybody, not even to Ottilie, and hardly even to herself.

27

Geddes Axe

Daniel had taken up his old job with Henley Motorcycles in Birmingham, despite his several years' absence from the firm, and, as before, was having to return to Eltham on his combination every Friday evening, because, as before, Rosie was repeatedly putting off moving up there with him. The work was interesting enough; he was supervising some experiments with belt rather than chain drive, and testing some JAP engines, but he had quickly returned to the state of burning rage that he had experienced before they had left for Ceylon, and it was as if he had travelled an immense circle back into the grind from which he had escaped. He had begun to think of exercising his right as the children's legal guardian, of removing them to Birmingham, and employing someone to care for them whilst he was at work. What held him back was the feeling that it would, somehow, simply not be right. He knew that they needed their mother as much as they needed him, and neither could he, despite his anger, bring himself to cause such a catastrophic hurt to Rosie. He was also a man of his time. Since the middle of the nineteenth century the conventional wisdom had entirely reversed, and now it was assumed unquestioningly that children belonged with their mothers. It had become as socially obvious as the flatness of the Earth had been before the Renaissance.

His agitation had been seriously compounded upon hearing that Christabel and Gaskell had decided to move to France for six months in order to photograph and paint the old battlefields. He was dismayed, excited, guilty and perplexed. He had become more than fond of Christabel during his many trips to Hexham. Their lovemaking had been intense and poignant, and she had said things to him that took him back to Samadara, whose delicious memory was already fading into a languorous dream of a vanished Eden.

Now he suddenly began to feel used and discarded, and had to fight to persuade himself that this was not the case, despite the many fond and newsy letters from Christabel and Gaskell that arrived at his address in Wootton Wawen. 'I've been a damned fool,' he often repeated to himself, and he wondered if Christabel would be receiving him as passionately as before, when he finally came up to Hexham to meet his 'godchild'. Perhaps her passion would be like her sister's, only evident when a child was in the offing. And how was he to cope with having a child at such a distance, one who was being brought up by someone else, and did not even know him for a father?

To make matters worse, the Honourable Mary had been visibly thrilled upon his return. She had begun to go a little grey, her face was showing its first lines, but she was the same warm and comely woman, with the same poetic Irish lilt in her voice, and the same patient willingness to put up with Mrs McCosh's erratic ways. Being a 'lady maid' had been a confining but safe experience, and she kept herself consoled by the thought that one day she might find the right man, as Ottilie clearly had. Daniel's return had thrown her heart into unwelcome confusion. It seemed impossible for their eyes not to meet, and impossible for Rosie not to notice it one day.

Daniel became increasingly annoyed with himself for being attracted to her. 'My life is too damn painful and complicated already,' he would mutter to himself, as he motorcycled grimly back to The Grampians on Friday evenings. He was surprised by himself, and increasingly contemptuous. When he was young he had never contemplated the possibility of becoming a rake. He would get married, he would be faithful. What could have been simpler? But he had had two lovers already in the first years of being married, and the strange thing was that he had no feeling whatsoever of having done anything wrong. It had all seemed perfectly natural, and even meritorious. And now, here was Mary, with her big sorrowful eyes, clearly offering her unsatisfied heart to him, and here he was, tempted, even though his wife was in the house, and his wife's sister was in France, expecting his child. He did not know who to blame – himself, or these women with their complicated desires and adaptable sense of morality. He told himself that life had turned out to be far more complex than he ever could have imagined, and that no value did not have a countervalue. He missed his old certainties, when fornication was a shocking sin only committed by others, and adultery was the sport of the degenerate.

One Friday evening he returned home with presents for the children in his sidecar, to find Mary bent over a figure that was lying across the steps to the front porch. He killed the engine, lifted his goggles and dismounted. He knelt down on the steps next to her.

'Archie!' he said.

His brother was in a state of extreme dereliction, stinking of gin, in ragged and filthy clothing. The soles flapped off his shoes, and saliva dribbled from the corner of his mouth.

'Archie, what on earth are you doing here?'

Archie looked at him dazedly, without raising his head. 'Bloody Geddes Axe,' he said. 'Too many majors in the regiment. No damn promotions to colonel. The buggers have pensioned me off. Got to live off a pittance.'

'You've come home?'

'No, that's Peshawar. This is bloody England. What the hell am I to do here?'

'How did you get here?'

'Walked. Only took a few days.'

'You walked from Southampton?'

'Haven't eaten for days. Slept in barns, mostly. Damned hungry.'

'Why didn't you go to *maman* at Partridge Green?'

'Too ashamed, old boy. Knew I had to find you first.'

'And where's your luggage?'

'Had to leave it in a hedge. Ovington. Couldn't carry it any further. Sent a trunk up by train. Should be at Mottingham by now. Couldn't afford the fare.'

'Why on earth didn't you stay in India? Find something else to do?'

'Didn't occur to me, old boy. Should have thought of that. Too upset. A bit confused by the whole thing, really.'

Daniel looked sideways at the Honourable Mary, saw that she was crying, and was moved by her compassion.

'Let's get him inside,' he said. 'You run the bath and I'll get him undressed. I really don't want the children to see him like this.'

'Yes,' she said, wiping her eyes, and standing up, 'let's get him inside. Then I'll find Mrs Pitt and tell her what's happened. She'll certainly know what to do.'

'I think we should telephone Dr Scott,' said Daniel.

'Who's going to keep an eye on the bloody Afghans now?' said Archie.

'I have done the state some service,' quoted Daniel. 'Damn this country. He's been a Frontier Scout for years. He's got half a dozen decorations. He's got three bullets in him and a knife scar ten inches long. He's risked getting his balls cut off every time he went out. He got an MC in France. Damn this bloody country to hell.'

Mary put her hand on his arm and stroked it lightly, looking up at his face. 'Come on, my dear,' she said. 'Calm down. We've got some lifting to do. I think I'd better go and fetch Wragge. He's probably asleep in the wheelbarrow.'

28

A Bombshell in *The Times*

On 30 June 1930, ladies in immodest and brightly coloured swimsuits leapt into the newly opened Lido in Hyde Park, in London, for the inauguration of mixed bathing.

The Times reported on the withdrawal of French troops from the Rhineland, five years ahead of schedule, because the German Foreign Minister had successfully persuaded France that the years of German militarism had finally gone. A peaceful future for Europe was assured, and optimism was in the air.

Great Britain set the course for peace in the Middle East by recognising the independence of Iraq.

The paper was still reporting comment on the Simon Commission's recommendation of a federal India, and there continued to be much of a buzz about Neville Chamberlain becoming the chairman of the Conservative Party.

What caught Rosie's attention in *The Times* was none of these things, however. There was a report on the Lambeth Conference, and nothing could have interested her more. Under the chairmanship of Archbishop Cosmo Gordon Lang, racism was now expressly outlawed in the Anglican Church.

But there was also a new resolution about contraception, and she was dismayed by what she read. The conference had declared that, whilst abstinence was the obvious and primary method, it was lawful to use ordinary means of contraception, provided that it was done in the light of Christian principles. The measure had been carried by a majority of 126.

Rosie bridled. Although she could not quite articulate why, it was obvious to her that this was completely wrong,

It had taken her a great deal of effort to persuade Daniel that her attitudes were determined by her religious faith and not by any aversion to him, and now there was this.

Rosie read the rest of the newspaper, and then took it outside and consigned it to the incinerator, in case Daniel should see it when he returned.

29

Agatha

I was a little girl when I first went to see my father's grave.
Although my mother had died and I was sent to live with an
aunt, my father always remembered me, and sent me birthday and
Christmas presents, and would call in whenever he could. He
would throw me in the air and hold me upside down, until I
became too big, and then he would sit down on me and say, 'My
my, what a wriggly cushion this is. Whoever heard of wriggly
cushions?' and I would be giggling and stifling underneath, and
when he stood up I'd say, 'Daddy, Daddy, do it again! Do it again!'
Sometimes he'd clamp my legs under one arm and tickle my feet
until I almost burst.

He'd bought us a house in Notwithstanding, which is where
I still live. It's a medium-sized village on the border of Surrey
and Sussex, and back then it was still very rustic. There was a
local accent, rather like the one in Dorset, which eventually
disappeared completely.

I was living in the house with my aunt, who was a charmingly
dotty spinster with no children of her own, and you could say
that my mother's early death was the making of her. She had a
nice big house, and an income, like a retired mistress, and no one
ever knew that I was illegitimate. I've never thought of myself
that way, in any case. I was an orphan, that's all, an orphan who
was luckier than most.

My aunt had a Swift Convertible, which I am still using to
this day. I've left it to the brothers at the garage, on condition
that they service it for nothing, just as I've given this house to
the vet in return for an annual income, as one sometimes does
in France, I'm told.

One day when I suppose I was about eight, my aunt said, 'Let's
go and visit your father's grave, my dear.' I think she must have
been very bored to want to drive so far just to visit the grave of

someone she barely knew, but she did love driving. She was the kind of person who adored going to fancy-dress parties, enjoyed swing dancing, and she loved driving dangerously. Eventually she taught me, and sometimes I can't help being a little bit naughty on the road, as she was. When the police stop me I just pretend to be a bit silly and confused. Recently I went over the double white line on the way to Guildford because I was overtaking a tractor, and the policeman who stopped me just wanted to see under the bonnet of the car, because it's such an antique. He let me off with a gentle remonstrance.

In those days it was an awful long drive from Notwithstanding to Eltham. It took absolutely hours, going through Dorking and over Box Hill and everything, but it was a nice day and we had the canopy down. My aunt said, 'Don't worry, my dear, I'm sure we'll find a hotel somewhere,' and she waved her chequebook and crammed a large hat on her head, which she secured by means of a length of tulle tied under the chin.

We found my father's grave right up against the wall at St John's, and it had fresh flowers on it. I stood there feeling very quiet and sad, looking down at the turf, and reading the inscription over and over again, and my aunt took my hand and squeezed it, without saying anything. We'd brought daffodils all the way from Surrey, and we laid them down, and my aunt said, 'Well, there he is, the old rascal.'

I became aware of a woman sitting quietly on the bench up against the church wall, observing us. She had chestnut hair and very blue eyes, accentuated by her blue dress, and I suppose she was about thirty years old. It was one of those spring days when it's very warm for about a week, and then it becomes chilly again, and she had bare arms, with a very pretty silver bangle in the form of a serpent around her upper arm. She was looking at us so hard that I began to feel uneasy. Then she got to her feet and approached us. She stood beside my aunt and said, 'This is the grave of my father.'

My aunt thought quickly, and said, 'It's a lovely grave. We were just admiring the flowers.'

'Do you have a loved one buried here?' said the woman.

'No,' said my aunt, 'I just love graveyards. I so enjoy their melancholy.'

'I miss my father terribly,' said the woman. 'I came back from Ceylon to be with him when he died, and then it happened very suddenly when I wasn't there. I come here every day. My mother does too.'

'Oh, how awful for you,' said my aunt. 'I am so sorry.'

'You can't replace a father like that,' said the woman, and we could see that she had tears welling up in her eyes.

My aunt held out her hand and said, 'I'm Virginia Clydesdale. And this is Agatha, my niece.'

The woman took her hand and said, 'I'm Rosie Pitt, one of his daughters.'

'How many daughters and sons are there?' I asked.

'I have three sisters, and I have about ten half-brothers and -sisters. I've never met those ones.'

'Gracious me!' said my aunt. 'I had no idea!'

'No idea? Well, why should you? What do you mean?'

'I had no idea that one might have such a large family these days,' said my aunt lamely.

'I'm going now,' said the woman, adding rather drily, 'Thank you for putting flowers on my father's grave, even though you didn't know him.'

She leaned down and kissed me on the cheek, and said, 'Goodbye, little Agatha. It was very good fun to meet you. I do hope you have a long and happy life.' I've never forgotten how gentle and sad that woman was.

That evening at the hotel I asked my aunt why she had lied about her name being Clydesdale, rather than Feakes.

'Because it's my favourite kind of horse. They're lovely, don't you think?'

'Why have I got about fifteen brothers and sisters and I don't know any of them?' I asked.

'That's life,' she said, 'and why worry if you've got a nice aunt?'

All my life I've wondered about my long-lost mysterious siblings. Having met only one of them, I always meant to try and find the rest, but I never did get round to it. In the final analysis it's too expensive to hire a private detective, and I don't suppose I wanted to have to share the old man, even in retrospect.

I've still got a set of his clubs in the cupboard under the stairs, and a box of Hesketh golf balls, and his old brogues with hobnails hammered into the soles.

30

Daniel at Hexham

Daniel looks down at the tiny baby in its cot, wrapped in woollen shawls, its mouth working rhythmically on its own thumb as it suckles in its sleep. Its thin dark hair is plastered against its pink skull. The sweet warm smell of infancy rises up, reminding him of Esther and Bertie when they were tiny.

Gaskell is holding Daniel's left hand in her right, and Christabel is holding his right hand in her left.

'So this is Felix,' he says.

'Do you like it? The name, I mean. Is it all right with you?' asks Christabel.

'It's a perfect name,' says Daniel, and suddenly his face crumples. Gaskell puts her arm around his shoulder and squeezes him.

Daniel says falteringly, 'I had no idea that this would be so hard to take.' He pauses, and then asks, 'I really can never tell anyone he's mine?'

'Think of Rosie, and Bertie and Esther,' says Christabel. 'And I absolutely couldn't face Rosie.'

'What we've done is really very shocking,' reflects Gaskell, 'but strangely enough we don't care at all.'

'We wouldn't feel guilty unless we were found out. We're such scallywags,' says Christabel brightly. '*C'est la vie.*'

'I don't know how I will be able to be apart from him,' says Daniel. 'It's bad enough not being with the other two. What are you going to tell him when he's older? Have you thought of a story?'

'We have years to think of a story,' says Gaskell drily.

Christabel leans down and gently lifts the baby out. She arranges the shawls tenderly, and then holds him out to Daniel, who takes him to the window. Felix blinks in the light, and Daniel sniffs the top of his head. 'Nothing smells so sweet and delicious as a baby's head,' he says.

162

'I know. Isn't it gorgeous?' says Gaskell. 'It compares very well to behind a cat's ears. Or a golden retriever's.'

Daniel says, 'I think I have unintentionally set myself up for a lifetime of sadness and regret.'

Christabel says, 'But you've made Gaskell and me delirious with happiness.'

'Yes,' says Gaskell. 'We really couldn't be more overjoyed. We'll never be able to thank you enough. And we so much want you to come here as often as you can. To be with Felix as much as you can.'

'And we don't want to stop at one,' says Christabel.

Later, in the studio that was once a ballroom, with Felix becoming heavier in his arms, Daniel looks at their latest work. Christabel has taken photographs of Gaskell's parents, lying newly dead on their beds, having met their grandchild and then miraculously contrived to die within two days of each other. 'I hope you don't think it's too morbid,' says Christabel. 'It seemed like the right thing to do at the time.'

'There's no tragedy in a peaceful death in old age,' says Daniel. 'You'll be able to remember them at peace. In repose.'

'They got madder and madder,' says Gaskell. 'They so much enjoyed the ends of their lives.'

'A consummation devoutly to be wished,' says Daniel.

He goes to look at the paintings and is disconcerted to see half a dozen portraits of a reclining naked woman, executed in bold, thick brushstrokes, depicting the progressive stages of pregnancy. He instantly recognises Christabel's body, because it is a body he has grown to love, but the head is Gaskell's. Her extraordinary green eyes gaze out of the canvas with an expression of disdainful confidence and defiance. There is a plain black ribbon about her neck, as there is on Goya's Naked Maja.

Daniel takes her arm and says, 'That's my girl.'

At that moment he suddenly understands with complete clarity that it will only be in the spirit of renunciation that he will be able to be a father to this child.

Later that evening, he and Christabel are in the conservatory alone, because Gaskell wants to paint by candleglow in order to see what the colours will look like the next morning. She has recently realised that her left eye sees colours differently from her right, and so she is trying experiments in painting first with one eye and then the other, in all the different kinds of light. Daniel and Christabel are looking out on a quiet night with a full moon rising above the elms. She has her arm threaded through his; he can smell her hair, and the French scent that she likes to dab on the insides of her wrists. Christabel and Gaskell have made a practical little nest in almost every room, where the baby can be set down. In the conservatory, a drawer has been pulled out of the old chest that is otherwise full of string, trowels and small brown-paper packets containing seeds. Felix is asleep again, suckling his thumb.

'I have to ask you something,' he says.

'What about?'

'Fidelity.'

'Oh.'

'What are we to do?'

'I can't ask you to be faithful,' says Christabel. 'I can't be faithful to you, can I? Well, I can be faithful in the sense that you're the only man I'll ever have. Or want, probably. And I don't want any father for my children except you. But it can't be enough for you, can it? Is there someone else?'

Daniel hesitates, and says, 'The Honourable Mary.'

'Oh Lord,' says Christabel. 'Oh well, I suppose it shows that you have good taste.'

'Nothing's happened yet, but it's very obviously coming on.'

'She'd have to leave Mother and The Grampians.'

'Your mother's become completely impossible,' says Daniel. 'Mary says she has to go anyway, for the sake of her own equanimity. She hates the way that Rosie tries to keep the children from me, and says that she just has to keep biting her tongue. I'm sure she could find plenty to do, wherever she is.'

'But you can't marry her. Won't she want children? And she won't want to live in sin, will she? She's not a cynical reprobate, like me.'

'No, she won't. She's quite conventional. She isn't innocent though. She had a fiancé who was killed at Beersheba. They thought they might never see each other again.'

'Don't you mind?'

'Only in theory. When I see the loss ... the sadness in her eyes, I can't mind. And I couldn't be less innocent myself, could I? In the end one can't be a hypocrite. What about us?'

Christabel is suddenly alarmed. 'You can't tell her about me.'

'I mean, what about our next child? You say you want more children. So do I.'

'You'll just have to be unfaithful,' says Christabel with determination. 'Whatever happens, I'll still know that you love me, and Gaskell and I will still love you. And, look on the bright side, by that time Lady Mary may have given up on you and upped sticks.' Christabel falls silent, then adds, 'But it really would make my heart ache, the thought of you with someone else. It would be hard to bear.'

'Christabel,' says Daniel, 'when I was younger I had absolutely no idea that it's utterly impossible to live without so much subterfuge, so many compromises, and secrets and lies.'

'You can perfectly well live a dull life without them,' she says, 'but who wants a dull life? When I'm on my deathbed, I don't want to be lying there thinking about all the things I never did.'

31

The Honourable Mary FitzGerald St George

I was with Daniel for several years, and moved to be with him
when he found work at Brough's, in Nottingham.

Of course I had to confess to him that I wasn't an 'Honourable'
at all, and neither was I a St George. I worked up to it for months,
and when I finally told him, one Sunday morning when we were
lounging in bed with a cup of tea, he just laughed, and said,
'What a tangled web we weave.'

Daniel absolutely worshipped George Brough and his motorcycles. He called Mr Brough 'St George' and he had two of
the motorcycles for himself, which he called 'George the First'
and 'George the Second'. They were guaranteed to do at least
one hundred miles per hour, and kept breaking speed records.
He told me that every Brough motorcycle was a one-off, built
for a particular customer, and each one was built twice. It was
put together once to make sure that everything fitted and
worked, taken apart for chroming and painting, and then re-
assembled. I'm afraid that when he explained their virtues and
specifications my eyes would just cloud over and I could feel
my brain closing down, but I do so well remember the lovely
low burbling note of the exhaust, and how I never seemed to
get tired or uncomfortable on a long run, and the only times
it broke down were when we had punctures caused by horse-
shoe nails. Daniel developed quite a vehement hatred for horses,
although he said he'd become very fond of a bay horse in
Ceylon.

At first we lived in Lenton, a village that's been somewhat
swallowed up by the city, but it was still a proper village, in
between the Clifton Hills and Peveril Castle. There was a gorgeous
little river called the Leen, and in the church was an absolutely
massive Norman font made out of one big block.

We chose Lenton because we liked it, but we hadn't realised that it was where Captain Albert Ball had come from. Daniel had known Captain Ball quite well, and often spoke of him, although it was always an annoyance to him that Ball was the only British ace that anyone seemed to have heard of. He died when he was only twenty years old, having won the Légion d'Honneur, the Order of St George of Russia, the Victoria Cross, and the DSO three times.

Daniel said that Ball was wildly brave, so recklessly courageous that the enemy didn't know how to cope with him, but he mainly remembers him as a young man who was completely passionate about flying, who would sing his heart out all the time that he was aloft. He used to light a fire at night and circle it, playing his violin to the flames. Like Daniel, he was somewhat obsessed by mechanics and machinery.

I remember the first time we went into the church and saw the memorial plaque. Daniel just stood before it, clenching and unclenching his fists. I left him there to grieve.

We left Lenton after a few months because it was difficult for Daniel to get to Haydn Road by crossing the centre of the city every day, so we moved to the north, to Arnold, near Cockpit Hill. The church had a memorial to William Johnson, another VC.

I found myself a humble job as a solicitor's secretary. Oddly enough, I enjoyed it in a quiet and mundane sort of way. Working for Mrs McCosh had never felt like proper work. Daniel was doing terribly well at Brough's, and he bought me a tiny two-seater Morris Tourer. It cost him £120, plus £10 if you wanted the bumpers, and it looked like a little sports car, but it could only do fifty-five miles an hour, and the steering was so imprecise that it wandered all over the road, especially if it wasn't a level one. It didn't have a boot or even a dicky, and you had to carry anything you had behind the seats. It was a lovely British racing-green colour, with black mudguards, and red leather seats. We'd tried out an Austin 7 on the same day that Daniel bought it, and the Morris was definitely miles better. I often wonder whether Enid Blyton got the idea for Little Noddy's car from the Morris Tourer.

Bucketing around with Daniel in that quirky little Morris was just the most fun I've ever had. In the summer we'd go out with the canopy off, all goggled up, and our hats firmly clamped down on our heads, and drive up to Dorket Head to have a picnic and enjoy the views. He insisted on my driving it most of the time, because proper vehicles had handlebars or joysticks. I would sit there on the rug, look at my false wedding ring glinting on my finger in the sunlight, and be two-thirds happy.

For a while Daniel was a friend of Lawrence of Arabia, who was also a Brough fanatic, and owned several different models in succession. Daniel used to scoff about Lawrence pretending to be Aircraftman Shaw, when everybody knew perfectly well who he was. I know he used to rib Lawrence about it. He was deeply envious, not of Lawrence's heroic past, but of his stainless-steel petrol tank.

Lawrence came to stay with us one weekend, and I had been expecting a thrilling time, with tales of derring-do and blowing up railway lines, and encounters with sheikhs and their camels, but the two boys just talked about the latest aircraft and Brough Superior Motorcycles. They went on and on about Castle forks and mousetrap carburettors, and Enfield brakes, and the torque effect of rotary engines. Never in my life have I experienced so much difficulty in restraining my yawns, and I was really dreadfully pleased when our guest finally left. Even so, I was saddened and shocked to hear the news when Lawrence was killed, riding one of his beloved Broughs.

I never regretted leaving The Grampians. The fashion for lady maids had long gone, and it had been a stultifying occupation in many ways. It was beneath my intelligence, and it wasn't living, it was existing. I'd become completely bored with pretending to be a lady, and Mrs McCosh's relentless obsession with the royal family had been driving me up the wall for years. She almost made me a republican. She was a hopeless snob about absolutely everything, including whether or not the butter knife was silver or silver-plated, and if there was no butter knife at all she just wouldn't have any butter, and if there was marmalade in somebody else's house she wouldn't eat it if it had come from a shop. She went shopping with a Harrods bag even if she was just nipping out to buy a darning needle. She had also become accustomed to brandishing her air rifle whenever she found an annoyance in me, and of course I know it's difficult to kill someone with such a weapon, but I didn't relish the prospect of having an eye put out. In any case, I was scarcely needed any more because Rosie was there with the children.

That was another reason to move, of course. Daniel was a kind man who adored the children, but she treated him as if he had leprosy. After he moved out she would do anything to prevent him from seeing them, even telling him blatant lies about them being ill, or being somewhere else, or not wanting to see him. I caught her more than once burning his letters to them, until the letters stopped arriving at all. Of course I found out later about the arrangement with Mrs Pendennis, but at the time I thought that Daniel must have given up in defeat, and it made me terribly sad. I couldn't say anything to Rosie, so had to bite my tongue.

Daniel didn't deserve to be treated so badly. Quite apart from having made a name for himself in the Great War, he was energetic and humorous and hard-working, and he loved having fun. A fun-loving man is difficult for a woman to resist, especially when he is compassionate, and as much concerned with your pleasure as he is with his own.

I don't feel comfortable talking about that kind of thing, but it matters, it really does. If he had been more disappointing, perhaps it would have been easier to leave him a great deal sooner.

The main reason I left The Grampians was that Daniel and I fell in love. We came together because for a couple of weeks we had to look after his brother Archie, who had fallen on hard times and was terribly sick. It was then that I realised what a tender heart Daniel had, and in his case I suppose it was obvious that a man in his situation needs some consolation. I was very beautiful when I was young, and that is a most convenient shortcut to a man's heart, as everybody knows.

It was no easy thing, having his wife in the house, and she treating him so badly, and expecting me to be supportive. After a great deal of havering, Daniel and I realised that it was quite impossible for us to have any kind of life together unless I bit the bullet and left, and that's how it came about that I had to swallow my pride and agree to become his mistress.

It was not such a bad thing to be the mistress of a man as amusing and appreciative as he was.

Sometimes he brought his rather antiquated two-seater Avro down from Hexham, which was such fun, and we did seem to spend an awful lot of time hurtling about with his combination, going sightseeing, or just out on jaunts. I still have a lot of photographs in a shoebox, and of course I kept all the little presents he gave me, like the 'wedding' and 'engagement' rings that we wore for the purpose of going to hotels, and my brooch in the shape of a honey bee.

We did all that at weekends, of course, because after I left the solicitor's, I found clerical work in the Northern and Provincial Bank. They thought I was a respectable but childless wife, and quite often I thought what fun it was that I was really the secret mistress of a great flying ace. It's surprising how quickly one becomes used to being unrespectable, as long as no one else realises.

Sometimes we went out into the sticks for weekends, because Daniel had a friend with an empty tied cottage. It was very small and cold, and we spent an awful lot of time cutting logs and humping them about. We had water from a well, and a thunderbox outside the back door that was just absolutely perishing in winter. Eventually Daniel found a stove, and used the workshops at Brough's to alter it so that a pipe went through the back to a tank upstairs that made enough hot water, and of course the pipes heated the house a little bit too. Daniel said it would work on the 'thermosyphon' principle, and it really did. To this day I have never got round to finding out what a 'thermosyphon' is. I felt I couldn't ask Daniel in case he thought I was just another silly woman. Sometimes it's best just to nod wisely.

When we were there we lived mainly off pheasant and partridge and wood pigeon, and trout from a stream in the woods. Daniel would go out with a twelve-bore or a fishing rod, and not return until we had some supper. I remember picking whole bathfuls of blackberries and never being able to finish them before they began to go mouldy.

We did have a wonderful time for several years, despite his frequent absences when he went to see his children. He quite often went to Hexham too, to fly his aeroplanes and see Gaskell and Christabel, who were becoming more and more outlandish and successful by the day. He was terribly fond of Christabel's adopted children, and would talk about them rather a lot. It was 'Felix said this, and Felicity did that' and Christabel used to send him letters about how well they were doing. It was very much easier for him to see his godchildren than it was to see his own. When he came back from Hexham he was always agitated or sad, or both, and I suppose that that was the reason. Obviously Daniel couldn't take me too, although I am certain I would have loved it there, and I'd always been fond of Gaskell and Christabel, and I was really not so easily shocked any more. The person who shocked me the most was me. I suppose Daniel couldn't really tell Christabel about me, no matter how 'modern' she was. He was married to her sister, after all.

It's difficult to be a woman in her early thirties, with fading beauty and no prospect of children or any kind of security. Daniel and I did talk about having children, but in the end it always seemed too fraught and difficult, and we lacked the courage. I did, anyway. I'm just not the bohemian type. Daniel was about as bohemian as is possible for a military man. We never did take the risk, however much we were tempted or got carried away. The worst thing was not being able to get married. I would have married him if Rosie had agreed to a divorce, but she doggedly refused every time he asked, on religious grounds. She accidentally blighted my life as well as his. No one does more harm than someone who's obstinately trying to stick to a principle.

And I also think that deep down she really and truly still loved him and wanted to be married to him.

She was a casualty of the war, the same as me. Her fiancé died in France and mine died in Mesopotamia. I did understand what was going on in her heart, I think. The thing is, when your fiancé dies, you've never had the chance to see their bad side, and so they're perfect forever. I tried not to be angry and bitter, and now I appreciate that my passion for Daniel was what laid the ghost of my poor dead soldier to rest.

In the end I began to feel stuck and panicky. I could see my youth fading away out of reach, and I saw a strangely empty future in front of me. What if Daniel should tire of me? Or get killed stunting in one of his rickety old planes? Daniel confessed that he'd had a native mistress in Ceylon, and sometimes I would look at him with all the adoring passion in my heart, and think, 'Oh, when all's said and done, I'm just another mistress.'

What happened in the end was that I went home to Edenderry for Christmas, to spend it with my father, and when I went shopping in Dublin I bumped into my teenage sweetheart. I found him sitting forlornly on a bench on the banks of the Liffey. We went and drank tea together, and it turned out that his situation was terribly sad. He had two children, but his wife had gone completely mad after the second, and fled to France, and laid her neck on a railway line outside Toulouse.

Fergus made it quite clear that his feelings for me would be easily revived, and one day I stood and looked at myself in the mirror. My hips were widening and my bosom was not as impudent as before. I still had my fine white skin and my girlish freckles, but I could see the bloom beginning to fade. Even my lips seemed less moist. I had one or two grey hairs amongst my brown curls, but I still had my big grey eyes that everyone commented upon, and which Daniel had loved so much. I knew that I had reached a crossroad and, that Easter, one morning after we had passed a very tender night, and after Daniel had gone to work, I left him a note to say that I was going back to Ireland, and that he would find the Morris in the car park at the station. I wept all the way from Nottingham to Dublin.

Fergus's children were very sweet, and after a while they thought of me as their mother. Then I had two more of my own.

Fergus was a wonderful husband, and I did grow to love him very deeply, in a comfortable and comforting way. It made such a difference that I'd been besotted with him before. I could be a teenager again, and the clock could be wound back to where it had all started. I've had a very good life, in retrospect, and I don't regret one moment of it. I think I really did belong in Ireland, despite being Anglo-Irish all at the wrong time.

When I left Daniel, it was obvious from his letters that it had thrown him into a deep slough. He wasn't angry with me; he entirely understood why I had acted as I did.

He decided to find a new job abroad, in the hope of having one last new start with Rosie. I was sad to think of him wasting his life with her, but I know he was trying to be unselfish, thinking mainly of the children. However much he loved me, and I know that he did, she was always the ghost at his shoulder.

I still shudder with rage to think of the stunt she pulled on him.

One day I was in Dublin, just before the war, and I heard a motorcycle go by that sounded just like his, and a huge wave of regret and nostalgia overcame me. It was so painful that I went into a hotel to sit down for a while, gather my thoughts, and order myself some tea. I had the two rings he'd given me in a small box at the bottom of my handbag, and I took them out and put them on, feeling guilty because I had to remove Fergus's first. Then I took out one of his letters, and read it.

We'd kept in touch, and his telephone number was on the header of his notepaper. Even though I was happy with my husband, I missed Daniel terribly, and I just wanted to hear his voice again. The line was dreadful and it was hard to talk, especially as it's always obvious when the operator is eavesdropping. It was a conversation full of painful silence, and awful fumblings when a new penny has to be dropped in. He told me that he'd discovered that poor Archie had been reduced to taking work as a roadsweeper in Brighton, and then he asked, 'Why did you call your son after me?'

I said, 'He isn't named after you. He's just got the same name.'

He said, 'Mary, I love you,' and then the last penny was used up, and the bleeps cut in, and the line went dead.

Even after all those long years in Germany, he said, 'Mary, I love you.'

32

Rosie (3)

I've often thought about the failure of my marriage to Daniel, and have sometimes even wondered if it really was killed off. After all, there was never a divorce, which is admittedly because I refused him one.

We did get off to a bad start, but then we had some glorious years in Ceylon, until I decided that we must come home. I don't think he ever forgave me for that. I didn't find out about his Tamil mistress until later, and he still doesn't know that I know, but although I was angry, I did understand it. I didn't want any more children, and he didn't want to give up his carnal pleasures. The same thing seems to have happened to my own father and mother. A man has certain rights in marriage, and a woman has certain duties. But hasn't that all been changing? I mean, a woman isn't a chattel any more. I don't think I should have had to cooperate if it went against the grain. Perhaps I just never had enough carnality of my own. That's probably it. But it's not my fault. I am as God made me. I've got my own nature. Ottilie and Sophie obviously have plenty of carnality, and God knows what Christabel gets up to, and God knows Daniel's mother had some opinions on this subject.

But in the end it's all about love, isn't it? Your love changes as time goes by. I still loved Daniel. Every time he came home my heart jumped a little bit in my chest at the sound of his motorcycle or the turn of his key in the door, and when he kissed me on the cheek and said 'hello, darling' I knew that his heart still leapt a little bit as well, because I could see that little glint of desire in his eyes before they clouded over again with anger and resentment.

But too much had gone wrong. Bridges get burned, too many apologies have to be made, there are too many false new starts and rotten compromises, too many bad habits that re-establish themselves the moment your back is turned and you've taken your eye off the ball.

I don't lack self-knowledge. In fact I know myself very well, and I don't even like myself. I wouldn't seek out my company if I was someone else. I do things that are selfish, and then find some justification for it in the Bible, or dress it up as something virtuous.

The very worst thing I did to Daniel happened at about the time that Christabel adopted her second child. It would have been in November of 1930. We got the letter from her on the same day that the papers were full of the news that a great many people had been injured by stampeding elephants at the Lord Mayor's Show. It was not long after the R101 crashed and burned at Beauvais. We actually saw it flying over the house and it seemed wobbly and much too low, and my mother ran indoors to fetch her air rifle, because it brought back memories of the Zeppelins. We let her pop away at it. It couldn't have been more harmless, and she was often quite normal (for her) after she'd had a little fit of barminess, so it was worth allowing her to let off steam.

For some reason Daniel had become terribly agitated. He'd found an even better job, with Brough's, and although he often went to see his godchildren in Hexham, he was mostly going back and forth to Nottingham. He was only able to be with us at weekends and on holidays, because I was still refusing to move there with him. I had my mad mother to deal with, and I loved it at The Grampians. I liked to visit my father's grave every day. I always took Mother with me, and we kept the grave tidy. I didn't really see the point in moving to Nottingham, when my husband didn't even like me any more and was always angry. He actually just wanted to be with the children, not with me, but children belong with their mothers, don't they?

My mother was alone because the Honourable Mary had left, so I had to look after her in her dotage. It was at about the time that she left that Daniel stopped even mentioning us moving up to Nottingham. The whole issue slid away. I suppose he realised that I was intransigent and that my mother really did need me.

Daniel would come home and spend the whole weekend ignoring me, just playing with the children, setting up stumps on the lawn, taking them to zoos and organising little picnics, and when he left on Sunday evenings Esther would cling to him and cry, and Bertie would just look angry and abandoned.

Once, when Daniel was infuriated, he told me that as the children's legal guardian, he could take them from me at any time. I said, 'How would you work and look after them at the same time?' and he said, 'Obviously I would have to hire a governess.'

I knew he wouldn't, however. He knew that he couldn't take the children, because they loved me too much, it would have been cruel. It would have been too cruel to me, as well. Daniel wasn't a naturally cruel man. Esther used to say that she wanted to live with Daddy, but I never believed it. Daniel probably wouldn't have been able to find a governess who would live in the same house as a solitary man, because she'd want to avoid getting a reputation. He knew he just had to carry on making the best of a bad job.

He once said to me, 'How can you keep saying that children belong with their mothers, when you yourself very obviously preferred your father?'

I denied it. I don't really see what else I could have done. I just knew that the children belonged with me, that's all.

One weekend Daniel came home and Esther was on his knee, sucking her thumb even though she was ten, when he announced that he'd been offered a plum job in Tanganyika, setting up a pioneering coffee plantation, with a sideline in importing motor-cycles. He also mentioned something about civil aviation. He told the children they'd see leopards and rhinoceros. He said he wanted the children and me to come too, and this would probably be our last chance to start again and set everything right.

I agreed. I had a sudden little fit of optimism, and I thought I could probably find someone to live with my mother. I wrote to the Honourable Mary, but never heard anything back, so I found someone at an agency.

What happened, and this was the worst thing I ever did to him, was that when we boarded the ship in Southampton, just a minute or two before the final klaxon, I sent Daniel to the cabin to fetch me a handkerchief, and then I took the children, one in each hand, and fled down the gangplank.

I remember Daniel dancing and shouting at the rail as the ship moved away, his face white with rage, and Esther waving to him and repeatedly asking, 'Why is Daddy going without us?'

Daniel tore the handkerchief in two, held up one half in each hand, and then let go of them. The wind caught them and carried them over our heads, fluttering away like doves, over Southampton.

For a few days I wondered if Daniel would go on to Tanganyika, but he didn't. He came back from Gibraltar, and demanded a divorce. I've never seen anyone so enraged, and I felt in danger of my life. Bertie was there, clinging to my legs, when Daniel was raging at me, shouting and stabbing the air with his finger, spittle flying, and I think it affected his feelings for his father forever afterwards, though he can't possibly remember it. He was only four. A child of that age shouldn't be subjected to the sight of his own mother being raged at. Daniel went upstairs and smashed the mirror and the windows in my bedroom with a chair, and then he threw the chair out and it broke in the driveway, and then he came down and kissed the children and drove away. He probably went to Partridge Green, as he'd had to give up his job and his lodgings in Nottingham.

Of course the whole family was on his side. Nobody understood what I'd done. I had very hurtful and unkind letters from Ottilie, Christabel and Sophie. All was now forever irreparable, and Daniel never stayed at The Grampians again. He booked lodgings nearby and would come and try to take the children out at weekends and holidays. He'd let me know when he was coming, and so I'd arrange for them to be somewhere else, or I'd say 'They don't want to see you' or 'They're ill' or 'They've got a party they're desperate to go to'.

One day Daniel turned up, and I saw him from the morning-room window. I sent Esther upstairs, and came to the door and talked to Daniel in the driveway. I said, 'They've got influenza, so I put them to bed, and they're really too ill to have visitors.'

Daniel said, 'Then why is Esther waving to me from the window?'

I looked up, and Esther was waving to Daniel and blowing him kisses. I didn't know what to say. She suddenly threw open the sash, scrambled out, stood for a horrifying moment on the sill, and jumped. My heart leapt into my throat, but Daniel caught her, and they both fell backwards onto the grass under the tree. Esther was laughing and kissing him all over his face.

Without a word to me, Daniel got out the little flying jacket, gauntlets and helmet that he kept in his sidecar, and put them on her. I didn't see them for another week, until he brought her back.

I called the police but they weren't interested. Apparently you can't be kidnapped by your own father when he is the legal guardian.

Bertie was very sweet. All that week he stuck to me like a limpet, saying, 'Don't worry, Mummy, I'm here. I'll look after you.'

Esther and Daniel had spent the time at the seaside, and she gave me a stick of rock when she came back, with a picture of Brighton Pavilion on the cellophane, and 'A souvenir of Brighton' all the way through it in red lettering. She said she'd been to Beachy Head, and her father had shown her the fulmars. For some months, she would run around the garden with her arms outspread, pretending to be a fulmar, and saying, 'Look at me! Look at me! I'm flying!'

After that, Daniel never believed my excuses and would just push past me into the house, to check for himself, so I had to find people who would have them for the weekends.

33

Daniel Goes to See Archie

Puttering about the backstreets of Brighton, Daniel had immense difficulty in finding Archie's lodgings. He was tired after his long ride, and had become extremely cold as a result of miscalculating the weather. When he had set out it had been warm and pleasant, but the wind had switched to the north-east and he felt sorely the lack of something like his good old Sidcot and flying gloves.

He had asked many people for directions and was finally appalled to find that Archie was living in a basement in a very poor corner indeed. Daniel stood before the building, looking at the wrecked guttering that hung from the eaves, the water stains on the unpointed brickwork, the rotting window frames, and the stunted buddleia growing out of the cracks in the walls. Ragged washing hung across the street from window to window, and he wondered at all the mutual agreements that must have been arrived at by the occupants of opposing buildings. A child of some eight years, with the soles flapping from his shoes, was holding a baby at the same time as kicking a football against the wall. The baby stared at nothing, its thumb in its mouth, as it was jolted about.

'Is this where Archie Pitt lives?' asked Daniel.

'Archie? The old posher? You best tap on that window down there, mister, 'cause no one won't come to the door.'

'Thank you,' said Daniel, adding, 'Why don't you get that ball stitched up? I'm sure a cobbler could do it in no time. If you keep kicking it about, the bladder's going to burst.'

'Can't afford it, mister. Anyway, Dad's at work, and anyway, he don't know how to sew.'

'And your mother?'

'Buggered off.'

'Oh,' said Daniel. 'I am sorry.'

'We're not.'

'And what does your father do?'

'On the bins, mister.'

'And why aren't you at school?'

The boy looked at him in astonishment, as if he were an idiot. 'Someone's got to hold the baby, mister!'

'I'm sure you do it very well,' said Daniel.

'I'm the best,' replied the boy. 'I've got Gracie indoors as well. She's three. Ain't much use yet, but she will be.'

'Will you keep an eye on my combination?' asked Daniel. 'I'll give you a shilling.'

'Cor, thanks, mister!'

Daniel went down the steps and tapped on the basement window. After a few moments, the door beneath the steps opened, catching and scraping on the flags. Archie said, 'Slack hinges – must do something about it.' He held out his hand to shake Daniel's. 'We're half French, remember?' said Daniel, sidestepping the proffered hand, embracing him warmly, and patting him on the back.

'Terribly British now, old fellow,' said Archie. 'Hardly remember a word of the old Froggy.'

Archie was thin and pallid. His grey moustache was brown from nicotine above the centre of his lips, and his formerly smart tweed suit was bare at the elbows and knees. He wore his regimental tie and a waistcoat, from which, Daniel noted, his fob watch no longer hung. His shoes were immaculately polished, as befitted an old military man, but the rest of him was shabby.

'Do come in,' said Archie. Daniel entered and surveyed the one room where Archie subsisted. There was a small round wooden table with four plain chairs, one of which was broken. There was no armchair or sofa, and the rug was thickly congealed with grime. There was a mousetrap in the corner, gripping the corpse of a desiccated mouse that had plainly been dead for several days. Against one wall was a truckle bed piled with old army blankets, but there was no pillow or sheet. Under the bed, Daniel could see the gleam of empty whisky bottles, stacked neatly in rows. The walls were papered with painted woodchip that sagged away at the juncture with the ceiling.

The worst thing was the smell. Damp plaster, rotting wood, mildew, urine. 'Cup of tea?' said Archie. 'Only got one point, I'm afraid. Have to disconnect the fire.'

'Oh, Archie,' said Daniel, 'how can you live like this? In this ...'

'Squalor?'

'Yes, this squalor.'

'No choice, old boy. No money. Pension doesn't stretch. Damned Geddes did for me. What does an old soldier do? I'm buggered, old boy.'

'You can't live like this,' said Daniel. 'It's not on. You're in a slum.'

'I'm good for nothing,' said Archie. 'What am I good for? Can't start a business. No one'll lend me a sou. Damned duffer at school, can't be a master. Might as well stick to being a sweeper. Only thing I'm fit for.'

'You were very good at Latin and Greek at Westminster, and you speak half a dozen Indian languages. You could teach French, for God's sake! There must be something.'

'*Rien du tout*,' replied Archie. 'Tried all the local prep schools. Nothing doing. I'm buggered.'

'There must be lots of people who would want private tuition. Archie, you've got to pull yourself together! Isn't it freezing here in winter?'

'Perishing. The water runs down the walls. Not as bad as the Kush, though. Got to keep things in perspective.'

'Where's the thunderbox?'

'Backyard. Have to go out the front and round the back. Not much fun. It's damned sordid and there's always someone in there shitting their heart out. Feel dreadfully sorry for the children. Grimy little buggers, hearts of gold though.'

'We're going out to lunch,' said Daniel. 'I've got bugger all as well, so let's go out and spend it.'

'That's the spirit,' said Archie.

In the Palace Hotel, Daniel watched as Archie tucked away an immense plate of ox liver and gravy with mashed potatoes and cabbage. He had plainly not eaten properly for a very long time. He felt saddened beyond measure by what time had done to his brother, a man who had been athletic and splendid, heroic and indomitable. Archie was now a starving drunk who had been repaid for his service to the Empire with penury and neglect.

'I'm going to get you away from here,' said Daniel, as his brother wiped his lips with a napkin. Daniel noticed that Archie's hands were trembling rhythmically.

'Wish you would, old boy,' said Archie. ''Fraid it probably can't be done.'

'Rubbish,' replied Daniel. 'You weren't born to live like this.'

'How's Rosie?' asked Archie. 'And the children?'

'Rosie does everything she can to make sure I never see the children. And she refuses to give me a divorce. I hardly know how the children are.'

'Must be dreadful. Did you say you want to get divorced?'

'Desperately. I'm trapped, completely trapped. I can't possibly be a bigamist, and I haven't yet met a woman who wants to live in sin forever.'

Archie seemed to perk up. His hands trembled a little more, and his eyes lost some of their alcoholic dullness.

'It's vile,' said Daniel. 'Every time I arrange to come and take the children out there's a new excuse. They're too tired or they've got a cold or it isn't convenient, or it's raining so I can't take them away in the combination, and no, I can't come in, or even that they don't want to see me. It's all piffle. And what can I do? Argue on the doorstep? Thrust my way in? Sometimes I come all the way from Nottingham and then have to go back again without seeing them, and Rosie says, "You haven't sent us any money recently." Bloody cheek! She wants me to pay her for kidnapping them? It makes my blood boil! And when I do send a cheque she doesn't cash it, just to show that she doesn't need me. And then when I'm leaving, I look up at the window and I see little Esther, waving to me. I've lost Bertie, I know it. I'm their legal guardian, and yet I am completely powerless unless I take them away from her altogether.'

'I do dislike it when you speak badly of Rosie,' said Archie.

Daniel looked at him and said, 'Archie, I do know, you know. I have always known.'

''Bout what, old boy?'

'Rosie. I know you have always adored her, from when we were boys. Even when she only had eyes for Ash.'

'Don't want to talk about it, old boy. Not unless I have to. Too much pain.' He tapped his chest. 'Gives me a pain. In here.'

'*Archie, mon frère, mon pauvre frère, tu dois parler. J'ai déjà tout compris.*'

'I can't,' replied Archie miserably.

Daniel gesticulated as if to take in the whole world. 'You never married, you never even had a flirtation as far as I know. You've let yourself go and you've given up hope.'

'Just drinking myself to death,' said Archie honestly. '*Jusqu'à la mort.*'

'Archie, I have to be honest. You must understand. *Elle* ... She is no good as a wife. She has no fire. She's the only one of the sisters who has no ... she may have had it for Ash ... she's ... Look, Archie, even if she and I divorced, she wouldn't marry you, because she doesn't want what marriage implies. If she did marry you, you would be utterly miserable, because all the affection and tenderness you can give her wouldn't make any difference. You'd be throwing your heart at the wind. You'd be as miserable as I was. *Elle manque la flamme. T'as compris?*'

Archie nodded slowly and put down his fork. He stared at his empty plate, which he had scoured clean with a piece of bread, *à la française*, and didn't look up for what must have been at least a minute. Daniel reached over and took his hand across the table. When Archie did look up, he had a tear coursing down each cheek. '*Néanmoins* ... even so ...' he said, 'I can't do anything. Never thought of another. *Jamais. Je ne peux pas. J'suis perdu. Perdu.*' He paused, looked at his brother levelly, and added in his clipped and aristocratic English accent, 'I am completely snafued and fubared, old boy.'

He stood up and pushed his chair back. 'Going out for a minute,' he said. 'Blubbing in public. Not very British. Conduct unbecoming.'

Whilst Archie was out in the yard recovering himself, Daniel reflected that his beloved older brother was two very different people, depending on whether he was being French or British. He knew that he was the same himself.

When Archie returned, he sat down and said, 'Got a coffin nail? I'm cleaned out.'

Daniel reached inside his jacket for his case, and noticed once again the inscription in elegant italics: '*With fond memories of some jolly decent scraps. Keep Flying. Fluke*'. Daniel had given up smoking years before, but he still carried his case with a few cigarettes in it. It was surprising how often someone asked him if he could spare a gasper, and how easy it was to break the ice by offering one. Archie took a cigarette and asked a passing waiter for a light.

Archie inhaled the smoke deeply. 'Did you know,' he said, 'that if you buy your own papers you can roll one new cigarette out of the butts of ten old ones?'

'Sounds pretty desperate,' said Daniel.

'I'm living like a tramp, *un vrai clochard*,' said Archie, looking directly at his brother. 'Do you know what I want? What I really want?'

'Apart from Rosie?'

'Yes, apart from Rosie. I want to go back to Peshawar. I was happy there. I loved it. I want to go back to Peshawar, even though it's too damned hot and full of assassins. I want to live there and die there and be buried there.'

'You should have married Ottilie. She was very sweet on you. She always asks after you. You missed a good chance. You could have been happy with her. She's a sweet girl.'

'I could give you similar advice,' answered Archie. 'You married the wrong woman, didn't you?'

'I didn't have anyone else who was sweet on me,' said Daniel.

He flipped open his cigarette case and gave the few that were left to his brother, sliding them into his breast pocket.

'I've got a plan,' he said. 'I'm going to take two weeks off. I'm sure I can swing it. Business is very slow, and I've been working my socks off. I'm going to take you to France.'

'*Oh, mon brave*,' said Archie, his face lighting up. 'Do let's go to Saumur.'

'And Limoges.'

'In Limoges we will eat *magret de canard*.'

'We will eat tripe in Caen and snails in Poitiers!'

'Tally-ho! Let's drink a toast!'

They raised their glasses, chinked them together, and said, '*Santé!*'

'*Fraternité!*' proposed Daniel, and they drank again.

On the way back to Archie's hovel they passed a small shop selling toys and sports equipment, and Daniel went in and bought a three-quarter-size football. He tucked it under his arm and found the little boy still kicking his ruined ball against the wall, with his baby sister in his arms. 'Have you been kicking that ball all this time?' asked Daniel.

'No, mister. We've been sitting in your sidecar, mostly. It's nice and cosy, that is.'

'Well, here's your shilling.' Daniel held out the coin, and the little boy took it eagerly. He bit into it and grimaced.

'It is real,' said Daniel, 'and I'm not sure that the biting test is any good.'

'It works for me, mister,' said the child.

'If I give you a new football, will you give me the old one for sixpence? I'll get it mended.'

The boy looked at him suspiciously. 'What's the catch?'

'The catch is that you get a new football and sixpence.'

'Blimey,' said the boy.

'Blimey indeed,' said Daniel.

'Can I see the ball, mister?'

Daniel handed it over. 'Corks,' said the urchin, 'it's a Comet, three-quarter-size.'

'Take my tip, and don't ever head it when it's wet. I did that in a game once, and it nearly took my nut off.'

'Thanks, mister!'

'Can I have your old one for sixpence, then?'

When the deal had been struck, and the sixpence bitten, Daniel tossed the bulging old ball into his sidecar, and then whispered in the boy's ear: 'You ought to play with Archie. He's wonderful in goal. And he hasn't got a son to play with.'

'He's always pissed,' said the boy in a whisper that was really rather too loud.

The boy ran indoors with his trophies, and the brothers looked at each other. 'I'll be in touch soon,' said Daniel. 'We've got a trip to organise. I'll drop you a line or send you a telegram.'

They stood with nothing further to say, until Daniel broke the silence with 'Remember what I said. About Rosie.'

'*Elle manque la flamme.*'

'*Tout à fait.* She only knows how to create unhappiness. She has the cruelty of saints. *Je t'assure.*'

'Even so, you know how it is,' said Archie forlornly. 'And it really isn't her fault, you know. Ash getting killed. She's never got over it. *Ça explique, n'est-ce pas? C'est la faute de la guerre.* It was the war.'

'I know how it is,' said Daniel sadly. 'Of course I understand about Ash. How could I not? We all remember how wonderful he was. But all the same … *elle m'a raté la vie. Sans vouloir.*'

This time Archie did not hold out his hand. They embraced and kissed each other's cheeks.

On the way home Daniel realised that he didn't even know whether or not Bertie liked to play football. He tried to quell the rage that welled up inside him so often and so uncontrollably.

34

A Letter from Willy and Fritzl

Kirchenstrasse 104
Dortmund
Westfalen

11 November 1930

Our dear Captain Daniel Pitt,
We are you for your recent letter very much thanking. My name is Gretchen Brand, and I am this letter on behalf of Willy and Fritzl writing, because I have good English, and it for them is too difficult. Willy my special friend has become, and this happiness.

Willy me what to write is telling. He says 'Good greetings, old comrade', here Willy is. We all very sorry that life for you shit has become, because of no job and a woman departed. A broken heart and at the same time no job indeed shit is, but all to eat you a kilo of shit before you die, not true?

Old comrade, Fritzl and I like to invite you again to Germany. Germany not very good, big mess, big politics, too much chaos, too many election, all buggered and scunnered. But to Germany we you invite, because all of us getting too old are becoming, and it twelve years since you us captured did and us saved from being in battle killed. We happy memories of captivity in Scotland. We have still a wee dram in the evening afore bed.

Still we you for not shooting us down when we helpless were grateful forever are, and we once more to embrace you wish and in our own homeland to honour. We of drinking your health tired are when you not here are.

We, Willy and Fritzl, a new shop for motorcycle here in Dortmund have begun. We hear of British motorcycle many good things, and we too have very excellent. We, Willy and Fritzl, wish to British here sell, and in England our good German. A swap!

Also we will maintenance and repair do, and that our bread and butter will be.

OK, Germany economy at the moment in big shit, and our idea very stupid, and it will not at all work, but, our dear Captain Daniel Pitt, anyway come, and we will eat and drink and sing and on motorcycle adventures, and old days remember.

We, Willy and Fritzl, would like gladly a Brough Superior to see. The best famous of all! We are very jealous envious, and is our secret intention to bury you in the woods, and the Brough keep. We joke.

Come, even if only holiday. We have Rhein wine for broken hearts, and Gretchen will to you songs sing, and beautiful women we have who also for broken hearts.

Farewell greetings!

Your best friends who to see you again very big pleasure,

Willy, Fritzl, and me Gretchen who this writes, and I of you from Willy and Fritzl have very much heard and I too you invite.

35

Daniel Writes to Esther

Villa Primel
Waldstrasse
Dortmund
Westfalen

5 June 1931

My dearest darling daughter,

Well, here I am in Dortmund! Who would have thought it? It took me days and days and days to drive here, but luckily the Brough didn't break down and my luggage didn't get too wet in the sidecar. I didn't get lost very much on the way, and I only had one tummy upset, which I think was caused by a mischievous omelette near Lille.

I expect you remember me telling you that I am here to see Willy and Fritzl. I captured them and their Walfisch in the Great War, and we remained friends ever since, by post of course, because I haven't seen them for about thirteen years. Longer than you've been alive! They came up with a plan to set up a business importing our motorcycles to Germany, and exporting theirs to Blighty and France, and in the meantime to establish a nice workshop for sales and repairs. I have been very much looking forward to getting my hands on a German motorcycle, just to see how it compares. I have high hopes for the morrow, but I don't honestly think that the importing idea is going to work, because nobody in Germany has the money for a new motorcycle, but that does mean that you are always busy repairing the old ones.

I've had a big welcome here. Willy has got fatter and Fritzl has got thinner, and we all have less hair, and what's left is going grey at the edges, and our complexions are not particularly rosy, as they were in 1918. Willy and Fritzl are still the same underneath, though. We are at present communicating in French, although theirs is terribly bad, and so I am setting about the serious business of learning German. Willy has a girlfriend who is ten years younger than him (lucky dog), and she is a Wandervogel. 'Gracious me! What's that?' I hear you enquire. Well, Willy's Wandervogel paramour has a guitar disguised as a lute, and she likes to roam about with her friends in picturesque parts of the country, especially the hills and mountains, singing songs about the beauties of Germany, and its many mystical connections with all that is praiseworthy and noble and brave. She is very pretty and has long blonde hair and blue eyes, and strong ankles, and always wears a dirndl, and, I must say, she does looks very sweet in it. She reminds me of pictures of milkmaids. I am going to buy you a dirndl and bring it back for you. The girl is called Gretchen, and she gave me a posy of flowers which she picked for me on a song-filled expedition to a hillside (valderi valdera), and she said they were the most beautiful flowers in the world. They're exactly the same as ours, but I decided not to tell her so. Next Sunday we are all going to go on a Wandervogel expedition together, and I expect to be taught some rousing Teutonic choruses as we roam the byways, and chew blades of grass, and occasionally skip like newborn lambs.

I should pick up German quite quickly. Just think, I will soon be able to speak in Pashtun, English, French, Tamil and German! How will I find the space in my head? By forgetting ever more Pashtun and Tamil, I fear.

Germany is all in a fidget because of a little strutting and yelling Austrian fellow called Adolf Hitler. Dortmund isn't too bad, but elsewhere there are flags everywhere with swastikas on, and people marching about in columns, wearing uniforms. You will see that I have drawn a swastika at the top of the page. Dortmund is a communistic kind of place, so I don't think the National Socialists are ever going to get anywhere, but they come out on the streets in gangs and look for gangs of Communists who are out looking for them. There are terrible brawls and melees, which are quite fun to watch … from a safe distance. Bottles get broken on people's heads, and windows get smashed. Everyone thinks that Germans are very orderly and disciplined, don't they? But they would soon be disabused of that idea if they were to come here on a Saturday night. What is certainly true is that Germans have a great passion for slogans and uniforms. At present there is a certain amount of bloodshed, but so far not many have actually been killed. They say it's much worse in other towns.

Willy, Fritzl and Gretchen have all joined Hitler's National Socialist Party. I have taken up lodgings with a Jewish family, who are terribly nice and have two very pretty daughters of a dangerous age. Willy and Fritzl (and Gretchen) are very sharp about Jews, because they say they lost the last war on account of them. They keep talking about the 'stab in the back', and that they lost because of the Jewish subversives on the home front. I don't understand their logic. I seem to remember that it was us who defeated them, and we didn't have any Jews in our squadron, as far as I can remember. I don't feel I can say much, without causing a brouhaha, and anyway my German isn't good enough yet, and their French is painful, and their English comical. They've talked themselves into the idea that absolutely everything is someone else's fault, and that someone else is always a Jew. If you slip on some dog muck, you can be sure it was a Jewish dog! A great many people act as though they are suffering from some kind of drunkenness. You know, glassy eyes and fixed smiles. I suppose they are still punch-drunk because of the war, and then the ghastly financial crash, and of course, if you feel humiliated, it's always nice to think you're the wronged hero, isn't it?

Anyway, the man of the house (and the father of the pretty daughters of a dangerous age) is a Herr Wolff. He is a philosophy professor, and he is very gloomy. He is a logical positivist, apparently. I have no idea what that means yet, but he seems to worship Science rather than God, and frets constantly about what a fact is. I said to him, 'If you find a proper theory of what a fact is, how will you know whether that theory is in fact itself a fact?' and he said, 'Ah, my boy, this is the greatest puzzle of all.' Frau Wolff is a small lady with dark eyebrows and a worried look. She is terribly bustly, and a real tittlemouse. She says, 'Ach, Herr Pitt, alles! Alles!' I think that means that she is dismayed by everything.

They have a nice comfortable house in a suburb, but recently some young men have started throwing stones at their windows, and even doing nasty things in their garden, and putting things through their letter box. Your daddy went out and punched one on the nose on his third night here, and since then they haven't been back, but a policeman came round to tell him off, and then he puffed out his cheeks and said that Germany was going to the dogs again, and the policeman's advice was to get out and go home, and he wished he could come with me. He advised Herr Wolff to wear his medals from the last war. He won the Iron Cross at

Verdun. There is a nice slang word for the criminal police, which is 'Kripo'.

Now, chérie, my little champignonne, let me tell you what is happening. During the holidays Mrs Pendennis next door will be our poste restante. I have told her about our problem with Mama not letting you have my letters and presents, and she is very sympathetic, so all you have to do is pop next door, see the old lady, and read the letters. Do always remember to give her my best regards. You mustn't ever lie to Mama, but on the other hand you don't have to tell her everything either, so I think it would be a good idea not to mention our arrangement. Mrs Pendennis doesn't speak much to Mama any more, so our secret is safe with her, and she doesn't mind if you leave the toys and things with her. Poor Mrs Pendennis lost all her sons in the Great War, so for her it is both terribly nice and terribly sad to have children in the house. She doesn't have any grandchildren, so do try to be like a little granddaughter to her so that it helps to fill the gap, and take Bertie round too.

During term time, of course, you will get my letters as normal. I hope you're enjoying Effingham House, by the way, and I am so proud of you getting into the hockey 3rd 11, even though you are only eleven yourself! The weather is bracing on the Sussex coast, is it not? And do you like Latin? I didn't, but now I wish I'd paid more attention. Uncle Archie was awfully good at Latin and Greek. He should have been a classical scholar, really. Please do make a special effort in French, won't you?

Your dear headmistress is also very understanding about our difficult situation, and she has agreed that I can come and take you out on weekends which are not officially exeats. I shall probably come home by train and boat, and my plan is to come back for two weeks every three months. That way I can have fun with you, keep an eye on your Uncle Archie and Gran'mère Pitt, and even go and see my little godchildren at Auntie Christabel's ... and go flying with Auntie Gaskell too! The three aeroplanes are fast becoming antiques, and will probably have to be rebuilt yet again. When that happens I shall come home for a couple of months so that I can have fun joining in and making sure that everything goes smoothly. I shall have to find a friendly shed for a spare motorcycle somewhere near the harbour, or I could buy a small car, as long as it's very fast and has wings that come out of the side.

Dortmund is a nice city despite all the smoke and smells from the iron foundries and steelworks. Luckily we have lots of waterways and woodlands, and there is a very nice lake at Hörde, just south of here, and there is Westfalenpark and Rombergpark. We've got no less than six castles, and there's an opera house too, so soon I am going to go and see my first opera. I am hoping to see some very loud and fat ladies dressed as ancient warrioresses, with bosoomers so capacious that they have to be carried before them in a wheelbarrow, and when they sing loudly enough, the windows will shatter for miles around.

There is a nice church near me called the Reinoldikirche, which has a very pointy spire like a needle poked at the sky, and there's another nice church called the Marienkirche.

A great many people here have Polish names, but they all swear they are true Germans. In the evenings I am eating big mounds of something called Himmel und Erde, which means 'heaven and earth' but it is really a sort of black pudding with apples and mashed potato. There's a nice kind of goulash called Pfefferpotthast, and if you want a snack you have a potato pancake with apple sauce. After every meal here you feel as if you have just eaten a medium-sized family saloon. A Morris Tourer, perhaps.

Mr Wragge is here with me. He didn't want to stay with Granny because she does things like throwing his garden fork over the wall, and threatening to get His Majesty to put him in the Tower, and once she shot him in the backside with her air rifle, and then told him not to wear grey trousers because when he was bending over she thought he was a pigeon. It was very stingy and left a big bruise, but luckily the pellet didn't penetrate. Mr Wragge wasn't being paid very much, and he is an excellent mechanic, so I persuaded him to come.

He is a great asset to us, and loves nothing more than stripping a machine down and cleaning every little piece. This place is dedicated to coal, steel and beer, but Mr Wragge is mainly interested in the beer, and is quite often 'clever side up' in the evenings. He has taken lodgings in an attic, which he seems to like very much, because he has a good view over the rooftops, and the sparrows come to his window for crumbs. He says there is one sparrow that likes to sit on his finger, but he holds it out of the window until it relieves itself, to make sure that it doesn't do so when invited into the room. He has a landlady who, he says, is 'most obliging' and I shall tell you what that means when you are a little bit older.

And when you're older, we shall be able to do as we please. But I don't want you to get older. I love you as you are. I miss you so much, and we have already lost so much time. Let's have special fun when I come to get you from school in a fortnight! Let's eat too much ice cream at funfairs! Let's go to the beach and cook sausages on a Primus in howling gales!

I hug you so tight that all the little bones in your spine go 'crack crack crack' and all the bones in your ribs too. And I tickle your feet. And I brush your hair a little bit too hard, so that the brush gets caught, and you make a face, and then I push you too high on the swings, and then I put you on my lap and get stuck halfway down the slide because my derrière's too wide.

With all my love from your best and one and only ...
Daddy

PS Yes! What wonderful news about Auntie Ottilie!

Effingham House
Bexhill-on-Sea
Sussex

12 July 1931

Darlingest Daddy,
I am just back at school and I have bad news which is that naughty Bertie told Mummy about the letter you wrote to him care of Mrs Pendennis, and now she says that we can't go next door any more, so what I did was wait at the window until I saw Mrs Pendennis in her garden, and then I ran out and opened the blue door in the wall, and I talked to her without going next door at all. Aren't I the clever one?

She came in and she went to talk to Mummy, and they were talking very loud to each other in the drawing room, but I didn't listen because I was frightened. Now Mummy says that she is not a friend of Mrs Pendennis any more, even though Mrs Pendennis used to be like an extra mother, and Mummy used to be engaged to her son.

I waited 'til Mummy went out, and then I went to talk to Mrs Pendennis at the blue door, and she was very huffy about Mummy, and said she would leave your letters and presents in a tin box just inside the door on her side, and I was to be very careful not to go and look unless I was sure that Mummy was out. She told me that she would post any letters I wrote in the holidays, and not to mind about the stamps, and I could leave them in the box, and she sends her special regards.

My best friend from last term has stopped being my best friend, and says she wants to be best friends with Helen Anstruther instead, so my new best friend is Violet Construction. It's such a funny name, but she says it's her real name and she's got to put up with it. She likes sports and reading Girls' Budgets, the same as I do, and when we are older we are going to be film stars. We are going to try for parts in the school play so we can practise. I want to learn tap dancing, but so far I have only learned waltzing, with me pretending to be the man. Violet has brown eyes and black hair and is very pretty, much prettier than me, but I don't mind.

The dorm is very cold at night, and in winter we have frost on the insides of the windows in the morning, and we have to wash with a jug of water and bowl, and it's my turn at the moment to get up early and fetch the jug of hot water and put some in each bowl, and sometimes the hot tap doesn't work, and we have to wash with cold. Brrrrr! Mrs Clodson says it will make us tough and hardy, and I suppose I might need to be tough and hardy if I am to be a film star, because I might have to be in the jungle, or learn to fall off galloping horses, or do sad scenes in the rain, because in films rain stands for tears.

We have boring old chapel twice a day, but I like the singing. I am thinking of asking to learn the piano, because the best girls sometimes accompany the hymns, and singing and playing are very good things for an actress to learn, for the stage anyway. Dearest Daddy, would you pay for my lessons? Mummy has a piano, and I can practise in the holidays, can't I? I can already play 'Frère Jacques' even though nobody taught it to me. I want to learn all those sad songs about Way Down Upon the Swanee River, and Poor Old Joe, and I am quite fond of 'Widecombe Fair' because of all the names.

I am trying extra hard in French, just to please you and so we can talk in secret, and of course I have French Bear that Gran'mère gave me when I was little. He is very worn-out, and in the holidays Mummy sewed a white patch on his arm where the stuffing was coming out, and she painted a red cross on it so that he looks as though he does first aid, and she bought me a pretend nurse's uniform for Christmas so we can be first-aiders together. Granny gave me a junior air pistol because she wants me to start helping her to shoot pigeons, but I don't really want to, and I feel sorry for the pigeons, so I am saving it for Bertie, because I expect he'll like it a lot when he's older. I don't know if you have ever noticed, but pigeon blood is very scarlet.

We play lacrosse on Wednesday afternoons, but we call it lax, and I get injured quite a lot. I had six bruises after the last game. It's the dangerousest thing for girls to do.

I can do a handstand without leaning against the wall, and I can walk on my hands from the dorm to the thunderbox on the corridor, but I only do it when I have culottes on, because otherwise everyone can see your knickers and it's not very ladylike.

I can say 'amo amas amat amamus amatis amant' and 'bella bella bella bellorum bellis bellis' very quickly, and I know nominative vocative accusative genitive and dative and ablative, and I know adverbs of manner. I hope you are proud of me. Oh, and I have found out that Timbuktu is a real place, and learned a poem by Robert Burns that goes 'Scots wha hae with Wallace bled'. I am half Scottish as you probably know.

Dearest Daddy, I think you should stop bothering to write to Bertie. He just tells Mummy, and she gives him chocolate drops for being a good boy, and then she puts your letter on the fire, so there's no point really. You should spend the extra time writing longer letters to me.

Thank you for Emil and the Detectives. I read it straight away and I like that it's not at all fairylandy, and the bad people are properly bad, and Emil got his money back in the end because of the pinholes, and then there was the reward too. If you meet Mr Erich Kästner in Germany, please tell him I would like another book about Emil, but please can it be about twins, because I do wish I had a twin instead of Bertie, who is a bit annoying. He follows me around ALL the time and tells Mummy every time I even do something innocent. Someone older would be bossy, and someone younger is just a nuisance, and that is why I would like a twin.

I am sorry that being in Germany is a trial, and I am glad to hear that Mr Wragge has a nice landlady, now that I know what a landlady is. I had to ask Mrs Clodson.

Now I have used up my letter-writing time and it's Sunday lunch. I hope it's Dead Man's Leg and custard for pudding, and not stewed plums again. For main course we always get meat in gravy with wet vegetables, and you can tell that the meat was cooked in the reign of Willy the Conk. At supper we sometimes get just two tinned tomatoes on a piece of toast.

Your half-starved loving daughter,
Esther

PS I expect you heard Ottilie's new baby is going to be called Mary, but everyone's calling it Molly already. Ottilie loves it in India. She says she's coming back for three months every year, but I'm not sure that she will, because India is rather far.

36

Oily Wragge (1)

Germany turned out to be a bleedin' nightmare, eventually, though I liked it well enough at first. The idea came up because one day I was raking the gravel round the front, when the Captain turned up on his Brough, and he had a row with his missus on the front doorstep because she said the children had gone away for the weekend, and he knew they hadn't. He was demanding the address of where they had gone, and she was stumped for an answer, so he just pushed past her and came out with a kid in each hand, but he ended up just leaving with Esther, because the little boy was tied to his mother's apron strings, and I happen to know she'd told him that motorcycles were too dangerous for little boys to go on, so he was kicking and screaming and holding on to his mum. She took him in and slammed the door, and Esther got into the sidecar good as gold and smiling all over her little face, and the Captain said to me, 'I'm sorry you had to witness that, Mr Wragge.'

I liked it that he called me Mister. Most fellows in his position would've called me 'Wragge' and have done with it, but he knew I'd been a warrant officer in the Norfolks, and I was entitled to be Mister if anyone was. I'd had a conversation with him, and he said, 'I'm going to call you Mr Wragge, if you don't mind, because somehow I can't bring myself to call you "Oily",' and I said, 'And if you don't mind, as you're an officer and a gentleman, I'll call you Sir.' So we shook hands on it, and that's how it stayed to the day I last clapped eyes on him.

After Mr McCosh died of happiness on the golf course and after Lady Mary left, there was no one except Cookie in the house, and Miss Rosie and the tiddlers, and it was always Mr McCosh that kept his old lady on the straight and narrow, but after he died there was no one to keep her anywhere near normal. She did what she bloody well liked, and after that day when I was bending over and she shot me in the arse with her air rifle, and told me I shouldn't be wearing trousers that made me look like a pigeon, I decided I was going the moment something came up.

He wasn't a Captain by the way, he was a Flight Lieutenant, but he didn't like the RFC becoming the RAF, so he stuck to Captain, because that's what he was when he was a soldier and the RFC was still a corps of the army.

Anyway, he told me that he was going to Germany to set up a motorcycles business, and said, 'You're an excellent mechanic, Mr Wragge, why don't you come too?' so I jumped at the chance, didn't I? I'd heard from an old mucker that German women were a damn fine thing. 'Thing' isn't the word he used though; it was another word beginning with F. It turned out to be true.

The Captain had a spare Brough, and we drove them all the way to Hunland, loaded up with spares in case we broke down, but we never did. I swear those Broughs were the best thing on two wheels ever.

Captain Pitt got lodgings with a professor, and I was proper envious because he had two daughters, a bit young though. I got a room in a house with a landlady who rented most of the rooms to single men like me, and what you might call semi-professional girls. This landlady used to have a rich husband, and that's why she had this enormous house, but he was killed in the Spring Offensive in 1918, and now she was forced to let out all the rooms, and we had to share the kitchen and bathroom, which were a terrible mess, and we were always squabbling about who stole someone else's soap or bread, or whatever.

I wouldn't say she was a madam, this landlady, and these girls didn't have pimps as far as I could see. They were doing what they did because they had jobs that hardly paid them anything, and Germany was a right mess in those days. The money was worth less than pebbles, and you had to spend it the moment you had it before the value fell again, and you were better off stealing a chicken and buying things with the eggs. There were three girls I got on with, and I'd say that one was a full-time no-nonsense prossie, and she wore red shoes so the punters'd know she could do discipline, and there was a sort of part-timer who did it mostly for fun and got paid in presents and suchlike, and the third was a right goer who just did it for a laugh and had as many boyfriends as she liked. I got fond of those girls, and we'd sit in the kitchen swigging beer and smoking ourselves silly, but I didn't ever hop between the sheets with them because I was concerned about getting the clap again. I got it in Belgaum, back in India, before the war, and it was a palaver getting rid of it. For all I know those German girls were clean, but I wasn't risking it again. It was like pissing broken glass, and they put a contraption down my pisshole that opened up like a bleeding umbrella, and then they pulled it out. It was a scouring. Makes my eyes water just thinking about it.

I was doing it with the landlady. She was called Baldhart, and she was in her thirties and still firing on all six cylinders. She had lovely brown hair with golden bits, sort of streaky, and her nose turned up, and she had these hazel eyes that changed colour depending on the angle, and long thin fingers that were always a bit on the cold side, and that was something I liked, and she had lips that were small but sort of plump at the same time, and I'd say that everything about her was just about exactly the right size, and you know what? It wasn't long before she was saying '*Oily, ich liebe dich*' and at first I was thinking 'I know you like a bit of dick' but soon enough she got through to me, and it was really the first time in my life, because I never did feel that way about my wife before she went off with that Gordon Highlander. I'd married her because she got pregnant, and now I'm not even sure it was my tackle that did the damage.

Baldhart used to sing that song from *The Blue Angel*, you know, that flick where Marlene Dietrich gets her legs out. She must have seen it lots of times, because she knew all the words, and when she'd had a few schnapps she'd light an imaginary cigarette and sing it to me. '*Ich bin von Kopf bis Fuss auf Liebe eingestellt, den dass ist meine Welt, und sonst gar nichts. Das ist − was soll ich machen? − Mein Natur …*'

Well, she was a lovely woman, the best I ever had, so I was contented in Hunland at first, but Captain Pitt wasn't. He was glum most of the time, and only perked up when he was going home to see his kids, which he did quite a lot. I was left alone in Krautland for a month at a time, hardly speaking a word of Kraut. Of course I learned all the names for the parts of motor-cycles at the workshop, and the girls taught me everything filthy I needed to know. After a while I twigged, from little things that he said, that Captain Pitt'd been in love, and she'd packed him in, and that was why he'd done this madcap thing and come out to Germany, just to get away. He was a man in pain, and he talked like someone who knows that everything's got pickled up, because he said things like 'If I'd stayed in Ceylon, I'd probably be an estate manager by now', and he'd look into the distance and sigh, and say, 'You've no idea how glorious it was in Ceylon.'

He liked going to Berlin. It was really just a great big poxed-out whorehouse, but as far as I know he just wanted to see Josephine Baker and La Jana, and Margo Lion, and he was quite keen on all the plays, and once there was that little boy called Yehudi Menuhin who played the fiddle like a bleedin' angel, or so he said, and nowadays he's very famous. I remember how chuffed he was with *The Threepenny Opera*, and he knew all the songs from it. He must have seen it five times. Both of us learned most of our Kraut from songs. There was a stone lion in Berlin and everybody said it roared when a virgin went past it. It never roared, wouldn't you know.

We didn't do much business. I mean, Germany was down shit creek without a paddle and no leg to stand on, everyone'd lost all their savings twice, and once you'd added on the transport costs, there wasn't anybody who could buy a British motorcycle, no matter how good they were. And it was pretty much the same the other way round. The Huns made perfectly good motorcycles themselves, same as we did, but it cost a lot to get them back to Blighty, so we didn't sell many. We turned over a few DKWs and BMWs. I always liked those horizontal engines. The bike leaned over differently, depending on whether it was a right- or a left-hand bend. That was the torque effect, that was.

Captain Pitt's two friends, Willy and Fritzl, were a right pair of characters. He'd captured them in the war, and they'd become friends, and to begin with they just talked about what they'd done in the war, and about all the technical details of the planes they knew about, and they'd crack open a bottle of white after work, and toast all the dead aces together, and stagger home a bit late with their arms around each other's shoulders. I reckon that for them it was like being back in 1917.

Willy and Fritzl were proud of Captain Pitt, because the Captain was still pretty famous, and it wasn't too bad, having been captured by an ace and then become friends afterwards. It was all chivalry and knights of the air. I do remember one night in the pub when they got a bit wild and they started re-enacting an air battle using their chairs as aircraft, and ratatat-tatting like kids, and then the landlord called the Schupo and we all got slung out and we rode back into town blind drunk, and Willy and Fritzl stopped by crashing into the wall of the workshop and bent up their forks. Willy went over the bars and cracked his head on the wall, and he was out cold.

There was this stupid song about how my parrot doesn't eat hard-boiled eggs, and Willy and Fritzl did it as a duet, and they crossed their eyes and waggled their heads like idiots, and it always cracked me up. I can still sing it. '*Mein Papagai frisst keine harten Eier …*'

Those were the days.

Then in 1933 Hitler got elected, and it wasn't long before he'd given himself the two top jobs all at once. He was fond of referendums, that one. He got the people to do all his dirty work, and the mad bastards went along with it and gave him what he wanted.

You can sort of understand it. I mean, they'd been having an election every five minutes, and there was a dozen parties to vote for, and there was fighting in the streets, and they'd had that second bloody great depression in 1929, and there were queues for the dole a mile long, and there was eight million unemployed, and there was a plague of suicides. I think it was in 1932, they had that Bloody Sunday in Hamburg and it was a big barney between the National Socialists and the Commies, and sixteen people got killed. It was shocking. What they had in common was not being arsed with democracy, and wanting to knock it on the head. It was like they couldn't cope with not having a Kaiser. That's what Captain Pitt thought. We used to talk about all this stuff when we were on our tea breaks, and I'd say I got my opinions from him to begin with, until I knew more about it myself.

Well, Adolf was the Kaiser all right, multiplied by ten. Everything happened so fast. They dumped the League of Nations, Parliament got elbowed out, and they banned criticism, and they fired all the people who weren't like them, and the Bolshies started disappearing into camps, and a lot of people got banged up for their own protection or to stop them doing anything evil before they'd even thought of doing it, and they started their war on unemployment, and people left for the countryside in droves to do land help and labour service, and what have you. Then some clot set fire to the Reichstag, so they gave the rozzers a lot of extra clout, and Willy and Fritzl got all fired up and wrote to Himmler offering to execute the arsonist. And then there was the secret police on top of the Schupos and the Kripos, and this was the Gestapo, and you couldn't fart without some idiot denouncing you. It was Adolf giving the whole country the biggest kick up the backside it ever had, and it sort of worked. After three years, you wouldn't believe the difference. Even the Bolshies were impressed.

All around you people were like drunks, talking bollocks about how the Germans was the bee's knees, and everyone else was dross, as if they weren't just a bunch of loonies who went around starting wars. And they kept going on about how they hadn't really lost the last war, and it was all because of a stab in the back by the Jewboy Bolshies. We had these parades of SA Brownshirts, with their torches and their speeches from balconies. And I heard those shirts were only brown because brown was the cheapest cloth. Baldhart was going to join the NSF, which was the National Socialist Womanhood, because she was fired up like everyone else, but in the end she didn't, and I'll tell you why.

It was because the prossie woman in our house didn't give one of her clients what he was hoping for, and did give him something else he wasn't hoping for, and he went to the Gestapo. He said she was a streetwalker, which wasn't legal by then, even though she wasn't, and he said the house was a brothel, which it hardly was, and he said the girls were sleeping with foreigners and Jews and it was causing racial defilement and contamination, because what would happen if one of them got pregnant and the kid was half un-German?

The only thing he said that was true was that the girl was giving out the clap. Oh, and the girls slept with whoever they liked because if they liked someone, they wouldn't have given a toss even if he'd been an Eskimo.

Well, the Gestapo liked a bit of drama, so they always kicked the door down, and if it was open, they closed it, and then they kicked it down. And they always came in the middle of the night. So that's what happened. We were all woken up by shouting and crashing about, and Baldhart and me got dragged out of bed, and all the girls got dragged out of bed, and the men in the house too, and we got stuffed into a couple of vans and we got taken to their interrogation place that was like a bunch of sheds with a barbed-wire fence. We were there for flipping weeks, and this stupid sour-faced woman turned up in a doctor's coat, with her tape measures and calipers to measure our heads and the lengths of our noses.

It turned out that this place was for prossies, pimps, gypsies, tramps, abortionists, beggars, professional criminals, unemployable pissheads and people with the clap. They hadn't really got started on poofters, lesbos and pornographers by then.

I got off for shagging Baldhart because I was the right racial type and 'capable of Germanisation', and Captain Pitt somehow managed to find us and give those Gestapo a proper bollocking, waving his passport with that stuff in it about how His Majesty Requests and Requires, and talking about the War of Jenkins' Ear, and then Willy and Fritzl turned up and said that as they were good Nazis and had the papers to prove it, they wanted me back because the business was suffering.

Eventually it became clear that we had all been denounced just out of malice, and they went and got that man and put him in a re-education camp for three months. Served him right. I hope he got re-educated. From what I know now, he might never have come out of there at all, though.

And now I'll tell you why Baldhart never did join the National Socialist Womanhood. It was because the three girls we were so fond of didn't come back for a few more days. They got given this long lecture about sexual anarchy, and racial suicide and biological duty, and blood and honour, and Treason against the Race, and hereditary criminality, and then when they got back, it turned out they'd all been tied down and sterilised, because they'd had too many boyfriends and some of them were probably Jewish Bolsheviks, and it was to prevent racial contamination.

It knocked the stuffing out of them. I mean, a girl dreams of having tiddlers one day, doesn't she? Even a prossie.

37

Sandwiches

Gaskell and Christabel spent the whole of 4 October 1936 in Hexham making sandwiches, wrapping up apples and baking fairy cakes.

The women, now both in their early forties, had weathered well the storms and vicissitudes of their unconventional relationship. Christabel's long and occasional relationship with Daniel had survived the years of his being with Mary and then in Germany, because neither of them expected anything more than the pleasure and affection they could afford to give, and their weeks apart had always served merely to awaken an eagerness to see each other again. For Christabel, Daniel filled in the gaps left by Gaskell, who was as much of a husband to her as a woman could be.

As for Gaskell, she entirely failed to be jealous of Daniel. She adored him. He treated her exactly as she had always wanted to be treated. They went out shooting together, and Daniel was not ashamed to admit that she was the better shot. They painted stumps on a blank wall of the great house and bowled balls at each other, but most of all, they went flying. Daniel's aircraft were now at least eighteen years old, and had to be handled very tenderly, so for the most part they were lovingly kept idle in a barn on the estate. Daniel thought they were probably unsaleable because of their obsolescence, and they had even gone so far as to plan a Viking funeral for them, but on the evening of the ceremony, they had not had the heart to douse them with petrol. They went down to Shoreham and came back with a Southern Martlet, a lovely little biplane for stunting in, and a little while later they bought a Miles Falcon, because it was very fast and there was even room for the children. Gaskell had a plan to fly it to China, which, fortunately, she never had time to attempt because of all her artistic commissions, and then the outbreak of war.

The affection between these three was cemented by the children. Felix was now eight years old, and had been despatched to Dunhurst in Hampshire. This was a Montessori school attached to Bedales, itself a 'progressive' school which specialised in the education of atheists, liberals, bohemians, artistic types, the children of the louche, and stray Russian and European intellectuals. It did not suit Felix very well, as he was a quiet and conservative little boy. In later life he would look back on his education at these establishments as a somewhat perplexing sojourn in a menagerie, relieved only by being taken on frequent exeats by his particularly glamorous, kind and affectionate godfather, who treated him to bangers and mash with onion gravy in roadside cafes, and knew everything about aeroplanes. Felix lived for the holidays, when he would be back on the estate in Hexham, roving the increasingly wild grounds with a catapult in his pocket and a parcel of sandwiches, having been told not to worry about coming back until it was dark. Inside the house, Gaskell and Christabel got on with their nude portraits and strangely angled photographs.

Felicity was six years old, and sometimes went to stay with her Aunt Sophie in Blackheath, where she sat alongside the other little ones in the dame school, and learned to do sums on a slate. She listened wide-eyed as Sophie gleefully related all the most horrible episodes from the Bible, such as the decapitation of St John the Baptist, or Jael's murder of Sisera by driving a tent peg through his head whilst he slept. Sometimes she won Sophie's weekly prize for the most outrageous word of the week. Quite often Fairhead would come in and sit with the children, a cigarette smoking in the centre of his lips, to listen to his wife, and Crusty the dog would slumber under Sophie's desk, occasionally being startled awake by its own farts.

Felicity was a vivacious child, with blue eyes and black hair, who would, at the end of each day, count up the number of new bruises on her limbs and then invite people to inspect them. She was always up trees, or up ladders, or getting her head stuck between the railings, or losing one wellington boot in a dungheap. Daniel loved her clear, rippling laughter, and the way that she would run to him and leap up into his arms, putting hers around his neck, and plastering his face with kisses. She would be joining

Felix at Dunhurst in a year's time, and it would suit her very much better.

If there was ever a bone of contention between Gaskell and Christabel, it was because neither of them was particularly adept at avoiding entanglements with other women, and they had adopted the noble but inadvisable policy of being completely honest about it. Their artistic milieu consisted almost entirely of sexually polymorphic characters with interesting inclinations, and it was all but impossible not to get drawn in, because it was such fun, and, at least when one was tipsy, seemed so harmless at first. Their squabbles would end with Gaskell storming out of the house to drive her Bentley into the distance at suicidal speed, whilst Christabel sat up all night, sipping sherry and listening for the sound of the engine, hoping to see at last the sweep of the lights across the curtains as the car turned at the curve of the drive. As far as men were concerned, Christabel remained faithful to Daniel, as she always knew she would.

Christabel and Gaskell thought of themselves as socialists, but were in reality libertarian conservatives. They believed that one should do pretty much whatever one wants, but there should be a gentleman in Number Ten Downing Street, who speaks in properly constructed sentences, and that this gentleman should be paternally concerned with the welfare of the people. Accordingly, on this day, they were driving down to Consett, with its belching steelworks and permanent Martian cloud of red dust, and then on to Chester-le-Street, in order to be there for when Ellen Wilkinson led the Jarrow Crusaders in.

They were going to park up the Bentley at the Church Institute, and use it as a sort of kiosk, to serve cakes and apples, and partridge or pheasant sandwiches to the hungry and weary marchers. There would be a choice of hot tea, chilled champagne or home-made ginger beer from their battery of Thermos vacuum flasks.

38

Daniel, Felix and Felicity

D aniel came home early for Christmas in 1937. The entire
world seemed to be in a state of hysteria, and Daniel was
profoundly worried by what he was reading in the newspapers
and hearing on the radio sets in roadside cafes. It had been a
terrible year in almost every way imaginable. In the USSR Stalin
was continuing the show trials and mass killings that were to
make him one of the greatest murderers in history and the execu-
tioner of the Communist Ideal; Spain was in a state of civil war,
in which one side was killing priests and the other was killing
intellectuals; China had been invaded by Japan and subjected to
a campaign of sustained atrocity; Shanghai had been burned to
the ground by incendiary bombs; in May the *Hindenburg* had
exploded into flame in New Jersey; in September, Mussolini and
Hitler, equally fired up in their competitive quest for empire, had
filled a stadium with one million people at the Field of May in
Berlin; at home, Sir Oswald Mosley's blackshirts were meeting
violent resistance during their parading through London, and in
Liverpool Mosley himself had accidentally boosted his public
support by being knocked unconscious by a rock; Ramsay
MacDonald had died, loved and respected by everybody except
his own Labour Party.

The only good news was that Great Britain had acquired a
new monarch who was worthy of the throne, with a common-
sensical Queen beside him who knew how to make their lives
enjoyable.

Just before Daniel had left for Christmas, a Christian family in
Silesia had been successfully prosecuted for refusing to bring up
their children as Nazis, and it was this that had finally convinced
Daniel that his remaining days in Germany were few.

He had been writing to various motoring, aviation and engineering companies, offering himself for employment, whilst also

looking into the possibility of setting up a new company himself, which he envisaged as being somewhere equidistant between Eltham and Hexham. So far, he had received encouraging responses from de Havilland, Supermarine, Triumph and Bristol, and discouraging ones from Ariel, Matchless and Nuffield. Brough's said they would have loved to have him back, but that their future was at present too uncertain to know what their staffing requirements were likely to be. They had already been approached by the government with a view to suspending the manufacture of motorcycles, and converting to war work. Now that the Royal Air Force was being rapidly doubled in size, Daniel had also written to the Ministry of War to find out if he could be of any service.

The one thing holding him back was the residual loyalty he owed to Willy and Fritzl, and to Oily Wragge, who wanted to remain in Dortmund because he was happily embedded with his landlady, and greatly enjoyed his work.

Daniel himself had grown tired of Nazi Germany. Its philosophical certainties deeply perplexed and annoyed him, and it was burdensome having to keep one's mouth shut. The Germans were suffering from a kind of drunkenness that resembled the revelations of someone who has been perched on a bar stool for eight hours, sorted out the universe in its entirety, and finally reached the stage of righteous bellicosity.

In Germany he had found no lasting love, and everything that had been fun in the early years had become either stale or forbidden. Furthermore, he had not been making any more money than he could have done if he had stayed at home, and this fact alone made all his efforts over the past few years seem wasted. All he had done was make it difficult to be with the ones he loved. He told himself that never again would he allow his life to veer off course on account of a broken heart. From now on he was to be immune. He would love when he loved, and wave a resigned but cheerful farewell when it was over. When he thought of Mary FitzGerald these days, it was without rancour or regret.

He had begun to feel a deep ache of nostalgia for home, a longing to be closer to his children, and was deeply tired of the thousands of miles he had to drive every year, along the same old routes, just in order to keep the love alive.

On the estate in Hexham, Daniel walked through the woodland with Felix holding one hand, and Felicity holding the other. Felix was nine, and Felicity was seven. Behind them by fifty yards strolled Gaskell and Christabel, earnestly discussing a forthcoming exhibition in Dublin. They were both in a fever of excitement and anticipation because the photographs and portraits included many nudes in suggestive postures, and the thought of being arrested and deported by the Garda for obscenity was wildly entertaining. The exhibition was to be private, but there were certainly ways to get themselves into trouble all the same. Gaskell thought it might be a fine wheeze to write an anonymous letter of protest to Cardinal Joseph MacRory, just to get the ball rolling.

The children's hands felt very small in Daniel's, and their noses were red and dripping on account of the December weather. There was a sharp north-east wind, and a cold spit of rain.

'Uncle Daniel,' said Felix, 'is it true there's going to be a war?'

'I think so. But if there is, I hope that it happens soon.'

'Why?'

'Because you two would be too young to fight in it. You'd be fairly safe up here, I would think.'

'I like fighting,' said Felicity. 'At school I'm always in trouble for fighting. I hurt my thumb once when I bashed Rebecca Stephens for stamping on my teddy.'

'You punched someone? Gracious me! What a girl! When you punch someone, you should always tuck your thumb away behind your knuckles. But you wouldn't like the bullets and bombs kind of fighting,' said Daniel. 'That's almost entirely about who's lucky and who isn't.'

'Will you be fighting?' asked Felicity.

'I hope so. But they will certainly tell me I'm too old, and then I'll have to make a big fuss.'

'Why do you want to fight, Uncle Daniel? I thought you said it wasn't nice with bullets and bombs.'

'It's the most important thing you can do, fighting for what you know is right. Or what you think is right. And anyway, I'm forty-five years old. I've had an interesting life, and it wouldn't be too awful to leave a bit early. I don't really matter any more.'

'I don't want you to fight,' said Felicity.

'If you do fight, will you keep me some bullet cases, Uncle Daniel?'

'Of course I will.'

'Uncle Daniel?'

'Yes, my love?'

'Why've we got you instead of a father? Where's our father? Felix and me want to go and find him. When we're grown up. And where's our real mother?'

'You should say "Felix and I" when Felix and you are the subject of the sentence,' said Daniel. 'And I have no idea who your real mother and father are. But Auntie Christabel might know. And she might know what happened to them.'

'And we want to know,' said Felix, 'if we have the same father and mother. Because if we're adopted, why do we look the same?'

'And Auntie Gaskell is a funny kind of aunt,' said Felicity, following her own train of thought.

'What do you mean? She's the best aunt possible.'

'She's more like a "he", isn't she?' said Felix. 'She smokes a pipe and goes out shooting, and she's got a great big man's car. And she plays cricket.'

'She's still a she, and we all love her, whatever she's like or not like, don't we?'

The children nodded, and Daniel said, 'Ooh, look, there's a pair of buzzards.' He pointed out the two enormous speckled birds that were wheeling above, calling to each other. They reminded him of two RE8s on a reconnaissance.

Felicity said, 'Aunt Christabel lets us call her Mummy.'

'Or Mum,' added Felix.

'Does she?'

Felicity looked up and said 'Yes, she does. Uncle Daniel?'

'Yes, my love?'

'Can we call you Daddy?'

Daniel stood stock-still, his heart racing in his chest. 'Why don't we ask Auntie Christabel and Auntie Gaskell if it's all right with them? We wouldn't want to upset them, would we? Perhaps you could call me Daddiel, or Dannydad, or something.'

'Don't be silly,' said Felicity firmly. 'Those aren't words.'

Felix put his hands in his pockets and screwed up his face thoughtfully. 'You're the same as a daddy though, aren't you? You give us florins and birthday and Christmas presents, and you're here an awful lot, and you take us out and hold our hands and tell us to look right, look left, look right again. I can't tell the difference. What's the difference between you and a proper daddy?'

'And,' said Felicity, 'Esther and Bertie look like you, and you're their daddy. And you look like us. Who would know that you actually weren't?'

39

Oily Wragge (2)

It was mad, and it all got madder. The Krauts even started to have a special day called 'Eintopftag' and on that day you only ate one meal, and it was stew, and you gave the money you saved to the SS who came out rattling their tins, and it was supposed to go to something called 'Winterhelp' but it went for Hitlerhelp, in my estimation. And the police had a day every year, and it turned into a week once. There they were, smiling and shaking hands and collecting money, and all the time there were stories everyone knew about, which was the police overturning court decisions, and doing torture, and taking gyppos into the woods and making people disappear, and getting rid of degenerates and parasites and Poles and Jehovah's Witnesses, and talking about riff-raff who were unfit for community life, and poofters 'committing suicide' in prison. Then they started castrating the poofters, and suddenly if you nicked something, or if you couldn't be arsed with the Hitlergruss, it was high treason.

I don't know why we didn't leave sooner. Well, I do. In fact we started talking about leaving after National Boycott Day, when you were supposed to avoid any Jewish shops. Captain Pitt said it was all getting out of hand and going too far, and we should pack up and go. He said there was going to be another war, because no one was bothering to prevent rearmament. He started having big rows with Willy and Fritzl, and it got in the way of running the business. The Captain gave up all that wandering about in the countryside singing songs. Those two wanted to have another bash at War and Captain Pitt didn't endear himself by telling them they were a pair of loonies. Those two turned into parrots, just repeating slogans.

It was my fault that we didn't leave sooner. I didn't want to leave Baldhart behind, and the Captain said, 'Well, Mr Wragge, why don't you just marry her? Then we can take her with us.'

I said, 'Sir, you know I'm married already, and I never got round to divorcing the cow,' and he says, 'Yes, but we can probably get it all sorted out at the Consulate,' but I never did a thing because to tell the truth I'm not the marrying kind. Always got one eye open for what might be better, just coming along round the corner. We could have had a Kraut wedding and no one would've known about the last one, would they? And she would have got a visa. But I didn't do it. And anyway, she wasn't ready to give everything up and sell her precious house and go to Blighty. She didn't speak English, and she was doing all right, and she had her friends right there, in the house with her.

The other thing is, we were earning good money, and that's a bit hard to give up. Adolf got a grip, and fixed all the wages and prices, and put half the blokes in the army, and suddenly everybody had a job and a little bit of cash.

And another thing, Captain Pitt was exceedingly fond of that Jewish family he was staying with, and he was worried about them all the time. I know they loved him back, and those two girls used to look at him like he was John Gilbert or something. I don't know if he ever had his way with them. He was somewhat lethal with women, but they were a bit young, and he wasn't much of a chancer.

Everything got turned around in about 1935. There was a law all about the protection of German Blood and Honour. Herr Wolff got sacked from his job, and his mates who sacked him told him confidentially that he could continue to teach his Jewish students at his own house as long as they didn't know about it, and so that's what he did. It was proper lucky that his books had all been translated, because that way he got money from America. He gave me a couple of books, because he wanted to show his gratitude, and in the end books were all he had left. Look. This one's called *The Analysis of Atomic Propositions*, and this one's *The Nature of Scientific Progress*, and this one here is called *Rudolf Carnap and the Epistemological Paradox of Logical Positivism*. I mean, look at the first sentence. I don't even know what a proposition is if it isn't making a suggestive suggestion. I can't make head nor tail of it. I can hardly read anyway. But that professor was a nice old codger and he wrote me a dedication in each one, and that's the only bit of those books I ever get round to reading. Captain Pitt had actually met someone that the professor used to write to, on a train to Cambridge. Small world.

It was at that time that Captain Pitt started telling the Prof that he had to leave, but the Prof said that Adolf was too nasty and too mad to last for very long. The Captain said, 'You're wrong there.'

But the Prof was like Baldhart. He had a nice house he'd lived in for years, and he didn't want to go when he had nothing to go to. He said, 'But this is my homeland; I'm a Jewish German, not a German Jew,' and when he said that, he had tears in his eyes, and he had the Iron Cross to prove it, always pinned to his chest to give the bastards who abused him something to think about. He just stayed there and twiddled his thumbs whilst all his mates, like that Einstein with the mad hair, got up and left. The Captain said he should apply for a job at a proper posh university, like Princeton or Cambridge.

Well, it just got worse. The Prof got so poor that he had to sell his car. What happened was that Jews suddenly had to have a special number plate, so that when you drove around people could spit at you and throw stones, so what Captain Pitt did was that he bought that car off Herr Wolff, and then lent it back to him. The Prof had to go and register his wealth, and it was obvious they were going to take it off him one of these days.

They had a damned great bonfire of paintings in the square in Dortmund. Jewish and Degenerate Art, it supposedly was. And then they burned a load of books, and the Prof said they even burned his, and he said actually there was no point in burning books, because you'd never get every copy, would you? And you'd never get every Jew, would you?

And all the time the people got madder and madder, doing physical jerks in public and putting up statues of blokes with huge muscles and tiny dicks, and marching around to brass bands and singing songs, and they took a lump out of Czechoslovakia, and the SS wiped out the SA, just massacred all the leaders. One day I suddenly noticed that all the little carts that sold books in the streets had gone, and you could only buy one newspaper when there used to be hundreds. I liked those little carts. I liked looking at that Gothic script I couldn't make head nor tail of.

A lot of Jews became U-boats. That's what they called them. They just slipped out of sight under the surface. But you couldn't do that if you had a wife and two daughters.

What did it in the end was Reichskristallnacht. I heard it all going on, and Baldhart and I stayed in because we didn't like what we were seeing from the windows. There were trucks of Nazis going round smashing all the shops and windows on Jewish premises, and then getting back on the trucks and going off to smash up somewhere else. There was shouting and jeering and wailing and crashing and banging, and smoke drifting through the streets, and the police did absolutely nothing. Just folded their arms and stood and watched. A lot of Jews got beaten up, including the Prof, and Captain Pitt got whacked on the head with a cosh when he tried to intervene. He's still got the scar on his forehead where he fell down and got cut. Then they gave him a kicking, and then they took the car. They didn't smash it up or anything, they just stole it. It was a Hansa-Lloyd, really beautiful it was, and it was Herr Wolff's pride and joy. Everything in that big beautiful house did get smashed, though, and luckily the girls and the mother were up in the attic behind the chimney stack under a heap of old carpets, because God knows what might have been done to them otherwise.

It was the worst thing I can remember that didn't actually happen in a war. And you know what? Hitler said he was going to fine the Jews a billion marks to pay for all the repairs. Well, I suppose he had a sense of humour.

It was after that that the Gestapo turned up at the workshop and demanded to see Captain Pitt. They didn't kick the door down for once because we had big double doors and they were open. We had about ten men working for us by then, and they all just stopped work and looked up with their spanners in their hands.

There were three Gestapo, and one was tall and thin and one was a bit short and fat, and the other had glassy eyes, like he was on something, and they walked straight up to Captain Pitt and gave him the Hitlergruss, and he just held out his hand for them to shake, and that got them confused, but it softened them up, and they shook it anyway, and they said, '*Herr Kapitän*, we have a proposition. Either you help us with the Luftwaffe, or we lock you up, or you get on your motorcycle and go home,' and Captain Pitt said, 'Where's your warrant?' and the thin man reached inside his coat and brought out a pistol. He waved it in the air and smiled, and said, 'We are the Gestapo. Here is my warrant, *Herr Kapitän*.' Then he pointed it at the Captain's face, smiled again, and said, 'My friends here also have a warrant', and he turned to them and said, '*Nicht wahr?*' and they smiled and took out their pistols.

'You've come too late,' said the Captain.

'Too late?' said the thin man.

'Yes,' said the Captain, 'I'd already decided to leave.'

'*Das ist aber schade*,' said the thin man. 'You would have had a good welcome in the Luftwaffe,' and he put his gun back in his pocket.

'I'll be gone in a week,' said the Captain.

'And are you taking this man with you,' he said, nodding his chin at me, and I said, 'Of course I'm going. If he goes, I go.' My Kraut was pretty good by then, so I said it in Kraut, you understand.

After that it was a mad rush. We didn't get on with Willy and Fritzl any more, because you couldn't talk things over with them. They just shouted and strutted about and talked a load of balls because they'd got that Hitler up their backsides like they'd sat on hedgehogs, and they went on and on at Captain Pitt about how he shouldn't be lodging with Jews. There was no more getting pissed together and it wasn't fun any more. It was just business. At least they were decent enough to go to the bank and they got enough cash to buy the Captain out of the business, and they handed it over with a little bow and without a word, and that was the end of nigh on twenty years' friendship.

We spent a few hours getting the Broughs shipshape, and then the Captain went home to the Wolffs.

It turned out that those same three Gestapo had turned up at the Wolffs' and told them to get out of the house because they were enemies of the state, and the house was going to be sold at auction. And then the thin one got out forty marks, and he gave ten to each of them, and he said, 'That's for the house, because when you leave you're only allowed ten marks each.'

So the Wolffs had a week to sell just about everything they had, and obviously they got bugger all because everyone knew they were desperate, and there was a glut on the market because of all the other Jews having to bugger off, and people wouldn't give them anything anyway because their stuff was contaminated with Jewishness. Luckily that Herr Wolff wasn't stupid, and he'd been taking money out of the bank for a year and hiding it away, and this is what we did: he could only take out ten marks, but me and the Captain could take out as much as we wanted, so when we were getting the Broughs ready we stashed all his lucre inside panels, and we folded it up and put it down inside the forks, and we even took the tyres off and put notes between the inner tubes and the outer, and we found plenty of scope on the sidecars. The Captain welded false floors into both of them. Those Broughs were mobile bank vaults by the time we finished.

Herr Wolff wanted to go to Palestine, but it cost something like a thousand quid that you had to hand over to the Brits, and everyone else was asking for visas and having waiting lists and demanding payments, and it was just impossible, so the Captain went to the British Consul, who was weighted down already with people wanting visas, with damn great queues going round the block, and half of them had musical instrument cases in their hands, but luckily that Consul knew about the Captain because he was famous for being an ace, and the Captain had what you might call the habit of command, and he harassed that Consul until he had visas for the Wolffs. He said he had a guaranteed offer of employment for Herr Wolff back in Blighty, because there was a terrible great shortage of logical positivists in the Midlands. Of course that Consul didn't have a clue what he was talking about, and he got so fed up with the embuggerance he was getting from the Captain that he came up with visas in a couple of days.

There were four Wolffs and two of us, and that meant three on each Brough, with one on the pillion and another in the sidecar. We couldn't take hardly any luggage, and we couldn't take Baldhart even if we'd wanted to. We had to get those Jews out, that was the important thing. And Baldhart wouldn't have come anyway. She didn't have a passport, and she was still thinking everything would be all right, and she wasn't very short of cash any more, and she didn't speak a word of English, or even French, and by that time a lot of the shine had worn off, and we were just like any other couple, sort of just rubbing along.

Even so, we spent that last week in bed, because suddenly it all means more when one of you's about to go, and on the last night she took that rubber off me and said, 'Shall I wash it as usual, or shall I just throw it away?' and I said, 'Wash it, because I'm a coming back after the war,' and she said, 'What war?' and I said, '*Liebchen*, you know there's going to be a war,' and she hung her head and started to cry.

Well, I can't cope with a weeping woman, it makes me choke, and I started to feel sorry for her. I stroked her hair and I said, '*Ich liebe dich*,' and you know what? It was actually the first time I ever said it, in any language, and she said, '*Ich weiss es. Ich liebe dich auch.*'

I said, 'After the war I'll come back and find you, and we'll get married, because I can't imagine being wed to anyone but you.' And there were tears in my eyes.

'It's not too late to have children,' she said, and she gave me a little smile. 'I think I could have one.'

I nodded at that ugly old rubber that had done us some good service over the years, and said, 'Might as well throw that away then.'

And there we were, pissed and in a state of nature, all clasped together tight, crying, and saying, 'After the war, after the war, after the war', and when I left at dawn she was still fast asleep, and I kissed her on the temple, and I had this ring I'd bought from Mrs Wolff to help her out when she had no money for food, and I left it there for Baldhart on her dressing table.

40

Oily Wragge (3)

I had Herr Wolff and one daughter on my Brough, and the Captain had the other daughter and Frau Wolff, and we rode across the Rhineland. That countryside was just about as beautiful as I have ever seen in my life, what with castles up on hills, and old towns sitting like ducks on the edges of rivers, and all those vineyards, but it was seething with soldiers and military trucks, and that's when I fully realised, with absolutely certainty, that it was war again. It was proof enough.

It pelted with rain a lot of the time, and when it got too bad, we just stopped, because you can't keep going with rain running down your goggles, and the Captain and I were used to all that kind of thing, but the Wolffs just got too miserable. The girls quite liked all the riding, but the older Wolffs hated it. They'd been used to a nice big limousine, hadn't they? The girls went pillion, and the Wolffs went in the sidecars, and what little luggage there was was strapped to the racks on the back end of the side-cars, and we had throw-overs between the seats on the Broughs. We did everything in hops, quite a long way each time, but not too far. Luckily there were lots of barns, and some of the farmers were friendly, at least 'til they realised the Wolffs were Jews. I'd say they'd caught the sickness in the countryside even worse than they had in towns. Some of the villages had signs up that said 'Jews Unwelcome'.

The Captain said it was nice having a lovely young girl up behind him for hundreds of miles, with her arms around his waist. I got the second-best girl as my pillion, surprise surprise, but still, I was happy enough.

We went through Essen and Duisburg, not too far really, and then when we got to the Kraut side of Venlo, the Captain said we were going south and over a smaller border post. He said the little ones out in the sticks were much easier to get through. By the time we'd got close to Venlo the roads were full of poor exhausted stragglers with their cardboard cases and bicycles and even wheelbarrows, and they were all headed for the border like us. I was right sorry I couldn't give anyone a lift, they were that pathetic.

The Captain took us a few miles south and then down a road called the Rabenstrasse, and there wasn't much going on at that border post. There was a guard reading the *Völkischer Beobachter* and another one eating a sandwich, and one on the barrier, and he hadn't even shaved properly, the lazy bastard. He wasn't soldier-like.

Well, they looked at the passports, and the Captain even had two, because he was half French, and they looked at the visas the Wolffs had, and then they didn't bother me and the Captain because at that time Adolf was still thinking we were going to be on his side. Exactly the same mistake as the Kaiser. They tipped everything out of the luggage bags and the Wolffs' pockets, and they searched inside their clothes, but all they found was ten marks each. And then the half-shaved one said, 'I'm sorry, *Herr Kapitän*, you and your friend are all right, but these *Untermenschen* don't have the proper exit papers.'

'What exit papers?' asks the Captain. 'I thought you wanted the Jews to leave,' and the guard says, 'They still need proper exit papers', and it goes on like this until the Captain suddenly twigs, and he takes a wad of marks out of his wallet and he divides it into three, and that does the trick. The bags get repacked, and up goes the barrier.

We get about five miles into Holland, and then Herr Wolff indicates that he wants to stop, and he gets out and he kneels down and kisses the earth, and then he gets up and shakes my hand, and shakes the Captain's hand, and then the girls and their mother want to shake our hands, but the Captain takes their hands when they hold them out, and he bows down and kisses them. Sometimes he had so much charm it was actually annoying. Then the Wolffs go into a sort of huddle in a circle, and a strange noise comes out, and I realise they're all crying and wailing.

It was freedom, and safety, and relief, I suppose, and losing their homeland and everything they ever had. I felt like that when the

Light Horse turned up and I got released from that labour camp on the railway in Turkey, except I still had a homeland to go to.

In Eindhoven the Captain sent a telegram to the Fairheads: BRINGING FOUR REFUGEES STOP TEMPORARY STOP GOOD PEOPLE STOP DANIEL, and then it was off to Antwerp and Bruges. The Captain wanted to go and see all the places in Flanders he'd been in the Royal Flying Corps, and visit the grave of his friend Ash, but I said, 'Give over, sir, we've got to get these characters to Blighty. We've got no time for flippin' tourism.' I think he knew it was a pretty daft idea because he gave in straight away.

They winched the Broughs aboard at Calais, and by the end of the following day we were in Blackheath, and it was all avenues lined with conker trees, and mothers out with prams, and there was Miss Sophie and Fairhead, looking the same but older, with cakes all ready in the living room and the kettle full and waiting to boil, and beds made up upstairs, and a game of cricket going on just over the road. No damned great posters about Blood and Fatherland. It was so peaceful and nice, it hardly seemed real.

I asked the Captain why he'd brought them to Fairhead and Miss Sophie, and not to Miss Rosie, and he said, 'Because Fairhead and Sophie are proper Christians.'

'What's a proper one, then?' I asked, and he said, 'They do the deeds.'

Well, it turned out that the Fairheads and the Wolffs got on really well, and it was because Herr Wolff didn't believe a damn thing out of the Bible, and Fairhead was a chaplain with doubts. They set to and argued about it for months until Herr Wolff got too good at English and Fairhead couldn't keep up with all the philosophical jargon. Mrs Wolff couldn't stop cleaning the house, she was such a tittlemouse, so Miss Sophie put her feet up and read magazines. The two girls liked it in Blackheath because everybody felt sorry for them and treated them nicely, and the prettier one was more than a bit happy because the Captain kept turning up to see how everybody was getting on, and they developed this tendency to take the dog and go out together and walk on the heath. That dog was called Crusty, on account of having been very scabby in his youth. He was lucky, the Captain, he looked a lot younger than he was. Always did. I always looked older than I was, until I got to the age that I looked like.

Miss Sophie and Fairhead were sorry when the bombing started, because it was decided that the Wolffs would go up and stay in Hexham with Miss Gaskell and Miss Christabel. They had a huge great house with no one in it, apart from all the refugee tiddlers, and no one was going to bomb a country house outside Hexham, were they? Not on purpose, anyway. And then Miss Sophie went up there as well, to set up her little dame school in that house, and Fairhead came up when he could for a while, until he shut up that house in Blackheath, just for the duration, and went and got the chaplaincy in a hospital nearby.

And then Herr Wolff had a bright idea and he went to Oxford and he called in on all the logical positivists that were nineteen to the dozen there in those days, and before you could say knife they were all on a ship to America, and he ended up in some posh university getting paid handsomely for talking complicated folderol for the rest of his days. I think it was the one where that Einstein went. The Captain had a thing about Einstein. He kept trying to explain relativity to me, because I'm not stupid, but I never did understand it, and now I wonder if the Captain did either.

As for the Captain, when Hitler marched into Poland he went straight to the War Office and demanded to go back into the RAF. He was like me. Not being at war never felt quite right. It made us proper uneasy. It was like being in one of those gigantic department stores, with stuff everywhere, and no money to buy it with and no reason to choose one thing rather than another. War makes everything simple. There's a tunnel in front of you and you put your head down, and you struggle forward for the light at the end of it, one bloody impossible step at a time, and that frees you up somehow.

What I did was I went to Liverpool Street Station and I got on a train to Norwich, and I walked a good mile or two to Britannia Barracks, up on the side of the hill, and it hadn't changed a bit. I said to the guard on the gate, 'Sergeant Wragge reporting for duty,' and he said, 'Bless my soul, another one,' and he pointed me towards the sergeants' mess even though I knew where it damn well was.

Well, the Sergeant Major says, 'You're too old,' and I roll up my sleeve and I show him my tattoo of Britannia with '2nd Norfolks' under it, and my right tit with 'HOLY' written round it, and my left tit with 'BOYS' written round that, and I say, 'Listen, bor, I was a Barnardo boy, and I was at Shaiba and Basra and Kut. I got through Kut, and I got through a blinkin' death march for two thousand miles, and I got through a Turkish slave camp where they worked us to death, and I have been shot in the arse by a mad old woman who thought I was a pigeon, and I even drove a Brough Superior, which is the biggest and heaviest bike in the world, with two up and one in the sidecar from Krautland to flippin' Blackheath, and that was only last year,' and he blows his lips and says, 'Tough old bugger then,' and I says, 'Yes, I am a tough old bugger and I am a Holy Boy of the 9th Foot, and the Norfolks is my regiment, and the 2nd is my battalion, and there has never been a better man with a bayonet, and I am not bloody leaving 'til I'm back in.'

41

Where They All Were

On the morning of Sunday, 3 September 1939, the Reverend Fairhead came home from conducting a service at the hospital, to find Sophie waiting for him in the hall, seated on the cupboard bench inside of which they stored their useful rubbish, such as wrapping paper and Christmas decorations. When he came in he said, 'Hello, darling, what are you doing sitting there?'

Sophie stood up, put her arms around his neck and began to sob.

In Brighton, Archie Pitt poured himself a stiff glass of gin, even though it was only time for elevenses, and pulled the plug for his single-bar heater from the one electrical socket in the wall. He plugged in the radio, and caught the Prime Minister's broadcast just in time. It was like the sound of a bugle to an old cavalry horse. He stood up slowly, poured the gin back into its bottle, and went to look at himself in the mirror. Shaven, tatty, pathetically thin, but upright and respectable. He took his black air-raid precautions helmet from its hook on the back of the door, brushed a speck of dust from it with his fingers, and went out to report for duty, no longer a humble roadsweeper.

At the home of their decadent friends in Lewes, Christabel and Gaskell were draped over the sofas, nursing their hangovers. Felix and Felicity had got themselves up and given themselves breakfast and were wrenching quinces from the tree, to throw at each other. Their sibling screams of 'I hate you, I hate you' were ringing out over the river valley, from which an early-autumn mist had begun to evaporate. After they had listened to the broadcast, Gaskell said, 'What are we going to do? Paint pictures and take photographs?'

'I don't know,' said Christabel.

Gaskell thumbnailed her cigarette out of its holder into an ashtray, undraped herself, and went to the French window. She watched the children for a while, and said, 'We're going to go home to Hexham and open the house up for refugees. They'll be evacuating all the children from London now.'

Christabel came and stood beside her, taking her arm. 'It'll be the best thing we've ever done,' she said. 'I'll go and pack.'

Daniel's mother, Mme Pitt, wearing galoshes over her slippers, was in the garden in Partridge Green, deadheading the roses, when her neighbour popped her head over the garden wall. 'I thought you'd like to know,' she said. 'On account of Poland. We're at war. I just heard the Prime Minister. And France is in with us again.'

Mme Pitt took off her gloves and wiped her brow with the back of her hand 'Oh, mon pauvre pays,' she sighed. Then she looked up at her neighbour and said, 'I am selfish to think like this, I know, but at least my boys are too old to fight this time.'

'No one's too old,' said her neighbour. 'Well, begging your pardon, but you might be, I suppose.'

Mme Pitt gestured towards her flower bed. 'Je peux faire pousser les légumes between the roses,' she said. 'I'll grow vegetables.'

Mrs McCosh was with Cookie in the kitchen at The Grampians. Cookie was the last servant left, and the two women had been together for more than several decades. There was very little left of the relationship between mistress and servant apart from the formality of Cookie addressing Mrs McCosh as 'madam'. Cookie was completely reconciled to her employer's fits of extreme eccentricity, unembarrassed because they had become so completely commonplace.

'We'll get bombed again, won't we, madam?' said Cookie.

'I'm not leaving the house. I shall be buried in its rubble, if need be.'

'They'll fly straight over us to get to London, won't they, madam?'

'Last time,' said Mrs McCosh, 'the Kaiser declared war on his own family. The least you can say for Herr Hitler is that he doesn't have any relatives here.'

'I think we should bomb them first,' said Cookie, 'before they get a head start.'

'You should write and suggest it to the Prime Minister, Cookie.'

'Well, madam, I think I will.'

Rosie was at her father's graveside at St John's, after matins, when a passer-by waved to her cheerily, and said, 'It's war. I don't know if you heard.'

She went back into the church and knelt in the front row of the pews, but the prayers never came. She wondered how long the war would last, because Bertie might become eligible for it if it went on too long.

Bertie was upstairs at The Grampians wondering what else he could cram into his school trunk, and whether he could get away with taking some tins of pineapple from the larder.

Esther was brushing her hair and making faces at herself in the mirror, hoping that it was lamb for Sunday lunch. She suddenly remembered the ultimatum and went downstairs to the kitchen, where Cookie and her grandmother were sitting together at the table with one of the family cats between them. She saw their numbed expressions, and said, 'It's war then, is it?' She went out into the garden and realised that she urgently needed to see her father. He would know what to do.

Daniel Pitt missed the broadcast because he was out on his Brough, taking a joyride to Box Hill on the way to his mother; but when he stopped in a roadside cafe outside Reigate he caught the painfully halting and monotonous broadcast of the King. Nobody in the cafe spoke for the whole address, and then somebody said, 'Good old George.'

Daniel went outside. He had been expecting this for months, especially since the partial mobilisation at the time of Hitler's annexation of the Sudetenland. He was fortunate to have such a record from the previous war, and had been pulling strings for months. Now he was merely waiting for a telegram. The RAF would definitely want him, whether up in the air or not. Whatever happened he was determined to get back up in the air. He was thinking of the Air Transport Auxiliary. He'd be flying every kind of plane there was, and the thought of that was a little intoxicating.

Out in India Ottilie wondered if she could refresh her nursing skills and go back into hospitals, or whether she would be more usefully employed continuing to run her own little clinic for the poorer coolies, just when she was making progress in persuading them to accept inoculation. In any case there were the three children to think of. Frederick wrote to the War Ministry of the Indian government stating that he was a former naval officer, and asking how he might be useful.

Near Berwick, Young Edward, no longer as young as he was, wondered what he would do when the golf course was made into a training ground. They had already built a pillbox on it and an anti-aircraft emplacement that as yet had no gun. There was even talk of turning the par fives into airstrips. Life had suddenly become too serious for golf, and his rigid leg and damaged hip made any military career seem improbable. All the same, he was going to volunteer for the LDV, even if they were presently only drilling with broomsticks. It occurred to him that if the course became an airfield he could give lessons to the young officers.

At the family house in Edenderry, Mary went to the window and looked out at the familiar rain. She calculated that Daniel was too old to fight now, but knew that he still would. She wondered if Ireland would be dragged into the war, and thought, 'Only if Britain is defeated. Or the Germans start sinking our ships.' She was sure that the Irish would enjoy the *Schadenfreude* of watching from a safe distance as British soldiers fell. The sadness of this thought made her regret all over again being neither one thing nor the other.

In Ceylon, when the news of war arrived in the hills of paradise a day later, Samadara stroked the head of her oldest son and remembered the man of whom he reminded her so much. She smiled sadly and wondered if the war would bring him back, and what it would be like if it did, and whether she would even know, and if he were even still alive.

42

After All These Years

Esther met her father at the Ritz. It was her plan to spend her last five-pound note. A good cream tea at the Ritz seemed like an excellent way to arrive at utter destitution until the end of the month, which was not too far away.

They were shown in by a footman in immaculate uniform, who, despite his impeccable respect, made it quite clear by his manner that no one short of the King himself might be considered an equal.

'Daddy,' said Esther, once they were settled and spreading jam on their scones, 'I really think you should come and talk to Mummy.'

He was startled. 'What on earth for, Shompi? So we can shout at each other?'

'I just think that you should.'

'But why?'

She paused and then said, 'I want you to.'

'Is that a good enough reason? You're not hoping we'll be reunited, are you?'

'Of course I'd like you to be reunited, but I know how you feel about it. I know how she feels about it.'

'She thinks I'm an irresponsible God-hating wastrel addicted to disgusting sensual pleasures.'

'And what do you think of her?'

'Well, I can't stand her piety for one thing, and I can't forgive her for marrying me when she was still in love with a dead man, and I can't forgive her for refusing to leave home and make a life with me. And abandoning me at Southampton. And I will never understand why she thinks her dead child was a punishment and not just bad luck, and I will never understand why she insisted on living with her mother. I found it all intolerable, and that's putting it mildly.'

'Gran's not very well,' said Esther.

'What is it?'

'Ever more senile. Mummy couldn't leave her now even if she wanted to. She thinks I'm Princess Elizabeth.'

'What fun.'

'It is quite. I don't try to put her right. It's not worth the trouble. And she does have periods of complete clarity. And the most terrible snobbery.'

'And is your mother better now?'

'They removed it.'

'I know, you told me when you wrote. There's no sign of it returning?'

'It can take ages.'

'Fingers crossed then.'

'It must be absolutely horrible ... having one of them cut off like that. I can hardly imagine it.'

'Luckily your mother never had any vanity about her body. She was always covered up. In all circumstances. Like the wife of Montaigne.'

'Daddy, I don't really want to know about those kinds of things.'

'I'm sorry. It's just that you and I have something special, don't we? All that heartbreaking separation; I missed so much of your childhood, but you never forgot me and I never gave up hope.'

She leaned across the table and patted his hand. 'I missed bags and bags of fun not having you. And I still remember all the characters in the stories you used to tell us at night. Like Boris Clapperbang.'

'Who stole iron manhole covers so that people would fall into sewers? And what about Mr Cratchett, and Snuffles the dog, and Mrs Poorpong? And the giant mole who objected to light bulbs? And Cyril Nutsack who stole people's lawns? And Knickerless Knickernicker?'

'Who stole knickers from washing lines? And what about that story about pushing us on a swing so hard that we flew to the moon ... ?'

'Where the souls of all the dead cats go when they die? And Gran'mère is there, having a picnic, and you then have to find the lunar trampoline in order to fly home again.'

An idea occurred to him. 'We've got a dance next month. Not in the mess. It's been bombed. But it will be somewhere nearby. Do come. I'll pretend you're my little doxy.'

'I'd have to come all the way from Scarborough! Much as I love you, it's a bit far. And we're obviously going to be posted somewhere soon. I don't know where. Wouldn't you rather take one of your poor gullible little floozies?'

'The Wrens get sent to Gibraltar and Malta, don't they? And as for floozies, I'm afraid the Yanks have got all the best ones. It's the nylons and steaks and the big dollar pay packets. The rest of us have to make do with three-legged squinters and bearded ladies and oddities from freak shows. God knows what the other ranks make use of. They probably take the bungs out of barrels.'

'Daddy! Did you hear the one about why picking nuts is like a pair of nylons?'

'No. Why is picking nuts like a pair of nylons?'

'One Yank and they're off!'

There was a moment of silence between them, and then Daniel said, 'Shompi, you know I was driven out, don't you? You know I never would have deserted you of my own free will. I adored you. I always did and always will. Losing you was the greatest sorrow of my life. As it is I have lost your brother permanently, because of never having had him in the first place. He doesn't even remember me from when we were a proper family. Bertie once said something terribly intriguing when he was tiny. He said, "I can feel the earth moving. It's moving very slowly." I can't remember anything else he ever said because I wasn't there to hear him say it.'

She looked up at him and saw that his eyes were dark with pain. She felt the same thing happening to her and she reached into her bag for a lacy handkerchief. She sniffled into it and said, 'Daddy, you never lost me. You know you didn't. And I've been working on Bertie for years. He knows I'm right, but he loves Mummy too much to admit it.'

'I didn't see you for six months once. Every time I arranged to see you I got a message at the last minute saying that something had come up, and I couldn't. I can't tell you how desperate I got. And angry. The rage was unbearable. I went for ten-mile walks in the rain just to tire the fury out of me so that I could sleep. At times I felt like committing murder, and at other times I just wanted to kill myself.'

'I know, Daddy. And now Mummy has to live with knowing that she didn't do the right thing. She isn't happy. I don't think she ever will be. She knows that Bertie and I could have been happier. She knows that you're lots of fun, and we didn't have enough time with you. You're happy now, aren't you? You won out, really, didn't you?'

'I'm happy,' he replied, 'but I have holes that I can't fill. One is shaped like you, and the other is shaped like Bertie. I've got the kind of happiness that comes after you've been through so much that you can't feel it any more and are forced to rise above it. And I enjoy being at war. It gives me something to concentrate on that really feels important. They've given me a Hurricane to get around in, but I'm not allowed to initiate combat. It's not a very good one, unfortunately.'

'Well, I'm having a fine time in the Wrens. Join the Wrens! Free a man for the Fleet! Just think, I'm a third officer now, and all the lower ranks have to salute me! Great hairy sailors, saluting me! And I'm a fully qualified radio telegraphist!'

'Good for you, Shompi. I'm so proud of you. If you're lucky you'll get sent back to Ceylon. Trincomalee. You'd love it.'

'The sailors call us Jennies.'

'Why's that?'

'Jenny wrens, of course!'

'Oh. Silly of me. It's obvious, isn't it?'

'Bertie's working on the fire watch because he's too young to do anything else.'

'Really? I must write to say that I am proud of him. Do you think that would help?'

'I don't know. It might. You know he helped to put out the fire on the roof of Eltham Palace?'

'Did he, by God?'

'He did. He was the only one with the guts to go up on the roof. And one day he was left to guard an unexploded bomb in the middle of a crater on Court Road. He thought nothing of it. Do you know Steven Courtauld?'

'Well, not personally, but I know of him of course.'

'Bertie says he's a terrible funker. He's supposed to be in charge of the fire watch, and every time something happens he's nowhere to be found.'

'The only thing I know about him is that he had a pet lemur that had its own fireman's pole for getting downstairs.'

They laughed, and then she said, 'Come home and say hello to Mummy. You can say you were worried about how she is after the operation.'

'I was worried. I am. And in fact there is something I have to talk to her about. I've been steeling myself, but somehow I'd rather face a horde of Huns than bring it up yet again.'

'What is it?' she asked, and when he told her, her face fell.

'You're still hoping then?' he said.

Rosie was both astonished and vexed when she found herself face-to-face with her husband in the hall of the house. She had come out of the drawing room upon hearing the turn of Esther's key in the lock and was eager to see her. She was feeling very weak, and even small separations were difficult these days. The bombers only came over at night, but you still worried about anyone who was even a fraction later than you expected.

Daniel made as if to kiss her, and she hesitated before offering her cheek to him. He was half French, after all. The French even kissed people they didn't like or hardly knew. She looked at him and her heart lurched when she saw that he had barely changed in twenty years. He was grey, and his hair was thin, but he was still slim and handsome, with an athletic air and the same glint in his eye. She felt an immediate association with Ash, and her sense of loss doubled.

'You're looking very well,' said Daniel, 'you've hardly changed at all.' They both knew he was lying. She was greying and her skin had sagged. Her body had lost much of its shape, and she was dressed without any sense of style; practical shoes, darned stockings, a plain frock, and her hair pinned up in a practical bun. He had kept his youth, but she had lost hers.

'I wasn't expecting you,' she said, adding, 'Bertie's out.'

'I asked him here. It was my idea,' said Esther. 'And he wants to talk to you about something.'

'Come into the drawing room,' said Rosie. 'I'll make tea. I expect you know, Cookie's become a little old and helpless. I do almost everything now. It's funny when you think back. The house used to be swarming with servants ... when I was a girl.'

Daniel looked around. It was a strange feeling to be back in this house that had once been so familiar, that had intermittently been his home for years. He saw that the beautifully delicate and elaborate cornices were as fresh and white as they had ever been, and the family portraits on the walls still gazed down with the same knowing, impassive inscrutability. The huge Bible still stood on its lectern in the morning room. The difference was that the carpets were worn out and nothing sparkled any more.

Daniel and Esther went into the drawing room, to be confronted by a virago. Mrs McCosh was ensconced in a high-backed armchair with one quivering hand resting on the ball of her cane, got up in the same black dress she had worn almost every day since the death of her husband. Her white hair was piled up on her head, topped off with a small white mob cap, and she wore a white lace ruff about her neck.

Upon looking up and seeing Daniel, she sprang to her feet and pointed her cane at him. 'You!' she exclaimed.

'How nice to see you again,' said Daniel, approaching as if to kiss her on the cheek. She poked him in the stomach with the silver tip of her cane and cried, 'Scoundrel! Ne'er-do-well! Traitor!'

'Oh Lord,' said Daniel, backing off.

'Gran, what's the matter now?' asked Esther, taking the old lady's arm and trying to encourage her back into her chair.

'I'm not going to call him "Your Grace",' explained Mrs McCosh. 'He is a dis-Grace. I will never bring myself to call him "Your Grace".'

'But who, Gran? Who are you talking about?'

She waved the tip of her cane at Daniel. 'Running off with that American slut! How dare he come here and show his face? Letting us down like that! Traitor!'

'Oh my, she thinks you're the Duke of Windsor,' said Esther.

'Explain yourself!' demanded Mrs McCosh.

'I can only apologise,' said Daniel, glancing sideways at Esther. 'Sometimes one is led astray by love.'

'Love! Love! It was lust! Pure greedy, naked, lubricious, salacious, lascivious lust! They say she has certain skills. Do you think I'm to be taken in by talk of love?'

'It was indeed lust, madam,' said Daniel. 'I do most heartily apologise. When it wears off I shall have to endure a lifetime of regret.' Esther put her hand to her mouth and giggled.

Rosie entered pushing a trolley sparsely laden with a teapot and a few biscuits. Daniel looked at it and remembered the sumptuous teas they used to have in the old days, before rationing had made it easier to avoid the appearance of poverty.

'We can't have tea in here, Mummy,' said Esther; 'Gran's peeved. She thinks Daddy's the Duke of Windsor.'

'Oh dear, we'll go in the morning room then.'

'Goodbye, Mrs McCosh,' said Daniel.

'Be off with you,' said Mrs McCosh. 'And thank God we got a better king in your brother.' She turned, arranged her skirts and sat down, gazing resolutely at the fireplace, in which no fire was burning.

In the morning room they made polite and strained conversation about the various relatives that one or other of them had not seen for years. She learned that Daniel was back in the RAF, and that Mr Wragge had gone back to Norwich.

'It's horrible to see all the bomb damage, isn't it? It's far worse than last time,' said Daniel eventually. 'I do hope you have a decent shelter.'

'At the bottom of the garden,' said Rosie. 'Just an Anderson. But it's quite impossible to get Mother to go down there. She thinks it's a mine and she thinks it's beneath her to have to consort with miners. She kicks up a fuss and runs back to the house. We have to sweat it out in the shelter while she stands in the garden with her air rifle and shoots at the aeroplanes. Still, I don't think we're important enough to bomb, really.'

Daniel was horrified. 'That's not how it works. In the first place bombers accidentally-on-purpose drop their load early because that's how they avoid having to face the ack-ack over the target zone. In the second place the Huns really are just bombing civilians quite randomly because they think we'll get downhearted, which is exactly what they did in the last war, and it didn't work then either, and thirdly, bombers drop their spare bombs to lighten the aircraft and get home quicker. There was a one like that just recently in Bungay.'

'Bungay?'

'Little place in Suffolk. Someone got killed and someone else lost their legs. You really ought to go down to the shelter. Leave your mother if you have to.'

'Daniel!'

'Anyway, it certainly makes Zeppelins and Gothas look tame, eh? Oh, I've had an idea! About your mother.'

'Oh yes?"

'Why don't you write to the King and ask him to send her an order that she has to take shelter during air raids?'

'Write to the King? Daniel, whatever next?'

'Lots of people do,' said Daniel. 'The King has dozens of people to write replies for him. It might be worth a shot. Oh, and it's often been noticed that the safest place in a raid is in the cupboard under the stairs. When you look at the wrecks of houses, the staircases are usually still intact. If your mother won't leave the house, why don't you make her a bed in there and put all the clutter in the attic?'

She nodded and sipped her tea. 'What did you want to talk to me about?'

Daniel asked his daughter to leave, and she held up both hands with the middle fingers crossed over the index. 'Good luck,' she said.

After she had left he said, 'I'm sorry, I really am, but I need to bring up the subject of divorce. Again.'

'You know my views.'

'But I can't start again. Yet I have to start again, can't you see? It's not fair on the women I fall in love with. They want to marry, of course they do. And I can't marry them because you won't let me go. I want children I can actually live with. You have no idea how I suffered from being deprived of the children, absolutely no idea. My son still hates me. Why? Because you've been denigrating me for years.'

'What do you mean "them"?' asked Rosie.

'I have loved and lost several times. Nice girls. Honest, affectionate women. Because of you. What am I supposed to do? I refuse to be a bigamist.'

'No,' said Rosie. 'I made a vow when we married. 'Til death do us part. And I didn't make the vows to you. I made them to God. Have you no thought of how disgraceful it is to break a promise that you made to God? I can't do it. I won't. Not even if it makes the whole world unhappy. Not even if it disappoints the little waifs and strays you're going round with who want to be Mrs Daniel Pitt.'

Daniel bridled. 'You and your wretched principles! Do you really think you know what God wants?'

'It's all written,' said Rosie. 'It's all in the Book.'

'The Book where everyone looks for what they want to find, and everybody finds it!' exclaimed Daniel. 'Like every other Holy Book there's ever been. There should be a bloody great bonfire.'

'Do we have to have the same arguments over and over again, even when we've hardly talked for years? I'm not changing my mind. You made the promise too, so you've got to keep it.'

'You broke your wedding vows anyway,' said Daniel.

'What? I never did!'

'With my body I thee honour,' quoted Daniel, 'and it says in the preamble that marriage is for people who don't have the gift of continence.'

'It says that marriage isn't to satisfy men's carnal lusts and appetites like brute beasts that have no understanding. And I did honour you with my body. We had two children, remember?'

'Three,' said Daniel. 'You forget the poor little thing that didn't live.'

'How could I forget him? It still cuts me to the quick to think about it.'

'You switched off the moment you had all the children you wanted, and then you pushed me away. You came up with all that rubbish about prevention being against God's law. I don't know if you noticed, but shortly afterwards the Church of England changed God's law and made it perfectly all right.'

'I did notice. I still don't think it's right. And the Roman Church hasn't changed.'

Daniel got to his feet and paced about, irritated and frustrated. 'For God's sake, give me a divorce! Please! I'm begging you!'

'I certainly can't do it for God's sake,' said Rosie primly.

'Fuck God!' shouted Daniel. 'I hate Him! I hate what He's turned you into! He's a gorgon, He's turned you to stone. He's filled you with poison! He's watched us get drenched in carnage twice in one century, and you still think He's good? You'd kill your own child if God told you to!'

'I'd know there was a good reason,' said Rosie. 'No one thinks badly of Abraham for agreeing to sacrifice Isaac. It's admired.'

'What? Are you mad? If God told me to kill one of my children, I'd tell Him to fuck off. I'd tell Him I'd rather be tortured in hell forever. What kind of depraved bastard tells you to kill your own child? And what kind of depraved bastard would agree to it?'

'You'd better leave now,' said Rosie stiffly, avoiding his furious gaze. 'You can't go insulting God and the patriarchs. Not in front of me.'

At the door, Daniel turned and said, 'I apologise for the profanity.'

'I've heard worse during amputations,' said Rosie. They looked at one another for a few moments, both wondering how and why it was that the love between them had never really gone, even after everything was beyond repair. Rosie said suddenly, 'Can you explain why it is that Felicity and Felix both look like you, and why you go to Hexham so often?'

Daniel felt a small surge of contempt. 'No,' he said, and turned on his heel.

239

On the way out he kissed Esther on the cheeks and hugged her tightly to his chest, her head on his shoulder. 'I should have listened to Fluke,' he said mysteriously.

'How did it go?' asked Esther.

'Perfectly snafu and fubar,' he replied, patting her on the cheek.

At that moment Mrs McCosh burst in, brandishing the very air rifle with which she had despatched so many copulating pigeons over the years. 'Out!' she cried. 'Out! Traitor! Marry a foreign slut, would you? Out before I shoot!'

'In the long run a slut might be infinitely preferable to a saint,' said Daniel drily. He kissed Esther on the forehead, said, 'Goodbye, Shompi sweetheart, let's see each other soon.'

'After the war, Daddy, let's go on a long holiday somewhere. I'm dying to go to Canada. And South Africa. And Australia. I can protect you from all the ravening women, and you can protect me from men, and other wild beasts.'

'After the war,' repeated Daniel, remembering how that had been everybody's mantra the last time round. 'This one won't be over by Christmas either,' he said. He embraced her again, kissed her three times, and then he was gone.

When he had gone, Rosie sat very still for a long time, feeling numb inside. She had almost always felt numb, apart from those happy months in Ceylon, but now she felt like a failure, and even suspected that Daniel might be in the right. She closed her mind quite deliberately again, because without God's approval and support she would have no sanction for living. She went upstairs and took her Virgin and child from under the bed. She realised that she had no one to hide it from any more, and set it on the mantelpiece. She rummaged again and took out the parcel of Ash's uniform. For the same reason she put it in the bottom drawer of her chest. She looked briefly at her charred bundle of letters, and then inspected her hands. You'd never know they'd been burned. She wondered what had happened to Dr Scott. He must be dead by now.

Rosie decided to go back into nursing. It had been impossibly gruelling and difficult work in the last war, but it had been the one time when she had been able to forget herself completely. She had loved the men, and they had loved her in return. She went to her desk and wrote to the commandant of the hospital at Netley, explaining that she had recently been operated on for cancer and had no idea how long she had to live, but that she wanted to do her bit during whatever time was left.

If she had to leave her mother, then so be it. Cookie would still be here.

43

Two Letters

7 November 1940

From My Secret Address
But your mother knows what it is

My dear Bertie,

Shompi told me that you have become a fire warden and that you were instrumental in putting out the fire at the palace. She told me about the bomb in the crater, too.

I just wanted you to know that I am most wonderfully proud of you for bravely doing your bit before you even have to. Remember that you are a quarter French and half Scottish, so you have three countries to fight for!

I would like it very much if you would come to the aerodrome sometime to see what I am up to, and to meet some genuine heroes. They are as fine a bunch of men as I ever served with in the last bagarre. *I could take you up in a trainer and we could buzz the house as we did in the old days. It isn't far.*

Looking forward to hearing from you soon.

Your loving father,

Monsieur DP

5 December 1940

Dear Father,

Thank you for your letter.

Unfortunately I am tied up just about every day in the holidays with my duties on the fire watch, and the rest of the time I am back in school.

I did have to go up on the roof of the palace to put the fire out. I think that in future I shall never want to go quite so high again. The bomb in the middle of the road was quite big, and it just sat in the hole with its tailfins sticking out. I had to stand guard and tell people to keep away.

I am learning to shoot with Grandma's old air rifle that she shoots pigeons with.

I hope you are very well.

Bertie

44

Two Letters from Sandringham

24 January 1941

> Sandringham
> Norfolk

Dear Mrs Pitt,

Your letter about your mother has caused me some considerable entertainment in these very dark times. His Majesty saw it himself when he came into the office yesterday, and it certainly did raise his spirits. He remembers his father, the late King, mentioning a persistent correspondent named Mrs McCosh, who even wrote to him about dog mess on the Esplanade at Ryde. She must be your mother. He has therefore authorised me to compose the letter which will go directly to your mother under separate cover, and which, I trust, will arrive in the same post as this. Obviously the order cannot have any official signs of validity, but I shall seal it and make sure that it displays the best possible flourishes.

Yours truly,
J. J. Wilberforce
Senior secretary

> Sandringham
> Norfolk

His Majesty King George the Sixth by the Grace of God King of England Scotland and Ireland Emperor of India and of the Dominions of Canada and Australia and of his other domains Defender of the Faith etc etc by these presents ordains requires and commands that his beloved servant Mrs Hamilton McCosh of Court Road Eltham shall without fail let or hindrance and invariably obey her daughter Mrs

Daniel Pitt when required by the said Mrs Daniel Pitt to take shelter on the occasions of enemy attack so that the said Mrs Hamilton McCosh may continue safely in the service of His Majesty to the end of her natural life.

Le Roi le veult.

45

The Bombers Will Always Get Through

On 7 September 1940, Operation Loge began. Fortunately the phoney war had given people time to make shelters, although the Underground would not be opened at night for a further two weeks.

Some say that the Blitz was Hitler's hyperbolic revenge for an RAF raid on Munich, but it was a hyperbole very much diminished in its effects by the fact that the British had already built dozens of fake airfields and industrial sites. Germany's bombers were too small, and methods to confuse their navigation beams had been discovered and put in place. Above a childless London there floated hundreds of barrage balloons, and almost no lights twinkled below, on account of the elaborate and strongly resented blackout procedures.

Perhaps the oddest thing about the Blitz is that, just like the Zeppelin raids of the previous war, it had the opposite effect on the British that Hitler and Goering had confidently expected.

One night in January of 1941 at The Grampians, only Cookie and Mrs McCosh were in residence, and hitherto the latter had, very much against her inclinations, obeyed the apparently direct command of the King to take shelter during raids. She was now a very old lady, suffering from bouts of immense passion and confusion, who had, as her long life had unrolled, become more and more herself until she resembled her own caricature. Like the late Queen she dressed entirely in black and made a cult of her deceased husband. Her own patriotism and royalism had, if anything, become more fanatical, and her stated reason for hating the Germans was that the Kaiser had declared war against his own family in the previous conflict, and thereby vitiated his entire nation forever, rather as the original sin of Adam and Eve had corrupted humankind.

246

As the bombers thundered over The Grampians and the bombs crumped in the distance, Cookie and Mrs McCosh sat together in the Anderson shelter with only one candle between them, and sipped on cocoa that they had made on a Primus. The air was heavy with the fumes of methylated spirit and candlewax, but on this day Mrs McCosh's mind was unusually clear. They were dressed in overcoats and hats, and would have looked very like each other had Cookie not been wearing a scarf, whereas Mrs McCosh wore a fox-fur stole with its glass eyes glinting in the yellow light. The candle flame cast heavy shadows, and the flesh of their ancient faces glowed golden yellow. Sitting on the edge of the narrow truckle bed, Mrs McCosh calmed her trembling fingers and played the violin to her cook, who, over the years, had become completely familiar with her employer's repertoire. Mrs McCosh played 'The Swan', the 'Meditation' from *Thaïs*, and three pieces of Kreisler's, concluding with 'Schön Rosmarin'. The old lady swayed and made the strings sing quietly and intimately, on account of the confined space, and Cookie listened raptly with sentimental tears gathering at the corners of her eyes. Afterwards, there was nothing for the two old women to do but talk.

'I probably shouldn't play Kreisler,' said Mrs McCosh. 'I strongly suspect him of having been German.'

'And how is Miss Rosie, madam? Back at Netley?'

'Yes, so I hear. A letter came this morning. It seems to be a more comfortable place than it was in the last war. Very much less crowded, apparently.'

'Wasn't they fun, the old days, madam, when Miss Rosie and the others were all little, and Master Daniel and Archie used to come over the wall, and the Pendennis boys came in and out of the blue door, and the littl'uns were like a tribe of savages?'

'And Bouncer was still alive. And the master. Those were our salad days, Cookie.'

'It's cold, isn't it, madam?' said Cookie. 'Do you think it'll be fine tomorrow?'

'I dare say it may be, Cookie, but personally I have always loved this time of year, whatever the weather.'

'Me too, madam. It's so nice when the russets ripen up, and there's the blackberries, and the first fogs, and the little shrews come out to die, and you find their little corpses on the paths, and the rosehips are turning red, and suddenly all the flies have gone from the larder.'

'I have written to the King, Cookie, to advise him on some strategies for winning the war.'

'You should have sent it to Mr Churchill,' said Cookie. 'The King will only pass it on to him, won't he? I mean, it's Mr Churchill in charge of winning. You could have saved His Majesty some bother.'

'I understand that Mr Churchill is half American,' said Mrs McCosh. 'I am not entirely sure that I approve of him. And the Dardanelles were hardly a triumph. And Mr Churchill sees His Majesty every week, you know. I am certain that his best ideas actually come from that quarter.'

'I expect so, madam.'

'Cookie?'

'Yes, madam?'

'You have been very good, you know.'

'Very good?'

'Yes, Cookie. You have been very staunch. A faithful servant for a very long time. I hardly think of you as one.'

'Me neither, madam.'

'You have seen us through thick and thin.'

'Well, you could see it just as easy the other way round. I've had a sort of family, haven't I?'

Mrs McCosh patted Cookie's hand. 'How good of you to say so.'

'Not at all, madam.'

'I am leaving you money in my will, you know.'

'I know, madam, you have often told me, practically every day, but it would be quite all right with me if I were to pop me clogs first. Perhaps you could send my effects to my sister in Shropshire.'

'It's "my" not "me", Cookie. "My clogs", not "me clogs".'

'Quite so, madam.'

'Precision in speech is important, Cookie.'

'I'm sure it is, madam.'

'The bombers are returning,' said Mrs McCosh. 'I can hear the engines getting louder again.' She reached out for her Britannia air rifle that had brought about the demise of so many dozens of indecently copulating pigeons over the years, and which had first seen action against the Kaiser's Zeppelins.

'Don't go out, madam. You know there's no chance of hitting one, and if you do it'll be like water off a duck's back, and there might be more bombs.'

'I am quite confident of getting one, one of these days, Cookie.'

'Yes, madam, but that thing's only got a few yards' range, and you still shouldn't go out. You know what His Majesty said.'

'Indeed, Cookie. He has no more loyal subject than me, as you know, but on this occasion I feel that I may make an exception, as neither you nor I is very likely to tell him, and I am only doing my duty. Make sure you shut the door behind me, for your own protection. I shall return very presently.'

Mrs McCosh put ten lead pellets in her mouth for reloading, opened the door of the shelter and ducked out of it. On the lawn she breathed in the crisp air, and felt the droning of hundreds of bombers vibrating in her own bones. She raised the air rifle to her shoulder and fired upwards against the shadows, then reset the spring and opened the breech, removing a pellet from her mouth to place in it.

High above her, a young German aircraftman from Cologne finally worked out why the bomb hatch of his Heinkel had not opened, and informed the pilot. The pilot's opinion was that it was better to leave the bombs somewhere in England, rather than carry such a heavy load home again at greatly reduced speed, and so the bomb hatches were duly opened, and a long stick of bombs released.

For the second time in a century, the glass of The Grampians' conservatory was shattered.

By the time Cookie found Mrs McCosh, still clutching the Britannia, in the rose bed by the blue door where she had been thrown by the blast, she had already bled to death, her head cracked against the wall and her neck sliced through by a plate of glass. Cookie could see the heavy pool of blood glowing thickly in the darkness, and she took off her scarf and patted at it, as if by this she were doing something to be helpful to the dead woman.

Cookie knelt down and placed her head on her mistress's chest. 'Oh, madam,' she said, 'I did tell you not to go out.'

Cookie took the air rifle from her mistress's hands, and raised it up against her shoulder as a last stray bomber passed above. She had never fired a gun before, but she pulled the trigger and felt the sudden kick against her collarbone.

She propped it carefully against the blue door, and manoeuvred her heavy body down next to that of Mrs McCosh, lying beside her amongst the roses. She held her mistress's rapidly cooling left hand to her cheek, weeping quietly, trying not to get prickled, and confusedly working out how many years they had been together in this house. It must have been something like fifty.

'Just think, madam,' she said, at last, 'you've gone out in exactly the same way as your friend Myrtle, all those years ago. In 1917.'

When the all-clear sounded, she went out through the house to try to find help, and it struck her that when Mrs McCosh went to her funeral, she ought to have that gun on the top of her coffin. Yes, she should, she should have that there gun on top of the coffin, where it rightly belonged, and there ought to be a union flag.

46

The *Aguila*

The first SS *Aguila* was sunk by the submarine U-28 in 1915, but its owners optimistically caused a new one to be built, which spent its heyday carrying passengers and fruit to and from Lisbon and the Canary Islands.

On 13 August 1941, with a cargo of naval personnel, the SS *Aguila* left Liverpool with Convoy OG 71, bound for Gibraltar, accompanied by a Norwegian destroyer, a sloop and six corvettes.

Two of the ships were Irish, and so they did not black themselves out, much to the irritation of the other crews. Because of these blazing lights, the convoy was soon spotted by a Focke-Wulf Fw 200.

During the first ever U-Boat wolf-pack attack, the *Aguila* became the third ship to be sunk. Some of the crew were saved, only to be killed shortly afterwards. The twelve Wrens from the base in Scarborough went straight to the bottom of the sea.

The U-201, the submarine that had sunk the *Aguila* was itself sunk on 17 February 1943 by HMS *Viscount*, off the east coast of Newfoundland, with the loss of all of its crew of forty-nine, but its captain had already moved on. By the end of the war, *Kapitänleutnant* Adalbert Schnee had sunk at least twenty-three ships, and won the Knight's Cross of the Iron Cross, With Oak Leaves.

He spent six months after the war helping to clear mines, and died in 1982. Whether or not he had any regrets is unknown.

47

The Cliffs

After the Stuka attack on Tangmere aerodrome that destroyed the east wing of the officers' mess, the new and very sensible policy of dispersal meant that Daniel was in the mess at Shopwyke House when he was handed the telegram by an orderly, a few days after Wing Commander Bader had had to bail out over France. He read it several times, unable to take in its enormity, and then, all rational thought impossible, he went straight outside, fired up the Brough, and drove to the airfield to see Wing Commander Paddy Woodhouse.

He found the Wing Commander outside one of the hangars, saluted, realised that his throat was closed, and silently handed him the telegram. Woodhouse looked at it, and said, 'My dear Daniel, I am so very sorry. I suppose you need a while to take it all in.'

Daniel nodded.

'Can't speak, eh? Can't say I blame you. You must have compassionate leave. Of course you must. Will ten days be all right? We've got a lot on, as you know. You can hardly be spared, but under the circumstances … go back to Shopwyke and I'll have somebody bring the pass over in an hour or so, is that all right?'

Daniel nodded again, and Woodhouse stood and held out his hand for Daniel to shake. '*Bon courage*,' he said. 'I really can't tell you how very sorry I am. When you come back we'll keep you busy. In times like this, the trick is to keep busy, I've always found.'

Daniel was able to make the long journey from Tangmere to Beachy Head because he had long ago given up smoking and had been trading his weekly tin of fifty cigarettes for petrol. In wartime one has to improvise, and he felt guiltless about it. Other people used their cigarettes to obtain chocolate, or vice versa. He

252

was careful with his fuel and never wasted it on trivial jaunts, but from time to time he needed to go to Brighton to check up on Archie, or to see his mother at Partridge Green, who was scarcely managing any more. He would take her treats from the NAAFI and do whatever maintenance jobs needed to be done about the house and garden, directed by Mme Pitt, who, on her bad days, was largely confined to her bath chair.

On this September day, however, he would pass both Partridge Green and Brighton without a thought for his mother or his brother. The tears and the rain made it impossible for him to drive the combination with his customary elan, and he felt a pressure inside his head that was maddening and intolerable, as if someone had inserted a jack inside his skull and was piti-lessly winding it up. He could feel the pulse in his temples hammering, and his throat was so constricted he could barely breathe. He had to take short breaths to keep going, and for once the sheer exhilaration of being out on the open road on a motorcycle completely failed to enthral him. His mind was empty of reason, his usual stray thoughts suppressed, replaced by a hideous, tormenting numbness that was as irresistible as a spring tide. He was drowning in it, and there was only one way out.

Daniel stopped for a short while above Cuckmere Haven. Its tranquil beauty, its lovely meadows and oxbows of water, had never failed to move him and fill him with a sense of natural wonder, until today. He stopped only to say a cold farewell to it, as if his soul had risen above the merely beautiful.

When he arrived at Beachy Head immediately afterwards, the loss of forethought that comes with overwhelming grief brought him up short. He had forgotten that there was a war on, and he perceived now that the clifftops were crammed with equipment and personnel. A chicane had been set up in the road with a Canadian guard who was checking the papers of everyone passing through. Daniel halted and shut off the engine.

He produced what he had, and the guard asked, 'And do you have a warrant, sir?'

'A warrant? For what?'

'A warrant for whatever you are a-doing of,' replied the guard.

'I'm not really doing anything, Corporal,' said Daniel.

'And might you have a warrant permitting you not to be doing anything, sir?'

Daniel looked up into those eyes that were both cynical and humorous, and said, 'I have compassionate leave, as you see.'

'I'm sure sorry you should have needed it,' replied the guard, 'but this is a reserved area. I can't let you through. You'll have to get to Eastbourne by going round the back way.'

'Bugger Eastbourne,' said Daniel violently. 'It was here I was hoping to come to.'

The guard looked at him suspiciously. 'But do you have a warrant, sir?'

At that moment a passing British lieutenant decided to take an interest. He saluted Daniel, and took the papers from the guard. After a moment he said, 'I thought so.'

'Thought what, Lieutenant?' said Daniel.

'You're Daniel Pitt, aren't you? *The* Daniel Pitt? The flying ace?'

Daniel nodded. 'I suppose I must be. How on earth did you know?'

'Cigarette cards, sir.'

'Cigarette cards?'

'Player's, sir. My father smoked Player's, and I kept the cards; Great Footballers of the World, Great Explorers, Flying Aces of the Great War. I memorised all of them; twenty-five victories, in Pups, Camels and Snipes. You shot down a Gotha bomber, didn't you, sir?'

'Forced it to land,' said Daniel. 'I forced a Roland Walfisch down once, and after the war, the two fellows on board became personal friends. I don't know what happened to the Gotha crew.'

'I am so pleased to meet you,' said the Lieutenant. 'May I shake your hand, sir?'

Somewhat confused by all this, Daniel held out his hand. The Lieutenant shook it vigorously, saying, 'You've always been one of my heroes, sir, if you don't mind me saying so, sir, and everyone says it was really a lot more than twenty-five.'

'I had no idea I'd been on a cigarette card,' said Daniel.

At this point the guard, who had been waiting for all of this to begin to make sense, asked, 'Excuse me, sir, but if you weren't going to Eastbourne, why were you coming here?'

'I just wanted to come to Beachy Head, Corporal, but of course I remember it from peacetime. I should have realised it would be like this. It was stupid of me.'

'You must meet Captain Roberts,' said the Lieutenant. 'He'll be thrilled to meet you.'

It was from the inside of his surreal psychological fog that Daniel had to shake hands with half a dozen officers and be shown around the clifftop, attempting to show a polite interest whilst suppressing intense and sickening waves of grief, and the strange impatience of the condemned man to have it all over and done with. It was a bright and windy day, with small clouds scudding across the sun, so that from minute to minute it was either chilly or hot.

Captain Roberts was a solid man with a greying but soldierly moustache, who had come back into the army after ten years of being a solicitor in a small Cotswold town. The Lieutenant, on the other hand, was a small lively man with sleek black hair, who had grown up in Shropshire, 'Mary Webb country' as he called it, in response to Daniel's polite enquiry as to his origins.

'My wife loved Mary Webb,' said Daniel, and he thought briefly of Rosie, wondering what she would think of his intention. 'She would just think it was a sin,' he thought bitterly. He still thought of her as she had been in their youth, chestnut-haired, freckled and bursting with poetry. He thought about their brief period of happiness in Ceylon. The memory brought with it another pang of loss.

The three men stood, not looking over the cliff, but at the peaceful and beautiful farmland behind it. 'This is what it's all about,' said Captain Roberts, waving his swagger stick.

'I'm half French,' said Daniel. 'I've had two countries to fight for, just like the last time.'

'We've got some Free French here,' said the Lieutenant. 'They shout insults at the German aeroplanes. And yesterday five young Frenchies turned up on the beach in canoes. That's the spirit, eh, sir? Two pairs of brothers, and a spare. Another little poke in the eye for Adolf.'

There seemed to be something of everybody up there on the cliff. There were Home Guard manning aircraft guns, a great many men from the Observer Corps, and a colony of WAACs operating a radio station. There was an establishment monitoring transmissions from the Eiffel Tower, which the Germans were using to broadcast to their troops in France, so that there was a small group of people who were condemned to spend the entire war listening to appalling German light entertainment, without ever discovering one useful secret. To the west, a company of Canadians was executing a mock attack on a stubby disused lighthouse which was already pocked with bullet holes, and divots carved out by mortars.

The two officers left Daniel to his own devices after a runner appeared with a message, and he took the opportunity to wander along the cliff edge, only to feel the full force of his despair wash over him again. It was so overwhelming that he had to sit on the grass.

He wrapped his arms around his knees and looked out over the sea. He was reminded of Tennyson's poem about the eagle; 'The wrinkled sea beneath him crawls'. The sea did indeed seem wrinkled. In places it was black from the shadow of the tiny clouds, and in others it sparkled so brightly that it was almost impossible to look upon it. A huge full moon hung above France.

He dropped his head on his knees and closed his eyes, but a sense of drowning, of being overwhelmed by water and panic, overtook him, and he was forced to look up. There really was only one way out.

He stood, peered over and saw the stones hundreds of feet below. He felt a kind of vertigo take hold of him, as if some malign spirit was pushing him in the small of his back, and he swayed. It would be so easy to give in to it, to close his eyes and topple forward, but at the same time it seemed infinitely hard. He realised that it would take more courage than he had ever needed before in his life, because this time he was not fighting with others but with himself.

On the other hand, he was contemplating the most extreme liberty of all, the only liberty that was both infinite and truly desirable. It occurred to him that he could sit at the cliff edge, facing the downs, and just go over backwards, as if getting into bed. On the other hand, he could take a run, and fly for the last time in his life, making the leap to freedom joyously and spectacularly. Or he could simply step forward, as if going for a stroll, and go quietly, with dignity.

It was a death he had faced daily in the Great War. If your aircraft was on fire, rather than burn, you would unbuckle, flip the machine over and fall to Earth. The force of the impact was so great that every bone in one's body would be shattered, and all one's internal organs turned to a paste. Death was instantaneous and probably painless. He had seen dozens of such deaths. He had seen both enemies and comrades die in that manner.

Daniel had carried a revolver, like so many others, just in case his machine could not be flipped, and now he suddenly wondered why he had not simply walked out onto the airfield and put a pistol against his temple or in his mouth.

But that was not a real airman's death. That was a second-class death. He stepped up to the brink and looked at the moon over France. Death in flight; this was a real airman's death. 'Goodbye, world,' he thought. 'I won't miss you.'

A quiet voice behind him said, 'I wouldn't jump there if I were you. The cliff isn't vertical, and it's studded with flints. You don't go down like a thunderbolt; you bounce all the way and get shredded. You might end up on a ledge. It can take several hours to die. There's a much better place further along. You might even consider Seaford Head.'

Daniel did nothing. The voice seemed as though it might even have been inside his own head. He looked down at the beach far below and felt the cliff drawing him over. It had its own hunger; it needed him to be crushed, bloody, and gone.

Daniel watched two black birds squabbling on a small ledge.

'They're choughs,' said the voice. 'People think they're jackdaws, or crows, but they have red legs. They're cliff-dwellers. Have you ever seen *King Lear*? Where Edgar describes the Dover Cliffs?'

'You're disrupting my peace,' said Daniel, without looking round.

'How fearful / And dizzy 'tis to cast one's eyes so low!' continued the voice.

'The crows and choughs that wing the midway air
Show scarce so gross as beetles; halfway down
Hangs one that gathers samphire, dreadful trade!
Methinks he seems no bigger than his head.
The fishermen that walk upon the beach
Appear like mice, and yond tall anchoring bark
Diminished to her cock, her cock a buoy
Almost too small for sight. The murmuring surge,
That on the unnumber'd idle pebble chafes,
Cannot be heard so high. I'll look no more,
Lest my brain turn, and the deficient sight
Topple down headlong.

'I have often wondered why Shakespeare made that mistake about samphire. Samphire grows in muddy estuaries. People did gather seagull eggs, though. I imagine a great many people perished like that. Of course he and Gloucester weren't at the cliff at all. Did you know that once an entire village committed suicide here, during a famine? Can you feel your brain turn? The cliff does turn the brain, doesn't it? You'd better step back before you topple down headlong.'

Daniel sighed and looked out towards France. Above him, at barely more than a hundred feet, three of the new Spitfires from his own airfield roared by, performing a victory roll to the cheers of the gunners. 'They must have got a Junkers or something,' thought Daniel, and that thought made him step back from the edge. He suddenly wondered why he had not simply waited for a scramble and gone up in his obsolete Hurricane. That would have been an airman's death.

'Unfinished business,' said the voice. 'France isn't free yet.'

Daniel turned, and found himself facing the tallest man he had ever seen, in the late prime of life, with his forage cap tucked under his arm so that his straw-coloured hair shone in the sunlight. He was slender, almost epicene, and his eyes were golden brown. He looked as though he had probably never had to shave. He smiled and held out his hand, saying, 'You don't have to mention how tall I am.'

'I imagine that everyone does,' replied Daniel.

'People like to enquire about the weather up here.'

'And call you "Titch"?'

The man nodded. 'I'm Captain Raphael. Chaplaincy. Attached to the Medical Corps.'

'A sky pilot,' said Daniel. 'In the RFC we called them sky pilots.'

'I spotted you out here and knew straight away what you were thinking of doing. I'm sorry to interfere, but I felt I had no choice. I suggest we go to the pub. There are one or two nice ones in Eastbourne. I'd just about fit in your sidecar, with my knees tucked under my chin.'

Twenty minutes later they were sitting face-to-face across two pints of beer in a smoky pub that was full of Home Guardsmen and fire wardens. Captain Raphael said, 'You'd better tell me about it. I don't mean to intrude. What I mean is, you can tell me about it if you'd like to.'

'As long as you don't bring God into it,' said Daniel. 'He and I avoid each other's eyes when we pass in the street.'

'I won't bring up God,' said the Chaplain. 'God brings Himself up, in His own good time.' He paused, then said, 'I suppose you must have lost someone, someone very dear to you. When I saw you standing at the edge I thought I'd never seen anyone radiate so much anguish. I'm very sorry if I spoiled your plan for a beautiful, quick and easy exit, but when I was watching you I felt, um, compassion. I thought, "There is a man who has more to do. Who has life left over." As I say, I felt I had no choice.'

'Compassion?'

'Yes. I had to intervene. I felt the pain, and I wanted to end the pain in myself as much as in you. I'm very sorry. I've been a busybody, rather a self-regarding one.'

'You're not going to tell me that suicide is a sin?'

'No.'

'You remind me of my brother-in-law,' said Daniel. 'He was an army chaplain, and he doesn't seem to believe in any of it.'

'Theology is the feeble wisdom of those who are terrified of mystery and want to build castles in the air in all the empty spaces, just for the sake of filling them up.'

'That's the sort of thing Fairhead says. This is all very strange,' said Daniel.

'Who have you lost?'

'How do you know I've lost someone?'

'Well, you have, haven't you?'

Daniel nodded slowly, and with great difficulty said, 'Esther. My daughter. She was a Wren.'

'You must have loved her very greatly, if you can't imagine life without her.'

'I can imagine life without her ... But it's not a life I want.'

'What happened?'

'Torpedoed.'

'Oh, in the *Aguila*?'

'How do you know about the *Aguila*?'

'I can't tell you how I know. I just do. Contacts in high places. One hundred and fifty-three dead, of whom twenty-one were Wrens. It went down in ninety seconds, apparently. On the way to Gibraltar. Am I right?'

'I don't know. You seem to know a lot more about it than I do. All I have is a telegram.'

Captain Raphael sat back and sipped on his beer thoughtfully. 'All those lovely young women,' he said at last. 'So full of life. What a terrible waste. All the children that won't be born. I am so very sorry. Now I understand why you were up at the cliff. There's no love greater than one's love for a child, is there?'

'You have children?'

'I seem to have a great many. They're not all equally easy to love, I have to say. Do you have any other children? A wife?'

'I have a son, Bertie, but my wife has turned him against me. He treats me as if I were a stain. A smudge on his existence. He's at Sandhurst, training for the Armoured Corps. It's impossible to love someone who treats you with contempt. My wife is not well, in my opinion. Like her mother. We've lived separately for years. I don't know if she knows about Esther yet. I assume that she must have been sent a telegram too.'

'You have no other children?'

'No,' said Daniel, before suddenly remembering, with an evanescent burst of happiness, that of course he had Felix and Felicity.

'Would you show me the telegram?'

Daniel reached into the breast pocket of his tunic and handed it over, folded in four. Captain Raphael looked at it and made a wry face. He put his hand into his own pocket and brought out a cigarette lighter. He flicked it alight and showed Daniel the flame, which was ochre flecked with green. 'I want your permission to burn the telegram,' he said.

'Burn it?'

'Yes. It's always the best thing to do. Otherwise you will keep looking at it for year after year, and everything will keep coming back over you with renewed force, and you will wish you could get rid of it but you won't be able to bring yourself to, and it will hang on to you like a succubus, so it's best if you let me destroy it. Esther has gone, so let this be gone too.'

'Burn it,' said Daniel.

The Captain flicked the lighter again, and Daniel heard the distinct scrape of the carbide wheel on the flint. He watched as the flame enveloped the paper, turning black at the edges and glowing orange. Captain Raphael inverted it so the flame would not touch his fingers, and then, when it was almost down to nothing, he dropped the remainder in the ashtray. He stood, picked up the ashtray and carried it out of the door, where he checked the direction of the breeze, raised it to his lips, and blew the ashes into the air.

'You were watching the flame very intently,' he said, when he had reseated himself. 'Did you see anything?'

'See anything? No.'

'I've always found that if you watch a flame like that, you begin to see things. It's a kind of scrying. Do you have brothers and sisters? A mother? A father?'

'My father is dead, two of my brothers died in South Africa, and my remaining brother is an alcoholic, but he's got himself into the ARP in Brighton, and my mother ...'

'Yes? Your mother? You don't want to say anything about her?'

Daniel pictured his ancient mother, out in her garden, a trug basket over her arm, wearing her shabbiest clothes and a broad-brimmed hat. He wanted to go and see her. It was obviously what he had to do next, because somebody had to tell her the news about Esther. 'My mother, well ... I don't know ...'

'I do,' said Captain Raphael. 'You have just realised that your mother is one good reason that you cannot commit suicide. She's already lost too much. At her age, it would be a devastating blow. Am I right?'

Daniel was dumbfounded.

'I have a suggestion. Because of this war, there will be hundreds more Esthers killed. The sooner we end it, the fewer Esthers will have to die. Do you follow me?'

Daniel nodded and the priest continued. 'Well, just grit your teeth and put your head down, and get on with the war. And on the day of victory, then you will be free to decide whether or not to go over the cliff. Does that make sense? There's too much necessary work to do for you to indulge in the luxury of killing yourself now.'

'I do see your point.'

'You must sacrifice your own preferences, as, I imagine, you always have. Is it agreed?'

Daniel nodded again, and then suddenly got to his feet. 'Please excuse me,' he said, and, accidentally knocking over his chair, he fled to the lavatory, where he sat on the closed lid and buried his head in his hands. The room was tiny and malodorous, with water dripping from a rusted pipe, and a rank puddle on the floor, but it was good enough to grieve in. The disappointment of having been deprived of his death overcame him, and his temples ached dully. His shoulders began to shake, and when he finally surrendered and gave himself permission to cry, he wept until he was so exhausted that he felt purged.

He had no idea how long he was in there, but when he came out, feeling lighter, he saw that Captain Raphael had gone, leaving behind him a small heap of coins on top of a piece of notepaper, upon which he had written in the most beautiful italic script: 'Cheerio and good luck. The beer's on me.'

Daniel went outside and put his flying gear back on. He adjusted the choke and the advance/retard lever, and tickled the carburettor until petrol began to whelm out of it, finding solace and purpose in this routine little ritual that he performed so well, so thoughtlessly and so often. He kicked the Brough into life and set off for Partridge Green, taking the back roads to avoid having to pass along the cliff. On a fast straight he tipped the sidecar so that its wheel left the ground, and remembered how Esther had loved him doing that when she had been the passenger as a tiny girl, clinging on to the sides of the cockpit, screaming with delight.

48

Necessary Work

Daniel spent a quiet and melancholy week with his mother. She knew that something terrible had happened the moment he took off his flying helmet and goggles, and reached out his arms to her, saying '*Chère maman*'. She had been weeding amongst the roses in the beds at the front of the house, and was wearing her tattiest old gardening clothes, including a hat that had been magnificently glamorous back in 1912, but now had its lid flapping and was tied beneath her chin with a strip of tulle. Over her shoes she wore the rubber galoshes that made her feet look comically large. She was an old woman beyond the reach of vanity, or rather, to whom vanity has become an amusing and very occasional distraction.

She had heard the sound of the motorcycle as it came through the village, and had lifted her head like a deer that senses one's presence in a forest. The engine had the sound of her son about it and her heart leapt a little at the thought. She put down her trug basket and reached for her walking stick, which she had propped against a standard rose. She stepped gingerly over the little wall, only two courses high, that Daniel had once built for her to retain the soil, and was at the gate, ready to open it, when he turned in.

Daniel embraced her tenderly, and said 'Come inside, *maman*. I've something to tell you.'

Mme Pitt was already trembling by the time that she sat down in her armchair. 'What's happened?' she asked, looking up at her son. 'Is it Archie?'

Daniel knelt down before her and put his hands on her knees. 'No, *maman*,' he said. 'It's Esther. She's been lost at sea. Torpedoed. On the way to the Med.'

She raised a shaking hand to stroke his cheek, and said, 'Oh, my poor son. She's been too cruel for you, this life. *Tu ne sauras jamais comment je suis désolée.*'

'I've just come back from Beachy Head,' said Daniel, 'but then I was reminded of you.'

The old woman looked at him with a puzzled expression, until his meaning suddenly dawned on her. 'I am too old to live for, *mon fils,*' she said, '*c'est pas la peine.*'

'*Non, maman,* you're not too old to live for.'

That week, Mme Pitt spent long hours sitting silently in her rocking chair, with tears coursing down her cheeks, repeating, '*C'est trop dur, c'est trop dur,*' whilst Daniel wrote long letters to Sophie and Fairhead, Christabel and Gaskell, Ottilie and Frederick, to Archie, and, finally, to Rosie. In his letter to Rosie he said:

Our daughter embodied all that I most love to remember, all that I most cherished, and all that for which I most loved to hope. Now that she has gone, for me the world has emptied out almost completely. You still have Bertie, for that you can be thankful, although God knows if he'll get through once he's finished with OCTU. It seems most likely to me that he'll be going to Italy, because that's where the Royal Armoured Corps is likeliest to be busy for the time being.

Incidentally, it was remiss of both you and him not to tell me about his passing-out parade at Sandhurst. The manner in which you have succeeded in excluding him from my life is cruel both to him and to me. Perhaps I cannot speak for other men. I know there are many who apparently don't give a damn, but in my case, paternity has been the most precious thing of my life, and your attempts to sabotage it are and always will be unacceptable and unforgivable. I heard about the parade from Esther, and wrote to the Commandant, explaining that I was estranged to you both, and he very generously allowed me to watch from a window in Old College. I was extremely proud when he received the Sam Browne, but I left forlorn because of being unable to speak either to him or to you. I shall always do my bit for him, despite his long-standing and deeply hurtful indifference, amounting to hostility.

I thought you looked very fine in that blue dress, and more than once thought how preposterous it is to have to observe one's own wife and son through binoculars.

If I get through this war intact, there may perhaps come a time when all I feel is gratitude for Esther's life amongst us. For the time being I am in utter darkness. Perhaps you are there too, although your faith no doubt bears you up. I embrace you for old times' sake, remembering when we were happy and hopeful enough together to create such a lovely girl and bring her into the world.

In the last war I was ready to die because it seemed an absolute certainty that I would do so. In the Flying Corps there was almost no chance of making it through. It gave us a kind of mad gaiety that I still remember with pleasure. To tell the truth, we had more fun than our minds and bodies could take. In this war I am sorry that the prospect of death is a little more remote. I go up in my battered old Hurricane, but I have a parachute this time, the Battle of Britain is over, and the skies are very much safer than they ever were on the Western Front. Even so, I no longer care whether I live or die. If there is the slightest chance that our little daughter will be waiting for me on the other side, then I'll be glad enough to go.

When Daniel's leave was over he returned to Tangmere, having decided not to go and see Archie in Brighton. His brother lived in such appalling squalor that it seemed unkind to arrive without notice. At least Archie should be given the chance to line up the whisky bottles against the wall, empty the ashtrays, and sweep the mouse droppings from the floor.

Archie was still a roadsweeper, but these days he was also on the Fire Watch, and perhaps that would have the effect of pulling his life back together. There is nothing more soul-destroying for a valiant old soldier than to live inside a crippling sense of uselessness.

49

Oily Wragge (4)

Well, I did get back in, in a manner of speaking The Norfolks ended up with about seventeen battalions, and I stayed in Norwich and got hooked into setting up the local LDV, that turned into the Home Guard, and we had a little book called the *Home Guard Manual*, and it had information about how to turn a shotgun into a musket by taking the shot out and putting a ball there instead, and you could get moulds for making the ball, and it was accurate to about eighty yards, which was just about perfect for nobbling deer. Put it this way, during all those times in Thetford Forest, my platoon didn't go short of venison.

When they wound us up because Adolf was losing, I went up to Hexham because Miss Gaskell and Miss Christabel had a flipping great estate with no workers, but dozens of evacuee tiddlers, and Miss Sophie and Fairhead were there too, and it was a right jungle, so we had plenty of venison there too, and enough bunnies to make you sick, and I was out on a tractor a lot of the time, and we even planted a couple of acres of taters. I got just about as brown as I was in Mespot, and I got whopping great muscles in my forearms.

It was just as well I didn't get back in the 2nd Battalion. In 1940 they got captured by the 1st Battalion, 2nd SS Totenkopf Regiment, and marched into a field in column of threes, where there were two heavy machine guns, and not one single Holy Boy marched out again, but there were two men who crawled out, and it was thanks to them that the news got known, and that Kraut officer who did it was hanged after the war. It was a place called Le Paradis. Well, that's a funny one.

Still, the Norfolks got more VCs in that war than any other regiment. Those are my boys.

I was in Norwich when the Huns bombed it, and it brought tears to my eyes to see what they did. It was about thirty raids

267

in all. On the first one they got five girls from Colman's Mustard, wheeling their bikes up a hill, including Gladys Sampson who I happened to know, and was a sweetheart. After that, the attacks were regular. We set up shelters and feeding centres, and went round telling people how to pour sand on incendiaries, and we arranged a swapping system so that you had a house to go to if yours was wrecked. Then there were the two Baedeker raids in 1942, when Caley's chocolate factory went up in flames, and after that we dug a lot of spare graves in Earlham Road Cemetery, just in case. On the second raid they got the synagogue, and I bet Adolf would have been proud of that. Some people reckoned that Norwich had it almost as bad as Coventry, and we had trekkers, who were people who left the town in the evening, and came back in the morning, and quite a lot of them were camping in tents in fields or kipping in barns and whatnot. You could hear the raids going on in faraway parts. It was like the distant rolling of drums all night.

But I didn't have too bad a time of it in the second war. I've got fond memories, like gallons of sweet hot chocolate, when it was available, and bloody great wedges of bread covered in golden syrup, nights out under the stars, and those lovely bossy girls from the WVS bustling about, and the searchlights criss-crossing the sky, and those little bints on the anti-aircraft guns with their blonde curls escaping from under their tin hats, and the Duke of Kent coming up to visit and strolling about being interested with his hands behind his back. Mrs McCosh would've been impressed.

After the war I began to think about Baldhart again, and I couldn't get her out of my head. It was like being haunted.

50

The Temptation

On the morning after his return to Tangmere, Daniel received a letter from Gaskell, saying that she had applied to join the Air Transport Auxiliary, and his first thought was that she would have made a very fine fighter pilot, given the chance. Gaskell said that she was positively crowded out at the house in Hexham, what with all the children, and Sophie and Fairhead, and she needed to get up into the air alone, preferably for hours at a time. She was planning to travel with a pad of cartridge paper, and make a great many sketches that she could work up to canvas after the war.

He folded the letter up, put it in his pocket, and reported for duty to Wing Commander Woodhouse, hoping to be sent off somewhere in his Hurricane, only to be told: 'I'll need you to report back here at 1700 hours. There's someone who very badly wants to see you.'

'Can I take the bus up for a spin, sir?'

'Yes, but make sure you're here at 1700. It's very important, very hush-hush. Don't go looking for trouble. This wouldn't be a good time to get shot down.'

Accordingly, Daniel took the bus up and went to buzz his mother's house in Partridge Green. It might give her a little pleasure to know that her son was back aloft, and not going to give up old habits just because there had been a tragedy. Then he went and stunted over Beachy Head for the Canadians and the Free French and Captain Raphael, if he was still down there. Stunting still made him feel nauseous, but it was a habit that was impossible to give up if you had ever been in the Flying Corps, and you never admitted to the nausea anyway, even to yourself.

That early evening he went to the Wing Commander's office, and found him there with a middle-aged man in the service dress of the Royal Engineers. He was grey-haired and silver-moustached, but plainly still very fit. Daniel guessed that, like him, he was a survivor of the last war, and still sound enough for this one. He was introduced as Colonel Ericson.

After the ritual exchange of salutes, Wing Commander Woodhouse invited the two men to sit, and remembered not to offer Daniel a cigarette. He said, 'Colonel Ericson has a proposition for you, Daniel.'

The Colonel coughed to clear his throat, and leaned forward. 'First of all, I am truly damned sorry to hear about your daughter. I've got two myself. One's a land girl and the other's ATS. With any luck they'll never go to sea.'

Daniel nodded dumbly, and the Colonel continued. 'I understand that you can speak German. Are you fluent?'

'Not really. I wouldn't say so. I'm on the cusp of fluency, really. I can understand it all quite well and I can say what I want to say, but my accent is pretty poor. I learned it in Westphalia.'

'But you can get by. Could you get by as a Frenchman who speaks German? No pretence of being German at all? As if you were, let's say, from Alsace?'

'Yes, that would be pretty easy. You do know that I'm half French?'

'Of course. And incidentally, it's a great honour to meet you. I've been an admirer since 1918. Since you captured that Gotha, in fact. Quite a feat. A David and Goliath exploit if ever there was one.'

'Thank you. May I ask what you're leading up to?'

'Well, you're a bit long in the tooth, but clearly very fit and active, with a long record of resourcefulness and courage, and you speak three languages.'

'Five, sir. I used to speak Pashtun and Tamil, and could pick them up again quite quickly.'

'Hmm, well, we'll bear that in mind, but at present we need people for the European theatre. Did you do Greek? At Westminster?'

'I hated it, sir. I didn't pay any attention, and now I regret it.'

Wing Commander Woodhouse intervened. 'I've got a young man here who you might talk to. Warren. Bunny Warren. He's a classics scholar, very fit and confident. Knows how to use a parachute.

Rowing blue at Cambridge. He recites the battle scenes from *The Iliad* when he's three sheets to the wind. I wouldn't want to lose him, but he doesn't really have the makings of a great flyer. He's the kind who breaks the undercarriage and clips trees. It won't be the Huns that get him.'

'Ah, really? I'll speak to him later if I may.' Turning to Daniel he asked, 'Have you ever flown a Lysander?'

'No, but I imagine it would be exactly like flying an RE8.'

'It's a great little plane, the Lysander. It can land and take off on a sixpence, just like a Sopwith. How are you with night flying? Mainly by moonlight?'

'I've never tried it, sir. The Night Camels did all that sort of thing last time. I've always been a daylighter.'

'Are you willing to try?'

'I'm not keen, but I'm willing.'

'And how about parachuting? I know you've never done it. Are you willing to learn to do that? At night?'

'In the dark? Good God. Well, I've always wanted to try it. It looks like tremendous fun. Are you asking me to become a spy?' Daniel felt his stomach churn with fear and excitement.

'Well, as far as possible you would always be in uniform.'

'So they can't shoot me when they catch me?'

'Precisely. But they probably would anyway. The Huns seem to have fewer principles than ever this time.'

'Don't you think I'm too old for this?'

'No. There would be extensive training. And when you're not in uniform, it will be less suspicious if you're older rather than younger.'

'So I would sometimes be in mufti?'

'Yes. Sometimes.'

'And then I could be shot as a spy?'

'Yes. Indeed you could.'

'I think you're asking me to commit suicide.'

'That's what one's country always demands in time of war.'

The Colonel leaned forward and said, 'There's necessary work, and very few who are capable of doing it. You're one of them. And I'm guessing that after what's happened ... your terrible loss ... you might be ideal for us.'

'Ideal?'

'I apologise if this sounds cruel, but you have less to live for now,' said the Colonel levelly, 'and in addition to all your other qualities, that's a hell of an asset to an enterprise like ours.'

'I've realised that I do have people to live for,' said Daniel, 'and I do have some conditions.'

'Hmm, I thought you might. Everybody does. Some people demand a decent store of cyanide capsules. What do you want then?'

'I want to be based here at Tangmere.'

'Well, as a matter of fact, you would be. You must have noticed all the Lysanders going in and out. Or heard them at night. You don't even have to move your billet.'

'Secondly, I want to keep my Hurricane, fully armed, and no one else is to use it.'

'No one would want to use it,' said the Wing Commander. 'It's completely obsolete. We're all in Spitfires now.'

'It isn't obsolete to me. It's a hell of a lot tougher than a Spitfire. I'd rather crash a Hurricane any day.'

'You'll really have to stop taking on the enemy.'

'My orders are not to initiate an attack. I can't help it if they keep turning up on my tail.'

'It is generally believed that you interpret your orders somewhat flexibly,' said Colonel Ericson. 'But do we have a deal? If so, you have until Monday to change your mind. No one is ordering you to commit suicide. That remains entirely voluntary. By the way, I have some news that might interest you. Your old mucker, Fluke Beckenham-Gilbert, has returned from Argentina. He's back in, at Hendon.'

'Flying?'

'Well, he's doing the same as you. Flying around giving pep talks. Apparently he wouldn't fly a monoplane or anything with a retractable undercarriage, so they've given him a Gladiator. His pep talks are a little oversimplified; he repeats the word "attack" rather a lot. They're hoping to make him shift over to the ATA, but then he'd have to reconcile himself to monoplanes.'

'Good old Fluke,' said Daniel. 'I haven't seen him since about 1919. I'll have to look him up. Do you need anything delivering to Hendon?'

On the way out Daniel passed somebody coming in, a slimly built man in middle age, with a long face and a salt-and-pepper moustache. He looked strangely familiar. Both men did a double take, and paused in their step. 'Skipper?' said Daniel.

'Good God, Pittsy, it's you. What are you doing here?'

'I'm flying around in a Mark I Hurricane, doing pep talks.'

'And I'm flying around in a Hurricane organising training.'

'How do you like the Hurricane?'

'Hmm, very solid and reliable. Not as much fun as a Bristol Fighter, though. You were a Camel man, weren't you?'

'Pups, Camels, and then Snipes. I've got a Snipe and a Pup rotting in a barn in Hexham. They're a pitiful sight.'

'I wish I had a Bristol Fighter.'

'You never went back to New Zealand? You've still got a whiff of the accent.'

The Air Vice Marshall shook his head. 'I'm reckoning on retiring there after the war. In the end, a man has to go home. And I'm getting sick of banging my head against a brick wall. The higher you get in this game, the less of a soldier you are, and the more you have to be a bloody politician. I had Bader and Leigh-Mallory throwing this entire sector into confusion with their damned Big Wing, and instead of them getting a bollocking for bloody-minded perversity, I got shifted downwards and sideways to a training group.

'They'd take hours to form up, and by then the enemy would have dropped their eggs and gone. It's like Richthofen's bloody flying circus, but half as effective. How come Richthofen did it twice as fast, and didn't even have radio? Leigh-Mallory thought he was in some kind of competition with me, and I never could get on with Bader. He's ... well ... I can't think of a diplomatic way of putting it.'

'An arrogant *espèce de merde, un vrai couillon*,' said Daniel.

'Very diplomatic. I suppose you heard the rumour, about how he got shot down?'

'I'm almost certain it's true. It's what the Huns are saying.'

'Well, it wouldn't surprise me in the least. What's the news with you?'

Daniel thought of saying nothing, but blurted out, 'My daughter just got killed. Torpedoed. She was a Wren.' He suddenly wished he had kept it to himself.

Keith Park's shoulders drooped. 'Oh, Pittsy, empty chairs. I'm so sorry. Makes my troubles seem a bit piffling. Come and have a drink. You can tell me all about the time you captured that Gotha.'

'We can talk about the times we got shot down.'

Keith Park put his hand on Daniel's shoulder, and said, 'Look, we don't have to talk at all. I don't mind just sitting there saying nothing. I'm at Goodwood. My driver'll bring you back.' He paused, then said sympathetically, 'There are so many ways to get shot down, eh?'

Three hours later, Daniel went out for a long walk in the darkness to clear his head, setting off in the direction of Chichester. It had been very strange, but also comforting, to sit with Keith, mulling over old times. They had never been particular friends, but had often bumped into each other during the last war, and had occasionally got drunk together in Amiens. Daniel reflected somewhat ruefully that if he had stayed in, as Keith had, he too might have been an Air Vice Marshall by now. He wondered if Keith had thought they were all worth it, those intervening years. If you have been embroiled in a war in which you confidently expected to die, what were you supposed to do with so much life unexpectedly left over? There were so many ways of passing the peace, and you would never know what they would have been like, those roads not taken.

A Lysander flew slowly overhead, like a rumbling owl, on its way to Normandy. They only ever went out when the moon was bright. Daniel shivered, and talked to himself and the moon, imagining it to be a visible manifestation of Esther. He had always thought of it as young and virginal. He could see the black silhouette of the cathedral spire against the deepening indigo of the sky. He still had Keith Park's advice repeating itself in his head: 'Look, Pittsy, the only thing you can do at such a terrible time is keep yourself as occupied as possible. Keep yourself busy. Busy busy busy.' He thought about all the comrades he had lost in the last war, and of the women he had loved, of Rosie, Samadara, Christabel, Mary; of his mother, alone and grief-stricken in Partridge Green, and of his brother, rotting slowly from self-hatred in Brighton; of solemn Felix and sparkling

Felicity, both still at school, who would never know that he was their father; and of his truculent legitimate son who would soon be a sitting duck in a tank with a derisory six-pound gun.

He thought about how, if you have no faith, there is no meaning in anything unless you put it there yourself.

And he made his decision.

Acknowledgements

My heartfelt thanks to Sanath Ukwatte, chairman of the Mount Lavinia Hotel, Colombo, and to Merrill J. Fernando of Dilmah Tea; their hospitality and helpfulness were beyond anything I could have deserved or hoped for; also to Professor Kingsley da Silva, of Kandy, for giving up so much of his time to enlighten me about Ceylon under British rule; also to Shevanthie Goonesekera, who greatly facilitated my second research trip, and ensured that we were always full of tea.